Join the army of fans who LOVE Scott Mariani's Ben Hope series . . .

'Deadly conspiracies, bone-crunching action and a tormented hero with a heart . . . Scott Mariani packs a real punch'
Andy McDermott, bestselling author of *The Revelation Code*

'Slick, serpentine, sharp, and very very entertaining. If you've got a pulse, you'll love Scott Mariani; if you haven't, then maybe you crossed Ben Hope'
Simon Toyne, bestselling author of the *Sanctus* series

'Scott Mariani's latest page-turning rollercoaster of a thriller takes the sort of conspiracy theory that made Dan Brown's *The Da Vinci Code* an international hit, and gives it an injection of steroids . . . [Mariani] is a master of edge-of-the-seat suspense. A genuinely gripping thriller that holds the attention of its readers from the first page to the last'
Shots Magazine

'You know you are rooting for the guy when he does something so cool you do a mental fist punch in the air and have to bite the inside of your mouth not to shout out 'YES!' in case you get arrested on the train. Awesome thrilling stuff'
My Favourite Books

'If you like Dan Brown you will like all of Scott Mariani's work – but you will like it better. This guy knows exactly how to bait his hook, cast his line and reel you in, nice and slow. The heart-stopping pace and clever, cunning, joyfully serpentine tale will have you frantic to reach the end, but reluctant to finish such a blindingly good read'
The Bookbag

STAR OF AFRICA

Scott Mariani is the author of the worldwide-acclaimed action-adventure thriller series featuring ex-SAS hero Ben Hope, which has sold nearly two million copies in Scott's native UK alone and is also translated into over 20 languages. His books have been described as 'James Bond meets Jason Bourne, with a historical twist.' The first Ben Hope book, THE ALCHEMIST'S SECRET, spent six straight weeks at #1 on Amazon's Kindle chart, and all the others have been *Sunday Times* bestsellers.

Scott was born in Scotland, studied in Oxford and now lives and writes in a remote setting in rural west Wales. When not writing, he can be found bouncing about the country lanes in an ancient Land Rover, wild camping in the Brecon Beacons or engrossed in his hobbies of astronomy, photography and target shooting (no dead animals involved!).

You can find out more about Scott and his work, and sign up to his exclusive newsletter, on his official website:

www.scottmariani.com

By the same author:

Ben Hope series
The Alchemist's Secret
The Mozart Conspiracy
The Doomsday Prophecy
The Heretic's Treasure
The Shadow Project
The Lost Relic
The Sacred Sword
The Armada Legacy
The Nemesis Program
The Forgotten Holocaust
The Martyr's Curse
The Cassandra Sanction

To find out more visit **www.scottmariani.com**

SCOTT MARIANI

Star of Africa

avon

AVON

A division of HarperCollins*Publishers*
1 London Bridge Street,
London SE1 9GF

www.harpercollins.co.uk

A Paperback Original 2016

1

Copyright © Scott Mariani 2016

Scott Mariani asserts the moral right to
be identified as the author of this work

A catalogue record for this book is
available from the British Library

ISBN-13: 978-0-00-748620-5

Set in Minion by Palimpsest Book Production Ltd, Falkirk, Stirlingshire

Printed and bound in Great Britain by
Clays Ltd, St Ives plc

MIX
Paper from
responsible sources
FSC www.fsc.org **FSC™ C007454**

STAR OF AFRICA

Prologue

Salalah, Oman

Hussein Al Bu Said stood at one of the tall, broad living room windows of his palatial residence and gazed out towards the sea front. The sunset was a mosaic of reds and purples and golds, cloaking its rich colours over the extended lawns and terraces of his property, reflecting gently off the surface of the pool behind the house, silhouetting the palm trees against the horizon. Beyond the landscaped gardens he could see the private marina where his yacht was moored, its sleek whiteness touched by the crimson of the setting sun.

Ice clinked in his crystal glass as he sipped from it. Pineapple juice, freshly pressed that day. Hussein was a loyal and devout Muslim who had never touched alcohol in his forty-four years. In other ways, he knew, he had not always proved himself to be such a virtuous man. But he tried. God knew he tried. Insha'Allah, he would always do the best thing for his family.

He smiled to himself as he listened to the sounds of his children playing in another room. Chakir had just turned twelve, his little sister Salma excitedly looking forward to her eighth birthday. He loved nothing more than to hear their happy voices echoing through the big house. They were his life, and he gave them everything that he had been blessed with.

'You look as if you're very deep in thought,' said another voice behind him. Hussein turned to see his wife Najila's smiling face.

'And you look very beautiful, my love,' Hussein said as she came to join him at the window. Najila was wearing a long white dress and her black hair was loose around her shoulders. She put her arms around his neck, and they spent a few moments watching the darkening colours wash over the ocean.

Nobody had to tell Najila she was beautiful. She was his treasure, soulmate, best friend. Hussein was a dozen years older, but he kept in good shape for her and was still as lean and fit as the day he'd spotted her and decided she was the one to share his life with. They'd been married just weeks later. Hussein was also about twice as wealthy as he'd been then, even though he'd already been high up in Oman's top twenty. Their home was filled with the exquisite things he loved to collect, but Najila was by far the most wonderful and precious.

Hussein set down his glass and held her tight. He kissed her. She laughed and squirmed gently out of his arms. 'Not in the window,' she said, glancing through the ten-foot pane in the direction of the cluster of buildings that were the staff residence where the security team lived. 'The men will be watching us.'

'I gave them the night off, remember?' Hussein said. 'It's Jermar's birthday. The three of them went into town to celebrate.'

'You're too nice to them. What's the point of having security men if you let them go off partying all the time?'

Hussein smiled. 'All the more privacy for us.' He drew her in and kissed her again.

With typical timing, their embrace was interrupted by the twelve-year-old whirlwind that was Chakir blowing into the room, his sister tagging along in his wake. Chakir was clutching the handset for the remote controlled Ferrari, his favourite of the many toys he'd had as recent birthday presents. 'When can I get a real one, like yours?' he was always asking, to which his father always patiently replied, 'One day, Chakir, one day.'

'Please may we watch TV?' Chakir said.

Hussein knew Chakir was angling to see the latest Batman film on the Movie Channel. 'It's nearly time for dinner,' he replied. 'You can maybe watch it later, after your sister has gone to bed.'

Chakir looked disappointed. Salma pulled a face, too, and it was obvious that her brother had got her all worked up about seeing the movie.

Najila bent down and clasped both her daughter's hands. 'Why don't you go and look at that nice picture book your father bought you?'

'I can't find it,' Salma said. She had the same beautiful big dark eyes as her mother, and the same irresistible smile – when she wasn't pouting about not being allowed to watch TV.

Najila stroked her little heart-shaped face and was about to reply when a loud noise startled them all. It had come from inside the house.

Najila turned to Hussein with a frown. 'What was that?'

Hussein shook his head. 'I don't know.'

'Did something fall over?'

Hussein thought that maybe a picture or a mirror had dropped off the wall in one of the house's many other rooms.

He didn't understand how that could happen. He started towards the living room door that opened through to the long passage leading the whole length of the house to the grand marble-floored entrance hall.

Then he stopped. And froze.

The door burst open. Three men he'd never seen before walked into the room. Europeans, from the look of them, or Americans. What was happening?

Najila let out a gasp. Her children ran to her, wide-eyed with sudden fear. She wrapped her arms protectively around them. Little Salma buried her face in her mother's side.

Without a word, the three intruders walked deeper into the living room. Hussein stepped forward to place himself squarely between them and his family. 'Who are you?' he challenged them furiously, in English. 'What are you doing in our home? Get out, before I call the police. You hear me?'

The oldest of the three men was the one in the middle, solid, muscular, not tall, in crisp jeans and a US-Air-Force-style jacket over a dark T-shirt. His hair was cut very short, and greying. Probably prematurely. He probably wasn't much older than Hussein, but he had a lot of mileage on him. His features were rough and pockmarked and his nose had been broken more than once in the past. A very tough, very collected individual. He was giving Hussein a dead-eyed stare, unimpressed by all the angry bluster. He reached inside the jacket and his hand came out with a gun. The men either side of him did the same thing.

Najila screamed and hugged her terrified children close to her. Hussein stared at the guns.

'Now, Mister Al Bu Said, this doesn't have to be hard,' said the greying-haired man. 'So let's take it easy and do it right, and we'll be out of here before you know it.' He had an American accent. He was very clearly the boss out of the three.

'I . . . What do you want?' Hussein stammered.

'I want item 227586,' the man said calmly.

Hussein's mind wheeled and whirled. How could these men even know about that? Then his eyes narrowed as it hit him. Fiedelholz and Goldstein. This was an inside job. Had to be. He should never have trusted those dirty Swiss dogs with his business. Now that he'd changed his mind about selling, the bastards were betraying him. It was unbelievable.

'I don't know what you're talking about.'

The man sighed. 'Sure you don't. Oh well, I guess some people have to be difficult.' And he shot Hussein in the left leg, just above the knee.

The blast of the pistol shot sounded like a bomb exploding. Najila screamed again as she watched her husband fall writhing to the floor, clutching his leg. Blood pumped from the wound onto the white wool carpet.

The other two men stepped over Hussein. One of them put a pistol to Najila's head and the other grabbed hold of twelve-year-old Chakir and ripped him away from his mother. The boy kicked and struggled in the man's grip, until a gun muzzle pressed hard against his cheek and he went rigid with terror.

'Now, like I said,' the older man went on casually, gazing down at the injured and bleeding Hussein, 'this doesn't have to be any harder than it needs to be. You got a safe, right? Course you do. Then I guess that's where you'd be keeping it, huh?' He reached down and grasped Hussein by the hair. 'On your feet, Twinkletoes. Lead the way.'

'Take what you want,' Hussein gasped through clenched teeth as he struggled to his feet. The agony of his shattered leg had him in a cold sweat and his heart felt as if it was going to explode. 'But please don't hurt my family.'

'The safe,' the man said.

'Tell this bitch to quit howling,' said the one with the gun to Najila's head. 'Or I'm going to put one in her eye.'

Hussein looked at his wife. 'It's going to be all right,' he assured her. 'Just do as they say.' Najila's cries fell to a whimper. She closed her eyes, tears streaming down her face, and clutched her trembling daughter even more tightly to her.

Hussein limped and staggered across the room, leaving a thick blood trail over the carpet. The safe was concealed behind a $250,000 copy of a Jacques-Louis David oil painting on the living room wall, *The Death of Socrates*. It was a big wall, and it was a big painting, and it was a big safe too. Sweat was pouring into Hussein's eyes and he thought he was going to faint from the pain, but he managed to press the hidden catch that allowed the gilt frame to hinge away from the wall, revealing the steel door and digital keypad panel behind it. With a bloody finger he stabbed out the twelve-digit code and pressed ENTER, and the locks popped with a click. He swung the safe door open.

'Please,' he implored the leader of the three men. 'Take what's in there and leave us alone.'

'Oh, I'm going to take it, all right. Out of the way.' The grey-haired man shoved Hussein aside and Hussein fell back to the floor with a cry of pain as the man started searching the shelves of the safe. Stacks of cash and gold watches, business documents and contracts, he wasn't interested in. Just the one item he was being paid to obtain.

He found it inside a leather-covered, velvet-lined box on the upper shelf. When he flipped the lid of the box and saw what was inside, his dead-eyed expression became one of amazement. You had to see it to believe it.

'Bingo,' he said. He took it out and weighed it in his hand for a second, keeping his back to the other two men so they couldn't see what he was holding. He slipped it into the leather pouch he'd brought with him, then slipped the pouch into his pocket. It would be transferred to the locked briefcase later that night, before they got the hell out of Oman, never to return.

'Now you have it, go,' Hussein gasped. The agony was burning him up. He was losing blood so fast that he felt dizzy. The bullet must have clipped the artery. The white carpet all around where he lay was turning bright red.

The man stood over him, the gun dangling loose from his right hand. 'Pleasure doing business with you, Mister Al Bu Said. We'll be out of here in just a moment. One thing, before we go. I need to ask – you wouldn't even dream of calling the cops and telling them all about this, now would you?'

'No! Never! Please! Just go! I promise, no police.'

The man nodded to himself, and a thin little smile creased his lips. 'Guess what? I don't believe you.'

The gunshot drowned Najila's scream of horror. Hussein Al Bu Said's head dropped lifelessly to the blood-soaked floor with a bullet hole in the centre of his forehead.

Then the living room of the palatial family home resonated to another gunshot. Then two more. Then silence.

The men left the bodies where they lay, and made their exit into the falling night.

Chapter 1

Paris

It should have been a simple affair. But in his world, things that started out simple often didn't end up that way. That was how it had always been for him, and he'd long ago stopped questioning why. Some people had a talent for music, others for business. Ben Hope had a talent for trouble. Both attracting it, and fixing it.

Which was the reason he was sitting here now on this chilly, damp November afternoon, parked under a grey sky on this unusually empty street in the middle of this bustling city he both loved and hated, at the wheel of an Alpina BMW twin-turbo coupé that had seen better days, smoking his way through a fresh pack of Gauloises, watching the world go by and the pigeons strutting over the Parisian pavements and the entrance of the little grocery shop across the road, and counting down the minutes before trouble was inevitably about to walk back into his life.

He wouldn't have to wait much longer. It was thirteen minutes past three o'clock, which meant the deadline for Abdel's phone call had been and gone exactly thirteen minutes ago. Precisely as Ben had instructed Abdel to allow to happen. If the Romanians anywhere near lived up to the image that was being painted of them, then such an act of open defiance would not be tolerated. They'd be here soon, ready to do business. And Ben would be ready to put the first phase of his plan into action. It might go smoothly, or then again it might not. That all depended entirely on how Dracul decided to play it. Either way, it wasn't exactly how Ben had planned on spending this brief return visit to Paris.

Naturally, things just couldn't be that simple.

When Abdel's broken deadline was twenty-one minutes old and Ben was two-thirds of the way through his next cigarette, the silver Mercedes-Benz turned sharply in out of the traffic and squealed up at the kerb outside the grocery shop, right across the street from where Ben was sitting. Both front doors opened at once. Two men got out, slammed their doors and converged on the pavement, glancing left and right.

Ben followed them with a watchful eye, and knew immediately that he was looking at the Romanians. They were both in their late twenties or early thirties. One was darker in hair and skin, with sharper features that hinted at gypsy ancestry. The other had more Slavic blood, or maybe Hungarian, with a long face and fairer hair. Ethnic variations aside, they could have been clones: big, heavy, hand-picked from the pages of the rent-a-thug catalogue, dressed to intimidate in leather jackets and big stompy boots and putting on a theatrical air of menace as they walked up to the shop entrance and pushed their way inside.

Dracul's enforcers, come to deliver on their promise of violence, bloodshed and broken bones. They looked more than up to the job. Little wonder they had Abdel and the rest of the neighbourhood spooked.

Ben took a last draw on his Gauloise, crushed the stub

into the crowded dashboard ashtray, picked up his bag from the passenger seat and got out of the car.

'Here we go again,' he muttered to himself. Then he crossed the street and walked into the shop after them.

It was Ben's first visit to Paris in well over a year. He hadn't been planning on coming back any time soon – not out of any kind of deliberate avoidance, but because he had few plans of any kind at all. For some time now, for reasons that he preferred not to dwell on, his had been a rootless, meandering existence that took him wherever chance and circumstance led him: he'd wandered aimlessly around Europe, never lingering long in one place, never quite sure why he'd come or where he was going next. He wasn't a tourist, being fluent in the core European languages and conversant in most of the others, but he wasn't a native either, and there seemed to be no place he could settle and feel at home. Sometimes he stayed a day here and there in cheap hotels; sometimes he roughed it in the kinds of solitary wild places he'd always liked to spend time, away from the complexities of life, away from hustle and bustle – most of all, away from trouble.

At least, that was the idea.

Jeff Dekker, Ben's old friend and former partner, still ran the business they'd built together in Normandy, and still thought that Ben had lost his mind. Back in the day, Jeff had done his stint in the Special Boat Service, the Royal Navy's equivalent of Ben's old regiment, 22 SAS. Years later, after Ben had gone to live at the former farm near Valognes, a place called Le Val, he and Jeff had teamed up to carve out a prestigious niche for themselves teaching their specialised skills to military, security, law enforcement and anti-terrorist operatives from across the globe. They'd reached the point in their careers where they could enjoy the fruits of all those years of extreme risk and back-breaking hardship.

That was how it worked in their world. Special Forces was like some kind of super-university where the learning curves were tough, the lifestyle tougher, the possibility of sudden violent death never far away, and the pay on a par with a schoolteacher's salary. But those who survived the experience ultimately emerged from it as life members of the most exclusive club in the world, with their real careers still ahead of them. Former SAS and SBS guys were in high demand for plum jobs as senior security advisors in Iraq, Afghanistan and elsewhere, with earning potential running into hundreds of thousands a year, tax-free, for a fraction of the workload they were used to, and virtually zero risk. Others did what Ben had done for several years after quitting the military, go freelance as what he'd termed a 'crisis response consultant', before Le Val had entered his life.

In short, for men of their qualifications it was a world of opportunity. Le Val certainly had paid off on everyone's expectations. So as far as Jeff was concerned, to have put yourself through the living hell they had, come through it alive and then invested all that hard-won knowledge and experience into the best private tactical training facility in Europe, just to abandon it and go wandering off into the sunset like some kind of half-arsed nomad, was completely nuts. It was an opinion he'd frequently expressed to Ben, in increasingly strong terms as it became increasingly apparent that Ben wasn't coming back.

Ben respected his old friend's point of view, and had always felt bad for having left Jeff holding the baby. But he felt he'd had no choice but to walk away from Le Val. Only

Ben understood the deep inner restlessness that troubled his soul and drove him to do the things he did.

Lately, though, a growing shadow of doubt had been hanging over him and Jeff's words were often in his mind. The trouble with walking away from a lucrative little enterprise like Le Val, with no other employment on the horizon, was that unless you were a millionaire it was no kind of an effective long-term financial proposition. And the Lord knew Ben Hope was no millionaire – never had been, never would be, never wanted to be. Technically speaking, he remained part-owner and a sleeping partner in the business, and could therefore be drawing an income from it if he'd so desired. But to Ben's mind, if he wasn't doing the work he didn't deserve to benefit from the profits, and had insisted on not receiving a penny from Le Val since the day he'd quit, choosing instead to support himself independently from his savings. He'd known, of course, that they wouldn't last forever, and he'd been careful. But the laws of simple economics couldn't be cheated, and slowly, slowly, his funds had dwindled away until worryingly little remained, leaving him to face some key decisions.

The first of those decisions was that he needed to sell his place in Paris. He'd occasionally toyed with the idea in the past, but now the time had finally come to put it on the market. The one-bedroom apartment had been a gift from a former client, years ago, and for a long time had served Ben as a base while travelling in Europe. He'd called it his safehouse, because it was so tucked away among a cluster of backstreet buildings that you'd never find it if you didn't know it was there. On more than one occasion, it had lived up to its name when he'd needed a place to lie low. But now it was nothing more than a pointless luxury, and a financial asset he could no longer afford to hang onto. Ben had reckoned he could get it all fixed up himself, without having to spend a fortune. A patch-up repair here, a lick of paint there, and he was confident it could make an ideal pad for a single guy or gal, perhaps even a young couple looking to get into the property market.

And so, with some regret, Ben had come to Paris to do the necessary.

And that was when the trouble had started.

Chapter 2

The first thing Ben had noticed on his return was how rundown the whole neighbourhood looked. Shop fronts that had been scrubbed and spotless last time he'd seen them were now covered in graffiti. A striking number of windows were boarded up where they'd been broken and never repaired, as if the local business community had fallen into some kind of collective apathy. The secondhand bookstore he'd often spent hours browsing in, just up the street from the apartment, was closed down. So was the great little patisserie where he'd always bought his morning croissants. Once bustling with life, the streets seemed weirdly empty. The few people Ben did pass looked furtive and anxious.

The area had never been the most prime location in Paris, by any stretch of the imagination – it wasn't Avenue Montaigne or the Champs Élysées. But something was different. Not just visibly, but tangibly. Like something in the air, a chill or a shadow, the dropping of a barometer needle signalling a change in pressure and things set to turn stormy. He could sense it like a bad smell. It was the oddest thing, but he put it out of his mind as he made his way from the underground car parking space and up the steps to the familiar old apartment entrance.

Ben had been away from the safehouse long enough to

find everything inside covered in a fine layer of dust. Still, it felt like part of him, like a comfortable old shoe, and he hated thinking he'd soon have to part with it. He fired up the heating to get some warmth into the place. Rooting in the kitchen cupboard he found an unopened pack of ground espresso not too far past its sell-by date, brewed up a mug of coffee, strong and black, the way he liked it, and then said to himself, 'Right. Let's get to work.'

He'd spent the rest of that first day cleaning up and surveying each room in turn with a critical eye, trying to see it from the perspective of a potential buyer, and making mental lists of what needed doing to bring the place up to scratch. It was fairly spartan and he'd never done much to try to furnish it beyond the absolute basics, but it wasn't in terrible shape. The most obvious first step was a general freshening-up of the decor, so the morning after his arrival, Ben had gone out to pick up the necessary supplies.

After paying a visit to the local hardware store for some decorating sundries, he'd headed for Abdel's grocery shop just around the corner from the safehouse to buy in some food provisions for the few days he expected to be around. Ben had known Abdel for years, and liked him a lot. They'd long ago got into the habit of conversing in the Algerian's native Arabic, which Ben spoke almost as well as he did French. Abdel was a good-natured guy, invariably cheerful, grinning a mile wide and ever ready with a funny anecdote.

Not today. The moment Ben had walked into the shop, he'd sensed the same change he'd been sensing everywhere.

And when he'd quizzed Abdel about what was wrong, it soon began to make sense. At first nervous and reluctant to talk, Abdel told Ben about the Romanian criminal gang who had steadily been taking over the neighbourhood during the last year.

'I have nothing against immigrants,' Abdel said. 'Why should I? My parents came here in '65. But these people are like animals. They have come here only to take and destroy. They are greedy for anything they can get. Stealing from tourists isn't enough for them any more.' He explained how the Romanians' enterprise had swelled and their confidence grown at such an alarming rate that within a matter of months they'd started leaning on local businesses and extorting protection money out of them, using the threat of vandalism as their incentive. Now Ben understood why he'd been seeing so many broken windows everywhere. The nearby hardware store he'd visited that morning had been no exception. An assistant had been sweeping glass off the floor as Ben had walked in.

Abdel explained how the Romanians had now started stepping up the pressure, bringing in their heavies to enforce the extortion racket with threats of broken legs, beatings and arson. Meanwhile, they were flooding the neighbourhood with cheap drugs and getting deeper into allied rackets like car theft, burglary and prostitution.

'Everyone is terrified of them. We are hardworking, decent people. We don't deserve this. Look what's happening out there. The streets are empty. People are afraid to go out. Hardly anyone comes into my shop any more, because they're scared of what might happen if the Romanians turned up.'

'What about the police?' Ben asked.

Abdel shrugged. 'What about them? Some of us got together and made an official complaint. We even told them the address where the gang are all living together like a bunch of bandits, making disgusting films and selling women and drugs. We told them the name of the leader, too.'

'Which is what?' Ben asked.

16

'He calls himself Dracul.'

Dracul. Ben shook his head. How trite. 'It means "devil" in Romanian,' he said.

'Why would he call himself by such a name?' Abdel asked, frowning.

'Probably because he thinks it sounds scary,' Ben said.

'He *is* scary. A big, big man, with long black hair and a scar on his face. He's easy to recognise. We gave the description to the police. They made us fill out a form and said they would be in touch. Nothing happened. Nobody gives a damn about us little guys.'

Ben sighed. You turned your back for a year, and this was the result of it. The neighbourhood falling into the control of a violent criminal gang wasn't going to do his chances of selling the apartment any favours, either.

There was more. Abdel told Ben that the Romanians wanted two thousand euros from him, a new monthly payment demand Dracul called 'respect tax'. They'd given Abdel a number to phone to say he was agreeing to cough up the money. If he didn't call by three o'clock that afternoon, they'd told him they were going to come and break one arm and one leg. That was so he could still work. Generous. He'd still have to pay, of course. Then if the following month's payment was late, it would be the other arm and the other leg. The next time after that, they'd promised, Dracul was personally going to have his fun with Abdel's fourteen-year-old daughter, Faridah, before handing her over to the boys to be gang-raped and beaten to a pulp. Or maybe they'd drug her up and make her the starlet in one of the hardcore movie productions they were selling on the side.

Ben was very unhappy to hear that. It made his fists tighten.

'What am I going to do?' Abdel said desperately. 'I have no money to pay them. I can't protect my own family from these people.'

'Do nothing,' Ben said. 'Don't call them. Wait for them to come to you.'

'But I told you what they'll do.'

'Everything will be fine,' Ben assured him.

After which Ben had gone back to the apartment, started stripping wallpaper, smoked some cigarettes and drunk some coffee, eaten a tin of cassoulet for lunch and bided his time until the afternoon.

Just before three, he'd left the apartment again and walked to his car, taking with him a few hardware store items he'd tossed inside his bag. He'd made the short drive and parked across the street from Abdel's shop to wait for the Romanians to turn up.

And now here they were, bang on schedule.

Chapter 3

As Ben stepped inside the shop, the two big guys were already standing shoulder to shoulder in front of the counter, glaring at Abdel. There wasn't a customer in the place. The Algerian looked pale. He became even paler when Ben walked in.

At the sound of the tinkling door chime, the Romanians turned in unison to give Ben the dead-eyed warning look that said, 'Stay out of this if you know what's good for you.'

And for a second the pair must have thought it had done the trick, because Ben turned around and walked straight back to the door. Except he didn't walk out of it. Instead, he popped the latch closed and flipped the sign around to say FERMÉ.

Then he turned back around to face them. He smiled. They were giving him their full attention now, arms folded and brows creased with impatience. Ben said in Arabic to Abdel, 'These two won't trouble you any more.'

'Who the fuck are you?' said the Slavic-looking one.

'My name's Ben,' Ben replied, switching to French. 'What's yours?'

'This is your last chance to get the fuck out of here, fuckhead.' Cheap gangsters didn't generally require a very wide vocabulary.

'You should be careful how you talk to me,' Ben said.

The Romanians exchanged glances. The darker one was grinning and shaking his head in amused disbelief at the impudence of this guy. The Slavic one didn't seem quite so confident. Evidently the smarter of the two. 'Yeah? Why's that?' he asked.

'Because I have a gun,' Ben said. He unslung his bag from his shoulder and took out the staple gun he'd bought that morning. A pressed-steel box with a spring-loaded squeeze mechanism. Handy for all kinds of jobs around the home. And outside it.

The Romanians stared at him. Ben aimed the stapler at the Slavic one, squeezed the handle with a *clack*, and the tiny steel staple went pinging through the air to bounce off his big chest.

That was all the provocation the Romanians needed. They both went for him at once.

Four seconds later, both were stretched out side by side on the floor. The dark one was still conscious, but Ben fixed that with a tap to the head with the toecap of his boot.

'*Ya ilahi*,' Abdel gasped, staring down at the inert bodies and wringing his hands. 'Look what you did.'

Next, Ben took out the big roll of tape, then the scissors, followed by a thick black marker pen. He cut off lengths of tape and used them to bind the Romanians' wrists, ankles and knees together. When they were securely trussed up and gagged with more tape over their mouths, he asked Abdel for a sheet of paper.

Abdel tore a blank page from a cash book. Ben scissored it into two halves. Using the marker pen he wrote on one half of the paper the greeting *SALUT*, in big blocky capital letters. On the other he wrote the Romanian gang leader's name.

Hello, Dracul. A clear enough message, sufficiently simple for even the lowliest kind of thug to comprehend, and opening the way to the next phase of Ben's plan. The bodies had to be correctly arranged left to right for it to read properly, but that wouldn't be a problem.

Then Ben used the staple gun to tack each half of the paper in turn to each of the men's foreheads. The hardened steel staples punched out with enough force to drive into wood or plaster, and had no problem biting into bone. They'd need to be prised out with a screwdriver.

Clack. Clack.

Abdel could hardly look. 'You can't do this,' he said.

'I just did,' Ben replied.

'They'll come back. It'll be worse than ever.'

'Trust me, a bunch of miserable cowards like this will leave you alone after today.'

Ben let himself out of the shop, telling Abdel to lock up after him and go and open up the back. Two minutes later, Ben had driven round to the shop's rear entrance, reversing up the narrow alleyway where delivery vans did their drop-offs, and found Abdel standing nervously by the back door. Ben went inside, grabbed one of the unconscious thugs by the ankles and dragged him like a sack of potatoes out to the back, then hefted him into the boot of the Alpina. Then he did the same with the other, and slammed the lid shut on them.

'Now, give me that address and number,' he said to Abdel.

Five minutes later, he turned down the dingy backstreet, past litter bins overflowing with garbage and crumbling walls daubed with obscene slogans and gang marks, and pulled up outside the two-storey corner building in which Abdel had said Dracul and his crooks were holed up. It certainly looked like their kind of place. The ground floor was a disused copy shop with boards for windows, plastered with flyers advertising the services of call girls. The upper windows were grimy and curtained and there was no sign of movement up there, but someone was home. A black Mercedes was parked at the kerbside below, and behind it a white Range Rover. No matter what kind of scummy ratholes gangsters seemed content to live in, they always kept their cars spick and span.

Ben parked the Alpina on the corner, killed the engine and got out, taking his bag. The only person in sight was a junkie stumbling along at the end of the street. Thudding music was coming from the crummy apartment block opposite, pulsing like a headache. A dog was barking somewhere. The wail of a baby, the angry yells of a man and woman arguing. Those weren't the only things Ben could hear. By now, the two thugs inside the boot of his car were awake, their muffled yells and struggles plainly audible from a couple of metres away. Which was exactly what Ben had intended.

Ben walked away from the car, leaving it unlocked, and crossed the street to the apartment block's entrance. He stepped inside just far enough to be half hidden behind the doorway, then leaned against the wall, took out his phone and dialled up the number the Romanians had given Abdel.

The voice that answered after just two rings was deep and gruff. 'Yeah?'

Ben said, 'You don't know who I am, but I know who you are. Take a peep out of your window. I left a present for you outside.'

Chapter 4

Ben cut the call off before the voice could say more. He lit a Gauloise and watched the windows opposite. The flicker of a curtain caught his eye. Behind the dirty pane, a face briefly appeared, scanning the street below. Someone was at home, all right. It wouldn't be long before they came out.

When they did, Ben knew that what would happen next was going to cause heat for him. He wasn't planning on being too gentle with these guys, because that was a language they wouldn't understand. Assuming they could still hold a telephone by the time he was done with them, or get someone else to do it on their behalf, he fully expected them to call the police and start crying victim. And, things being what they were, it was perfectly likely that the grievances of such upstanding citizens could potentially land Ben in more trouble for what he'd done than these guys ever would be for the crimes they were committing every day against the community. It could be a good time to get out of town for a few days. The safehouse was a little too close to the heat. Ben didn't want the expense of checking into a hotel; but there was another place he could stay until the heat died down.

Still watching the building across the street, Ben dialled the number for Le Val. After two rings, a voice Ben had never heard before replied. Last time he and Jeff had spoken, Jeff had said something about hiring a new guy to man the office. Ben thought he spoke with a slight Jamaican lilt to his accent, but he wasn't sure.

For brevity's sake, and because Ben didn't like having to explain himself on the phone to strangers, and also because even speaking to a stranger in what used to be his home felt odd and uncomfortable to him, he didn't say who was calling.

'Jeff there?'

'He's on the range with Jude,' the new guy said casually, obviously assuming from Ben's tone that he wasn't a client. 'Take a message?'

'That's okay, I'll call back,' Ben said. As he put the phone away, he was frowning. *On the range with Jude?* What was Jude doing at Le Val? Ben was thrown by the news for a second, wondering what the hell *that* was all about.

Ben felt suddenly bad that he hadn't even thought about Jude lately. He knew the young guy was at something of a loose end these days, having decided after a year and a half that a degree in Marine Biology from Portsmouth University was not for him, and jacking in his studies. Ben had no idea what he'd been up to since then.

But he didn't have long to think about it. At that moment, a door opened across the street and two men stepped out of the building and started walking towards the parked Alpina. One of them was Dracul.

Abdel's description had been on the understated side. Even from a distance, Ben could see the spectacular scar that looked as if it had been made with a hot poker and stretched from the Romanian's puckered brow to the corner of his mouth, distorting his left eye. For such an ugly guy, he evidently took good care of his thick mane of curly black locks, which hung over his broad shoulders. He was at least six-three, probably two-fifty. He was clutching a stainless steel Taurus nine-millimetre in his right fist, carrying it in plain view as he and his henchman strode towards Ben's car. So much for law and order.

Ben retreated a step further back inside the apartment block doorway, where he could peer around the wall without being seen. As he watched, Dracul and his man stopped near the car. Seeing it was empty, they glanced up and down the street. Then, right on cue, they turned back to stare at the car, and Ben knew they must have heard the muffled noise from the boot.

Dracul signalled to his guy to open it while he covered it with the pistol. The boot lid popped open. The two gangsters stared at what was inside, long enough for the hello message stapled to the captives' foreheads to register.

By that time, Ben had emerged unseen from his doorway and walked up behind them, drawing the shiny new rubber-handled claw hammer from his bag. He didn't waste time introducing himself. First rule, the man with the gun goes down first. Ben clubbed Dracul in the side of the head. It had to be a well-judged blow, because a claw hammer could too easily kill a man with a single hit, and Ben didn't want to kill anyone. Not today.

Dracul went down like a felled tree trunk. His henchman was half-turned towards Ben when the hammer caught him across the cheekbone and his knees folded under him. Two for two. They lay slumped on the pavement.

'Face it, boys,' Ben said. 'You just haven't got the hardware.'

Spectators were starting to appear at the apartment block windows overlooking the street. Ben ignored them. He relieved Dracul of the Taurus, clicked the safety on and slipped it in his belt. It wasn't that he wanted a gun, but he couldn't responsibly leave the thing lying around in the street for some kid to pick up and start playing about with. Next he used the hammer to knock out the two men in the boot again, then hauled each one out in turn and dumped them on the pavement next to their boss.

Once that was done, Ben grabbed Dracul's jacket collar and yanked him into a sitting position against the copy shop wall, and slapped his scarred face a few times until the Romanian's eyes fluttered open. Dracul blinked and tried to shake his head into focus. He seemed about to say something, then let out a sharp cry as Ben's boot toecap landed hard and square in his testicles.

'Consider yourself lucky you get to keep them,' Ben told him. 'Normally, depraved losers who want to molest innocent young girls should have them sliced off. But I don't like to get my hands all blooded up.' He knelt beside the groaning Dracul. 'Now listen to me carefully, because you'll hear it only once. Here's what you're going to do. You're going to disband your merry men and wrap up your operation, lock, stock and barrel, effective as of today. Then you're going to return all the money you took, with interest. Then you'll apologise in person to the people you hurt, begging for their forgiveness. After that, you're going to get yourself into a better line of work and never bother anyone again. If I hear you didn't do any of that and decided to play sillybuggers behind my back instead, you won't see me coming, because you'll already be dead. Now, what did I just say?'

Dracul grimaced in pain and groggily repeated back what Ben had told him.

'Excellent,' Ben said. 'Now you're going to go sleepy-byes for a while. Your new life begins from the moment you wake up.' He whacked Dracul over the head with the flat of the hammer. The Romanian's eyes rolled back in their sockets and he went limp.

Taking the scissors from his bag, Ben grabbed a handful of Dracul's thick black hair and sheared it roughly off, close to the scalp. He kept scissoring away until the pavement looked like the floor of a dog grooming parlour and the gang leader resembled Samson in the Old Testament story, after Delilah had chopped off his hair and robbed him of his superhuman power. For quite some time to come, whenever Dracul looked in the mirror, he'd be reminded of the promise he'd just made.

Ben left the piles of black curls lying around next to him to find when he came to. More people were staring from the apartment block. A couple of people cheered. Others might not be so happy to see their local dealers being put out of business.

Ben was nearly done. Just a couple more finishing touches, and he'd be gone before the police turned up. Lining up the unconscious bodies in a row, he used the heel of his boot to break all their wrists and ankles. Snap, snap, snap, snap, four times over. Sixteen fractures, with about ten years' worth of healing between them. That seemed a reasonable amount of punishment. The final icing on the cake wasn't going to hurt them, at least not physically. Ben reached into his bag for the half-litre tin of buttercup-yellow paint he'd bought to refresh his kitchen door with. The kitchen door would just have to wait. He levered the lid off with the claw of the hammer, tossed it away, upturned the pot and poured the paint all over Dracul and his men. Yellow, the universal colour of cowardly little bullies, extortionists and rapists.

'That should do the trick,' Ben said to himself, standing back to survey the final humiliation. Then he walked back to the car, climbed in, fired it up and took off with a squeal of tyres.

Chapter 5

It was dark by the time the Alpina bumped down the track to the security gate that barred public entry to the complex at Le Val, three hours and twenty-two minutes later. Ben still had a pass card, and fed it into the scanner to open the gate and drive on through.

The November drizzle had been thickening steadily since nightfall. A cold mist swirled around the beams of his headlights as Ben drove into the main yard of what had once been his home. It seemed weird to be back after such a prolonged absence.

The dogs were the first to notice his arrival. The four German shepherds that freely roamed the twenty-acre compound like a pack of wolves would have been enough to petrify any unauthorised visitor, but the sight of them charging towards him out of the mist as he stepped from the car brought a wide smile to Ben's face.

'Storm! Mauser! Luger! Solo!' He greeted them warmly in turn, crouching down to give each a hug as they swarmed happily around him, slapping him with their big hairy tails and panting their hot doggy breath all over him and slathering his face and hands with their lolling tongues. Storm was the pack leader out of the four, and had always been Ben's particular favourite, often accompanying him on long runs and rambles through the Normandy country-side. Ben hadn't seen him in such a long time that he hadn't been certain if the dog would even recognise him. Storm's delight at his master's return almost brought a tear to Ben's eye – not that he'd ever have admitted as much to Jeff.

The fifth dog to come bowling out of the darkness to meet him was less of a customary sight at Le Val. It was Scruffy, the wiry-haired terrier of indeterminate breed and independent spirit who, if he could be said to be anyone's property, belonged to Jude Arundel and lived with him in the English country vicarage where he'd grown up. Ben patted the terrier affectionately. 'Hey, Scruff. What the hell are you doing here?' Then what the new guy had told Ben on the phone had to be true. 'Where's Jude?' Ben asked the dog, but Scruffy wasn't telling.

Just then, floodlights on masts burst into life and illuminated the whole inner compound and buildings: the big stone farmhouse and annexe, the training yard, the residential huts, the killing house and storerooms. Ben gazed around him, filled with all kinds of memories.

'Ben?' yelled a familiar voice. Ben turned to see Jeff Dekker running down the steps from the house. Jeff was wearing his usual winter attire, old-pattern DPM combat trousers and a submariner-style jumper. His eyes were huge with surprise, and a grin wider than the radiator grille on a '58 Chevy Impala was spreading over his face. 'Christ, it is you. Welcome, stranger.'

'Hello, Jeff.'

'Well, fuck me sideways. You're about the last person I'd expected to turn up out of the blue.'

'Lucky you,' Ben said. 'I did try to call to say I was coming.'

'Are you staying? Or running off again?'

'I just popped over to check you haven't totally destroyed the place in my absence.'

'Oh, I think we're scraping by okay,' Jeff said, grinning even more widely. 'Come inside. I just opened a bottle.'

'Scotch?'

''Fraid we don't carry much of a stock of the hard stuff since you buggered off and left us. Make do with wine?'

'Good enough,' Ben said.

Jeff had moved out of his quarters in the annexe after Ben's departure, and taken up residence in the farmhouse. He led Ben into the familiar old stone-floored rustic kitchen. Gazing around him, Ben saw that nothing had changed. The solid fuel range was lit and filling the kitchen with a rosy glow of warmth.

'Cold tonight,' Ben said.

'Colder than a witch's tit in a brass bra,' Jeff said. Jeff had always had that way with words. He grabbed an extra wine-glass from the side and set about filling it up from the open bottle of Côtes du Rhône. They sat at the table where the two of them had spent many an evening drinking, playing chess, and sharing ideas about how they were going to make Le Val a success. Jeff slid Ben's glass to him over the worn pine table.

They clinked. 'Cheers,' Jeff said. 'To old times.'

'Old times.'

'And future ones, maybe,' Jeff said.

'We'll have to see about that.'

'So, dare I ask to what we owe the pleasure of your company?'

Ben savoured a gulp of the wine. 'You can ask,' he said. 'Let's just say I'm staying away from town for a few days.' Dracul's Taurus was still in his belt. He slipped it out, ejected the mag, locked back the slide to make the weapon safe and laid it on the table. 'Might want to stick that in the armoury when you get a moment. Its owner won't be needing it any more.'

Jeff gazed pensively at the gun. 'On second thoughts, mate, I'm not sure I want to know.'

They spent a few minutes catching up. Ben had little to report on his activities since they'd last seen each other, even though there was enough there to fill volumes. He especially had nothing to report on the love life front. He wasn't hiding anything on that score.

For his own part, Jeff revealed with a coy grin that he'd recently met a woman he liked. Her name was Chantal and she was a primary school teacher in the nearby village. It sounded serious, which was a departure for Jeff, whose long string of part-time, on-off, short-term girlfriends had been scattered across most of Lower Normandy and had seldom ever been brought home to Le Val – partly because he'd never met one he wanted to get too permanent with, and partly due to the sensitive nature of the business that went on there.

'How is business?' Ben asked, reaching for his cigarettes and Zippo lighter.

'Oh, you know, booming.' Jeff spent a few more minutes updating him on all the latest developments at Le Val, while Ben smoked and helped himself to more wine. Final touches were being put to the extended rifle range and the new classroom facilities, and they had contracts coming in from all over the place with a five-month waiting list because they couldn't cram it all in.

'If things keep up at this crazy pace, we're going to outgrow this place and need to start up another, just to meet demand,' Jeff said. Just when things had been getting ridiculously busy, Paul Bonnard, who had been with the team since the beginning, had left to take a job at the renowned Gunsite tactical training academy in Paulden, Arizona. Jeff had employed two new staff members to fill the gap left by his departure. One was Ludivine Tournoy, a sixty-year-old former bank manager's secretary from the nearby village who was now coming in part-time as an office assistant.

The other was a young British ex-infantryman who went by the name of Tuesday Fletcher. He was twenty-four, had done three years with the Royal Fusiliers and seen some warm action in Helmand Province, Afghanistan. His ambition, though, had been to become the first British Jamaican ever to qualify for 22 SAS. An ambition he might have achieved, if he hadn't taken a bad fall during the endurance phase of selection testing in the Brecon Beacons. Tumbling down a rocky hillside with fifty kilos of gear on his back, Tuesday had broken four ribs, his left wrist, his left femur and his tibia in two places. When he'd bounced back two months later, still temporarily on crutches after complications and surgery, his military career was over.

'He got a shitty deal from them, if you ask me,' Jeff said. 'But that's the army for you. Won't be long before they've got more Health and Safety officers than they have combatants.'

'What's he doing here?' Ben asked.

'Sniper trainer,' Jeff said. 'He's got some skill with the rifle, I tell you. Better than anyone I've ever seen. Better than you, even.'

'No, I mean, what brought him here?'

Jeff smiled. 'He wanted to work with you, Ben. I had to tell him your absence was just temporary, or he wouldn't have taken the job. Said they still talk about you in the Sass. Said you're his idol. Said—'

'I get the message,' Ben said irritably.

Jeff smiled wider. 'You never did take compliments well. Tough shit, 'cause I've got another one for you. I suppose you must've heard the news about old man Kaprisky?'

Auguste Kaprisky was an eighty-one-year-old Swiss-French billionaire with a château and estate near Le Mans, who couldn't spend enough on personal security. While still at Le Val, Ben had provided advanced VIP protection training to his small army of bodyguards.

'No, what about him?' Ben asked.

'It was all over the TV for a while. You must have been, um, busy.'

'You know I don't watch TV.'

'Papers?'

'You know I don't read those either.'

'How can you know what goes on in the world if you don't follow the news?'

'Because the less you follow the news,' Ben said, 'the more you know what goes on.'

'You're weird, you know that?' Jeff shrugged. 'Anyway, couple months back, a business rival of his went crazy over some lost deal or other that cost them a packet, got hold of an Uzi from somewhere and took a pop at the old boy.'

'Is he dead?'

Jeff shook his head. 'About a thousand holes in his house, but the ninjas took the bad guy down in short order. Nice job, too. Kaprisky swears he wouldn't have survived it if we hadn't trained up his team so well. You got a very nice letter of thanks, which I took the liberty of opening in your absence. Usual kind of thing, "Ben Hope saved my life; Ben Hope kicks arse; Ben Hope walks on water", etc., etc., blah, blah, and there's nothing he won't do for us in return. He's also recommended us to a bunch of his rich pals, three of whom have already been in touch wanting to make bookings.'

Ben disliked the spotlight, but he was pleased to hear things were going well. So far, though, he noticed, Jeff hadn't said anything about Jude being there. Which Ben thought was a little odd, so he decided to raise the subject himself.

'I gather you have a visitor?' he said. 'Someone I might know?'

Jeff's hesitation in replying gave away what Ben already suspected. 'He told you not to tell me, didn't he? Why? Where is he?'

'He's not here,' Jeff said.

'Don't fuck about with me, Jeff.'

'I'm not. He *was* here, for the last seven weeks. But you missed him. He's gone.'

'What was he doing here?' Ben asked. 'Seven *weeks*?'

'He wanted to do some training. That's what we do here, isn't it?'

'Training for what?' Ben said suspiciously.

Jeff looked at him. 'What is it with you two? First he's all cagey about you finding out he was here. Now you're firing questions at me, like it's such a big deal. Why get so het up about what Jude wants to do? He's over twenty-one, isn't he?'

'Just.'

'So what? I know you were close with his folks, but—'

'Training for what, Jeff?'

'Navy,' Jeff said with a sigh. 'Why he asked me not to tell you, it beats me. But now I have, so do me a favour and keep it to yourself, okay?'

Ben set his wineglass down. 'He wants to join the navy?'

'That's what I said. He's serious, too. Got the initial interview lined up in February, then the medical and PJFT two weeks later.' Jeff was talking about the Royal Navy's strenuous pre-joining fitness test, which all recruits had to pass before they could even commence the ordeal of basic training. 'So when he called me and said he wanted to get in shape and talk to me about what navy life was like, I said no problem, come over.'

'I see,' Ben said, tapping his glass with a fingertip.

'He's a natural,' Jeff said. 'Always saying how much he loves the sea, so I took him up to the Pointe de Barfleur to watch him swim. He's like a bloody fish in the water. Then we did weapons training, physio, technical knowledge, the works. He won't have a problem getting past the tests. In fact I'll eat my boots if he doesn't come top of the class in all of them. Where he gets it from, vicar's son and all that, who knows?'

Ben frowned.

Jeff went on, 'So, yeah, he hung around for a few weeks, helping out around the place to earn his keep. I enjoyed having him here, and he had a good time too, even if I worked him like a bastard. Like I said, you just missed him. He left for Africa this morning.'

Chapter 6

Ben blinked and thought for a second that he must have misheard. 'Africa?'

'Strictly speaking, he left here for Oman,' Jeff said. 'And he won't be *in* Africa unless he goes ashore when they touch at port, he'll be *off* Africa. South from the Port of Salalah, around the horn and down the east coast to Mombasa. He's got himself a crewman gig on the MV *Svalgaard Andromeda*.'

'A merchant vessel?'

Jeff nodded. 'Big Yank container ship, one of the Svalgaard Line. It's a good way for him to get the feel of things, learn about life at sea before he goes in at the deep end, so to speak. Wants to put a bit of money under his belt, too.'

'And I suppose it was you who set this up for him?' Ben asked.

Jeff nodded again. 'I know a guy who knows a guy, the usual thing. All it took was a couple of calls. Where's the bloody harm?'

Ben felt his rising frustration reddening into anger. 'Jude doesn't need to take a job like that to earn money. He has plenty already. He inherited everything from his parents when they died.' It still upset Ben to think about his old friends, and the car smash that had claimed both their lives that terrible December night, just a few miles from their village in rural Oxfordshire.

'Not what he told me,' Jeff said. 'He said he's skint. Doesn't have the nails to scratch himself with. All he has is the house, and he doesn't want to sell it. They didn't leave him much else. I don't think vicars earn a heck of a lot.'

'Anyway, that's not the point,' Ben said irritably. 'I don't want him joining the navy. Or the army, or the RAF, or anything else.'

'What's wrong with it?'

'It's just not the kind of life I see for him,' Ben said.

'The kind of life *you* see for him? What's that supposed to mean?'

'You heard me,' Ben said. Their voices were rising. 'I'm not happy about this, Jeff. You should have cleared it with me first.'

'Oh, right. Like I needed your permission to show him a few things and help him on his way doing something he's got his mind set on?'

'That's the whole point,' Ben said. 'He's stubborn, and he's wilful, and he'll throw himself into any risky situation that comes his way without a second thought. And you went and encouraged him, behind my back.'

'What are you getting so uptight about anyway? Jesus Christ, you talk as if he was your bloody son.'

Ben was silent a beat.

Then said, 'Jeff, he *is* my son.'

Jeff sat back in his chair, stunned. 'Are you kidding me? How can that be?'

'It just is,' Ben said.

Jeff stared at Ben, scrutinising his face as if he was seeing him for the first time. 'It's obvious, really, when you think about it.'

'Fancy that.'

'He's got your eyes. And your chin. Hair colour too.'

'If that was all he had of mine, it wouldn't be a problem.'

'But now I'm confused. Only a minute ago, you said his parents left him money when they died.'

'That's just what Jude thought.'

Jeff frowned, even more confused. 'So . . . his father wasn't a vicar at all.'

'That's the whole point, isn't it?' Ben said. 'I wish he had been. Simeon was a good man. A better one than me, that's for sure.'

'Then . . . what about his mother?'

'His mother was his mother. Michaela Arundel.'

'Then you and she—'

'You're the last guy I'd imagine believing in Immaculate Conception,' Ben said. 'Obviously, yes.'

'When did this happen?'

'Uh, at a rough guess, I'd say Jude's age plus nine months ago,' Ben said. 'It was when we were all students together, long before she and Simeon were married. Simeon knew all about it. She never tried to pretend that it was anything other than it was.'

Jeff was staring at him in amazement. 'And what about Jude, does he know?'

'It was agreed to keep it secret from him. He only found out the truth by chance, after they died. It was a bit rocky at first, but he accepts it.' Which wasn't strictly accurate, but it was the best Ben could do to describe their faltering relationship without getting into the painful details. The reality was that they hadn't spoken in well over a year, and Ben could easily imagine more years going by before they spoke again, if ever. The last words his son had said to him still resonated in his mind.

'Oh, just fuck off, *Dad*.'

Jeff was still stunned. 'Who else knows about this? Does Brooke know?'

Ben nodded.

'And Boonzie?'

'Him too,' Ben said.

'Then how come you never told me?'

'You were there when I told Boonzie.'

'When?'

'Right after the thing in the Gulf of Finland. Can I help it if you weren't paying attention?'

'I'd just taken a bloody rifle bullet in the leg,' Jeff said.

'It hardly touched you.'

'I was unconscious, for Christ's sake.'

'Then you should have woken up. I can't be repeating myself all the time.'

'It's not fair. How come I'm always the last to know these things? How come the others never told me either?'

'Maybe they thought you lacked the emotional maturity to be able to handle it,' Ben said. 'So now you know. And that's why I don't want him joining the damn services. The last thing I need is Jude following in my footsteps. Next thing he'll be wanting to do something even more stupid, like get it into his head to try out for Special Forces.'

Back in Ben and Jeff's day, SAS and SBS recruits had undergone separate selection processes; nowadays it was all run together under the joint auspices of UKSF. The few who survived the ninety percent failure rate were then streamed into their different divisions. In addition to the torture of hill marching, jungle combat, parachute, survival, evasion and resistance to interrogation training, Special Boat Service candidates were put through battle swimming and progressive dive tests in order to qualify as Swimmer Canoeists, before ultimately going on to join an operational squadron.

Jeff went quiet.

Ben narrowed his eyes. 'He didn't. Did he?'

'He did. I'm sorry. He went on about it quite a bit.'

'And of course, you didn't try to talk him out of it. Did you, Jeff?'

'Give me a break. He wanted to know what it's like in the SBS. How to apply to get in, what the training involves, what it takes to get badged, the kind of life it is, and all that sort of stuff. What was I supposed to do, refuse to tell him? He could've found most of it out online anyway. All I did was add in a few details. The kind of stuff you'd only know about if you'd been there and done it. I had to give him a proper idea, didn't I? I mean, he asked me, for fuck's sake.'

'Jesus, Jeff.'

But Ben knew there was little point in arguing. Jude was gone, and as usual, Ben hadn't been there for him. It was the story of their whole relationship, from day one.

'He's got a fire in the belly, Ben. Just like we had at his age. You can't stop him, if that's what he wants to do. Maybe it's in the blood.'

'Yeah. I know,' Ben said. 'That's exactly what I'm afraid of.'

Chapter 7

Port of Salalah, Oman
Two days later

When he climbed out of the taxi, still lagged from the long flight, and followed the directions he'd been given through the thirty-degree heat and clamour of the bustling port to where the *Svalgaard Andromeda* lay moored at the dockside, Jude's first impression was of the ship's sheer enormity. He'd expected it to be large, but checking out images on Google and seeing it for real were two completely different things.

For a few moments, planted on the dock clutching his backpack and surrounded by busy workers running here and there, forklift trucks zapping to and fro and the general noisy activity of the largest commercial seaport in Oman, all Jude could do was boggle at the overwhelming vastness of what was to be his home and workplace for the next little while.

It looked more like a floating city than a boat. Stretching over nine hundred feet from end to end, it was longer than the Trump World Tower in New York laid on its side. The black, rust-streaked sides of its hull towered over the dock with SVALGAARD LINE, the name of America's fifth-largest shipping company, painted in white letters twenty feet high.

Most of the vessel was deck, which by the time Jude arrived at port was already in the final stages of being stacked high with cargo by the ship's on-board forty-foot cranes. As he already knew from his web browsing, *Andromeda* had been built in 2007 and was listed as a Panamax-class vessel rated at 4,000 TEU capacity, which meant simply that she could accommodate four thousand twenty-foot-equivalent units of intermodal shipping containers. As he would later learn, the mixed cargo on this voyage consisted of vast quantities of electrical goods, generators, building supplies, agricultural equipment, tyres, and a million other items due for delivery to the various ports they would be visiting as they cruised southwards across the Indian Ocean on what was known as the East Africa run: stopping off at Djibouti, the Kenyan port of Mombasa and, finally, Dar es Salaam.

'Well, here I am,' Jude muttered to himself. This was it. There was no turning back now. The slight nervousness he'd felt ever since Jeff Dekker had lined him up with this job was intermingled with excitement at the prospect of going to sea for the first time as a real mariner, one of the ABs, short for able-bodied seamen, who crewed the ship along with the engine room team, the mates and the captain himself.

As he walked up the gangway he was met by a ruddy-faced, sandy-haired American wearing an open-necked khaki shirt and a look of harassed urgency, who briskly welcomed him aboard and introduced himself as Jack Skinner, ship's bosun.

'No time to give you the guided tour right now,' Skinner explained. 'Just do what you're told and try not to get in the way, okay?' Which was fine by Jude, even if the guy's manner was a little short. Jude figured he'd have to get used to that kind of thing if he wanted to join the Royal Navy.

Skinner quickly handed him over to an older AB called Mitch, whom Jude guessed to be from one of the southern US states – not that he was an expert on accents, but the Confederate flag T-shirt was something of a giveaway. Mitch seemed happy to get a few moments' break from his duties to grab a quick smoke and lead the new recruit to his quarters on C Deck. C Deck was the second floor of the looming seven-storey superstructure towards the rear of the ship – Jude had made a mental note to try to use nautical terms like 'stern' – that was known as 'the house'. Jude had seen smaller apartment buildings.

'You a Limey, right?' Mitch asked with a gap-toothed grin. 'I sailed with Polaks, Krauts, Gooks, Jappos, Eye-ties, all sorts. Never sailed with a Limey before.'

Welcome to the United Nations. 'Got a problem with it?' Jude said.

Mitch shrugged. 'So what's your story? You don't look like no sailor to me. More like a college boy. Daddy's a lawyer, right? Or a doctor. Wants you to join the family firm and this is your way of telling'm to go screw himself.'

'I'm not a college boy,' Jude said firmly. 'I'm anything but that.'

Mitch grinned again and punched him in the arm. 'Hey, just fucking with you, man. Lighten up. Betcha I'm right, though, huh? The daddy thing?'

Jude felt like telling him to keep his nose out of his business, but that didn't feel like the best start to a happy working relationship with his fellow crewmen.

'My father's dead,' he said after a beat, and then repeated it, as if somehow he had to make it doubly true. To have lost one father, only to discover another you didn't want to know – that had been a difficult and confusing time and he wanted to put it behind him. Closure was the best way. 'My father's dead. So's my mother. There is no family firm. No family at all. Just me.'

'Shit, man, sorry to hear it.'

'Yeah, whatever,' Jude said, looking around at his new quarters. There wasn't a lot to see. Being the most junior of the crew, he had been lodged in what he suspected to be – and later discovered was – the smallest and most cramped of the cabins allocated to the ABs. He had no problem with that, however. He intended to enjoy every minute of this adventure to the full. After stowing his backpack in the locker next to his berth, he followed Mitch back down onto the cargo deck and was immediately plunged into the hectic activity of helping to load the rest of the containers on board prior to shipping out.

Mitch, the amiable bigot who liked to poke into people's personal lives, quickly turned out to be not such a bad guy at all, to Jude's relief. 'Don't you mind Skinner,' Mitch advised him as he showed him how to lash down a container to prevent it from slipping in heavy weather. 'He's one mean, tough, hard-assed sonofabitch and a hell of a screamer, but do your job, keep your head down and your nose clean and he won't give you too much shit.' Which was good to know.

'What about the other officers?' Jude asked.

'We don't call 'em officers in the merchant marine. You got Frank Wilson, the chief mate. We just say "the mate". He's okay, I guess. Between you and me, he likes a drink. Starts every trip with a full case of Jim Beam. Catch'm on a good day, you wouldn't know it, but . . .' Mitch rolled his eyes knowingly. 'Then you got Diesel, he's what we call the chief. Chief engineer,' he explained for Jude's benefit. 'He's only about a million years old, knows every nut, bolt and rivet of this ol' tub like you wouldn't believe. Guzman, second mate, he's a slob, eats like a hog and he's so full of lard he can't hardly move. The boys call'm the Guzzler, but not to his face, okay? Then you got Ricky Marshall, the third mate. Real straight-up guy. You ask me, he oughta be captain.'

'Got it,' Jude said, making mental notes of it all. 'And what about the captain? What's he like?'

Mitch gave a noncommittal shrug. 'I sailed with Cappy O'Keefe a bunch of times, been loop the loop around the damn world together twice, three times, maybe more. He's comin' up for retirement. Ain't the guy he used to be. Spends most of his time in his cabin, writing long emails to his wife back home in Indiana, while he leaves it to Wilson and Skinner to do all the hard work. Then Wilson and Skinner pass it all down to the rest of us. That's pretty much the system here, kid. Better get used to it. You'll earn your money on board this ship, believe me.'

Jude was unafraid of hard work, which was just as well, because Mitch hadn't been joking. By the time the *Andromeda* was finally loaded up and ready to set off, Jude was drenched with sweat and fit to drop from exhaustion – and his first day on board had barely even begun. He watched from the deck as, to the deep throb of the diesel engines, they made their way out of the port and through the lesser shipping towards open sea. It was a heady feeling for Jude, and tired as he was, he couldn't keep the grin off his face. Before long, the land sank out of sight and they were alone under the vast empty bowl of the sky, with nothing but the deep blue-green waters of the Indian Ocean from horizon to horizon.

The voyage had begun.

And if Jude had known then how it was going to end, he would have dived straight into the sea and started swimming back to shore.

Chapter 8

Before now, Jude had never been on any kind of boat for longer than a few hours at a time, and he'd wondered about things like ocean sickness. But the Indian Ocean was as smooth as an endless sheet of blue glass, and after a couple of days he'd found his sea legs and the gentle movement of the ship felt as natural as being on land.

It might take him a little longer to get used to the heat, which was oppressive and humid everywhere except on the outer deck, where it was just scorching. And the three hours' sleep a night, four if you were lucky, took some adapting to as well. No time in the merchant navy to lounge on deck with a gin and tonic in your hand, admiring the view and counting dolphins. That was for sure.

He was getting to know his way around a little better, as well as getting to know his fellow crewmen. The mess and canteen were situated down on A Deck, two floors down from his quarters, where a lot of tired and hungry sailors would gather to recuperate from their shifts, to eat, smoke, gulp gallons of coffee and shoot the breeze. There were fourteen ABs aboard including himself – although, as far as he could see, some of them didn't really seem to be that able-bodied at all after so many years at sea. A number of the sailors were in their sixties, work-hardened and leathery as hell but beginning to show the strains of a lifetime of physical hardship. For many of them, this was the only life they'd ever known, and Jude quickly learned that it was one that seemed to attract some very colourful characters. The casual, totally non-uniform dress code among the ABs wasn't exactly what he could later expect to find aboard a Royal Navy ship, either. Tatty sweatshirts, faded jeans, military surplus gear, anything went. Steve Maisky, an ageing hippy who for reasons best known to himself insisted on being known as 'Condor' and claimed to have been hopping ships ever since dodging the draft for Vietnam in 1972, jangled with beads and bangles and had grey hair in a ratty ponytail that hung halfway down the back of his Grateful Dead T-shirt. He was benevolently disapproved of by Lou Gerber, a white-bearded ex-US Marine five years his senior, who strutted about in khakis and combat boots with a shapeless fatigue hat jammed on his balding pate to protect him from the sun.

Jude had developed a liking for Mitch and thought he could learn a lot from him. During work and breaks, the older man regaled him with all manner of colourful and sometimes improbable tales from his twenty-odd years in the merchant navy. Mitch had seen the world, all of it. There was, he claimed, not a bar or gambling den or whorehouse in any port town on the face of the planet that he hadn't frequented and in some way left his mark on. He'd been thrown out of many, barred from several. He'd been carried back comatose to his ship on a wheelbarrow more than once or twice. He'd been knifed in the ribs over a card game in Sri Lanka and shot at by a disgruntled pimp in Hong Kong. He'd won more bare-knuckle fights and arm-wrestling bouts than he'd lost, made a ton of money on them, too. He'd had more women, and probably fathered more children, than he could count or remember. It had been, he told Jude with a contented grin, one hell of a crazy run and it wasn't nearly over yet.

'What the hell for?' he asked when Jude told him of his own ambitions to join the Royal Navy. 'Do yourself a favour, partner. You don't wanna get in with that bunch of tight-assed dipshits. You wanna sail the world, Jude, then this is the way to do it. There is,' he added grandly, 'no better life for a free man than this one right here.'

'A free man?'

'You ain't got no wife back home, do you? Not at your age, right?'

Jude shook his head. 'Girlfriend. Nothing that serious.' The truth was, he was pretty certain his thing with Helen, who'd been a year below him at university, was dead and buried now that he'd dropped out of his studies. Her parents disapproved of his 'dissolute ways' and were a little too much of an influence on their daughter. He still wore the little bracelet she'd given him, a string of beads that spelled her name. He hadn't had the heart to throw it away.

'I'm not one to go givin' advice,' Mitch said, happy to go on dispensing it freely. 'But don't go gettin' yourself saddled. I finally had the good sense to walk away after number four. Lord knows there ain't no ocean as cold nor no mountain on this earth as hard as a woman's heart. These days I keep the bitches strictly on a payin' basis, if you get my drift.'

'I'll take your word for it,' Jude said, with a smile.

For all that he was making friends and feeling more comfortable by the hour in his new environment, Jude wasn't so sure about all his fellow crewmen. In particular, a chisel-faced, greasy-haired ex-biker called Scagnetti, who wore a grimy wife-beater T-shirt to show off his muscles and tattoos, and whose moods fluctuated between being silent and sullen, then argumentative and prone to lash out at the slightest provocation. He had been a Harley mechanic somewhere down in New Mexico before he'd gravitated to stealing choppers, nearly got caught and fled to sea. Everyone had a story, it seemed.

Mitch had already warned Jude not to get too close to Scagnetti. 'Dude's a decent enough mariner but there's something ain't quite right up here' – tapping a finger to his head. 'Watch'm, is all I'm sayin'.'

Another crew member Jude quickly warmed to was Hercules, the ship's cook, a larger-than-life black man with a laugh that could vibrate the hull from stem to stern, and who always wore the same frayed old army jacket that was spattered with a thousand grease stains. Hercules's constant companion in the galley, the mess, and everywhere else, perched on his shoulder, was an evil harpy of an African grey parrot that went by the name of Murphy and possessed an even more scatological vocabulary than most of the sailors. Not everyone appreciated the bird, especially after being screeched at repeatedly and at maximum volume to *get the fuck out of here!* – its favourite expression.

'If that vulture of yours shits in my plate, I'm going to chew its goddamned head off and spit out the beak,' complained Gerber, absolutely serious. Which, Hercules later confessed to Jude with a grin, earned Gerber a dollop of green parrot excreta mixed in with his gravy. Gerber either didn't notice, or thought it was an improvement on the usual slop the galley served up. Jude had to secretly agree that, whatever else Hercules might be, he certainly was no chef.

Strangely, Murphy never swore at Jude. On the third day of the voyage, the bird even flapped off its master's shoulder to swoop across the mess and perch on Jude's. 'First time he's ever done that,' Hercules said, mightily impressed, while Jude sat very still and hoped the thing wasn't about to rip his earlobe off with its nutcracker beak.

'Murph has real good taste in people,' Hercules chuckled while pouring Jude a mug of stewed coffee later that day. 'If he don't take kindly to a guy, that's how I know they's an asshole. He's like my early warnin' system.'

'Everyone seems okay to me,' Jude said, playing the diplomatic newbie. 'Mostly, anyway.'

'Ain't such a bad bunch crew on this run,' Hercules said. 'Just that lousy prick Scagnetti and the three a-holes up on D Deck.'

D Deck was where the engineers and mates had their slightly more comfortable quarters than the common crewmen, and for a moment Jude thought Hercules must be referring to some of them.

'Nah, man. Talking about our esteemed fuckin' passengers. Bird don't think too much of them neither, believe me.'

This was the first Jude had heard of passengers on board. No mention of it had been made by anyone until now, which struck him as being odd. 'I didn't realise merchant ships carried anybody but the working crew.'

Hercules sniffed. 'That's 'cause we don't, not as a rule leastways. I been at sea twelve years and I ain't never seen it. This ain't no damn cruise liner. Ain't no Sunday picnic neither. Like I don't already got enough to be doin' down here without I've got to carry up their meals twice a fuckin' day. What, are their asses too high an' mighty to chow down here with the rest of us? Ain't no room for freeloaders in this here merchant marine. Everybody pulls their weight or they ain't got no right bein' here in the first place.'

'What are they, friends of the captain?'

'You bet I already asked the bosun the same question 'fore we shipped out.'

'And what did he say?' Jude asked, wondering whether maybe Jack Skinner wasn't quite as unapproachable as Mitch had suggested.

Hercules grunted. 'Didn't say shit. Just gave me the look that says, don't even fuckin' ask.'

Chapter 9

As he went about his duties that day, Jude kept an eye open in case he might spot one of the mystery passengers. He saw no sign of them, and presumed they must be confining themselves to their quarters and choosing not to mix with the others on board. But what he did start to pick up more signs of were the grumbles of resentment among the crew against the unknown, nameless, faceless freeloaders up on D Deck. None of his business, he decided, reminding himself that he, too, was just passing through and only here thanks to some favour called in, some string or other pulled by one of Jeff Dekker's connections in the maritime world. He wasn't one of these guys. He was only here to gain knowledge and experience.

Which he was doing, every waking moment. Jude had always been a fast learner, effortlessly remaining top of his class at uni before he'd decided that Marine Biology was not what he wanted to spend his life doing. He was constantly full of questions for Mitch and the others, though careful not to overdo it. He soon filled in the gaps in his knowledge concerning the roles of the senior crewmen. The impressively named Henry Hainsworth O'Keefe was, as he'd supposed, the supreme authority aboard ship, directing things from his throne room up on the bridge. Frank Wilson, the chief mate, was responsible for overseeing the loading and unloading cargo, as well as handling security and the general day-to-day running of the ship. The chief engineer, Diesel, was a rare sight above decks, he and his assistants seldom emerging from their domain in the engine room down below. When not filling his already capacious belly, Guzman, second mate, was the so-called 'paper mate' in charge of navigation, charts and all the electronics up on the bridge. The third mate, Marshall, acted as an assistant. And as Jude had already inferred, the fearsome Skinner's job as bosun was to mediate between the mates and the rest of the crew, as well as ensure discipline on board.

In addition to learning about the men he was sailing with, Jude was also getting to know the ship pretty well. His first impression of a floating city had been perfectly right: you could lose yourself for days in the bewildering, endless maze of passageways and storerooms both above and below decks. Maybe it was because he was the youngest and most fleet of foot out of the crew, or maybe it was just because he was the new meat; either way, Jude found himself running back and forth all day on gopher duty. Clattering up and down rusty iron steps. Fetching this, fetching that, passing messages here and there.

On his errands about ship he was constantly intrigued by the heavy steel-mesh gates that barred virtually every external walkway and ladder, coming up from the deck to the superstructure. Every time you passed through one of the gates, you had to close and lock it behind you. It meant you couldn't go anywhere without first getting a set of keys from the bosun, and returning it afterwards. Unable to think what purpose the gates served, Jude quizzed the old salt Gerber on the matter.

'Those are pirate cages,' Gerber explained with a bristly scowl.

'Pirate cages?'

On the flight to Oman, Jude had contemplated the possible dangers of a voyage down the east coast of Africa. Typhoons, reefs, sharks, heatstroke, getting arrested in port for unruly behaviour and ending up incarcerated in some African jail had all occurred to him. He hadn't once thought about pirates. How could they even still exist, in this day and age? Terrorists, sure. But pirates? To him, the word conjured up images of snarling buccaneers with cutlasses and eye-patches, and the Jolly Roger flying at the masthead. Wasn't that ancient history?

Gerber, however, seemed very certain of the risk. 'Yup. That's what those are, all right. So's if we get boarded by the little darlings, they can't get access to enough key points, the bridge especially, to take over the ship. Only way we can even try to keep those scumsucking bastards off our asses. That, or hose 'em with water as they come up our sides. Some ships pour oily foam on 'em, gunks 'em up good. Needless to say, we got jack shit except a bunch of flimsy wire mesh.'

To Jude's amazement, Gerber explained how little shipping companies did to protect either their property, the cargo they carried or the men they paid to ferry it from the risk of violent armed pirate attacks that kept growing year on year in certain waters. Ships on the East Africa run, Gerber added bitterly, being one of the primary and most frequent prey, targeted by waterborne bandits operating mainly from the Somali coast.

'That's just how it is,' he told Jude. 'Personally, I'd like to see a whole damn locker of M16s on board. Been saying it for years, but who'd listen? Those corporate sonsofbitches would rather leave us out here like sitting ducks than trust us to defend ourselves.'

Jude hated to ask the inevitable question. 'What happens if pirates manage to get past the cages and take over the ship?'

Gerber shrugged. 'Best case, all they want is cash. Every vessel carries a few thousand bucks' worth in reserve in the captain's safe, for emergencies and such. If you get lucky, you might be able to just pay them off, and they'll beat it back to shore to get rat-assed and whored up, and you can go on your way rejoicing. That's how it used to be, more often than not, but it's rare you get off so lightly now. See, when these shit-eaters first started showing up twenty years ago, you were dealing with a few rag-tag fishermen making six hundred dollars a year, who thought five, ten thousand was the haul of a lifetime. Didn't take 'em long to figure out you could make a whole lot more by snapping up the whole ship and holding the cargo and crew for ransom.'

Jude was staring at him. 'They kidnap the crews?'

'This is all news to you, huh, sonny? Sure, these fuckers would kidnap their own mothers for a buck. They're taking hundreds of millions a year now in ransoms. It's big business. Instead of wooden skiffs they're coming out in speedboats, tooled up to the nines with Kalashnikovs, high as kites on fuckin' khat and ready to murder anyone who gets in their way. And they don't just cover a few miles out from the coast like they used to. Not when they can use stolen vessels as mother ships and hunt over the whole ocean looking for a juicy tanker to knock off. It's a whole other ball game now, and it's about goddamn time someone did something about it.'

'I had no idea it was so bad.'

Gerber pulled a disgusted face. 'Well now you have. Bring 'em on, I say. They want a fight, they'll get a fight like they won't believe. I'd rather be dead than wind up a hostage in

55

some Somali stinkpit, or sold as a fuckin' slave to work in a damn copper mine.'

Jude's head was still spinning from what Gerber had told him when he sat down to eat later with Mitch, Condor and another AB called Lang. 'Hey, s'matter, English? You don't think my jokes are funny any more?' Mitch said in a mock-hurt voice after Jude failed to break up at some stupid crack. Jude admitted what was on his mind.

'That old fart Gerber's just looking to scare your Limey ass,' Mitch said.

'Can't get it up no more, so he wants to play *Platoon* instead,' laughed Condor. 'Thinks he's still in 'Nam. You know why they don't issue weapons to merchant crews? So that trigger-happy dudes like Gerber can't shoot the crap out of every bunch of poor schmuck fishermen that come within a thousand-yard range, and call it self-defence. Who's gonna insure us for that?'

Jude wasn't sure. It had sounded pretty plausible the way Gerber described it.

'That's right, man, don't listen to his cranky bullshit,' said Lang, munching loudly on a bacon sandwich and spitting bits out as he talked. 'Sure, the pirates might hit a vessel now and then, but we're talking small trawlers and private yachts mostly. Few years back, they took a pop at a German naval tanker thinking she was a merchant and those Krauts chewed their asses up something terrible. I'll bet ol' Gerber didn't tell you what happened last time a pirate crew touched an American ship, did he?' Lang dragged his forefinger across his throat and smiled wickedly, bits of bacon stuck between his teeth. 'I got two words for you. Navy SEALs.'

'What happened?'

'Let's just say, our boys went home. The bad guys wound up as fish bait.'

'These waters are safe as houses,' Mitch said, ramming home the point. 'Hell, safer. Naval destroyers patrol up and down the coastline the whole time. Thank your fellow Limeys for that one. We even so much as smell a pirate, all Cappy O'Keefe has to do is dial up UKMTO on the sat phone, and the cavalry'll be all over us before you can say Jack Robinson.'

'Who the fuck *was* Jack Robinson, anyway?' Condor asked.

'Fuck should I know?' Mitch shot back at him.

'Always wondered about that,' Condor said absently.

Jude already knew about United Kingdom Maritime Trade Operations, the clearing house that governed shipping security in the Persian Gulf and the Indian Ocean. But he still wasn't entirely convinced.

'Okay,' he said, dubiously. 'Then if we're so safe and there's no risk, then why do we keep the pirate cages locked all the time? And how come these attacks are still going on?'

Mitch waved it away. 'Chill, dude. Ain't gonna happen to us.'

Chapter 10

The young woman's eyes were wide with terror and pleading as she tried to scream out from behind the tape that covered her mouth. Her bleached hair was all awry, her hands tied, her blue chequered shop assistant's uniform ripped at the neck from the struggle with her attacker who, presumably, had already wiped out the rest of her colleagues in his murderous spree.

The hostage taker stood half-concealed behind her, using her body as a shield with one arm clamped tightly around her neck. Was he a terrorist, or just another crazy on the loose? It didn't matter either way. He was the threat, and he had to be neutralised. He was wearing a black sweatshirt and his eyes were hidden by dark glasses that glinted in the morning sun. He was clutching a stubby pistol that was aimed over the woman's shoulder and pointing at the hostage rescue team who had come to save her.

Milliseconds counted. At any instant, a desperate man like this, all out of options and wild with panic, might turn the gun on her at point-blank range and blow her brains out.

Brrrpp . . . Brrrpp. The ripping snort of two short bursts from the silenced submachine gun, punctuated by the *clack-clackclack* of the weapon's bolt and the tinkle of spent cartridge cases hitting the ground. The hostage's left eye disappeared as the nine-millimetre bullets punched a jagged line from her throat up to her temple.

Then silence. The smell of cordite drifted on the cold morning air. A small trickle of smoke oozed from each of the bullet holes. The hostage taker's pistol was still pointing at the assembled HRT operators fifteen metres away.

'Cease fire,' Jeff Dekker said. 'Make your weapon safe.'

The shooter flicked on his safety catch and frowned at the woman he'd just killed.

'Shit.'

'Okay,' Jeff said. 'Your hostage is dead, and so are you, or maybe one of your teammates.'

'I'm sorry.'

'Tell that to her kids.' Jeff stepped up to the firing line and took the smoking subgun out of the shooter's hands. 'Ben? You want to give us a demonstration?'

The shooter stepped aside, angry with himself and shaking his head. Without a word, Ben took the gun from Jeff, walked up to the line and waited for the buzzer. Jeff pressed the remote button. At the signal, almost too fast for the eye to follow, Ben had the weapon up to his shoulder and on target with a single burst.

Brrrpp.

The hostage taker's sunglasses shattered into fragments. Shreds of high-density polyurethane foam flew from the back of his head and littered the grass like confetti. Less than three-quarters of a second from the buzzer, he wasn't going to be harming any more innocents.

Ben lowered the gun, made it safe and handed it back to Jeff, keeping the muzzle pointed downrange. 'Something like that,' he said to the first shooter, who was still shaking his head and staring in amazement at the tight grouping of holes between the bad guy's eyes.

It was just another morning at Le Val. The class were a group of twelve French police SWAT trainees who'd been sent out on a three-day instruction course in close-quarter shooting and hostage rescue tactics. The highly realistic, lifesize 3-D self-healing foam targets were a recent innovation Jeff had come up with, in conjunction with a Normandy plastic mouldings firm who couldn't manufacture them fast enough to meet the demand from law enforcement and military training units all over Europe.

'You want to break down for the group how you just did that?' Jeff asked Ben.

'We need to look beyond the accepted principles of combat shooting in order to become really fast and accurate,' Ben told the class. 'Forget what you've been taught about focusing on the sights of the weapon. And don't think too much about it. When you've shot enough to develop the right reflexes, muscle memory will bring the firearm to alignment instantly and without conscious thought. Even at twenty-five metres we've found it's possible to get good, solid hits in less time if you let the sights fuzz out and focus on the target instead. You'll also have better peripheral vision awareness of hostage movement or additional threats. Okay?'

'Okay,' came the muttered replies from the group.

'Let's try it again,' Jeff said.

'Just like old times,' Jeff said to Ben as the class broke up for lunch.

Ben said nothing, because he knew Jeff was angling for him to stay on permanently. He didn't want to commit to anything. His plans were unchanged: to wait a couple more days to let things settle down in Paris, return there to finish doing up the apartment, and go looking for an estate agent.

But Ben privately couldn't deny that, after a few days back

at Le Val, it was beginning to feel like home again, almost as if he'd never left the place. Initially, he'd resisted Jeff's invitation to get involved with the training side of things, and instead made himself useful elsewhere. He'd helped the decorators finish painting the new classroom building, driven into Valognes in the old Land Rover to fetch supplies, and mended part of the perimeter fence that had blown down. The rest of his time, he'd spent sitting by the fire in the farmhouse kitchen smoking cigarettes and reading with a glass of wine at his elbow, or revisiting his old running tracks through the wintry Normandy woodland with Storm trotting along at his heel. In the evenings, he and Jeff dined together and drank more wine and talked about everything except Ben's coming back to work at Le Val.

Tuesday Fletcher, the new recruit, was a dynamic addition to the team. He had a quick wit, a lively manner and a ready smile that dazzled away the wintry cold and drumming Normandy rain. Ben liked him at once, and watching him spatter cherry tomatoes for fun at six hundred metres with an L96 sniper rifle, he had no problem conceding to the younger man's superior marksmanship skills.

'Sorry to hear what happened on your selection,' Ben said to him as they were packing the gear away in the armoury room.

Tuesday shrugged. 'Just one of those things. Would've been nice to have been the first black kid in the SAS.'

'I always used to think it was wrong that we didn't have any,' Ben said.

'Don't know what they're missing. We're great for night ops. Nobody can see us coming in the dark,' Tuesday joked.

'Tuesday – is that a nickname?'

'Nope. It's what it says on my birth certificate.'

'Seriously?'

Tuesday laughed and gave another of his patented room-brighteners. 'I was born Tuesday, March third, 1992. Mum said they called me that so I'd have a birthday every week instead of just once a year like all the other kids. Truth is, she wanted to call me Troy and Dad wanted Sam. After I was born they fought over it for six weeks, until they were about to get fined for not registering me quick enough. So they both caved in and just called me after the day of the week I popped out. If that hadn't happened they'd still be fighting over it now. Stubbornness runs in the family.'

Join the club, Ben thought.

That got Ben back to thinking about his own family. Jude was on his mind a lot over those days, as he reflected about the past and all the regrets he had about the way he'd handled things. If there was a league table for fathers, they'd have to invent a new bottom place just for Ben. The only thing he'd ever given Jude was the birthright of his own wild temperament. Hardly much of a legacy to pass down from father to son.

It was painful to contemplate all the ways he'd been such a letdown as a parent, just as it hurt to think about all the missing parts of their relationship. He'd never seen the boy grow up, never got to know him properly, or had the chance to do the things a father should do to bond with his child. He'd inherited Jude just as Jude had inherited him, two strangers brought together by a tragedy brutally foisted on them by the car crash that had ended the lives of Michaela and Simeon Arundel. Ben missed them both deeply, but he knew that Jude's pain was deeper still and would never go away. Yet they'd barely ever talked about it. Ben regretted that too.

He wished Jude could be here now. He blamed himself for having missed him before his departure, and was trying not to blame Jeff for not having told him sooner that Jude was at Le Val, even if he understood Jeff's reasons. Then, of course, there was the undeniable fact that Ben hadn't exactly made himself easy to get in touch with. But seven whole weeks! If he'd only known, he'd have been here. They could have spent that time together. Maybe tried to start again.

Or maybe it would just have made things worse. He worried that it was too late to try and repair things between him and his son, just as it was probably too late for Ben to fix the profound rift between him and his ex-fiancée, Brooke Marcel. Ben already believed in his heart that Brooke would never speak to him again.

If Jude never wanted to either, then Ben would just have to accept that, too.

Chapter 11

On the morning of the fourth day since leaving Salalah, the *Svalgaard Andromeda* completed its south-westerly route down the Yemeni coast and arrived dead on schedule at the Port of Djibouti. Under the watchful eye of the bosun and a sun so searingly hot that the sky was burned almost white, Jude and the rest of the crew laboured and sweated for most of the day unloading cargo. When the gruelling toil was finally done, word came down from the captain that they were free to hit port for a few hours that evening before setting out again the following morning.

Condor and Mitch were first off the ship, in gleeful search of cheap beer and loose women – both of which, being old hands on the East Africa run, they knew exactly where to find in sufficient quantities to gorge themselves to the maximum. Even the dour-faced Scagnetti was smiling at the prospect of being let loose on land for a while.

Jude resisted all invitations to come ashore and have a good time with a polite smile and a 'That's okay, you go and have fun.' He spent the evening instead in his cabin, relaxing with a book. The next morning, he was predictably one of the only crew members who wasn't suffering a thudding headache and queasy stomach from a serious night on the town. Nobody had been stabbed, robbed, or detained by the port police. Scagnetti appeared to have managed to go the whole night without getting into any bar brawls.

The ship departed from Djibouti shortly after 9 a.m. and cruised back out into the infinite blue on a north-easterly bearing that would carry them around the Horn of Africa before turning south.

Mid-afternoon, the first of that day's incidents occurred.

Jude was far forward on the cargo deck, one of a small party of mostly hungover and groaning ABs working to clear up after the previous day's unloading, when he happened to glance over the rail at the expanse of ocean ahead, and thought he saw a dark, strangely angular shape bobbing on the surface of the water directly in the ship's path. It was only visible for a fleeting moment; then it was gone. He blinked and went closer to the rail to take another look.

Jude hadn't been imagining things. As it turned out, what he'd seen was a discarded forty-foot steel shipping container apparently lost from another vessel, so waterlogged that it was floating too low on the surface to be picked up by the radar. He quickly alerted Ricky Marshall, the third mate, who relayed the information to the bridge, and the ship changed course a few degrees to avoid the potential hazard.

Marshall was pleased with him, explaining that ships lost containers all the time, running into thousands a year world-wide, and often failed – illegally – to report them. While such floating debris posed no serious risk to the thick hulls of larger vessels like the *Andromeda*, it was always worth steering clear. 'You've got good eyes,' he said to Jude. 'Like to take a tour of the bridge?'

'Really?' It would be the first time Jude had ever been up there, and he lit up at the offer.

Marshall smiled at his excitement, and explained that especially observant ABs were often posted up on the bridge, as an extra pair of eyes always came in handy. 'Plus,' he added, 'I hear you're thinking of a naval career. You might be interested in seeing what goes on up there.'

And so, novice able-bodied seaman Jude Arundel followed the third mate up the steps and walkways to pay his first visit to the real nerve-centre of the ship, where he was introduced in person to Captain O'Keefe. The captain was a large, bearded man with a red face and a disinterested manner, who thanked Jude vaguely for having spotted the floating container and didn't seem to care one way or the other about Marshall showing him around. O'Keefe returned to the conversation he'd been having with Wilson, the chief mate, who had the wheel. Jude caught a whiff of a scent from Wilson that could have been cheap after-shave, but smelled more like bourbon.

The bridge was the very top floor of the ship's superstructure, accessible from an outer door and an inner hatch that led through to the rest of D Deck. It was shielded from the elements by tall windows that gave a commanding view for miles in every direction. On its roof was a railed open-air platform called the flying bridge, and extending some eighteen feet either side of it jutted steel observation walkways that overhung the ship's sides, used for fine steering adjustments while docking.

Inside the control room itself, Jude felt as if he was inside a giant greenhouse. The deck seemed very far below, and so narrow as to create the illusion that the ship must be dangerously top-heavy and about to keel over on its side.

'This is the conning station,' Marshall said, showing Jude the bank of electronic equipment at the centre of the bridge. The second mate, Guzman, was lurking nearby, munching on a sandwich and ignoring them as he pored over his charts. 'All these electronics are what we use for steering, nav and comm,' Marshall explained. 'Here you've got your GMDSS, short for Global Maritime Distress and Safety System, which feeds continuous weather updates. And this here is the radar,' he said, pointing at another screen, showing what looked like a greenish-hued circular clock face divided into quadrants, with a continually sweeping hand moving round the centre. 'The data stream on the right tells you the speed of any vessels we get close to, and their CPA. That's the Closest Point of Approach – basically how long before its path crosses ours. Keeps us out of trouble.'

Jude was running his eye over the screens, drinking everything in. 'This would be our position?' he asked, pointing at a set of coordinates displayed on a readout.

'That's right. Updated continually via GPS. So we don't lose our way.'

'And that?'

Marshall seemed happy to answer as many questions as this eager young sailor could fire his way. 'That's the EOT. Stands for Engine Order Telegraph. It's how the bridge tells the engine room to alter our speed. The panel next to it, right there, is the watertight door indicator. Every time a hatch seal opens anywhere on board, it lights up, green for open, red for shut. Alerts us if anything's open that shouldn't be in heavy weather.'

Fascinated by the wealth of equipment on board, Jude was about to ask more questions when the radar started to blip, drawing the attention of the mates. Wilson broke off from his conversation with the captain. The Guzzler swallowed the last of his sandwich and dragged his bulk over to the radar to take a look.

'Looks like a vessel coming right towards us, Cap,' he said. 'Three-point-six miles astern and closing fast. Moving it some.'

O'Keefe frowned and came over to peer at the screen, together with Ricky Marshall. Jude moved in behind, so he could peek between them at the display. Maybe he was being audacious, he thought, but everyone's attention was too fixed on the radar to take any notice of him. Onscreen, he could see a green dot moving towards the centre of the circle. As they watched, two smaller dots broke off from it.

'That's what I hoped we wouldn't see,' Guzman muttered. 'It can only mean one thing.'

'We're going to have company,' the captain said.

Chapter 12

Jude stared at the radar, remembering what Gerber had told him – how pirates no longer limited themselves to short-range raids from the coastline and now used stolen vessels as mother ships to patrol the whole ocean. 'Are we under attack?' he asked, unable to help himself from speaking out.

Nobody replied. Ricky Marshall just glanced at him, his jaw clenched. A whole minute passed, then another. The little green dots kept on coming. The two smaller ones that had broken away seemed to be converging on the centre of the circle at a slightly faster rate.

'Two-point-one miles, Cap,' Guzman said, looking intently at O'Keefe.

With an effort, Jude detached himself from the huddle at the radar and stepped over to the window. A large pair of binoculars was lying on a table. He picked them up. Again, the others were too focused on the screen to even notice him.

Scanning the distant ocean through the powerful binocs, Jude could just about make out the incoming objects on the water. The larger of the three was still on the horizon and seemed to be a sizeable vessel, while the smaller two were coming in much faster, black dots against the blue with white water visible at their bows. The way they were bouncing over the waves told him they were speedboats, which must have launched from the mother ship.

'They wouldn't dare touch a US merchant vessel,' Ricky Marshall said, but the expression on his face didn't radiate confidence.

'Course?' grunted O'Keefe.

'Two-twenty,' Guzman said.

'Take us one-seventy,' O'Keefe said, without looking up from the screen. Wilson turned the wheel to alter course.

'Further out to sea, Cap?' Marshall said with a raised eyebrow, obviously cautious not to question the captain's authority too directly.

O'Keefe ignored him. 'Give me a hundred and twenty-five revs, Guzman.'

'One-two-five,' Guzman repeated, getting on the EOT to relay the speed increase down to the engine room.

Jude seemed to have been entirely forgotten for the moment. He couldn't take his eyes from the binoculars. In what seemed a blindingly short time, the speedboats had closed the gap by at least a mile. He now could make out enough detail through the powerful lenses to see the tiny figures of men on board the approaching boats. There were at least six or eight men on each, all Africans. As they kept coming, Jude saw them alter course to follow the turning *Andromeda*. They were gaining.

Closer. Closer. Jude felt his mouth go dry as he realised the men on the boats were clutching automatic weapons. There was no longer any doubt. It was actually happening. The ship was under attack.

Jude's heart began to pound, and his mind began to swim.

'You want me to call up UKMTO, Cap?' Marshall asked.

'Too late for that,' O'Keefe muttered. 'They're coming in so fast.'

Jude couldn't believe what he was hearing. It seemed insane. Here they were, alone and vulnerable with an obvious pirate attack about to happen, and the captain didn't want to radio for help? What about the international navy patrols that were supposed to be out there guarding them?

Marshall turned to look at Jude. His face was full of strain, and Jude could see in his eyes that he couldn't understand the captain's unwillingness to call for help, either. 'You should get down there with the rest of the crew,' was all he said.

Jude nodded. He reluctantly put down the binoculars. Unmagnified, the incoming speedboats were just small dots once more, but growing larger every second. Jude left the bridge by the outer door, the way he and Marshall had entered, and stepped out onto the steel walkway. He glanced down at the deck far below, then at the speedboats and mother ship in the distance, and was suddenly gripped with the desire to get an even better view.

Without pausing to dwell on the knowledge that he was disobeying orders by not returning directly below, he thought, *What the hell*, and clattered up the narrow metal ladder that connected the walkway with the flying bridge, the very highest point of the ship.

It was like being on the top of a mountain. The ocean wind was strong, fluttering his shirt and ripping at his hair. Jude lay flat on his belly and peered through the railing. He didn't need binoculars any more for a clear view of the fast-approaching boats. He could hear their motors growing steadily louder over the thrum of the ship and the crash of the waves. He imagined he could almost hear the excited chatter of the pirates themselves as they got closer and closer to their prey. They couldn't be more than six or seven hundred yards away now.

Jude's heart was pounding faster than ever as he wondered what was going to happen. A voice inside his head was screaming at him that he shouldn't be up here watching the terrifying spectacle. He should be down there with his fellow crewmen, Mitch and Condor and Hercules, Gerber and the rest of them! If they didn't already know what was going on, he needed to warn everyone. *Now!*

Jude leapt to his feet, vaulted the rail and started tearing down the ladder. He could see O'Keefe, Guzman, Wilson and Marshall through the window, all with their backs to him. Thankfully, they hadn't noticed him.

Then, suddenly, the captain and mates were no longer alone on the bridge. An inner door opened. Three men Jude had never seen before walked in.

The man in the middle was older, with receding silvery hair cropped short like a soldier's. His body language was that of someone very much in charge. He was wearing a military-style combat jacket. In his left hand he was holding a small oblong aluminium flight case. Like the kind photographers carried cameras and lenses inside. Except he didn't look like a photographer. The case's handle was attached to his left wrist by a chain and steel cuff.

Who were they? Then Jude remembered what Hercules had told him.

The three a-holes on D Deck. Our esteemed passengers.

None of the three was smiling. The captain and mates didn't seem very happy to see them, either. But that might have been because of the pistol that the man with the case was holding in his right hand. It was pointing right at them.

'Carter? What in God's name do you think you're doing?' Jude heard Captain O'Keefe demand in a loud voice full of outrage.

Jude whipped out of sight, scrambling back up the ladder

and over the railing to the flying bridge. He froze there for a few instants, shaking and numb with shock at what he'd just seen. What was he supposed to do next? The rational part of him told him to remain hidden where nobody could see him.

To hell with rational. He had to keep watching.

He clutched the railing and let himself dangle head-first over the edge, terrified that the strong wind and the motion of the ship might cause him to slip and go plummeting to his death on the deck far below. Even more terrified that he might be spotted from inside the bridge.

Hanging upside down and clinging on for dear life, he peered through the glass.

The three mates were staring in bewilderment as the captain yelled at the man with the case. 'Lower that weapon, Carter, you hear me? This wasn't part of the deal.'

Those words hit Jude like a brick. *The deal?*

From the looks on the faces of Wilson, Guzman and Marshall, they had absolutely no idea what O'Keefe was talking about, either.

Jude hung on tight and kept watching.

The sound of the first gunshot almost made him let go.

The man called Carter showed not the smallest flicker of emotion as he shot the captain. O'Keefe clutched his chest and crumpled to the floor of the bridge. Then Carter turned the pistol on a stunned Frank Wilson and shot him in the head before he could react. Blood spattered the window.

Then the other two mystery passengers pulled out pistols of their own. Guzman took two bullets to the chest and one in the back as he tried to bolt for the outer exit. The last man standing, Ricky Marshall, made a valiant attempt to wrestle a weapon from one of the gunmen before he, too, was cut down and collapsed to the floor.

Paralysed with horror, still gaping through the bloody glass, Jude could barely breathe. As the speedboats kept getting nearer and nearer to the ship, he was realising that events much more complex and sinister than a simple pirate attack were unfolding. The *Svalgaard Andromeda* had just been hijacked from inside.

What happened next confused and bewildered him even more.

Chapter 13

The man sometimes known as Ty Carter, sometimes by other aliases as the sensitive nature of his work dictated, and rarely ever by his real name Lee Pender, walked calmly towards the bodies. Blood was already pooling thick on the bridge floor, spreading in rivulets this way and that with the motion of the ship. Carter disliked getting his shoes messy, and was careful to avoid the blood as he crouched over each body in turn and used his free hand to ensure none had a pulse. He had performed such checks many times before in his long career, and was as skilful as any surgeon.

Satisfied that all four were dead, he stood up and turned to his two accomplices with a nod. Their names were White and Brown, which amused him. They were mere hirelings, short-order trigger men paid to do exactly as he told them. So far, they'd proved perfectly capable at their job, and been equally good at taking his money without asking questions. To an operator like Pender, who trusted no one, secrecy was an essential part of life, and never more than now. Because if White and Brown had had any inkling whatsoever of what this was all about – the hit in Oman, the purpose of this sea voyage and, most of all, the nature of the item he was carrying inside the case attached to his left wrist – he was certain they would waste as little time killing him for it as he had in dispatching its former owner.

Which wasn't a worry for Pender, because he intended to beat them to the punch. The plan was about to enter its next phase. White and Brown had fulfilled their purpose and their services would no longer be required. Aside from anything else, after several days cooped up in their company on this vile tub, Pender couldn't stand them any longer.

'Thank you for your help,' he said to them. 'You're fired.'

He shot White first, because he'd observed that White was just a touch quicker on the uptake than Brown. The single bullet blew the back of White's head off and spattered the control console with blood and brains. Pender instantly turned the gun on Brown and pulled the trigger again. Brown caught it in the throat and dropped his weapon as he went staggering backwards, then slumped against the wall and slid to the floor.

Pender shot each of them once more in the head, just to be sure. Then put away his pistol and walked to the window to watch the fun and games that were about to begin. The boats were fast approaching. Khosa's men would soon be here, right on schedule.

Jude had witnessed the whole thing. Peering upside down through the window as the gunman opened fire on the second of his own accomplices, he decided he'd seen enough. He dropped down the ladder like a gymnast. For an instant he was certain he must surely have been spotted, and fully expected to hear more gunfire behind him: shattering glass and the shock of the bullet as he scrambled away.

But the killer was too busy slaughtering his own men to notice. Jude hit the deck at a sprint, his legs pumping faster and harder than he'd ever run in his life. No time to try to understand what he'd just seen, or what was happening. The angry buzz of the incoming speedboats was getting louder. It was all happening at once, and so fast. There was nothing Jude could do about the gunman who'd taken control of the bridge. Right now, all that mattered was keeping the attackers from getting on the ship. He had to find Mitch and the others, and alert them. What they could possibly do, he had no idea.

If the sound of pistol shots from the bridge hadn't already raised the alarm, the sudden crackle of automatic rifles and the splat of gunfire rattling off the side of the ship certainly did. Jude ran to the edge of the deck and peeked downwards over the rail, and his blood froze at the surreal sight of the two boats down below, coming right up alongside the *Andromeda*'s hull, crowded with pirates.

There were about fourteen or fifteen of them, but it might as well have been an army a hundred strong. They were thin and ragged in dirty T-shirts and shorts, mean and aggressive and visibly psyched up for war. Every one of them was armed with an assault weapon that Jude recognised from their distinctive banana-shaped magazines as Kalashnikovs. The mother ship, some kind of trawler, was still some way behind, but closing in rapidly.

As Jude watched the unthinkable happening right there in front of him, he saw muzzle flash from one of the boats and ducked back just in time before bullets whanged and sparked off the rail where he'd been standing a second ago. He rolled away from the edge, then sprang to his feet and went racing along the deck, frantically searching for his fellow crewmen.

Then he saw them.

A group of five crewmen, Mitch, Condor, Gerber, Lang and another sailor called Trent, were at the station just forward of the superstructure where the main high-pressure hose was kept, frantically getting ready to deploy the water jet in an attempt to repel the boarding that everyone knew was going to begin at any moment. The gunfire was almost continuous now, with bullets pinging everywhere and slapping off metal. The pirates seemed to know exactly where to concentrate their fire, making it impossible to get the hose over the side without getting shot to pieces. Running hard with his head down, Jude saw his friends were hopelessly pinned down on the deck where the upwards angle of the gunfire couldn't reach them.

'Where the hell were you?' Mitch yelled over the noise as Jude reached them. 'I was looking all over for you, man.' Mitch was clutching a bright red flare pistol, and his pockets were bulging with twelve-gauge flare cartridges. With his other hand he grabbed a fistful of Jude's shirt and yanked him down into a crouch next to the huddled group. His nose was an inch from Jude's and his eyes were wide. Gerber had a tight grip on the shaft of a fire axe and looked grim, with a 'didn't I tell you this would happen' glint in his eye. Condor's tanned face had gone white and he seemed ready to dissolve into panic.

'The bridge,' Jude yelled back. More flurries of automatic rifle fire burst from below, stitching the side of the house above their heads and ricocheting off the latticework of the number two cargo crane.

'Where's the Cap?' Gerber yelled.

Only then did Jude realise the full implications of the hijacking. With the bridge fallen to enemy hands, it meant there was nobody left up there to issue a distress signal. It meant the remaining crew were completely helpless and alone in the middle of the ocean, with virtually nothing to fight back against their attackers with except their wits.

Jude was so horrified by the realisation that he couldn't speak. At that instant, a movement caught his eye and he looked up to see something flying up over the side of the ship.

'Oh, shit,' Condor said, turning even whiter.

Twenty yards forward of where they were all huddled, the grappling hook dropped and hit the deck with a clang. Its steel claws raked backwards as the rope went taut, and then fastened themselves around the railing. It was quickly followed by another. The pirates only had to shinny up the sides. Within seconds they would be clambering aboard.

'No way,' Mitch yelled. 'Not this ship, you motherfuckers!' Before Jude could stop him, he was jumping to his feet and running like a crazy man towards the edge of the deck. Jude sprang up and chased after him, yelling at him to get back. Screaming in fury at the pirates, Mitch pointed the flare pistol down over the side and fired. Its boom was like a shotgun blast. The dazzling magnesium flare went off like a rocket and sailed downwards towards the boats, trailing green smoke. But Mitch's aim was wild and the missile hit the water, fizzling out instantly. Still roaring at the pirates he dug in his pocket for another cartridge to load.

The pirates had seen him and were training their fire on him. Mitch seemed oblivious of the bullets flying past and splatting off the container stack behind him. Jude grabbed his arm, trying to haul him back to safety, but Mitch jerked free and managed to load a second flare into his pistol.

'Mitch!' Jude shouted. 'Get b—'

Jude never finished. Mitch suddenly staggered and fell back towards him, nearly knocking Jude over. Jude felt something wet and warm slap across his face, and he tasted saltiness. He looked down and saw the blood spattered on his shirt, and for an instant he thought it was his own.

Mitch made a sound like 'Urgghhh', and collapsed at Jude's feet. Jude could hear someone screaming Mitch's name. He realised it was him. Mitch's body gave a jerk and rolled over. The side of his head was blown away.

Chapter 14

For what seemed like minutes on end, as if in a dream, Jude stared numbly down at his friend's body and the horrific red mess that had been his head. The gunfire rattling up the side of the ship; Condor's frantic yells of 'get down, get down!' coming from behind; the third and fourth grappling hooks shooting up over the side and getting a purchase on the rail: everything faded into the background. He was only dimly aware of Gerber running up next to him, axe in hand, swinging furious blows that struck sparks from the deck and severed one of the lines the pirates were using to shinny up the side of the ship. The rope parted and two boarders fell back and splashed into the foaming sea between their boats.

Only then did Jude come to his senses, and along with them came a flood of rage. He bent down and snatched up the fallen flare pistol. It was sticky with Mitch's blood. He didn't know how it worked, but he'd seen Mitch load it and he guessed you only had to pull the trigger. Teeth gritted, he leaned right out over the rail, pointed the gun vertically down at the nearer of the two boats, and fired.

The flare whooshed down the side and burst against the back of the boat in a flash of white flame that ignited the jerrycans of spare fuel lashed to the stern next to the outboard motor. The boat exploded in a blast that lifted it out of the water and sent a fireball and a wave of searing heat rippling up the *Andromeda*'s hull. Jude and Gerber both ducked back from the edge. A pall of black smoke enveloped everything. Jude could hear the screams and splashes as pirates hurled themselves into the sea to escape the flames.

For a few moments, it seemed as if they'd succeeded in beating them off. But it was a short-lived victory. The second boat had managed to power away from the explosion. With unbelievable speed, and before Jude even realised what was happening, the pirates were swarming up the ropes and leaping nimbly over the smoke-blackened rail to pounce on deck with their weapons ready and firing.

Jude wanted to shoot back at them, but then felt a powerful hand grip his arm and drag him back towards the cover of the container stacks. Gerber was in full-on soldier mode now and shouting 'Fall back, fall back!' as if commanding his troops to retreat in the face of an enemy charge.

There was no choice. Jude glanced back one last time at Mitch's body before he followed Gerber and the others at a run, down a narrow alley between container stacks and across a stretch of open deck towards the relative safety of the house. 'This way, this way!' Gerber was shouting over the crackle of gunfire, pointing towards the main hatchway leading inside.

One by one, they ducked through the entrance. Condor slammed the hatch shut behind them and spun the locking wheel. It was the same kind of heavy riveted iron door, streaked with rust, that were all over the ship. They were designed to seal tightly enough to keep out Force Ten storms. They could keep the pirates at bay – for now, at any rate.

From the other side of the thick metal they could hear running footsteps on the deck, clattering up the ladders, along the walkways. More gunshots, sporadic bursts of automatic fire coming from different points as the pirates rapidly spread all over. Jude edged closer to the door, pressed his ear to it and heard the raised voices and barked commands from the other side. He didn't think they were speaking in Arabic. It was an African language he'd never heard before. Somali?

The voices were drowned out as a rifle shot cracked out just the other side of the door, mingled with the very loud percussive impact of a bullet hitting the metal. Jude flinched back and saw the dent, like a raised bump, right next to where his ear had been. Two more shots hammered the door before the pirates gave up and moved on.

'They're gonna be all over us in no time,' Gerber muttered disgustedly. 'Those stupid cages ain't gonna hold 'em back more'n one minute.'

'What the crap are we gonna do?' said Trent.

Ignoring him, Gerber turned urgently to Jude. 'You were up on the bridge. Did you see the captain? Did they radio for help?'

Jude's mind was spinning so badly he thought he was going to throw up. He was the only one who knew just how bad their situation was. He had to break the news to the others.

'The captain's dead,' he blurted out. 'They shot him. And all three of the mates. They're all dead.'

'Steady on, son,' Gerber said. 'Slow down. Who shot them?'

'The passengers.'

'What?' Condor exploded.

'They're hijackers,' Jude said. 'Their leader is called Carter. He killed the other two.'

'Wait. You mean to say this guy Carter killed Cappy

83

O'Keefe and our guys, then killed his own guys?' Gerber said in disbelief.

'He's one of the pirates,' Jude said, struggling to talk coherently. They could hear activity and voices everywhere as the pirates took over the whole ship above them. 'It's all been planned in advance.' More questions were clotting his mind, one piling on top of another. What kind of deal did the captain do with the hijackers? Had O'Keefe deliberately failed to radio for help? What was in the case that Carter had cuffed to his wrist?

'Oh, shit, oh shit oh shit,' Condor kept repeating over and over. Gerber snapped at him to shut up.

'What the crap are we gonna do?' Trent said again, breathing hard.

'Get the hell out of here, is what,' said Lang.

Gerber nodded. 'We gotta get below, right now. Only chance. Down there with the chief and the others.' And Jude knew he was right. The pirates would quickly gain access to everything from A Deck upwards. But if their small group could beat them to the single stairway leading below decks to the engine room and holds, there was a hope that all the survivors might be able to seal themselves off down there together.

Gerber led the way, still clutching his axe, Jude right behind him, followed by Lang, Condor and Trent. At every turn through the twisting, constricted passageways, there was the terrifying prospect of running into a gang of armed pirates. Or maybe even worse, Jude was thinking, they might meet Carter. Either way, they wouldn't stand a chance.

They were just steps from the gangway leading below when a connecting hatch suddenly burst open and a large dark figure came piling through it towards them. Gerber raised the axe, ready to strike.

'Whoa, easy, easy!' It was Hercules. His old army jacket was spotted with fresh bloodstains and he was clutching a wicked-looking carving knife, the largest one he'd managed to grab from the galley before escaping. As he breathlessly explained, the pirates had stormed in as he'd been in the middle of serving coffee to Jack Skinner, the bosun. 'I don't know where Murphy is, man,' Hercules said in anguish, brandishing the knife. 'Just know if I get close to one of those mothers, they's gonna have a real bad day.'

Gerber had the good sense not to say, 'Never mind the damn parrot.' Pointing at the blood, he asked, 'Are you hurt?'

Hercules shook his head. 'It's Charlie's blood, man. They shot'm.' Charlie was the AB who sometimes helped in the kitchen. 'Skinner, too. Just opened fire. Sucker didn't have a chance. Me, I just managed to slip out the back way.'

Anxious looks passed between the others. Jack Skinner might not have been universally liked, but nobody was going to deny he'd have been a useful presence in a situation like this.

'Is he dead?' Condor groaned.

'I saw the man go down, homes. He's dead, all right.'

Jude quickly broke the news of the deaths of the captain and mates to Hercules, who just shook his head.

'They're wiping us out, dude,' Lang mumbled. 'We're fucked.'

'No we're not,' Jude said. 'We're going to get out of this.'

'Listen to the boy,' Gerber said.

'This ain't happening,' Condor said, on the verge of succumbing to panic. 'Pirates don't do this.'

'Not unless they want to take the ship for themselves,' Gerber said grimly.

'A ship this size? What the hell for?'

'You have any better ideas? Come on, let's keep moving before the bastards cut us off.'

As Gerber urged, the group kept moving. Six men out of twenty, with at least seven dead that they knew of above decks.

They could only hope that Diesel and his engine room assistants, Peters and Cherry, were still unharmed and without unwanted company down there.

As it turned out, the engineer and his guys were still very much alive, but not alone. They'd already been joined below by four more crewmen: Allen, Lorenz, Park the Korean, and Scagnetti, who'd bolted from their posts above decks to retreat to safety the moment the shooting had begun. Thirteen men crammed into the engine room and locked the hatch down behind them, safe for now. The heat in the confined space was stifling, the metal walls streaming with condensation. The sharp odours of oil and fuel, sweat and fear were heavy in the air.

An urgent conference immediately started, with Gerber announcing to those who didn't already know that the captain and mates had been shot to death, the vessel had fallen somehow into the hands of an unexplained coalition of hijackers and pirates, and there was no way to radio out for help. Diesel, a grizzled veteran of many trips under Henry O'Keefe, took the news grimly but silently.

Jude had never thought he'd be happy to see Scagnetti. Gerber didn't seem so pleased, especially when Scagnetti failed to suppress a crooked little smile on hearing of the captain's demise. 'We could have done with a little more help up there,' Gerber growled at him.

'You want to make something of it, Pop?' Scagnetti countered, instantly rising to the challenge.

'Cool it, boys,' said Diesel, thrusting a big arm between

them before it came to blows. 'Thirteen of us are still alive. It could've been a hell of a lot worse.'

'You figure?' Condor said. 'It's only a matter of time before they get to us down here.'

Diesel shook his head. 'Let 'em try. That hatch was built to keep a million tons of ocean out. You'd need a rocket to make a dent in it.'

'Then we'd best hope they ain't got any rockets,' Trent said.

'Face it, boys, we're screwed,' Condor said. 'No food or water, no weapons and no way to communicate jack shit to the outside world. Even if we could get to a radio, how many of us would even know what channel to use, or who to call?'

There was a murmur of anxious consent among some of the men. 'He's right,' Trent said.

'Buncha pussies,' Scagnetti sneered at them. 'Scared of a few raggedy-ass nigger pirates.'

Gerber gave him a hard look. 'You want to go up there and take 'em on all by yourself, Scagnetti, please, be my guest. Funny, I didn't see you up on deck when they were all comin' up the side.'

Cherry, one of the assistant engineers, put out his hands to quell the rising tension. 'Okay, look, we all know we can't fight them. Forget that shit. But there's gotta be something we can do. Maybe there's some other way we can get out a distress call.'

'We'll figure something out,' Diesel agreed. Though for the moment, nobody was offering any ideas.

Jude slumped down against the metal bulkhead wall, suddenly feeling completely drained. His hands were shaking. He closed his eyes, but however tightly he screwed them shut, he couldn't close out the image of Mitch's dead face, covered in blood and brains, or the vision of the burning boat hit by the flare that had been fired by his own hand. Men screaming, diving into the water. Jude had seen at least one of the pirates engulfed in flames. Could you survive that? Had he killed them?

Jude had never hurt a living soul in his life before. The remorse felt like a leaden weight in his stomach. He kept telling himself that he'd acted in defence of his friends. But did that justify it?

He thought about his father, his real father. Ben never talked about the people whose lives he'd taken. Jude knew there must have been many. But even though Ben had never said so, Jude always had the feeling that he lived with a private burden of remorse over the memory of each and every one of them, no matter how bad they'd been in life, no matter how little choice Ben might have had in killing them. To take away everything a person had, everything they would ever have. It was no easy thing. Now Jude understood that personally, and it was a weight he knew he would carry forever.

'You okay, son?' said a voice. Jude opened his eyes and tried to smile up at Gerber.

'I'm fine,' he said. It was a lie, but he swallowed hard and forced himself to make it true. He stood up and willed the trembling to stop.

'We'll get out of this, you'll see,' Gerber said. 'There'll be a way.'

That was when Jude suddenly remembered something Mitch had told him, while they were still in port in Salalah. It felt like a hundred years ago.

'What about sending out an email?' he said, speaking his thoughts out loud. Diesel and a couple of the others heard him, and turned.

'You mean like a text, from a cellphone? We're in the

middle of the Indian Ocean, son. You tried getting any reception lately?'

'I don't mean a text,' Jude said. 'I mean a real email, from a laptop with satellite internet access.'

Diesel shrugged. 'Well, sadly, I don't seem to have one on me right now.'

'But there's one on board,' Jude said. 'In the captain's cabin. Mitch told me O'Keefe was emailing his wife all the time.'

'So?'

'So,' Jude said, 'what if one of us was able to sneak up there?'

'One of us?'

'I was thinking of myself.'

'Without getting caught and shot to pieces?' said Condor, the eternal optimist. 'You want to tell me exactly how you're planning on managing that?'

'Son, it might as well be on Mars,' Gerber said. 'You'd never make it.'

Jude rubbed his chin and thought hard for a few moments. An idea was growing in his mind, and the more it grew the more he believed it could work. 'Diesel,' he said. 'This is the engine room, yes?'

'Last time I looked,' Diesel said, sweeping an arm back at the blue-painted mass of iron machinery, pipes and control equipment behind him.

'So we have control over the ship's power and they can't override us from the bridge in any way?'

If the answer was no, Jude's germ of a plan was dead before it was even born.

'Sure, we can throw the master switches on everything right here. Engine power, electrics, hydraulics, air, emergency generator, the works,' Diesel said, still staring at him, as were the others, apart from Scagnetti who had wandered off on his own to light a roll-up and pollute the unbreathable air of the engine room still further.

'What about the radar?' Jude asked.

'Uh-huh,' Diesel said, uncertain where Jude was going with this. 'We can knock that out along with every other instrument in the conning station. So?'

Jude could feel a smile spreading over his face as his confidence in his plan grew stronger. 'And if we cut the engines, the ship will stop moving and stay pretty much put?'

'As long as the sea's calm, sure,' Diesel replied. 'We'll drift, but not by more than a few points, depending on the currents. Cut to the chase, kid. What the hell is this about?'

'Listen,' Jude said.

Chapter 15

Jude's brainwave caused a lot of disagreement among the others. Condor thought he must be nuts to contemplate taking such a risk, with pirates almost certainly scouring every inch of the ship to murder each and every one of them. Gerber declared he had some balls on him and reckoned, on consideration, that it was worth a try. Nobody denied that Jude was the quickest and knew his way around the ship as well as any of them.

'It'll work,' Jude kept saying.

Scagnetti was sitting on a duct pipe, swinging his legs and puffing his roll-up. 'Who you gonna call in, Limey Boy?' he called out with a grin. 'Friggin' Double O Seven?'

'Shut it, Scagnetti,' Gerber warned him.

'Never thought I'd say it, but Scagnetti has a point,' Hercules said. 'You wanna take this kind of crazy-ass risk to send a lousy email? To who?'

'I have an idea about that,' Jude said. 'Trust me, okay?'

'It's not going to work,' Diesel said. 'The moment you shut down the power, the pirates will know something's up. These guys ain't stupid. They're sailors. They know ships. We cut the juice and engine power just like that, it'll give us away for sure. Like waving a big flag saying "Here we are!" They'll be all over us in two shakes of a lamb's tail.'

'I thought you said it'd take a rocket to get through that hatch,' Condor said.

'It would. But none of us wants to be out there with ten fuckin' Somalis blocking the way back with AK-47s.'

'We don't cut the power right away,' Jude said. 'I'll need it for the satellite hookup. Fifteen minutes, that's all I need, then throw the switch.'

'Then you have another problem,' Diesel said. 'We have to assume the pirates are all over the bridge, right? Which means that if the power's still on they'll be able to monitor the watertight door indicator. The panel of lights will show them exactly which doors and hatches are opening and closing below. It'll give your position away from the moment you start moving.'

Jude wasn't put off. 'I'll take my chances with the indicator panel. They probably won't even notice.'

'It's nuts.'

'Maybe so, but it's the only way,' Jude said. 'I'm going for it. Exactly quarter of an hour after I step out of that hatch, you pull those switches. I'll leg it back down below before they realise what's happening.'

'You're crazy, you know that?' Hercules rumbled, shaking his head. 'You gotta death wish?'

'Hey, if stupid wants to go get himself creamed, let'm,' Scagnetti said.

Diesel wasn't happy about it, but it was clear to everyone that Jude couldn't be dissuaded. Nobody had yet come up with anything better.

'Hold on,' Gerber said as Jude started opening the hatch. 'You can't go up there without some kind of weapon. Take my axe.'

Jude looked at it. 'I can't run about with that. It's too big.'

'How about this, bro?' Hercules said, offering Jude the butcher's knife.

The idea of using a knife on a living person made Jude's flesh crawl, but he knew how lame that would sound to the others. 'If I slip on a ladder and fall on it, it'll go right through me,' he said, by way of an excuse.

'You'll need this, at least,' Diesel said, handing Jude a long, heavy metal Maglite. 'It's going to get pretty dark below decks once the power goes off.'

Jude stuck the torch in his belt. 'Don't worry about me. I'm not planning on getting caught.'

'Good luck, son,' Gerber said as they unlocked the engine room hatch. Jude kicked off his shoes, thinking he'd be quieter without them, and padded barefoot through the open hatchway, his heart rate instantly quickening as he suddenly began to ask himself what the hell he thought he was doing.

Once the hatch closed behind him, there was no going back. Jude set off furtively down the narrow metal passageway to the vertical ladder they'd scrambled down minutes before. He paused at the bottom rung, peering up through the circular hole above him as he listened for approaching footsteps or voices. Hearing nothing, he took a deep breath and climbed upwards towards the next level.

The coast seemed to be clear, so far. He wasn't dead yet, although that could easily change at any second. His heart was in his throat as he padded gingerly to the next upward hatchway. He paused once more at the top, sweating. Then kept moving. Another bare metal passage with ducts and pipes running along the wall, another open-tread iron ladder.

It was as he was about to emerge onto the level above that Jude very nearly got caught for the first time. He ducked his head and shoulders down out of sight through the hatch and held his breath as a group of pirates appeared around a corner and passed directly above him, their footsteps clanging on the bare metal floor just inches away. There were three of them, heavily armed and apparently combing the ship for the rest of the crew, but they weren't taking it too seriously, as if mopping up survivors was just another part of the game to them. Jude could hear them laughing among themselves, and caught a whiff of something that wasn't tobacco smoke.

He waited until they were gone. When he could breathe again, he crept quickly onwards and upwards. Five minutes. Ten to go before Diesel shut down the power and the pirates would know something was up.

He was on A Deck now, into the bottom level of the house and approaching the heart of the danger zone. His pulse was escalating with every yard. Around the next ninety-degree corner was the mess room door, hanging ajar.

He drew breath as he saw the slick of blood on the metal step and across the passageway. The blood trail stopped in a pool that reflected the neon striplights above. In the middle of the pool, inert and spreadeagled on his belly, his head turned sideways with his cheek pressed to the floor and looking straight at Jude with lifeless porcelain eyes, was Jack Skinner, the ship's bosun. He'd managed to drag himself this far before he died from his gunshot wounds.

Jude was gaping at the corpse when the mess room door swung wide open. He ducked behind it just in time to avoid being spotted by the two armed Africans who stepped out and walked through the blood towards Skinner's body. They bent to seize a wrist each. Peering around the edge of the door, Jude was just three feet away from them, close enough to smell their sweat and the firing-range tang of cordite on their clothes. Their bare arms were muscled and lean and glistening. The pirate nearest him had his rifle casually slung over his shoulder, tantalisingly within Jude's reach, and for a moment he was insanely tempted to make a grab for it.

The pirates started dragging the bosun's body up the passage towards the external hatch that led to the main deck. The smeared blood trail they left in their wake made Jude want to throw up. He stood motionless until they were out of sight, then with legs like jelly he ran on towards the hatch for B Deck.

Up and up. Twice more, he froze as he heard voices and laughter, and whipped out of sight. By the time he reached E Deck his stomach muscles were clenched so tight that it hurt and he was cursing himself for having come up with this lunatic idea.

But they hadn't got him yet, and he'd almost reached his objective.

Eight minutes, thirty seconds. Six and a half minutes to go before the guys below threw the power switch. The sands were running fast out of the hourglass.

The door of the captain's cabin was shut, but not locked. Slowly, slowly, he eased it open and peered inside, ready to yank the big flashlight out of his belt and start flailing away with it as a club. As if it would do him any good against automatic weapons.

To Jude's relief, the cabin was empty. He slipped through the doorway and quickly bolted it behind him. If anyone came, he could always scramble out of the window, which was open just wide enough to admit a blessed breath of fresh air. Jude crept over and peered cautiously over the sill. He could see the whole length of the main deck from here. It was swarming with armed Africans. He swallowed hard, then harder as he saw what they were doing.

The pirates were dragging bodies across to the starboard

rail and dumping them into the sea. As he watched, the pair who'd almost caught him earlier heaved Jack Skinner's corpse up and over by the wrists and ankles, leaving a red smear on the railing as it slithered out of sight, followed a second later by a dull splash. Jude fought the urge to throw up.

The mother ship had come up alongside the *Andromeda*. It was a battered-looking fishing vessel, its hull more rust than paintwork. More pirates were milling about the trawler, every single one of them armed with the ubiquitous Kalashnikov. Then, as Jude kept watching, he saw two men walk up the deck of the cargo ship, deep in conversation. He instantly recognised one of them as Carter, still carrying the small aluminium case chained to his left hand.

The other was a demon.

The tall, powerfully-built African was the most frightening-looking man Jude had seen in his life. He was a commanding presence, dressed in a loose rendition of military uniform: boots, khakis, a red beret worn at an angle and a gunbelt with some kind of enormous handgun in a flap holster. Bandoliers loaded with pointed rifle cartridges hung crossways around both shoulders. His shirt sleeves were rolled up to the elbow, revealing thick, muscled fore-arms. The huge gold watch on one wrist caught the sunlight, as bright as a beacon against his ebony skin.

But it wasn't what the man was wearing. It was his face. Even from a distance, the sight of it made Jude draw a breath. He looked monstrous. Inhuman.

Jude had forgotten all about the ticking clock. He felt the same icy tingle of fear down the back of his neck that he'd felt as a young boy, when he'd sneaked downstairs in the dead of night to the living room of the vicarage to turn on the TV and be illicitly terrified by his first-ever horror movie.

At first glance Jude thought the African must have been burned or mangled in some kind of accident; then he realised what he was seeing was deliberate mutilation. Huge raised ridges of scar tissue ran in parallel lines up both sides of his face, from his jaw to where they disappeared under the red beret. More tracks had been carved in downward-pointing V shapes on his forehead, distorting his brow into a permanent expression of furious rage. They looked as if they had been gouged into his flesh with a hot knife. Patterns of lumps, like raised pockmarks, circled his eyes. Something had been done to his cheekbones to make them stand out like horns. Like something out of a nightmare.

The scarred man was unquestionably the leader of the pirates. While his men ran back and forth over the decks of both vessels, he stood calmly smoking a long cigar, breaking off from his conversation with Carter to issue orders and signals to the others.

The fifteen minutes were almost up. Jude managed to tear himself from the window, shaken by the sight and reminding himself of what he'd come here to find.

Captain O'Keefe had kept the personal belongings in his cabin in immaculate order, including the small desk set into an alcove in the wall. The Dell laptop was powered down, the lid closed, a light blinking on its front panel. Jude stepped over to the desk and flipped the laptop open. The screen flashed into life, showing the email program and the half-finished message that the captain had been in the middle of writing to his wife back home in Indiana when he'd left it to attend to his duties. It began: '*Dear Emily . . .*'

Jude felt a moment of shame for intruding on a dead man's privacy. He imagined the awful scene in store when Emily O'Keefe received the news of her husband's death. Remembering the captain's final words to Carter before the man had shot him, Jude found it easy to have more sympathy for her than for her late husband. Whatever kind of a deal the man had struck with Carter, it had landed them all in mortal danger. It had already cost the lives of Mitch and several other innocent men.

So burn in hell, Henry Hainsworth O'Keefe.

His time was nearly up. He was going to have to work fast. He deleted the unfinished email and clicked on COMPOSE NEW MESSAGE. He racked his brain to recall the position coordinates he'd seen on the readout in the conning station. As the figures came streaming into his mind, he started tapping keys and rushed out his message. There wasn't a lot to say. He didn't even know if it would work. By the time its recipient saw it, he and all his fellow crewmen might be dead and the ship stolen away to Christ knew where.

When he'd finished, he addressed the email to the only person he'd been able to think of to contact. The man who had got him here. Jeff Dekker.

Jude hit SEND and held his breath in a silent prayer as the email winged its way off into cyberspace. It was nearly twenty to five, his time. Two hours earlier in France.

Time up. Right on cue, Jude saw the power light of the laptop fade and die, and the battery light come on. The screen dimmed as it switched to its own power. A second later, Jude felt the ever-present low thrum of the engines go quiet. Diesel had been as good as his word. The ship was now effectively dead in the water.

Jude felt momentarily elated. The crew were still a long way from regaining full control of the ship, but they'd just scored a decisive little victory. It wouldn't be long now before Carter and the pirates twigged what was up.

He crept back over to the cabin window. Pirates were still

marching about the deck, but Carter and the terrifying African were gone. No telling where they could be now. Heading straight for him, maybe.

Jude grabbed his torch and hurried from the cabin. He had no idea whether he'd make it back down to the engine room alive. But he'd completed his task.

Now only time would tell whether it had been worth it.

Chapter 16

Business at Le Val had certainly been booming during Ben's long absence. He'd been happy to take Jeff's word for it, and it wasn't until early that afternoon when, bored and at a loose end, he'd wandered into the office where Jeff was at one of the two facing desks, tapping out an email to a client. Ludivine had the day off, and they had the place to themselves. Ben sat at the other desk and sifted through some files, amazed at all the new contracts that had been coming in over the last months. Money was pouring through the door, and with it increasing commitments and an expanding monthly timetable. No wonder Jeff wanted him back, if only to share the growing workload.

Something else for Ben to feel guilty about.

Going through the piles of paperwork, Ben soon discovered something else that didn't make him feel any better.

'You never told me Brooke was still coming here,' he commented to Jeff, keeping the surprise out of his voice.

'Yeah, so?' Jeff replied, still clacking away on his keyboard.

Brooke – or more properly, Brooke Marcel, PhD in Clinical Psychology, author of seminal papers on Stockholm Syndrome and a leading expert in Post-Traumatic Stress Disorder in long-term kidnap survivors – had once upon a time been a frequent visitor to Le Val, employed to give classes on hostage psychology. Ben had first met her back in his SAS days, when he'd attended one of her lectures and been highly impressed with her sharpness of mind, her humour and (he'd admitted to himself only in retrospect) her looks. It wasn't until she'd become a regular fixture at Le Val, some years afterwards, that their relationship had grown into something much deeper. When that relationship had later crumbled so disastrously, he'd assumed that she would never set foot there again. Yet there it was, an invoice of payment for lecture fees and travel expenses with her signature on it, stamped PAID and dated just two months earlier. And another, dated two months before that. Seeing her name, and knowing that she'd been here, made Ben's stomach flip and his throat go dry.

Jeff glanced up from his computer. 'What was I supposed to do, tell her not to come any more? You know as well as I do there's nobody better at what she does. Besides, I like having her around.'

'She's not due to turn up today, is she?' Ben asked, and immediately felt wretched and cowardly for even thinking it. But it couldn't be helped. If the answer was affirmative, he was ready to bolt for his car.

'Not for another couple of weeks,' Jeff muttered, returning to his message. 'Have to check the diary.'

'How is she?' Ben asked. Mr Nonchalant.

'Hmm? Oh, fine, fine.' Jeff wasn't always the most conversational of company.

'I mean, does she seem happy? Seeing anyone?' Ben didn't want to appear to be fishing, but, fully aware of how unreasonable it might be, that was exactly his intention.

'Think she was. Don't know.'

Ben almost gave a shudder as an awful thought struck him. 'Not Rupert Shannon, I hope.' Shannon was the stuffed

101

shirt of an ex-officer Brooke had been running around with for a time before she and Ben had got together. He couldn't think of a more unworthy suitor. The very idea made his flesh crawl with jealousy.

Jeff seemed to be barely listening and didn't look up from his screen. 'Like I say, I don't know. Didn't ask.'

'I see,' Ben said, quietly fearing the worst.

Jeff's computer gave a small *ping* as a new email came in. Probably another potential client, Ben thought, with mixed feelings. More income, more workload, more pressure on him to stay on.

Jeff lazily clicked out of whatever he was doing, and into the email inbox. He read, blinked, read again, and his jaw dropped open.

'Jesus Christ,' he said. 'Oh, no. No, *no*.'

'What?' Ben asked, with no idea what it could be. A surprise tax audit? A mass cancellation? The bank calling in a loan?

'You'd better fucking see this, Ben,' Jeff said.

Ben jumped up and moved around the desk to look at the screen. When he saw the email, he froze, blinked twice, then read it again.

He would read it many more times over the coming hours. It was unbelievable. But it was for real.

The email had landed at precisely thirty-nine minutes past two, local time. It had no subject header and was typed in capitals, a breathless one-line rush with no breaks, no punctuation, very clearly dashed off in a tearing hurry. All it said was:

JEFF SOS SHIP HIJACKED BY ARMED PIRATES CREW KILLED NEED HELP FAST NO RADIO MAINTAINING POSITION 3.530797, 54.381358 DO NOT REPLY TO THIS MESSAGE PLS HURRY JUDE

For a long moment, Ben and Jeff were stunned into silence.

Then the reaction hit. Pacing. Fretting. Wanting to yell and punch the walls. Ben's anguish. Jeff's horror. Ben's short-lived flare of anger towards his friend for getting Jude onto the ship in the first place. Jeff's remorse and readiness to take the blame, no excuses, no denials.

But there was no time for emotions here. Both men had learned a long time ago that emotions were the deadliest enemy at a time like this. Only the cold, calm, rational actions they took in the next few minutes would decide the outcome of the situation. Ben quashed his rising panic and took a deep breath. 'I'm sorry, Jeff. It's not your fault.'

'No hard feelings,' Jeff said, putting a hand on Ben's shoulder and looking him in the eye with as much reassurance as he could muster. 'I'd have felt the same. Fuck, a lot worse.'

'All right,' Ben said, fighting to stay calm. 'Let's take stock of this. What do we know? One, we know it's not a hoax. Jude wouldn't kid around. Two, we know that at least some of the crew are still alive. Or were, a few minutes ago when this message was sent.'

'Jesus Christ, don't say that,' Jeff muttered. 'Don't even think it.'

But Jeff was thinking the exact same thing, as Ben knew perfectly well. Anything could happen in a few minutes, with heavily tooled-up Somali pirates running amok on board and the crew resisting. Jude could be dead already. He could have been dead even before they'd read the email.

No. He's alive. Ben gritted his teeth and willed himself to hold that thought. Believe it, absolutely and without question.

Ben threw himself into a desk chair, yanked the computer

towards him, snatched a sheet of notepaper from the desk and dashed off the position coordinates from Jude's email. He plunged into a web search for Google Maps. Within seconds, he was feverishly tapping in the numbers. Moments later, he'd pinpointed the ship's position. A little red pointer, like an inverted drop of blood, marked the spot in the middle of the ocean where his son was, or had been. He was out in the middle of the Indian Ocean, just over one hundred and fifty miles east of the Somali coast.

'Two hours ahead of us, EAT, Eastern Africa Time,' Jeff said, peering over his shoulder. He glanced at his watch. '16.39 hours over there.'

Ben rattled more keys. Next he brought up the Commercial Crime Services section of the International Chamber of Commerce website. It was the home of the IMB Piracy Reporting Centre where all current and ongoing incidents were monitored and displayed around the clock. The website offered a single point of contact for shipmasters and shipping line owners all over the world to report piracy incidents. Its twenty-four-hour phone and email hotline was run from the central company base in Kuala Lumpur, from where the relevant maritime law enforcement authorities anywhere in the world could be alerted to a developing incident.

Ben clicked on the tab that said LIVE PIRACY MAP. A satellite image of the world appeared onscreen. It was dotted with a profusion of pointer arrows colour-coded by status, in increasing order of seriousness: Suspicious Vessel, Attempted Attack, Fired Upon, Boarded, Hijacked. The multicoloured arrows were mainly clustered around the east and west coasts of Africa, as well as a great many in the South China Sea, Malaysia and Borneo. A stunning number of the arrows were orange, designating 'Boarded'. It was incredible to think that at this very moment, so many ships' crews were facing the imminent danger of being overrun by armed bandits.

But in the location Jude had given, there was nothing but blank blue ocean. No markers anywhere close. If the incident map could be trusted – and Ben knew it could – there were two current piracy attacks taking place along the east coast of Africa. One was happening off Tanzania near Zanzibar, a thousand miles to the south of Jude's coordinates. The other stricken vessel was in the five-hundred-mile stretch of waters between Mozambique and Madagascar, a further thousand miles south again. Neither of them could possibly be the *Svalgaard Andromeda*.

The distances were impossible. Having set out from Salalah in Oman, it was extremely unlikely that the vessel could have reached Zanzibar by now, let alone the coast of Mozambique.

The obvious question came into Ben's mind. Could Jude have got the coordinates wrong?

Ben couldn't believe that. Firstly, Jude was a quick and precise thinker, with a superb memory for facts and numbers. He knew better than to make such a huge error. Besides which, the coordinates were too specific not to have come from the ship's own navigation computer. Ben was certain that, however Jude had been able to see them, he'd have noted them down correctly to the last number.

Which left two further possibilities. One, that the incident was in the process of being recorded by the IMB Piracy Reporting Centre. Or two, that they didn't yet know it was happening.

'Why wouldn't the crew have called it in before it kicked off?' Ben said. 'You can't miss an incoming pirate attack on radar. They must have known what was about to happen.'

Jeff just shook his head. 'Unless it all went down too fast.

Surprise attack? In open sea, I agree, it seems unlikely. But however it happened, the pirates must've gained control quick enough to prevent them from getting out a distress call in time, and cut off their radio access. Sounds like a seriously well-planned op.'

The scenario made sense to Ben. But Jude had somehow been able to get an email through. 'Why send the message here, to you?' he wondered aloud. 'Why not contact the authorities? The ship's officers would have known who to go to in this situation.'

It only took Ben another moment to realise what that had to mean. He glanced at Jeff, whose expression told him his friend was thinking the same thing he was.

'That's because there *are* no ship's officers,' Jeff said grimly. 'They're toast, and all that's left are the ordinary deckhands. Those blokes wouldn't have the first idea who to call in an emergency. They're on their own out there.'

Ben brought Jude's email back up onscreen, staring at it as though he could will the words to squeeze out more information. '"*Maintaining position*",' he read out, tapping the screen with a finger. 'What's that about?'

'What else?' Jeff said. 'They're not moving, that's all it means.'

'But why would he tell us? I know him. He's a planner. He wouldn't waste words on the obvious. He's thinking two steps ahead here.' Ben chewed his lip and struggled to think what it could be. An idea flashed into his mind. 'Where would the crew hide when the ship was taken?'

'Below decks,' Jeff said. 'For sure. That's where I'd go.'

'Me too. I'd head straight for the engine room. Chances are the guys already down there wouldn't even know it was happening at first, until the others ran down and told them. They'd bunch together. Strength in numbers.'

Jeff nodded, seeing where Ben was going with this. 'And the engine room has the strongest hatches to keep out water in an emergency. They could lock themselves down tighter than a fish's arse in there, and they'd have independent control over the engines and power. They could shut everything down and hold her steady, and there's bugger all the pirates could do about it from up top.'

'Which would mean we're looking at a sitting target,' Ben said. 'And assuming that Jude got these position coordinates just before, or just after, it all started going down, we know where to find it.'

'Give or take,' Jeff said, raising an eyebrow. 'It's the ocean. Things tend to drift around on it.'

Ben said nothing. He turned his attention back on the computer screen. His heart was thudding. He sat frozen in indecision for a moment, then grabbed the desk phone and started punching out the number. Then he stopped.

His whole career between leaving the SAS and starting up the business at Le Val had been predicated on the simple and well-proven fact that calling in law enforcement authorities was not always the most effective or advisable way to deal with a problem. Ben had been involved with several kidnap and hostage situations in which local police and paramilitary units had got there before him. Too many times, he'd seen the results of botched tactics, conflicting orders, poor communication and general inefficiency result in the wholesale slaughter of members of the raid team, the hostage takers and the hostages themselves. He did not trust these people. He was not going to let the same thing happen to his son.

Ben put the phone down.

Jeff's look was so intense that his eyes were like lasers. 'Are you thinking what I'm thinking?' he said.

'There isn't a lot of choice,' Ben said. 'And even less time. I'd better get moving.'

Jeff kept up the intense stare. 'What's with the *I*?'

'He's my kid,' Ben said.

'And he's my responsibility,' Jeff said. 'I'm the one he's asking for help.'

Jeff would never know how much that stung. Ben's guts writhed at the reminder that in such a moment of danger, Jude hadn't even been able to get in touch with his own father.

'I'm not asking you to come with me,' Ben said.

'And you'd better not ask me not to,' Jeff said hotly. 'I'm in, and that's it. Don't fucking fight me on this one, mate.'

Ben pursed his lips. There was no use arguing. And Jeff was right. There was no way one man on his own could handle this task.

'Okay,' he said after a pause. 'If we're going to get Jude out of there in one piece, we need to do it right. Full-on operation, no half measures. You know as well as I do what that's going to involve. A lot more than I can afford right now.'

Jeff looked affronted. 'Money? I can't believe you'd even talk to me about money. I got Jude into this. I'll do whatever it takes to get him out of it. I don't care if it costs every last penny in the bank.'

Ben lit a Gauloise. In ten seconds, he'd already smoked it down halfway. 'The biggest problem we have is getting there. We need to be over six thousand kilometres away, and we need to be there now. There's no time to mess about with visas. And the kind of hardware we're going to need won't pass for hand luggage. We'll need our own aircraft.'

Jeff spread his hands. 'That, as you say, is a problem.'

Ben worked on the cigarette a few more moments, puffing

great clouds of smoke. Then it came to him. 'Not when you can walk on water, it isn't.'

Jeff's face lit up. 'Kaprisky.'

Ben nodded. 'Time to call in that favour.'

Jeff was already looking up the number. 'You know, two is going in a bit light for a job like this. There's no shortage of blokes who'll jump in if we ask.'

Ben agreed. At least four names sprang to mind and were just a phone call or a text message away. Men he trusted, and whom he knew would drop everything to rush to his aid. But the clock was working against them. It could take forty-eight hours to scramble everyone together in one place. 'There's no time for that, Jeff. It'll just have to be the two of us.'

'You mean the three of us,' said a voice from behind them.

Ben and Jeff turned. Tuesday Fletcher was standing in the office doorway and he'd been listening to every word they'd been saying.

Chapter 17

Three more times on his way down from D Deck, Jude almost got caught. What saved him was the gloom in the windowless passages, now that the bright neon lights that normally burned day and night had gone out. The deeper he ventured into the bowels of the ship, the darker it would get. He didn't dare to use the Maglite until he could see nothing at all.

It was clear that the pirates were palpably more agitated now than before. The sudden loss of power to the whole ship was a real problem for them, and the fuss it seemed to be causing convinced Jude more than ever that they needed the vessel to be serviceable in order to steal it.

He was beginning to get a sense of their plans. If they'd wanted to hold it for ransom, he was certain they'd be keeping the crew alive to give them more bargaining leverage. But they weren't doing that. They were apparently set on killing everyone on board, which told Jude they had other intentions. To use it as a floating base, maybe, as Gerber had said. Or sell it. The cargo alone must be worth a fortune.

Those weren't comforting thoughts. Somehow, Jude kept telling himself, he and the rest of the crew were just going to have to hang on tight and hope that help arrived before it was too late.

Doubts were already crowding his mind. What if Jeff didn't receive the email? What if nobody came?

Looking in all directions, Jude reached the corridor where the bosun's body had been dragged away earlier. The floor was still slippery with blood. Jude gingerly sidestepped the trail of it and hurried on, past the open door of the mess.

He skidded to a halt. Crept back to the doorway and peered furtively through it.

Inside the mess canteen, a white man was standing with his back to the doorway. He was alone, bathed in the light from a porthole window and gazing out of it as if deep in contemplation, calmly sipping on a Coke and obviously unbothered by the blood all over the floor. The same small metal case Jude had seen him with before was still cuffed to his left wrist.

Carter.

Jude froze in the doorway, uncertain what to do. He desperately wanted to keep moving and rejoin his friends down below in the relative safety of the engine room. But he couldn't ignore the part of him that wanted to understand what was happening here, and who this guy Carter really was.

Jude stepped silently into the room and sneaked up behind Carter, terrified that the man might suddenly whip round, spot him and put a bullet in his heart. He hardly dared to breathe as he eased the heavy torch out of his belt.

He was just three steps away when Carter sensed the presence in the room, and turned suddenly. They stared at each other. Then Carter dropped his Coke and his right hand dived for his pistol and Jude closed in and lashed out with the Maglite. The solid aluminium tube thumped into the side of Carter's head with a dull meaty *crack*.

Carter dropped the gun. His eyes rolled back in their

sockets and he went over sideways, collapsed against a plastic chair and then slumped to the floor.

Jude ran and shut the door, then hurried back to the still body. For a second he was concerned he might have killed the man, but a check of his pulse told him Carter was just unconscious. Thankfully, the torch was still working after being used as a club. Jude started searching through the man's pockets for a wallet or a passport. He found a packet of gum, loose change, a loaded spare magazine for the pistol, and a ring with a pair of small keys.

Jude guessed that one of the keys must be for the handcuff on Carter's left wrist. The other, presumably, was for the case. Why would anyone go around with a reinforced metal box chained to them unless they were protecting something important? Jude wanted to know what. He soon found which key was which. The case had two locks. They opened smoothly and easily. With a glance at Carter to check he was still unconscious, Jude flipped up the lid.

The case was lined with black egg-box foam and contained five thick rolls of cash that between them added up to more money than Jude had ever seen before. Tens of thousands. Maybe hundreds. Beside the rolls, a collection of three US passports were banded together with elastic. Jude checked them each in turn. Each had the same photograph of the man he'd just knocked out, but all three had different names: Tyrone Carter, Larry Holder and Payton Bequette.

So which one of them was he, if any?

Under the passports lay a thick, sealed manila envelope. Jude pulled it out and ripped it open and found that it was stuffed with printed papers, some kind of legal documentation that was meaningless to him.

That was when he noticed, nestling inside the foam under where the envelope had been, a leather pouch tied with a thong. He let the papers spill to the floor, reached down and picked it up. Something hard inside. And heavy. It felt like a lump of stone, big enough to fill his hand. Jude untied the leather thong and opened the pouch. The thing inside was wrapped in tissue paper.

Jude peeled the wrapping open to reveal the object. He held it raised up on the flat of his palm, so that the light from the porthole shone on it.

What the—?

At first sight, it looked like a big lump of clear crystal, like one of those pieces of quartz his mother had once collected. She'd lined every window-sill and mantelpiece in the vicarage with a whole variety of ornamental rocks and as a young boy Jude had learned all their different names – moonstone, amethyst, haematite, jasper, citrine, rose quartz. This one was much larger and more uneven in shape, all angles and pits and sharp edges. But despite its roughness its clarity was like no crystal he'd ever seen before. It seemed to glow with an inner light of its own.

Jude swallowed. He felt suddenly dizzy with confusion. It couldn't be. It was way too big. Impossible.

Or maybe it wasn't impossible. He could think of only one reason why a person would carry something like this inside a locked box chained to their wrist.

Jude couldn't take his eyes off the thing. He couldn't believe it. He could have stared at it all day long – but then he remembered where he was. On a hijacked ship with armed pirates swarming from deck to deck looking for someone to kill. He hurriedly wrapped the lump of whatever it was back inside the tissue paper, replaced it in its pouch and jammed it into his jeans pocket. It only just fit in there. As an afterthought, he snatched up Carter's fallen pistol, which looked pretty much like the one Jeff Dekker had let him

113

shoot at Le Val. He remembered roughly how it worked. 'Designed for morons to use,' Jeff had laughed. 'And they do, so you shouldn't have too much of a problem.' Jude stuffed the gun into his waistband against the small of his back, dropped the spare magazine in his other pocket, then snatched up the torch and stuck it back through his belt, like a sword. He sprang to his feet, ran to the door and tentatively peeked out.

The coast was still clear, but Jude could hear voices and footsteps approaching from up the passage. With a last glance back at Carter's inert body, he slipped out and ran like crazy.

The others heard him pounding on the engine room door. 'It's me,' he panted. 'Let me in!'

The bowels of the ship were plunged into near-total darkness, and without the Maglite, Jude could have been groping blindly about for weeks through the maze of passageways. As the hatch opened, he was dazzled by a torch beam shining in his face. Unseen hands grabbed him by the arms and hauled him in through the hatch. It seemed eerily quiet and still down here, without the steady background chatter and vibration of the engines. When the hatch clanged shut behind him, it felt to Jude as if he was stepping inside a tomb. The heat and stench of enclosed bodies hit him. Shadows danced everywhere. The beams of several flashlights pointed at him from the darkness.

'We were worried as hell,' Gerber said. 'Those bastards must be all over the ship by now.'

'They are,' Jude said, nodding and gasping for breath, which wasn't easy in the airless atmosphere so far below decks. 'They started going apeshit when the power went down. But they didn't see me.'

'Did you manage to do it?' Everyone but Scagnetti was

crowded around Jude, anxiously waiting for the answer to the big question.

'I did it,' Jude said. 'The message went off without a hitch. That's the best we can do.'

There were grins and sighs of relief all round. 'Well done, son,' Diesel said, thumping Jude on the shoulder.

'So now what?' Condor asked nervously.

'Now we wait,' Gerber said. 'What the hell else is there to do?'

'Pray to God we make it through this,' said Trent.

Gerber gave a grunt. 'You go ahead and pray to that sonofabitch, if it pleases you. I stopped wasting my breath on him thirty years ago.'

'I need to use the bathroom,' Jude said, and Gerber motioned with his torch to show him over to a corner of the engine room where a bucket had been placed, out of sight in as private a spot as possible. It had already been used more than once. One bucket, for thirteen trapped men. As time went by, the smells inside the enclosed space would become horrendous.

In all the excitement, nobody had noticed the lump in Jude's pocket sticking out as big as a tennis ball. Now that he had a moment's privacy, he took it out and reopened the leather pouch to examine its contents more closely under the beam of his Maglite.

There was little doubt in his mind what it was he was holding. It was hard to believe the thing was even real. But it was real, all right. The more he stared at it, the more bewildered he became as questions layered up in his mind. Was this what the pirate leader was after, the big man with the awful scarred face? Or had Carter, or whatever his name was, been keeping it from him?

Amid all the uncertainty, one thing was for sure. If this

115

thing was what Jude thought it was, forget the value of the cargo. Forget the value of the whole ship and everything aboard. Jude was no expert, but he was pretty certain you could buy an entire fleet of ships for the value of what he was holding in his hand.

He spent a fevered moment debating with himself whether he should tell the others what he'd found. Gerber, Hercules and Diesel, he felt strongly that he could trust. Some, like Trent, Allen, Lorenz and Park, he knew much less well, and it worried him how they might react. As for Scagnetti, it would be running a huge risk. Jude remembered Mitch's warning. Scagnetti would be the first to slip a blade between your ribs for even a few bucks. With something like this, Jude wouldn't trust him any more than he trusted the pirates. He wasn't closed inside a steel box with them.

Jude decided that he should keep his secret to himself, at least for now. Then what was he going to do with it? He'd had no clear idea in his head when he'd picked it up, just a vague notion that he didn't want Carter to have it. Should he toss it in the sea, first chance he got? Return it to the hijackers and hope for leniency? Use it as a bargaining chip to plead for the lives of the crew? Some hope. The pirates would just take it and kill them all anyway.

If the pirates didn't, Carter certainly would. When the man came to and found it was gone, he was going to know exactly who took it, and he was going to want that person's blood. Jude had seen him personally execute four men as if it were nothing. What wouldn't he do to the thief who'd stolen *this* from him?

Even in the oppressive heat of the engine room, Jude felt a coldness wash over him. In taking this thing, he might have just made the worst mistake of his life.

Chapter 18

Pender let out a long, tortured groan as he opened his eyes and the agony shuddered through his skull. 'Jesus Christ!' He tried to shake his head to clear it, but that only made the pain worse. 'Mother*fucker*!'

He managed to prop himself up on one elbow. There was a burst of panic before he remembered that the blood on the floor had been there before, and wasn't his own. With that memory came the recollection of the last thing he'd seen before the white flash and the ensuing unconsciousness. It was the thin young blond-haired guy sneaking up behind him with the torch in his hand. The bastard who'd clobbered him. He could have busted his damn head open. Must have been one of the crew. Why wasn't he dead already?

Pender struggled into a kneeling position. As he moved, he felt the tug on his left wrist from the chain connecting him to the metal case. He had to smile. That was all that mattered. The crew weren't his problem. Headaches, he could deal with. What was a little knock on the nut? A man in his position could forgive and forget such minor transgressions with great magnanimity.

But then the smile dropped like a ton weight from Pender's face when he saw that the lid of the case was open. Someone had been through his pockets and got the key. The bundles of cash were strewn about. The thick envelope was torn open, the phony legal papers it contained scattered on the floor.

He didn't give a shit about the papers, not even about the money. With a despairing moan he yanked the case to him and delved inside. He blinked. It was empty. Empty!

No. No. It couldn't be. Please Christ oh Christ don't let it be. Pender searched frantically about the floor, but there was nothing there.

It was gone. His rock. Fucking GONE!

He wanted to scream. He did scream. A howl like a wounded dog.

His aching head was completely forgotten. He leapt to his feet and dashed from the mess room, running aimlessly in a breathless panic until he got a grip on himself.

Gone. Stolen. By the same dirty rotten little shit who'd sneaked up on him. Was this a targeted attack? How could he have known what was in the case? No, it was impossible. It was just some sailor.

Pender was floored by this unthinkable turn of events. For this to happen, after all he'd been through, after planning everything so carefully down to the last detail!

The plan had been so beautifully worked out. Starting with the escape from Oman, personally organised weeks in advance by none other than Eugene Svalgaard, heir to the shipping line dynasty, as the perfect way to smuggle out of the country what was possibly the hottest piece of stolen property in modern history. Who better to set up a passage for three anonymous stowaways on board a ship than the owner of the whole fleet? All it had really taken was a small donation to Captain O'Keefe's retirement fund. Fifty thousand bucks was a drop in all the world's oceans put together for a man as obscenely rich as Svalgaard.

Pender's fee for the job had been a little steeper, but then five million dollars was the going rate for hiring a professional mercenary and sometime jewel thief, never caught, to assemble a crew of hitters and carry out a home invasion robbery so serious that its perpetrators could never work again. The third-generation Dutch shipping magnate from New York hadn't even blinked at the cost. As both Svalgaard and Pender knew very well, five million was a ridiculously small investment to make in return for such incredible booty.

Of course, ol' Svalgaard had never had the faintest suspicion that, when he turned up in Mombasa for the rendezvous, there would be no ship, no Pender, and worst of all, no magnificent uncut rock the size of your fist waiting for him to collect and hustle home to his secure vault. The smug little crook was so used to getting his own way, it hadn't seemed to even occur to him that a common gun-for-hire like Lee Pender could outfox him and snatch the loot for himself.

Yet it had been so damned easy. Already drooling over the fifty-thousand-dollar bribe Svalgaard had slipped him to take on the unauthorised passengers, Captain O'Keefe hadn't needed too much persuading to accept a further hundred grand in cash from 'Ty Carter' to look the other way and make sure nothing was reported when the pirates appeared. Nobody would get hurt, Pender had assured O'Keefe. The pirates would help themselves to a few cargo containers and then go on their way rejoicing. It was just business. What did the captain care, anyway? This was to be his last voyage.

Pender had been a step ahead of everyone. The look on O'Keefe's face when the old fart clocked that he'd been tricked! And how that arrogant burger-stuffing hog Svalgaard would rant and rave on the dockside in Mombasa, when it hit him that he'd been double-crossed and that the fortune he'd been so sure of had just slipped irretrievably out of his hands, and he couldn't breathe a word about it to anyone! Pender hoped he'd have an apoplexy and drop dead on the spot.

Meanwhile Pender would be far, far away and laughing. Exactly where was the only part of his plan he hadn't finalised yet: with this kind of wealth, he could spend the rest of his life in any paradise he chose. Monaco or Mustique? Palm Springs or Tahiti? Such tough decisions. Why not all of them, he'd dreamed over and over again. He could just hop back and forth from one palatial beachside mansion to another in his jet whenever he got bored.

The most worrying part of his plan had been put in place weeks earlier, two days after Svalgaard had confirmed the ship's departure date from Salalah. That was when Pender had flown to Nairobi, Kenya, to meet with Jean-Pierre Khosa, known to hard-bitten veterans of African wars like Pender as 'the General'. General of what exactly, nobody knew for sure. Pender had never met Khosa before, but he'd heard the stories. Who hadn't? If even just half the stuff people whispered about the man was true, it was still enough to make you piss dust.

It hadn't been easy making contact with Khosa. Until the last minute, Pender had been nervous about whether he'd even turn up for the lunchtime appointment in the lavish suite in Nairobi's exclusive Fairmont The Norfolk Hotel. When the General eventually made his appearance, he was wearing a tailored Italian silk suit and accompanied by a pair of stone-faced bodyguards, who frisked Pender thoroughly for weapons and wires. Finally, the meeting was allowed to take place. Its purpose: to put the lucrative and highly illegal business proposition to Khosa, whom Pender knew to be badly in need of cash to further his own cause, one that Pender had no interest in.

He'd had to be extremely careful not to let too much slip with Khosa. The General might be one scary-looking sonofabitch, but he was also very, very smart. Over French cuisine and expensive wine, Pender had laid out the carefully concocted fiction that he was acting as a courier on behalf of a very rich client – that much was more or less accurate. Where Pender's story deviated from the truth was that he was tasked with delivering certain documents which, without going into all the boring details, were worth a vast amount of money to the client and legally too sensitive to be carried by normal means, hence Pender's involvement and the unorthodox means of transportation.

Khosa had just nodded through all of that. To Pender's indescribable but very well-hidden relief, the General was content to skim over the boring details. He was just waiting to find out what was in this for him.

The fiction continued: Pender's client had powerful enemies who stood to gain equally from the destruction of these documents, and thanks to new intelligence it was now believed that these people might have somehow infiltrated the client's network in an attempt to intercept the package on arrival in Mombasa, or possibly even sooner. This made it essential for the documents to be removed from the ship, either by helicopter or boat, before someone else got to them first.

The tale was all highly improbable, of course, but it was the best Pender could come up with, and he'd put on a good act of making it sound semi-plausible. A lawyer would have laughed – but the General was no lawyer (although he had allegedly ordered the murders of a few in his time, and good for him). Pender's hope had been that the promise of hard cash would be sufficient to distract Khosa from looking too hard for holes in the story.

And Pender's gamble had paid off. The offer of one-point-five million dollars, either in cash or wired to the account of Khosa's choice, had got the General's eyes twinkling exactly as hoped. For that sum, Khosa's task would be to supply the manpower and the means to whisk Pender and his precious 'documents' away, mid-ocean.

It was Khosa who had come up with the clever notion of the faked-up pirate attack, and Pender had jumped at the idea as enthusiastically as Khosa had jumped at the money. Piracy offered the perfect cover for the hijack. So many ships were already being knocked off around Africa that one more would attract very few questions. Pender's only concern had been that there were so many real pirate gangs hunting about the Indian Ocean for easy victims. What if one of them hit the *Andromeda* before Khosa showed up? It was a risk he had to take.

An aggressive negotiator, Khosa had imposed certain conditions to sweeten the deal his way: in addition to the flat fee, which was quickly bumped up to two million dollars, the General laid claim to both the ship and her cargo, as spoils of war to take away and dispose of as he saw fit. This would, of course, Khosa had added with a smile, include the crew, on the understanding that he could either just kill them all on the spot or put them to other uses of his own choosing. If Pender would agree to that, they were in business.

Pender had nothing to lose and everything to gain by going along with Khosa's whims. The $500,000 price hike had been expected and allowed for. He couldn't care less what happened to Eugene Svalgaard's valuable property, and he didn't give a rolling rat fuck if the General's band of cutthroats got their jollies slaughtering a bunch of ignorant sailors, either. Screw 'em.

And so, not without some trepidation, Lee Pender had entered into a binding agreement with the most notoriously unpredictable, grasping, violent and ruthless maniac in Africa. The phony legal papers purporting to be worth so much to his nonexistent client had already been forged, just in case he'd needed to show something to back up his cover story. White and Brown, the two expendables, had already been hired. The passage from Salalah was all set up with Svalgaard and O'Keefe. All that remained was to break into the home of Hussein Al Bu Said at the appointed time, take care of business there, snatch the rock, race undetected across the city to the port, jump aboard ship, endure a few days' discomfort cooped up in the company of White and Brown, wait for Khosa's dramatic entry and, at last, get the hell out of there a fabulously rich man. All the while letting not a living soul, least of all Jean-Pierre Khosa, know what he was really carrying. Piece of cake.

But for all its dangers and complexities, it had been the most beautiful plan. This had been the Big One that Pender had spent his life ready and willing to do anything to make happen. After surviving twenty-four years in the private military contractor business, he wanted out before his well ran dry or he met a bullet. At age fifty-five, with thirty more years of life expectancy, he'd literally wept with joy that such unbelievable good fortune could have fallen into his lap. He could walk away from the whole shitty world, the richest fugitive in history. Another new identity with passport and driver's licence to match, a nose job to alter his appearance a little, a high-rolling lifestyle of fast cars and beautiful women and casinos and more money than he could hope to spend if he lived to be a hundred, no matter how hard he tried. That was the intoxicatingly wonderful future he'd envisaged.

He'd been so close to the finish line that he could taste the Martini cocktails, feel the soft white warm sand between his toes and hear the giggles of the adoring bikini-clad girls.

And now everything was suddenly falling apart. Pender could actually visualise his plans cracking and raining to the floor in pieces like fragmented china.

He could already have been out of here, if fucking Khosa hadn't insisted on personally staying aboard the cargo ship until his guys finished off the last of the crew and sorted out the mysterious engine and power failure, instead of taking straight off in the fishing boat as first agreed. They were wasting time. What Khosa did with the ship was his business; Pender had been hopping with impatience to get on with his own. He'd been so disgusted with the circus up on the bridge that he'd wandered down to the empty mess room to find some coffee. And now look what had happened! Who let some young whippersnapper of a sailor go running amok like that? Pender couldn't believe that he'd survived decades of warfare and dodged bullets everywhere from Angola to Libya, only to get cold-cocked by some kid with a flashlight.

Now Pender was compelled to remain aboard until he got back what was his. He'd tear the vessel apart with his own bare hands if he had to.

Furious, still clutching his splitting head, he stormed up onto the bridge to marshal a few men to come help him find that little shit who'd clobbered him, take back what he'd stolen and then disembowel the bastard. About eight Africans were scratching their heads around the dead instruments of the conning station, debating in flurries of their own language what switch they could press or lever to pull to restore the power. Until they could figure out what had caused the shutdown, the ship was going nowhere.

'Maybe if you assholes didn't butcher everyone on sight,' thought Pender – the man who'd murdered the captain and mates – 'then you might have a clue how to sail the ship.'

He was about to start yelling at them in fury when he saw the formidable figure of Jean-Pierre Khosa standing by the windows, casually lighting up another of his giant Cohibas. Standing with him was his right-hand man, Zolani Tembe, tall and muscular and apparently made of granite. Tembe wore ammunition belts the way Los Angeles rappers wore gold chains. His personal weapon was an M60 machine gun that was never out of his huge hands. A long, curved machete was stuck crossways in his belt.

Pender swallowed and tried to play it cool. Only a very foolish man would vent his anger to the General's face. Pender had no wish to end up as chopped shark bait.

'You, you and you,' he said, jabbing a finger at three Africans who didn't seem to be doing much. 'Come with me.'

'What do you want them for?' Khosa said, in that deep, calm voice of his. Whenever he spoke, it was always with great deliberation, as if he considered every syllable in advance.

'I've been robbed.' Pender held up his left arm with the empty case dangling from it. 'One of the crew is running around loose, and he took my papers.'

Khosa's mutilated brow distorted into an even deeper frown. 'Why would he do this?'

'How the hell do I know what some illiterate deckhand would want with them? Use them to wipe his ass with, for all I know. That's not the point. I have to have them.'

Khosa roared with amusement amid a cloud of cigar

smoke. Then, turning to the puzzled gang at the conning station, he dropped the smile and laid a big hand on the dead electronic consoles. 'The problem is not with the equipment. The crew have done this. They are controlling the ship from the engine room. That is where we will find them. And that is where you will find your paper thief, messenger boy,' he added for Pender's benefit. He motioned at Zolani Tembe. 'Gather the men and find this engine room. We must get this ship working.'

'And the crew?' Tembe said.

'Bring them to me. We will take the ones that we can sell or use, and kill the rest.'

Chapter 19

The first of many urgent calls that day had an instantly positive outcome. The octogenarian billionaire Auguste Kaprisky was overjoyed by the chance to repay what he saw as his debt to Monsieur Hope for saving his life. His greatest fear, he told Ben on the phone, had been that Ben would never ask. Without any hesitation and not a single question about why it was needed, Kaprisky granted them full and free use of his private jet. The aircraft was kept in its own hangar at Le Mans Arnage airport, just a few kilometres from Kaprisky's estate, and he maintained two pilots on full-time salary, ready to fly at a moment's notice. The weather forecast was looking dicey, but they'd taken off in worse.

The old man upgraded his plane every couple of years. His latest acquisition, he proudly declared, was a brand new Gulfstream G650ER, capable of covering thirteen thousand kilometres at a stretch, travelling at a steady Mach .85 with up to nineteen passengers on board.

'That's more than plenty,' Ben said. 'I can't thank you enough, Auguste.'

'Anything for you, my friend. I mean it.'

Jeff was on his iPhone, cancelling clients and calling in the security firm they employed to look after Le Val when there was nobody around. With time so short, the rest of the plan was going to have to come together en route.

Kaprisky had additionally offered to send his personal Bell 407 helicopter up to Le Val to collect them, but Ben had declined, thinking he could make slightly better time by road in the Alpina. While Jeff was making the last of the calls, Ben and Tuesday set about transferring equipment from the armoury to the back of the car.

'I got to spend a little time with Jude while he was here,' Tuesday said, a little awkwardly, searching for the right words. 'I like him. I'm really sorry, you know?'

'He's not dead yet,' Ben said.

Le Val's armoury room was buried beneath several feet of reinforced concrete, with an armoured steel door and hi-tech security system. It housed scores of military-grade weapons and thousands of rounds of ammunition, all pains-takingly licensed by the authorities, itemised down to the last round and wrapped in enough red tape to tie up the French navy. One or two items stored down there, however, had never been registered officially, so that they could be set aside for a rainy day and never traced if things went awry or the guns had to be ditched. Over the years Ben had 'collected' four MP5 submachine guns and an assortment of shotguns, rifles and pistols whose serial numbers were unlisted. It was the pick of those that would be travelling with them to Africa.

Ben was still unsure about the wisdom of bringing Tuesday Fletcher along. The young guy had proved his worth as a soldier, no doubt about that, but he was an unknown quantity. 'How's that leg?' Ben asked him as they hauled the gear up from the armoury.

'Never better,' Tuesday replied, grabbing another case of ammo.

'This isn't going be a walk in the park. I don't want to be responsible for you if it goes south.'

'I get it,' Tuesday said with a frown. 'Just because I was invalided out of the service, you think I'm not fit for this, yeah? You worry about Jude. I'll worry about my leg. I won't let you down.' He paused. 'It's an honour working with you, man. You're a legend.'

'I'm just a person like anybody else,' Ben said, wishing Tuesday would shut up.

'Seriously. I heard stuff some of the older guys still talk about. Like the thing in Basra in 2003. That was the bollocks. I mean, forget the Iranian Embassy siege, right? Who dares wins.'

Ben put down the heavy kit bag he was carrying towards the car and turned to glare at him. 'What you've heard is bullshit. You want to know what your glorious SAS were really doing in Basra? Setting up false-flag bombing targets against civilians to create PR spin for the war on terror. Killing innocent people so that puppet leaders in the West could wave their bloody flags on TV and get re-elected. That's what we were doing. It's why I disobeyed orders and almost got myself court-martialled. It's also one of the main reasons I quit the regiment and never looked back. So you can stuff your "legend". Don't ever call me that again, okay? If you want to come, come. Just try not to get killed out there. I've enough crap to deal with already.'

Tuesday looked as if he'd been gut-punched. His smile vanished and he fell silent. When Ben's anger died down, he felt bad for having lashed out at the younger guy and thought about saying so, but didn't.

Minutes later, they were throwing hastily packed personal belongings into the back of the car and piling in after them. Jeff sat up front next to Ben, still talking on his iPhone, and

Tuesday clambered in the back. Ben fired up the engine, popped the clutch and scattered gravel as the BMW took off.

It was 3.16 p.m.

Le Val to Le Mans Arnage airport and the waiting jet was just over two hundred and sixty kilometres. For the next two hours, Ben concentrated on getting them there in one piece and not attracting unwanted police attention, while Jeff worked the phone and covered pages of a pad in his lap with scrawled notes and numbers.

The sky was darkening as the sun, invisible all day behind a blanket of grey cloud, now began to set. Ben kept his foot down hard while icy rain lashed the Alpina and the wipers worked hard to swat the deluge aside. The road was slick and shiny, too treacherous to be driving so fast. The taillights of other vehicles starred and flared on the wet windscreen as Ben blew past everything in front of him. Lost in his own anxious thoughts and chain-smoking one cigarette after another, he was barely aware of what Jeff was saying over the phone. Every minute felt to him like days. He gripped the wheel and fought to stay focused, telling himself over and over again that Jude was still alive. He was tough and resourceful. He'd hang in there. He'd make it through this.

'Okay,' Jeff said, after a series of long calls and internet searches. They were speeding at a hundred and fifty kilometres an hour along the Nationale 13, just past Caen. 'Here's what we've got so far. The plane is fuelled up and good to go the second we get the gear on board. There won't be any questions the other end. We wing it to Obbia – that's the nearest airport to where we need to be. It's right on the Somali coast, next to the town of Hobyo, 'bout five hundred klicks up from dear old Mog.'

The Somali capital Mogadishu had been the scene of

several incidents involving British and US Special Forces over the years, and wasn't a place much beloved by anyone who'd been remotely involved.

Jeff went on, 'Le Mans Arnage to Obbia is just a shade over six and a half thousand Ks. I just talked to Adrien, that's Kaprisky's pilot, and he reckons at a steady Mach point eight-five, depending on conditions, we're looking at less than six and a half hours in the air, point to point.'

'Not counting the hundred and thirty-plus nautical miles east to the ship's last position,' Ben reminded him.

'That's where it gets trickier. Hobyo isn't exactly a thriving metropolis, even by African standards. It's supposed to have a port, but I wouldn't expect to find much there. So the big question is, how do we get a fast boat from there to take us out the rest of the way? We'll be lucky if we can find a rusty fishing trawler.'

'There's got to be a bigger port where we can charter a speedboat or a fast cabin cruiser,' Ben said.

'Yeah, no problem, if we travel from Mombasa. I've already checked. World's your oyster down there. Only problem is, you're looking at over sixteen hundred kilometres distance. There isn't a small, fast craft that'll cover it.'

'How about the Seychelles? The islands are full of boats, and they're a little bit closer to where Jude is than Mombasa.'

'Thought about that already,' Jeff said. 'Not much in it, distance-wise. Same problem.'

Ben tossed the stub of his Gauloise through the inch-wide gap in the window and instantly lit another without taking his eyes off the road. His thoughts were rushing faster than the tarmac under the wheels of the speeding Alpina. 'Remember Chimp Chalmers?'

Jeff looked at Ben. 'Mate, Chimp Chalmers is a fucking lunatic.'

'I know he is,' Ben said. 'But he might be a useful fucking lunatic. We can't afford to get picky. Can you get his number?'

'I can ask around,' Jeff said reluctantly.

'Do it.'

'You don't want to deal with that bloke. He's not stable. And he's a crook.'

'Do it, Jeff.'

Chaz 'the Chimp' Chalmers, named as much for his physical appearance as for his ever-readiness to pull apart with his bare hands anyone who crossed him, had been one of the many who had quit the SF track to pursue a marginally safer and far more lucrative career in international security, and other things. Ben and Jeff hadn't heard from him in a few years, but rumour had it he'd jobbed around central and east Africa for much of that time, not always on the right side of the law. He was the kind of person who could thrive and make contacts in places most sane men would steer well clear of, which had made him a natural to drift into arms dealing. These days, he was reportedly based in Prague and had built himself up to be the go-to guy for anyone looking to get hold of anything from an ex-Soviet tank or attack helicopter to a Scud missile, delivered to the location of your choice, anywhere in the world, for the right fee. He had connections everywhere, an extensive bag of tricks and a magician's reputation for being able to pull rabbits out of hats, to order. Something as mundane as arranging a fast boat from Hobyo port should be a cinch for him.

Jeff got straight back on the phone while Ben, stealing a glance at the dashboard clock and wincing at the time, drove faster.

Chapter 20

It took three more calls before Jeff finally managed to dig up the number for Chimp Chalmers. He dialled it and was put through to Chalmers's offices in Prague, where he was put on hold by a receptionist before getting to talk to the man himself.

Jeff quickly explained what he required, managing not to reveal any specifics about their situation while stressing that it was urgent. The conversation lasted nearly ten minutes, during which the Chimp did most of the talking and Jeff did most of the listening, bent over his phone with a finger in his other ear to keep out the roar of the Alpina's engine.

'Hmm,' Jeff said to Chalmers after a long silence. 'We're not looking to buy it, Chaz. We just want to charter it. Day, maybe two.'

More silence. Jeff looked dubious and impatient. 'Okay. Okay. Then talk to your guy and call me back as soon as you know. Make it snappy, all right? We're on the clock here.'

'Well?' Ben asked as Jeff ended the call.

'That arsehole can't get enough of talking about himself,' Jeff said with a sigh. 'But anyway, we could be on to something. Chalmers deals with some bloke who deals with some other bloke who plays poker with the head of the port authority in Mog.'

'They can get us the kind of boat we need?'

Jeff shook his head. 'Not a boat. They have a seaplane in the harbour that was confiscated from a Somali smuggling gang the cops nabbed last month. It's been sitting there waiting for some legal clerk to sign off on a compulsory destruction order for it. Chalmers heard about it a couple of weeks back through the grapevine and was thinking of taking it off their hands to sell on, but the port authority guy was being awkward over the price. Theoretically, it's still up for grabs.'

'What kind of seaplane? What condition is it in?'

'Some kind of big ex-Soviet flying boat, he says. The smugglers souped up the engines and kitted it out with extra-large tanks for long range. It's old and tatty as fuck, but Chalmers reckons it's in good nick.' Jeff spread his hands and looked sceptical. 'I don't know, Ben.'

'How much does this guy want?'

'Unknown. The Chimp says he needs to make a couple of calls and get back to us.'

'We don't have a lot of time,' Ben said. They were three-quarters of the way to Le Mans now, and the minutes were ticking by faster than he liked.

'You heard me tell him that. We'll just have to wait, for what it's worth.'

Fifteen anxious minutes later, Jeff's iPhone started buzzing in his hand. He answered immediately. 'Dekker.'

Jeff listened, stone-faced. Ben glanced at him as he drove, trying to gauge what was being said.

'Let me think about it and call you right back,' Jeff said after a couple of minutes.

'What did he say?'

Jeff still didn't look happy. 'He talked to his guy. The port authority fella will rent us the plane, and he's got a local pilot called Achmed Mussa who'll agree to fly it the five hundred klicks from Mog and meet us at the port in Hobyo. Reckons Mussa can be on his way within the hour and be there waiting for us when we arrive. In with the deal, no extra cost, there's another local guy who'll drive us there from Obbia airport in his Land Cruiser.'

Ben was well aware of how things worked in Africa. You could get pretty much absolutely anything you wanted there, which was what made the place such a goldmine for the likes of Chimp Chalmers. Across much of the continent, laws were seldom observed and even more seldom enforced, especially when the odd palm was crossed with silver and the odd blind eye was turned, both of which were the norm. But that kind of handy corruption inevitably came at a price.

'Money?'

'Thirty thousand dollars for the rental, plus another ten for the pilot. Plus another ten as a finder's fee for the Chimp.'

'What?!' Tuesday exclaimed from the back seat.

Ben didn't blink at the extortionate price. There was no choice, and they were in no position to haggle. 'I'll pay you back,' he said to Jeff, immediately back to wondering how much he could get for his place in Paris.

'I'm not worried about the money,' Jeff said. 'I'm worried that we get there and this thing's missing its props and the fucking wings are about to drop off. I told you, Chimp Chalmers is a shyster. But it's your call, Ben. The money's in the bank. I can wire him the fifty grand online, right now. Take me half a minute.'

'Do it,' Ben said.

Without a word, Jeff got to work.

'It's done,' he said soon afterwards.

'We have a seaplane,' Ben said.

'We have a seaplane.'

135

'How do you want to do this?' Ben asked. He glanced away from the road to look quizzically at his friend, and could see from the look on Jeff's face that they were both thinking the same thing. Whether it was with an AK-47 or a rocket-propelled grenade, seaplanes weren't the hardest of things to blow out of the air. Assuming that they'd find the *Andromeda* at the coordinates Jude had given them, there would be no easy way to get close to a container ship loaded with heavily armed pirates. They'd be heard and spotted a mile away.

Jeff said, 'I'm thinking, MV *Nisha*, but underwater.'

'Me too.' Ben angled the rearview mirror to look back at Tuesday in the rear seat, and asked him, 'Can you swim?'

Tuesday's eyes met Ben's in the mirror. 'Black guys sink like a stone. It's a well-known fact. Yeah, of course I can swim.'

'Ever jumped out of a plane?'

'I've done the basic two-week army parachute course. Never got into the nitty gritty stuff of the SAS training, for obvious reasons.'

Ben nodded. That would have to be good enough. 'Do we still have dealings with that guy in Stuttgart?' he asked Jeff.

'Rudi Weinschlager? Time to time, yeah. I've got his number here on my phone.'

'Ask him if he's still doing deals on those ex-military DPVs. If he can promise to have two of them ready and prepped and delivered in time to meet us at Stuttgart airport, we can divert to pick them up on the way. Along with all the other necessary kit.'

Jeff hesitated. 'That's a lot of gear. What's the max takeoff weight of a Gulfstream?'

'We'll get off the ground,' Ben said. 'If we have to tear the seats out to lose weight.'

'Kaprisky's going to love us.'

Jeff dialled the number, and moments later was through to one of Europe's biggest suppliers to the police and security industry, trade customers only. Ben gritted his teeth and waited through the brief conversation. Then Jeff was back to wiring upwards of another twenty grand from the Le Val account, and the deal was done.

It was turning into an expensive afternoon, but Ben was past caring. He'd gladly have given ten times more to get Jude off that ship. He could only pray they could make a difference.

'What's a DPV?' Tuesday wanted to know.

'You'll find out soon enough,' Jeff told him with a grin. 'Best get ready to get your feet wet.'

It was coming together. A few quick calculations told Ben that with luck, they could make the whole trip from Le Mans to the last known position of the *Andromeda* in around ten hours.

All Jude had to do was stay alive until then.

Chapter 21

Down there in the darkness and the heat and the stink of sweat and fear, tobacco smoke and diesel oil and stale urine, they waited for something to happen, and tried not to think about what it might be.

It had only been three-quarters of an hour or so since Jude had returned from above decks, but it seemed as if hours had passed. The pitch blackness of the engine room just made it worse. The torches were all switched off, to save on batteries. The only light was the occasional flare of a lighter and the tiny red glow of cigarettes burning as anxious men tried to calm themselves by smoking. The engine room echoed to the sound of the eerie creakings that resonated through the hull of the immobilised ship, and the tick-tick of contracting metal as the shut-down engines gradually cooled. Diesel and his assistants had partially dismantled the machinery in a deliberate act of self-sabotage to deprive the pirates of any chance of getting the vessel back under power.

There remained nothing to do but sit it out. The silence was broken now and then by a nervous whisper, and the tune that Scagnetti kept quietly humming to himself, somewhere in the darkness. Scagnetti would occasionally break off from humming to mutter and cackle to himself. If he'd been deliberately trying to unsettle the others, he couldn't have done it better. Even Gerber had given up telling him to shut the hell up.

The only other voice that could be heard was that of Park. In between long silences, he would begin to mutter to himself in Korean and break into a whimper. The whimper would sometimes die away, or else grow into a tortured moan, like the whine of a sick dog.

Further away, they could hear the dull thud and clatter of running footsteps and hatches opening and closing as the pirates hunted through the bowels of the ship for the hiding crew. The sounds of movement and voices seemed to be drawing steadily closer and closer. Everyone knew that the pirates must have figured out the remaining crew members were hiding in the engine room, and that it was just a question of their locating it. The pirates were working their way down towards them methodically, level by level, investigating one compartment after another.

It was a big ship, but it wasn't that big. Not big enough. They would be here soon.

Jude could feel the tension growing among the others. It wasn't helped by Park, who was growing more nervous and vocal by the minute. It was obvious what the Korean was thinking, and he wasn't the only one. They were doomed. Nobody was coming to rescue them. The pirates were going to find them and butcher them, one by one.

Hunched cross-legged in a lonely corner of the darkness, Jude was finding it difficult not to believe it, too. He was the only one who'd personally witnessed the bodies of their dead fellow sailors being slung overboard like garbage for the sharks, something he had wisely chosen not to share with the others. He had to will himself to stay calm, which he did by mentally reciting over and over the words of the

139

message he'd emailed to Jeff Dekker. It was the only glimmer of hope he could cling to.

Jeff would know what to do. Jeff would find a way to help.

Just for something to help occupy his mind, Jude reached down and took the diamond – as he was now certain it was – out of his pocket. He fingered its rough contours in the darkness, and once more wondered what he was going to do with the thing.

He was lost in meditation when a torch beam suddenly shone into his face out of nowhere. Startled, Jude whipped the diamond out of sight as the figure holding the torch came up close and bent low to speak to him.

It was Gerber. 'Got a moment?' he whispered. As if he was butting into Jude's busy schedule. Gerber turned off the torch, settled himself down next to Jude and they sat in the darkness, shoulder to shoulder. Any other time, Jude would have welcomed the company. He was clutching the diamond tightly in both hands, jammed between his knees.

'I'm worried about Park,' Gerber said in a low voice.

'Yeah, I know. Me too.'

Right on cue, came another mournful groan from somewhere in the darkness.

'I think he's losing his mind.'

'Maybe.'

'It's the stress. Saw it in 'Nam. Some fellas just fall apart, you know? I think we should watch Park.' Gerber paused. 'What about you, son? How're you holdin' up?'

'Loving every minute of it.'

'Tell me something,' Gerber whispered. 'This Jeff guy you're in contact with. He's a cop, right?'

'Something like that.'

'Then he'll have known who to call. They should be here any time. Right?'

'Right.'

'Let's hope so,' Gerber said quietly.

Jude was getting cramps from sitting so long on the hard metal floor, and he still had Pender's pistol hidden in his waistband, where it kept digging into him. He shifted, trying to get comfortable. In the process, the diamond slipped out of his fingers and hit the floor with a dull clunk.

'What've you got there?'

'Nothing,' Jude said, quickly scrabbling in the dark for it. His fingers found it and clasped it tightly. It felt like a heavy burden, one that Jude badly wanted to share with someone. The pressure of keeping it secret was wearing him down. Lou Gerber was a good guy. He was a friend. Surely he could be trusted?

Jude wrestled with the idea, and relented. 'If I tell you, you have to promise to keep it to yourself,' he said in an extra-low whisper, leaning close to Gerber's ear.

'Sure. What?' Gerber murmured.

Jude took a deep breath, hoping it wasn't an unwise move to take Gerber into his confidence. He opened the fist that was clutching the diamond.

Just then, there was the thump of footsteps very close by, and the jabber of loud voices just the other side of the engine room hatch.

Gerber forgot all about what Jude had been about to show him. He gripped Jude's arm. 'They're here.'

More voices. The pirates were trying to spin the wheel that opened the watertight seal, but it was all locked solid from inside. When the lock wouldn't open, there was a pounding against the thick steel that sounded like a battery of lump-hammers and echoed loudly through the whole engine room.

Every single one of the thirteen men inside was up on

his feet, frozen. Nobody breathed or spoke, or dared to turn on a torch.

The clanging stopped as suddenly as it had begun. The voices receded. Could the pirates have given up so quickly, and moved on elsewhere?

Gerber relaxed his grip on Jude's arm. Jude sensed the older man turn towards him in the darkness. Gerber seemed about to say something. But whatever words came out of his mouth were drowned out by the huge, crashing explosion that seemed to rock the whole ship.

Jude's ears were filled with a high-pitched whine. Beside him, Gerber had staggered backwards and nearly fallen over. Jude grabbed his torch and shone it towards the hatch. The steel was buckled, the seal broken, smoke from the blast seeping in through the uneven gaps that had appeared around the edges of the door. But the solid hinges and locks had held. The door was still in place. There was a strong stink of cordite.

'Those crazy bastards!' Diesel yelled.

'RPG,' Gerber said. 'Gotta be.'

Jude had no idea what an RPG was. But he knew it was bad news. The pirates had finally located the engine room and they were determined enough to use artillery to break their way in.

Jude shone his torch around the room. Park was groaning continuously. Even Scagnetti had stopped humming and cackling. They all backed away as far as they could from the door.

Moments later, another stunning explosion punched Jude's eardrums and made him rock on his feet. The pirates had fired another missile at the door, but still, the door had taken the impact. Flames were licking through the widened gaps around the edges of the buckled steel. Fire had broken out in the passage. The pirates could be heard yabbering in a chorus of panic. After a few moments, there was the whoosh of a fire extinguisher, and the flames died down.

'They keep this up, they're gonna sink us,' Gerber said.

'Or burn us out and barbecue us,' Diesel added.

Jude shook his head. 'They're not about to destroy the engine room. They want to keep the ship. Why else would they still be here?' It was little comfort either way.

There were no more explosions. It took another ten minutes of voices calling out commands in their own language, and more footsteps and pounding and the scrape and rattle of equipment being lugged into the passageway, before it became apparent what the pirates were planning to try next.

They were going to cut their way through the hatch door with an oxyacetylene torch.

Chapter 22

The murky day had been merging into evening by the time the Alpina screeched up at the private terminal of Le Mans Arnage airport. Ben, Jeff and Tuesday were met by Auguste Kaprisky's men, who introduced themselves as Adrien Leroy, the chief pilot with whom Jeff had already spoken on the phone, and his number two Noël Marchand. Both appeared to be quick-witted and businesslike, and well aware of the urgency of the situation as they ushered them briskly across the tarmac to meet the waiting aircraft.

Ben explained the slight detour that was necessary to pick up equipment en route. Leroy said he would make the necessary adjustment to the flight plan, no problem. The Gulfstream was fully fuelled, and wouldn't need to touch the ground anywhere else. The only concern was weather. Sleet was forecast for Stuttgart that evening, but Leroy insisted that nothing short of a blizzard would prevent them from flying.

No questions were asked about the nature of the equipment they were picking up in Germany. Nor did either Leroy or Marchand pay any attention to the heavy bags that Jeff and Tuesday were loading aboard the sleek, white Gulfstream while they talked with Ben.

The aircraft was in the air just fifteen minutes later. Stiff from the fast two-hour drive and his neck and shoulders creaking with tension, Ben eased himself into one of the plush leather seats, closed his eyes and tried very hard to empty his mind of racing thoughts.

He didn't open them again until, just short of an hour later, they made their descent through the clouds and touched down on the glistening runway in a very cold and wet Stuttgart, for what might have been the quickest stop-off in civil aviation history.

Rudi Weinschlager had been as good as his word and come through with all their requirements, packed inside two large wooden crates and one bulging NATO-issue kit bag, in an unmarked black VW panel van that was waiting for them exactly as promised. With the van backed close by on the tarmac, Ben, Jeff and Tuesday hurriedly transferred the gear aboard. 'You still haven't told me what's in these boxes,' Tuesday grunted as they lugged the heavy crates aboard, each one more than six feet long. 'They weigh a bloody ton.'

'Why ruin a surprise?' Jeff told him.

The plane lacked any kind of cargo hold, but its forty-five-foot-long executive cabin offered some two hundred cubic feet of baggage space. The crates crammed the centre aisle, only just fitting between the seats and looking very out of place in the Gulfstream's luxurious interior. Adrien Leroy frowned at the extra payload but said nothing.

They left Stuttgart soon afterwards at 6.53 p.m., managing to get off the ground ahead of the forecast sleet, and without being bogged down by the weight of its unorthodox cargo. Jeff and Tuesday shared a plate of sandwiches offered to them by Noël Marchand. Ben could not eat, and returned to his seat for the longest leg of a journey that, so far, had progressed smoothly and precisely according to plan.

But was his plan the right one? With nothing else to do

but wait for the journey's end, he finally allowed himself to voice the question that had been growing in his mind like a dark shadow. So many times in the past, Ben had always trusted his instincts. Now, suddenly, with so much at stake, he wasn't so sure. Was this a mistake? Should he have called in the authorities, instead of jumping in with both feet and charging off to take care of matters himself?

Doubts hovered at the back of his mind, like voices nagging him from deep within his consciousness.

You're a fool.

You're going to make it worse.

You're going to get him killed.

Ben listened to the voices until they grew tired of taunting him. He didn't try to argue with them. Maybe they were right. But he could see no other way.

Just under six hours after leaving Stuttgart, at ten to three in the morning East Africa Time, the plane landed in a different world.

The tiny airport, little more than a cluster of tin-roofed huts straddling a narrow runway, was no more or less than could be expected in a fragile region still reeling from civil war and slowly crawling towards stability for the first time since the old kingdom of Hobyo was carved out by a Somali sultan in the nineteenth century. After the sultan had made the mistake of letting his nation become an Italian protectorate, it was finally grabbed wholesale by Mussolini's forces in 1925 and became part of Italian Somaliland until World War Two, when the British took control of the troubled colony. The shaky independence of the new integrated Somali Republic, declared in 1960, had lasted less than a decade before the nation had become mired in bloody revolution and entered a long and brutal cycle of wars and military dictatorships from which it had never fully recovered.

As Ben already knew very well from experience, in such frail and desperately impoverished countries you couldn't always expect things to go right. And from the moment they stepped onto the cracked runway at Obbia, things started going wrong.

Chimp Chalmers had assured Jeff over the phone that the Land Cruiser would be there to meet them on arrival. Its driver, a local man by the name of Geedi who apparently worked as a taxi driver and courier all over the area, had been put on standby hours earlier, at the same time as the seaplane pilot in Mombasa. But there was no sign of Geedi. Tuesday volunteered to scout around the airport grounds and up and down the road, just in case of a misunderstanding. He returned shaking his head.

'You didn't see him?'

'Saw a hyena,' Tuesday said. 'At least, that's what I think it was. It was eating something dead in the bushes. There's bugger all of anything in this place. No lights, not a soul in sight. I doubt they see more than a couple of vehicles a day pass through. We're stuck, guys.'

Three o'clock in the morning in an apparently deserted airport two kilometres away from a town that consisted of a few dismal buildings scattered over a few hundred metres of sand and scrub. It wasn't a good time or place to be stranded with no transport.

'What do you want me to do?' asked Adrien Leroy. He looked edgy and kept glancing about, as if expecting hordes of gun-toting Somalis to appear at any moment and pillage and strip his boss's precious Gulfstream to a skeleton right before his eyes. His anxieties were probably not all that unrealistic.

'Just go,' Ben said to him. 'I appreciate your bringing us this far. We'll manage.'

'Are you sure?'

'Absolutely.'

As the jet shrieked off into the night, Ben wished he could be so certain. He paced the empty runway and sucked the guts out of a Gauloise while Tuesday sat swinging his legs on one of the big wooden crates, and Jeff got on the phone to unload his anger and frustration on the Chimp. It was a short and unpleasant call, the upshot of which was that the driver must have got the time mixed up and would be with them shortly.

They waited. November temperatures could easily average over thirty Celsius in Somalia, but it could get chilly at night. 'I never thought you could freeze your arse off in frigging Africa,' Tuesday complained. Jeff stood with his hands planted on his hips, frowning and looking at his watch every twenty seconds. Ben went on pacing and smoking to pass the time and settle his nerves enough to keep from tearing the place apart, or what little there was of it. The clock in his head was ticking louder than gunfire.

After forty more agitated minutes, they heard the clatter of an approaching vehicle with a loose exhaust, lurching towards them out of the darkness by the light of its single working headlamp. Geedi had arrived. Whether he'd received an angry call to prompt him, or this was simply his idea of punctuality, they would never know. From the weaving, stop-start motion of the ancient Land Cruiser, it was instantly clear that something was up with Geedi.

Jeff stared at the approaching vehicle. 'Please don't tell me the fucker's—'

'Looks that way to me,' Ben replied tersely.

The Toyota coasted to a halt approximately nearby. Ben

strode up to the driver's door, yanked it open, and the obese hulk of its occupant fell straight out of the driver's seat and rolled to the ground, coming to rest with his fat arms splayed outwards and his enormous belly pointing at the stars. Along with him tumbled out an unlabelled open bottle that Geedi had apparently been clasping between his chubby thighs as he drove. It landed on the dome of his stomach, spilling some kind of pungent clear liquor over his grimy shirt. Geedi was too comatose to notice. The inside of the vehicle reeked of kill-me-quick African moonshine.

'He's completely fucking pie-eyed,' Jeff said, shaking his head in disbelief.

Ben grabbed Geedi's ankles and hauled his limp carcass away from the Land Cruiser. With any luck, he wouldn't wake up before he got run over by the next plane that landed.

With the equipment crammed into the back of the vehicle, the worn-out rear suspension was down to the stops. The three of them piled in, Ben taking the wheel, and the exhaust gave a death rattle as they took off. The Toyota looked, felt and drove as if it had very few miles left in it, but the port of Hobyo was mercifully close by. Even so, they had to roll the windows down to escape being intoxicated by the alcoholic fumes. Jeff was ranting and cursing Chimp Chalmers. 'I'm going to kill him.'

'Let's just hope the same thing won't happen with our seaplane,' Ben said.

'Yeah, right. If there is a seaplane.'

Chapter 23

To cut through an armoured steel door that was sturdy enough and thick enough to keep out millions of tons of seawater was a task that took hours. But out here in the middle of the ocean, with no sign of anyone coming to the ship's rescue, the pirates could afford to take their time.

The torture of waiting had now reached new levels of agony. The passage outside was brightly illuminated with some kind of portable lamps, whose light shone around the twisted edges of the door as the pirates worked. Sparks hissed and fizzed and the super-hot flame from the torch roared. After twenty minutes, the first red-hot spot appeared on the inside of the door. After thirty, the red had turned white and the first sparks were beginning to penetrate the steel. By the end of the first hour, the pirates had cut a five-inch slot along the bottom of the door, slowly working their way up and around to create an oval opening big enough to clamber through.

After the terror, and then the anger, came the crippling numbness. The crew fell into a state of passive acceptance as the fight went out of them, even out of Scagnetti, and they sat around in the darkness and waited for the inevitable. Escape was impossible. Capture was guaranteed, along with whatever would come next. All anyone could ask for was a quick death.

Hours came and went. The pirates ran out of gas and connected up a fresh bottle. The sparks went on hissing and fizzing, and the ragged slot grew longer. Ten inches. Eighteen. Two feet. On and on. Relentless.

Some time before five in the morning, Jude lost the struggle against sleep, and curled up against the iron bulkhead, mercifully far away in his dreams. But not long afterwards, he woke with a start as someone shook him. It was Condor, his face half-lit by dancing torch beams. He looked grim.

'It's Park, man.'

Two things had happened while Jude had been sleeping. The sea had grown much rougher and the ship was rocking more noticeably. Meanwhile, Park had given up hope. He had found a length of thin steel cable in a corner of the engine room. He had climbed up on the generator housing to loop one end around a pipe attached to the ceiling. Then he had looped the other end around his neck, and jumped. His body was swinging to and fro with the motion of the ship.

Jude helped Condor and Trent hold Park steady while Diesel fetched a pair of bolt-croppers and cut the cable. Park's dead weight sagged into their arms. They laid him on the floor and covered him with a tarpaulin. Someone said a prayer for the poor man. Come what may, Park was out of it now.

The pirates were almost through the door. Just six more inches, and the ragged cut would meet itself in a rough oval shape, four feet high and three feet wide. Jude stared at the white-hot flame slowly burning its way through the last inches of steel.

'Arm yourselves,' Gerber said through clenched teeth. 'Get ready, men. This is our last stand.'

As an unsettled red dawn broke over the Indian Ocean, Pender couldn't understand what the hell was taking so long.

He'd barged his way into the passage to watch as they finished cutting through the hatch. Now he was pacing up and down, cursing to himself and becoming increasingly restless. The sea was growing choppy as hell out there. The ship was pitching more than he was used to, making him nauseous, and he couldn't wait to get off it. What was taking so damn long?

Khosa had been watching Pender very closely, and taking a keen interest in his mood. He was beginning to wonder what the white mercenary was so worked up about. Whatever it was, the General was thinking, it was obviously worth considerably more than the paltry two million dollars Pender had paid him to stage the phony pirate attack. That offended Jean-Pierre Khosa's sense of pride. He and his men were not some rag-tag bunch of common fishermen who had taken to boosting ships for a living. Maybe one of those poor bastards would have fallen for this ploy. Not him.

Khosa did not like to be lied to, or tricked. Nor had he believed a word of Pender's convoluted tale about carrying legal documents for some vague and nameless rich client. It was insulting to him that the white man had thought he could feed him such a pack of lies. Khosa's intention all along had been to find out what this was really about, and what Pender had actually been keeping so close to him inside that case of his. He was looking forward to the moment.

Khosa returned to the deck, clutching the rail to steady himself against the yaw and pitch of the ship. Yesterday's marble-smooth blue-green ocean was now a heaving patch-work of white foam that rolled and crashed into the sides of the vessel with explosions of spray leaping up high. The smaller vessel alongside was tossing and bobbing on the waves as its crew struggled to keep it from being swept into the towering hull of the *Andromeda*. The dawn sky looked turbulent and menacing, as if it was full of angry gods ready to smite their wrath down on everything below.

Khosa envied them that power. He filled his lungs with the wind and relished the violence of the coming storm. The storm was him, or what he wanted to be. He was part of it, a force of nature. Men feared him just as they feared the elements. And they were right to fear him. One day, the whole world would understand, and would feel the fear. One day.

Such thoughts made Jean-Pierre Khosa happy.

Soon afterwards, Zolani Tembe came up on deck to tell him that they had finished cutting through the door. 'Good,' Khosa said with a smile that tugged at the mass of scar tissue down his cheeks. They had to raise their voices over the noise of the wind. 'Do not let the white man inside the engine room. Bring him here.'

'And the prisoners?'

'Bring them too.'

Jude and the others watched helplessly as the ragged oval cut-line finally met itself, full circle. The flames and sparks that had been roaring and spitting all night long now ceased. The white-hot edges of the gash in the steel rapidly cooled and darkened. A moment later came the pounding of heavy blows and what sounded like several men all kicking at the hatch at once.

Then, slowly, horribly, the cut-out shape in the steel door gave a lurch and began to topple inwards. It fell against the metal floor of the engine room with a loud echoing crash. Bright light from the pirates' portable work lamps shone in through the hole, blinding Jude and the rest of the crew after so many hours trapped in pitch-darkness.

The next moment, armed men were swarming in through

the hole and the engine room was filled with yelling as they advanced, waving their guns and ordering the crew in broken English to get on their knees and put their hands on their heads. Gerber's will to fight failed him, and he fell to his knees. Even Scagnetti threw down his knife. To fight them would mean certain and immediate death. They were mariners, not warriors. In moments like this, ordinary men always clung to whatever thin hope of survival they could pray for.

Jude's right hand strayed behind his back and for a crazy moment he wanted to tear out Pender's pistol and start blasting away. He flashed on a wild vision of himself taking the bastards down in quick succession, pulling the trigger over and over until every one of them was dead. But the reality would be very different, he knew.

There was nowhere to hide. As the pirates spread through the engine room Jude shrank into a corner and managed to drop the gun into the oily dirt of a recess behind a duct pipe before they spotted him. Acting on an impulsive afterthought he grabbed the leather pouch from his pocket and shoved it in there too, poking it out of sight with his fingers. He barely had time to do it before there was a rifle wagging in his face and an angry-looking African barking at him from the other end of it. He did what he was told, dropped to his knees and laced his fingers above his head.

The pirates pulled back the tarp to inspect Park's dead body. They kicked him in the ribs a few times to make sure he wasn't faking it. Jude wanted to scream at them to leave him alone, but he bit his lip and stayed quiet. Satisfied he was dead, the Africans lost interest in Park and got the remaining twelve on their feet.

Prodded and shoved like cattle with rifle barrels jabbing into their backs, Jude and the rest of the survivors were herded out of the engine room and into the bright passage

154

outside where the cutting equipment lay strewn messily over the floor.

'Move, move, move! General Khosa is waiting for you!'

Minutes later, they staggered out onto a main deck that was unsteady underfoot and appeared bathed in blood by the angry dawn light. Darker clouds were rolling in from the east. The storm was building by the minute. Waves lashed the hull and burst into leaping towers of spray that broke over the rail and rained down to soak them all to the skin.

'There, there, there!' commanded the barking voices. Jude felt another rifle jab the small of his back and followed the others to the clear area of deck where the pirates were making them all kneel. Condor was shaking uncontrollably. Hercules looked as if he was struggling to contain his urge to lash out at the pirates. Diesel was bowed over, staring resolutely at the spray-lashed deck and refusing to make eye contact with their captors. Jude and Gerber exchanged glances. A semicircle of rifles pointed steadily at them.

Jude counted fifteen pirates, plus two more. Their fearsome leader had been waiting for the prisoners to be brought on deck. Jude thought he must be General Khosa. General of what? He looked like a soldier, but in whose army? The hideously scarred African was leaning nonchalantly against the railing, smiling at them as if he loved nothing more than the rising storm. Beside him stood the man Jude knew as Carter, with the metal case still attached to his left wrist. He wasn't smiling. There was an angry weal across his face where Jude had hit him, and his right fist was clenching a different handgun, to replace the one Jude had stolen from him. A man like him probably had a whole arsenal of the damn things. He scanned the small crowd of kneeling prisoners as if he couldn't wait to execute them all personally. His gaze alighted on Jude, and something blazed in his eyes.

He pointed. 'You. Yeah you, you bastard. I know you. You're the sonofabitch who robbed me. Search him.'

Two of the Africans stepped up and shoved Jude face-first against the deck. One pressed a rifle muzzle against his head while the other bent down and started frisking Jude all over. He was very thorough. Jude was glad he'd emptied his pockets.

The pirate leader, General Khosa, was watching with a frown that made the terrible ridges on his face crinkle like a Halloween mask. 'Pender,' he said in a deep, calm voice that Jude had to strain to hear over the wind. Carter turned to look at Khosa.

Pender? Jude thought. It wasn't a surprise that Carter was a fake name. Maybe Pender was too.

'You told me this boy stole papers from you,' Khosa said, more loudly. 'The legal documents for your client.'

Pender turned a little pale and beads of sweat instantly appeared on his brow, despite the strong breeze. 'That's right.'

Khosa smiled. The scar tissue distorted the smile into a sinister rictus. 'How many paper files can he be hiding in his pockets?'

'It's – it's a digital flash drive,' Pender said quickly, and unconvincingly. 'It's tiny. He could be hiding it anywhere.'

'I see,' Khosa said. Jude could see the deep suspicion in his eyes as he gazed at Pender.

Finding nothing, Jude's searcher stepped back and shook his head as if to say, 'He's clean.' The rifle was pulled away from Jude's head. He eased himself slowly upright into a kneeling position.

Furious, Pender marched up to shove his pistol in Jude's face. 'Okay, no fucking around. Where is it? Give it back to me, right now.'

Jude's expression remained perfectly blank as he replied, 'I don't know what you're talking about. I took nothing from you.'

'Think you're pretty smart, don't you, huh, kid? Just what were you doing sneaking around the ship, anyway? Sending emails?' Pender gave a mirthless chuckle. 'What, you didn't think we'd find it?'

Jude's stomach clenched and he suddenly felt very cold. 'I don't know what—' he began.

'Oh, I think you do. Maybe you're not that smart after all, hmm, *Jude*?' Pender said, grinning. 'Should have deleted it after you sent it. Not that it's gonna make a spot of difference. Nobody's coming for you. It's just you and me out here. So give it back. Come on. You took a crack at me; I say, screw that. No hard feelings. I've been hit before, and besides you hit like a pussy. Just hand over my property, and we're cool.'

Jude said, 'I don't have it.' Which, as far as it went, was the truth.

Gerber was staring at him, as were several of the others. *What's he talking about?* was the question in the older man's eyes.

'You don't have it,' Pender said. 'Okay, so then maybe you'd like to tell me WHERE YOU PUT IT?!' Pender screamed the last words.

'I threw it overboard.'

Pender cast a horrified glance at the waves, but quickly recovered as he saw through the lie. 'Don't try to bullshit me, *Jude*. That would be a big fucking mistake, my sneaky little friend.'

'I don't remember what I did with it,' Jude said.

'Really. Let's see if this jogs your memory.' Pender swung the pistol away from Jude, randomly picked another target among the huddled prisoners, and pulled the trigger before Jude could react.

The gunshot cracked out and was whipped away by the wind. Diesel's eyes were wide and staring as a red hole appeared in the middle of his forehead. He slumped forwards on his face, blood pumping from the huge exit wound in the back of his skull.

'REMEMBER NOW, ASSHOLE?' Pender screamed at Jude.

Chapter 24

The nightmare was unfolding fast now, as fast as the rising storm. Jude gaped in mute horror at Diesel's body. He began to shake as waves of nausea gripped him. *Do something*, he thought. But what? He was certain that if he handed the diamond over, they would all soon be dead. If he didn't, someone else would be the next to be shot. What kind of choice was that?

Just then, Pender and a few of the pirates looked up, suddenly distracted. Jude could hear it too: the thrumming rumble of a propeller aircraft, faint but unmistakable. He craned his neck to gaze upwards, and saw what his captors were looking at, just as the storm clouds parted to reveal a crack of sky in the distance. It was still a long way off, just a tiny blob over the horizon, but it seemed to be heading their way. His horror deflated for a second as he felt a sudden stab of excitement. Could it be the police? The coastguard? Another passing ship might have seen something. They might have alerted the authorities.

Or it could be Jeff Dekker, riding in like the cavalry.

Pender had had the same thought. 'Who did you email?' he demanded. 'This Jeff guy, who the fuck is he?'

'He's – he's my . . . uncle.'

Pender stared at Jude as if he were an idiot. 'Your *uncle*?'

159

Khosa turned to face the ocean and observed the distant aircraft slicing through the clouds. The drone of its propellers could clearly be heard now. It was losing altitude to skim low over the waves, still more than a mile away. As Khosa watched, he thought he saw a tiny white splash hit the water in its wake, followed by a second that was just as quickly lost in the rough sea. But it was too distant to be sure what he'd seen. Then the plane picked up altitude again and banked away in a sloping curve.

Jude's heart sank into his boots as the plane veered off and quickly began to recede into the distance, its sound fading into the wind. It was nothing to do with them after all.

Pender turned back towards Jude, his feet braced wide to counter the rocking of the deck. 'Well, looks like Uncle Jeff decided to stay home and watch TV. Now, where was I? That's right. You were about to tell me where you've hidden my property. Maybe your memory needs refreshing again? No problem. Let's play eeny-meeny.'

He swept the gun over the huddle of prisoners. Diesel's blood was spreading over the deck, pink where it mingled with the seawater that rained down to soak them with each new wave that crashed into the side. Pender was swaying on his feet but his aim was steady as it settled on Gerber.

'How about you, old timer? You want to be next?'

'Fuck you,' Gerber said, staring up at him.

'Fuck me? Really? Let's see about that.' Pender stepped up to him and pressed the gun against Gerber's head.

Jude's eyes met Gerber's. 'I'm sorry,' he mouthed.

'*It's okay*,' Gerber's eyes replied. Then Gerber closed them and bowed his head, waiting for the white flash and the boom of the gunshot he would never hear.

'You have three seconds before I blow this guy away,'

160

Pender told Jude, pressing the gun harder against Gerber's temple. His finger tightened on the trigger. 'One.'

'You're making a big mistake,' Jude said. But it was just bravado. Just words. He felt empty, hollowed out. There was nothing any more between him, his friends, and death.

At that moment, Khosa's radio gave a crackle. 'What?' he barked into it, irritated at the further distraction. One of his men aboard the trawler was telling him they had picked up something on the fish-finder sonar. A pair of unidentified objects, moving together and travelling fast straight towards them.

Khosa scanned the empty waves beyond. The aircraft was now lost in the clouds, barely audible. Nothing there.

'Two,' Pender said.

'Engine room,' Jude blurted out. He quickly described where he'd hidden the leather pouch. 'That's where it is. I swear. Don't kill him.'

Pender took the gun away from Gerber's head and let it dangle at his side. 'You and you,' he said, pointing at two of the pirates. 'Go get it.' The two looked to Khosa. Khosa gave a nod, and the two hurried away across the lurching deck.

For five unbearable minutes, they waited as the storm continued to loom over them. The first raindrop spattered the deck. Then another. In moments, it was sheeting down thick and hard. Jude's hair was dripping and plastered over his face. His eyes were stinging from the salt spray as he watched Pender.

And Khosa was watching him, too. There was a nasty grin on the General's face. It was hard to tell what he was thinking.

Finally, the two pirates returned on deck. One of them was holding the leather pouch, grimy from where Jude had hidden it, and already wet from the lashing rain. Pender's eyes lit up at the sight of his prize.

'So now you have it,' Jude said. 'Let us go. You want to take the ship, fine. We can use the lifeboat. Please. You don't need to kill anyone else.'

Pender tucked his pistol under his left arm and grabbed the pouch from the pirate. He quickly opened his metal case, stuffed the pouch inside and clicked the catches shut as fast as he could, before anyone could notice what was inside. He whipped the pistol out from under his arm and thrust it at Jude's head.

'Thanks, kid. You made the right choice. But I'm going to blow your brains out anyway. Then I'm gonna kill all your pals, just because I feel like it. How's that grab you?'

'Wait,' Khosa said. He stepped up and snatched the gun from Pender's hand.

At first, Jude thought the African was trying to save him. But the pirate leader had no interest in Jude. He was looking at the case attached to Pender's wrist.

Pender froze.

Jude didn't breathe.

'Do you think I am an idiot?' Khosa asked Pender. There was no anger in his voice. The eyes set wide in that terrible face were perfectly calm.

'Of – of course not.'

'What is in the case?' Khosa said.

Pender turned white, then red. 'It's nothing that concerns you,' he blustered. 'I paid you to do a job. So do it. We're getting off this floating graveyard and getting out of here. Give me back my gun.'

Khosa shook his head. 'I do not think you give the orders here.' With a wave of his hand, there were suddenly two men standing either side of Pender, aiming rifles at his head.

'Open the case,' Khosa ordered Pender. 'I want to see

162

what is so small and can be so precious to you that you pay two million dollars for it as if it was pennies.'

'You don't understand—' Pender began.

'I understand that you are trying to take me for a fool,' Khosa said. 'That is a very big mistake. Have you forgotten who I am?'

Pender backed slowly away. The rifles followed him. 'Okay, okay. You want to renegotiate the fee, huh? Fine, I can go with that. I'll double your money. Four million. All right? That's the best deal you're going to get from anyone, anywhere.' If his face hadn't been slick with rainwater, it would have been pouring sweat. He was trying to brass it out, but Jude could see the terror in his eyes. Maybe he was thinking he shouldn't have killed his own men. They might have come in useful at this moment. Too late for those kind of regrets now.

'No negotiations,' Khosa said. 'Show me what is inside the case.'

Pender hesitated just a fraction too long.

Khosa snapped his fingers. 'Zolani. Bring it to me.'

A tall bare-chested African bedecked in gleaming cartridge belts stepped towards Pender and laid down the huge machine gun he was carrying. With no expression on his face, he drew the machete from his belt. Pender's jaw dropped. He backed away another step, but that was as far as he got before two more of Khosa's men seized his arms.

'No! What are you doing? Stop!'

For Jude and the others, the worst thing was knowing exactly what was about to happen. Khosa's men threw Pender to the gleaming wet deck. It took four of them to pin him down as he screamed and writhed. Taking hold of the case, a fifth man pulled it away to stretch Pender's left arm out, until it was fully extended across the iron floor. The handcuff bit into Pender's wrist and he screamed even more loudly, like a pig in a slaughterhouse.

The man called Zolani raised the machete and brought it down with a chopping sound that was all but drowned out by Pender's shriek.

Jude looked away and felt sick.

Zolani calmly picked up the case and took it over to Khosa. The severed hand and forearm were still dangling from the chain. Khosa took the case, laid it down on the deck, flipped the catches and opened the lid. He took out the leather pouch, upended it and its contents rolled out into his palm.

Even under the darkening storm clouds and the pouring rain, the diamond seemed to glitter like a small sun on the African's open hand.

'Now I understand,' Khosa murmured, gazing at the enormous stone. Pender was squealing and squirming and clutching his stump. It was jetting blood faster than the rain could wash it away.

'Kill him,' Khosa said, without taking his eyes off the diamond.

Zolani sheathed the machete and picked up his machine gun. He pressed the muzzle to the back of Pender's neck, pinning him down. The ear-splitting blast of fully automatic fire spattered Pender's skull like a rotten melon. The screams were instantly silenced. Pender twitched once, and went limp on the wet deck.

Jude watched the life go out of him. It was a terrible thing to see. He wondered if that was how he would look when he died, too. He cleared his throat and tried to make his voice strong.

'You have nothing to gain by killing us,' he said to Khosa. 'You have what you want. Let us go on our way.'

Khosa seemed not to hear. He closed his fist around the stone, clenching it tightly as if he dared anyone to try to claim it from him. He tossed the case over the rail, still trailing the severed arm. It disappeared over the side and its splash was lost in the roar of the wind.

'Execute them,' Khosa ordered his men.

Jude watched numbly as Khosa turned and started walking away. The men raised their rifles. He was drenched to the bone, but his mouth was dry as desert sand. Without thinking, he called out the first thing that came into his head.

'I'm rich.'

Khosa stopped. Slowly turned back to face Jude through the rain, grinning a demonic grin. 'So am I, white boy,' he said. He held up the fist that was clutching the diamond.

Jude swallowed. He fought the shake in his voice and the mad desire to rush for the opposite rail and hurl himself over it into the sea. 'That's nothing,' he said, pointing at the diamond in Khosa's hand. 'It's a bauble compared to what my family have. We wouldn't even bend down to pick it up out of the gutter. This ship? It's mine. And twenty more like it. You let me go, and my friends, and you can be the richest man in your country.'

Khosa's expression became serious and he studied Jude intently for a moment or two before the grin spread slowly back over his mutilated face. 'That was a very good try, my young friend.'

Khosa turned away again. His men pointed their guns.

Jude looked sadly at his crewmates, kneeling huddled and soaked together on the deck.

I'm sorry. I did everything I could.

He closed his eyes. This is it. This is where we die. He'd thought he would be ready, when the time came. But you could never be ready.

Jude felt a searing flash and a powerful force knocked him sideways.

He hit the deck.

He was dead.

Chapter 25

But if this was what it was like to be dead, it was the strangest thing. Jude blinked and gasped for air. He was stunned. He could feel the hard, cold, wet iron deck under him. He could hear noise all around him. Confusion. Men yelling. Guns firing.

No, he wasn't dead. He craned his neck upwards to see what was happening.

A second explosion made the *Andromeda* quiver and rock as if an earthquake had struck it. A violent eruption of flame as tall as the ship's superstructure shot into the sky, lighting the clouds. The pirate trawler alongside was lifted out of the water and ripped virtually in half by the blast. Its shattered hull crashed down into the foaming sea and disappeared amid a rolling mushroom cloud of flame and black smoke that poured across the deck of the cargo ship, so thick that the storm could barely disperse it. Pieces of wreckage rained down out of the blackness and spattered the deck like bullets.

Jude thought, *Am I dreaming?*

The pirates were in chaos. One lay on the deck, his legs separated from his torso where a piece of shrapnel had sliced him in two. The rest had been knocked flat, like Jude. Some of them were engulfed in the thick smoke. Others were back on their feet and discharging their weapons wildly and randomly towards the unseen enemy that was attacking them, no less stunned and disorientated than the cargo ship crewmen they'd been about to execute.

Jude staggered to his feet and saw Khosa. The General was clutching at the rail with one hand, the other still clasping the diamond. He was bent and sagging at the knees, as if the explosion had winded him. Without thinking, Jude charged him. Head low, shoulders bunched, like a bull. He rammed Khosa in the midriff and knocked him flat. Khosa let out a grunt as he went down, lashing out at Jude to bludgeon him with the rock. Jude blocked Khosa's wrist with his knee, stopping the blow with enough force to make the African lose his grip on the diamond. It hit the deck and bounced towards the rail. Jude dived onto his belly and caught it before it went overboard and was lost forever. Khosa's flailing hand gripped his arm. Jude pounded the diamond into the African's face, once, twice, with all the strength he had in him, and felt the hand loosen on his arm.

Jude scrambled away without looking back, clutching the lump of rock to his chest as he skidded across the slippery deck. Guns were firing all over the place, muzzle flashes strobing through the smoke and the deluge of rain.

'Come on!' he screamed at Gerber and the others, waving crazily at them to get behind the cover of the container stacks. Then the fuel lines aboard the shattered trawler ignited and a second, even thicker pall of black smoke rolled up over the side to swallow him. Blinded, guttering, choking, he ran headlong into the solid steel wall of a container and fell back, knocked dizzy by the impact.

Khosa came storming through the blanket of smoke like a man possessed. Blood was streaming from a gash on his cheek where the diamond had cut him. He saw Jude lying on the deck and came for him with his teeth bared in a snarl. 'I will KILL YOU!' Then his hands were around Jude's throat and his heavy body was crushing the air out of Jude's lungs. Jude managed to get his knee up so that it pressed against the African's chest, and shoved with all his might. Khosa went sprawling backwards and his head slammed into the corner of the container stack.

Jude started scrambling to his feet to escape.

But he couldn't get away. Something was stopping him, tugging at the back of his trousers and holding him back. For an instant he thought he'd snagged his belt on one of the iron fasteners that held the container stack fast to the deck. But when he glanced back over his shoulder, he saw with a jab of terror that Khosa was no longer alone in the fight.

Still clutching Jude's belt with one powerful fist, Zolani drew the machete from its sheath.

'Cut off his arms and his legs!' Khosa roared from the deck. He had lost his beret and he was bleeding from a fresh injury to his brow. 'I want to see him crawl like a worm!'

Jude struggled frantically, so afraid that his heart felt as if it was in flames. But he couldn't break Zolani's grip. It was like being snared by a machine. As if in slow motion, he saw the machete blade rise up in the air, glinting like a living thing from the flames that squirmed and danced through the smoke. He imagined he could already feel it slicing his flesh. First one arm, then the other. Then his legs. Reduced to a trunk. Crawling like a worm. He cried out.

The machete came down.

And tumbled harmlessly with a clatter to the deck.

Zolani's wide eyes stared into Jude's for a second or two before they rolled back white. He swayed on his feet. His knees gave way under him and he crumpled and dropped like a demolished tower.

Jude hadn't registered the gunshot and had no idea what was happening, until he saw that the top of Zolani's head was blown away, pink cauliflower brains bubbling out of the hole. He scrambled away from the corpse on his elbows and heels, bewildered. Then he looked up, and his confusion doubled.

The surreal black apparition stepped out of the smoke and the sheeting rain. It was the figure of a man, but he had no face. He was covered from head to toe in gleaming wet black skin, like a seal, and festooned with belts and straps and tubes and armament. His eyes were hidden behind goggles, their lenses filled with fire. In his gloved hands was the stubby submachine gun he'd used to shoot Zolani.

The frogman moved as fluidly as the water from which he'd emerged. He stepped up to Zolani and his silencer coughed out two more rounds into the African's head. Then he turned the weapon on Khosa, who was staggering to his feet, bloodied and unsteady.

For an instant, it looked as if Khosa was about to reach for the large revolver holstered at his right hip.

The frogman shook his head. *Uh-uh, pal. Don't even think about it.*

Khosa did think about it, but only for a second longer. The hand that had been snaking its way down towards the holster stopped moving. The frogman shoved him hard against the container stack, spun him around and held the subgun to the back of his head as he relieved him of the heavy revolver and threw it overboard. Then Khosa was on his face and his hands were being secured behind his back with a cable tie.

In what seemed like a matter of seconds, the gunfire on board the cargo ship had dwindled, the sharp, sporadic crackle of AK-47s giving way to the muted *BRRPP . . . BRRPP* of silenced automatic weapons. As the rising wind parted the curtains of smoke, Jude saw two more frogmen striding over the deck. He saw pirates on their knees, weapons thrown down, hands in the air. The corpses of those who hadn't surrendered sprawled here and there like dead rats, their clothing torn from bullet strikes and dark with blood and rain and seawater spray. The assault had been short, sharp and brutal, and now it was over. The ship was retaken. But that, for the moment, was all Jude knew.

'Who are you?' he asked the frogman. His voice came out as a thin, shaky croak.

The frogman reached up a gleaming black arm and peeled away his goggles. Jude stared into the glacier-blue eyes that locked onto his.

'*Ben?*'

Chapter 26

The truth was, if Jude hadn't been eight feet away and watching every move, Ben wouldn't have hesitated to empty the rest of his magazine into the big African in the combat khakis and the fancy gold watch who'd been threatening his son. There would have been no prisoners, no quarter. Ben wasn't in the mood for mercy that morning. But he held back, because it wouldn't have been the first time he'd killed a man in Jude's presence and he'd vowed to himself that he'd never do it again.

Ben took the gun away from the back of the African's head. He reached a hand out to Jude. 'Are you okay?'

Jude took the hand, and got unsteadily to his feet. 'I – I – I – what are you doing here?' His voice was weak and trembly. Ben could see the first stages of shock. Jude had reached the outer limits of his endurance, and now the traumatic stress was piling in on him.

'I thought maybe you could do with a little help,' Ben said.

Before Jude could reply, Jeff Dekker joined them. He was suited up in the same frogman kit as Ben, his goggles and breathing apparatus dangling from his neck, and grinning all over his face.

'Got your email, mate. Felt like a trip anyway. So here we are. In the nick of time, too, looks like.' Jeff glanced down at the trussed-up prisoner at their feet. 'Who's the arsehole?'

'Luckiest man on earth,' Ben said. 'Nearly ended up like his friend with the machete here.' He waved the muzzle of his gun at the corpse at their feet. The rain was already washing the deck clean of Zolani's blood.

'That one's called Zolani,' Jude said. 'And that one's called Khosa. He's their leader.'

'Funny kind of get-up for a pirate,' Jeff said, eyeing Khosa's military fatigues. 'Love the tribal scars, too. Looks like a fucking Klingon. Bet the girls love it.' Jeff's relief at finding Jude intact and safe had put him in a jovial mood, one that Ben wasn't ready to share just yet.

'I will kill you all,' Khosa said from the deck.

'I've had pretty much enough of this guy,' Ben said.

Jeff grinned. 'Be my guest.'

Ben knocked him out with a sharp kick to the head. Khosa's skull bounced off the deck and he went as limp as a dead fish.

'Don't hurt him any more,' Jude said. 'We're not like them.'

'You're right,' Ben said. 'We're nothing like these people.'

'Bad news for them,' Jeff said.

Jude could see a third frogman stalking the deck from one trussed-up prisoner to another, checking their bonds and collecting all their weapons, unloaded and made safe, into a heap that looked like a terrorist arsenal. He blinked as he recognised the face behind the goggles. 'I know him. That's Tuesday.'

'On-the-job training, the Le Val way,' Jeff joked.

'The plane,' Jude said, still incredulous. 'That was you? How did—?'

'We can talk later,' Ben said. 'We have a lot to do.'

Jude ran and found the rest of the crew gathered in a small crowd inside the main entrance passage to A Deck, where they were sheltering from the weather. Gerber, Hercules and everyone else except Scagnetti inevitably had a thousand questions about what the hell had just happened and who these three guys were that Jude had apparently summoned to their aid, just like that – but Jude had little time to explain. Nobody had yet mentioned the diamond. Jude sensed that would come later, too.

More pressing matters were at hand for the moment. Ben, Jeff and Tuesday joined them for a lightning conference, during which it was decided that getting the engines put back together and running again was a matter of urgent priority. The pummelling rain was falling even harder and the waves had grown up into towering mountains crested with white foam that rolled relentlessly towards them and shook the *Andromeda* with every crashing impact.

'We don't get powered up fast,' Cherry warned, 'we're gonna drift side-on to one of these big sumbitches and we'll broach and flip right over.' He and Peters had been Diesel's assistants in the engine room and they knew every twitch of every switch down there. It was quickly voted that Scagnetti should go with them, being a dab hand with a spanner. Jude was pleased to get Scagnetti out of the way. In the meantime, Trent and Lorenz, who both had experience, were to run up to the bridge, assess the amount of damage up there and take over the helm once the power was back on.

Other duties weren't going to be so pleasant. Jude and Gerber picked Hercules and Condor to help clear the bodies of their fellow crewmates that the pirates hadn't already slung overboard. That left Allen and Lang, who were assigned to help their rescuers take care of the prisoners. Ben issued them each a rifle from the captured store of arms, just in case of trouble.

The crewmen all hurried to their separate stations. As he and the other three in his group set about gathering their dead, Jude began to wish he hadn't volunteered for the grisly detail. It was sickening, but he felt partially responsible for what had happened to Diesel and the guilt spurred him to get on with it in grim silence. They carried the chief to the ship's tiny medical clinic, which housed an even smaller refrigerated morgue compartment. The body of poor Park was next. As they heaved the Korean up from below, they talked about what to do with the dead pirates still sliding around the deck.

'We can't just leave them there,' Jude said.

'Well,' Gerber told him, 'unless you want to wrap each one up in a Somali flag, say a prayer for his immortal soul and consign him to the depths with a full honours and a three-volley salute, I'd say we oughta dump their filthy carcasses over the side like they were going to do to us. Same goes for that sorry sonofabitch Carter, or Pender, or whoever he was.'

Jude was dead set against the idea. 'We're not animals. As for Pender, his body should be handed over to the police along with the rest of them. He's evidence of a crime.'

'Not the only evidence,' Gerber said, with a knowing tone.

Jude knew what Gerber was going to say next.

'That thing in your pocket, were you thinking of handing that in to the cops too?'

'Yeah, that ain't no glass paperweight, man,' Hercules said.

175

Jude stopped and let go of Park's body as he shone his torch at them each in turn, appalled by the insinuation. 'Why, you think I was planning on keeping it for myself?'

'Certainly kept quiet about it all night long. Just my observation, son. I'm not accusing you of anything.'

'I was going to tell you,' Jude protested. 'Down in the engine room, before they stormed us. Here, you want it? Take it. I wish I hadn't laid eyes on the damn thing.'

'Not me,' Hercules said, as if Jude was offering them a lump of plutonium. 'That's a whole lotta trouble I don't need.'

Gerber showed his palms. 'Nor me, son. I've had enough excitement to last me the rest of my life, and now I just want to get home in one piece. All I'm saying is, and I'm no expert, if that there rock is what I think it is, I'd be damned careful if I were you. We weren't the only ones in this crew who saw it, if you get my meaning. Better watch your six, before *someone* puts a knife in your back.'

After the crew had hurried off to attend to their duties Ben took a quiet moment to himself on deck, feeling that familiar old sense of post-battle melancholia as the adrenalin slowly oozed out of his system. The blood-red dawn had darkened like evening as unbroken black clouds scudded menacingly overhead, blotting out the light. Ben had seen tropical storms like it before. At this time of year in these waters, they could sweep in out of nowhere with shocking suddenness and not burn themselves out for days on end.

He stood at the rail, lashed by salt spray and craving a Gauloise, which wouldn't have stayed lit for long in this gale. Far below him, the wreckage of the pirate trawler was dispersing on the waves. Its shattered hull had long since sunk to the bottom – or what was left of it after the

176

high-explosive limpet mine, supplied by their man in Stuttgart, had done its destructive work. The two ex-military Rotinor Diver Propulsion Vehicles that had propelled them swiftly and silently underwater for the last mile of the journey would soon be joining the wreckage on the sea bed, if they hadn't already. Ben felt a pang about consigning twenty grand's worth of equipment to Davy Jones's locker, but it was a momentary regret lost in a sense of relief so overpowering that he almost wanted to cry.

It had been a close run thing. The delay at Obbia airport had filled him with dread that the seaplane might not materialise either; that Chimp Chalmers had diddled them; that they wouldn't make it. But Ben's fears had been allayed when they found the aircraft floating just offshore at Hobyo port, ready to take off at a moment's notice. Geedi's Toyota had served its purpose as an improvised amphibious transport to deliver their cargo to the plane, before being abandoned half-submerged in the surf. Geedi would mourn the loss of his vehicle, but to hell with the drunken bastard.

From there, everything had gone smoothly except for the unexpected turn in the weather. They'd located the ship just a couple of nautical miles from the coordinates in Jude's email. The tricky bail-out at low altitude into heavy seas had gone without a hitch. Tuesday might have balked at his first-ever underwater assault, clinging wild-eyed to a two-man diver propulsion vehicle as it sped thirty metres beneath the waves to zero in on their target, but he'd taken it in his stride and Ben was pleased with him.

And now it was over. They'd pulled it off.

Most importantly of all, Jude was safe. Until this moment, Ben hadn't allowed himself to fully consider the alternative. The mind can work in strange ways. Now that he knew it wouldn't happen, the worst images bubbled up in his imagination as if the brain needed to release the pressure of keeping them stored up. It hit him like a brick. His throat tightened up, his stomach was knotted and his hands shook. He gripped the rail and closed his eyes for a few moments, suddenly so washed out with feeling that he could have lain down and curled up right there on the rainswept deck. Sensing Jeff's presence behind him, he kept his back turned so that his friend wouldn't see his emotion.

'You all right?' Jeff said, joining him at the rail. He had to yell to be heard over the wind.

Ben nodded wordlessly.

Jeff clapped him on the shoulder. 'Got the shakes? Fucking bet I've got them too, mate. We haven't had a run like that in a while.'

'Not since the last time. Thanks, Jeff. I couldn't have done it without you.'

Jeff laughed it off. He looked up. 'Christ, I've never seen the morning sky so black. Blacker than the inside of the devil's arsehole.'

'You're a natural born poet, Dekker.'

'So everyone tells me. Any sign of Mussa?'

Ben had tried to raise the pilot several times, but he was out of handheld radio range. He scanned the sky once again, and would have been very surprised if there'd been any sign of the aircraft circling overhead somewhere in those clouds. The plan had been for Mussa to double back and land alongside the ship once the pirate threat was neutralised. Then, after spending the minimum amount of time making sure the ship was secure, they were going to leave it to its own devices, load Jude on the plane and return to Obbia to call Adrien Leroy and wait for the Gulfstream to carry them back home.

All of which had been assuming a successful outcome to

the mission. And none of which had reckoned on the dramatic downturn in the weather conditions. The sea had been slick and bright with starlight when they'd left Hobyo port.

'Not a chance. Headed back to land, if he's got any sense. This crap isn't going to lift in a hurry.'

'Then it looks like we're stuck on board this tub until it does.'

Ben nodded. 'Yup. Let's get to work.'

Chapter 27

Ben's first and main priority was to stow the prisoners securely under lock and key. Of the sixteen African pirates who had been aboard the ship at the time of the rescue assault, nine were still alive including their leader, Khosa. Those who had stayed on board the smaller vessel could be presumed drowned or blown to bits. Ben, Jeff and Tuesday hurriedly stripped off their dive apparatus and wetsuits. Once they had changed into combat trousers and T-shirts and swapped the cumbersome flippers for the lightweight assault boots they'd packed in the watertight kit bags along with the rest of the gear, Tuesday took charge of guarding the prisoners while Ben and Jeff hunted about below by torchlight for a suitable temporary cell space. They soon found a storage compartment in the aft cargo hold that would serve as a makeshift brig.

Three at a time, the prisoners had their ankle bonds slashed and were frogmarched below at gunpoint and bundled into the pitch-black hole that would be their home for the foreseeable future. Allen and Lang were stationed on sentry duty outside the door.

'I don't like it much,' Jeff said. 'That room isn't half secure enough to hold them. Especially Scarface. I look at that guy, I see trouble.'

They were making their way back up through the pitch-darkness below decks when the electrical power flickered on and the winding passages, hatchways and stairways that honeycombed the vast bowels of the ship were lit up in a stark neon glow. Seconds later, they felt the thrum of the restarted engines and the vibration of the ship's massive twin screws resonate under their feet. Cherry's guys had done their work and the *Andromeda* was back in business.

Ben's next priority was to check on the bridge. Now that the power was restored, he needed to make sure that the two crewmen up there, Trent and Lorenz, didn't do anything stupid like radio the coastguard and inform them of the attack. If the storm should suddenly abate, the last thing he needed was for a squad of trigger-happy Somali police to show up in a fast cruiser and spark an international incident when they discovered an unofficial hostage rescue team on board, with enough small arms to start a war.

Ben needn't have worried. When he stepped onto the rocking, swaying bridge he found Trent and Lorenz bent anxiously over the bullet-holed remains of the long-range radio receiver. 'It's fubar,' was Trent's technical assessment. Lorenz looked at Ben. 'Mister, I hope you know how to fix this or we're cut off from the whole freakin' universe.'

Ben examined it. One time, in his early days with 22 SAS, he had been on patrol in the Middle East when his unit's radio operator lost the top half of his body to a high-explosive 30-mm cannon shell. Even though much of the radio set had been pulverised along with him, Ben had managed to twist enough loose wires together to get it operational again. But that had been years ago, when they were still making technology he could understand. This thing was all circuit boards and computer chips, reduced to tiny shards of silicon that lay like dust in the metal casing. He could tell from the holes that two large-calibre handgun bullets had smashed through the electronics, ploughing through just about everything they needed to hit in order to ruin the radio beyond salvation.

'You're right,' he told Trent. 'It is fubar.' The whole freakin' universe would have to do without them for now.

Ben found Jeff and Tuesday below on A Deck. Smelling the scent of freshly brewed coffee, they followed their noses to the mess canteen where Jude and two of his crewmates sat huddled at a table knocking back as much hot coffee as they could swallow. Jude looked ashen and shaken up. The mood was that strained mixture of elation and sombreness that comes when danger has passed and nobody quite knows whether to celebrate the fact of their own survival or mourn the loss of those who didn't make it. It was an atmosphere Ben had shared in many times before.

They pulled up three more chairs and sat together. The floor of the mess canteen was rocking from side to side so much from the weather that the sailors had to hold their mugs to stop them sliding off the table. Ben put his hand on Jude's arm and gave him a look that said, 'You okay?'

Jude quietly nodded, but he didn't look okay. His face fell even more when Ben broke the news to them about the damaged radio. First the attack, then the storm, and now this.

Jude broke the dejected silence with introductions. 'This is Lou Gerber,' he said, nodding at the older man at the table. 'And this is Condor.'

Jeff smiled. 'Condor?'

'That's right, man, just Condor.' Condor's face was the colour of a long-dead fish and he kept clutching at his stomach as though he was about to throw up.

'Call yourself a mariner,' Gerber snorted. 'Seasick, at your age?'

Jude went on with the intros. 'This is Tuesday Fletcher—'

'Welcome to the silly names club,' Tuesday said.

'—and this is Jeff Dekker—'

'Uncle Jeff,' Gerber said with a thin smile.

Jeff raised an eyebrow. 'That's a new one on me. I've never been an uncle before.'

Jude motioned towards Ben. 'And this is . . . this is . . .' As if he couldn't bring himself to say the words 'my father'.

Ben respected that. He had never deserved the title, anyway. 'Ben,' he finished for Jude. 'Jude and I go back a long way.'

The happiest person in the mess canteen was the large black man introduced to Ben and the others as Hercules. He couldn't stop chuckling and grinning as he navigated across to the table and served more mugs of steaming coffee for the honoured guests. A grey parrot with a red tail and suspicious eyes was perched on his shoulder, regarding them all with great disdain.

'I see you got reunited with Murphy,' Jude said, forcing a smile.

Hercules tenderly held up a finger for the parrot to gnaw at. 'Yeah, he was the only one of us who had the sense not to let himself get caught by those motherfuckers.'

'Who's a pretty boy, then?' Jeff said to the bird.

'Up yours, buttcrack,' the bird shot back, giving him a look that would terrify a hawk.

'He's a charmer, isn't he?' Jeff said.

'He don't like to be patronised,' Hercules said.

'Sorry I spoke.'

Ben smiled and took a sip of the coffee. It tasted like something that had been ladled up from the recesses of the ship's hold and mixed with engine oil, but it was strong and hot and that was good enough.

'Speaking of those motherfuckers,' Gerber said when Hercules had gone weaving off over the listing floor, 'I'm not going to ask you fellas how you did it, where you came from or who you are. But I am going to thank you, on behalf of all of us, for saving our bacon, which you well and truly did.'

'Yeah, man,' Condor mumbled. 'We were dead meat.' The thought of actual dead meat almost made him vomit, and he went back to groaning and clutching his stomach.

Jude looked solemnly at the three of them. 'I don't know what to say.'

'Then say nothing,' Ben said.

'We do this kind of thing all the time, dear boy,' Jeff said.

'That's right,' Tuesday laughed. 'Piece of cake. Especially the hanging-on-like-grim-death-to-a-manned-torpedo-with-eighty-pounds-of-RDX-high-explosive-strapped-six-inches-from-my-bollocks part. I'd do it again tomorrow.'

'Let's hope we won't need to,' Ben said. 'And let me just say this, that the person everyone should be thanking is Jude. He's the one who sent the message.'

'Jude already knows how grateful we are,' Gerber said. 'But hey, does no one else know about this?'

'Not that we're aware of,' Jeff replied. 'And we'd prefer to keep it that way until we're off this ship, so as to avoid any unwanted, uh, *entanglements*, know what I mean?' Turning to Jude, he said, 'Seriously, mate, I feel like shit that I got you into it. If I'd thought there was the slightest risk of you getting hit by pirates—'

'It wasn't pirates,' Jude cut in. 'This was no ordinary attack.'

Ben looked at him. 'What are you saying, Jude? How do you know that?'

The rest of them sat in silence and sipped coffee as Jude

laid it all out, starting with his visit to the bridge, the radar alert and the appearance of the three passengers who had turned out to be hijackers and murdered the captain and ship's mates right in front of his eyes.

'Pender, he was the one in charge, except he was calling himself Carter. I think he bribed Captain O'Keefe to let them on board in secret. O'Keefe said something about a deal. I think he knew what was about to happen. I think he was paid to let it happen. That's why he seemed to turn a blind eye when the radar showed up the boats heading towards us. But he didn't realise they were going to kill anyone, least of all him.'

'Fuckers,' Condor breathed. Gerber looked sombre. They were hearing this story for the first time, too.

'You're saying this Pender hired Khosa and his men to attack the ship?' Ben asked.

Jude nodded. 'That's what it looks like to me. Then after he killed the captain, he killed his own accomplices. But then when Khosa saw *it*, he double-crossed Pender and tried to take it for himself.'

'Slow down,' Ben said. 'You're not making any sense. Saw what? Tried to take what?'

'This,' Jude said. '*This* is what this whole thing is all about.'

He took out the diamond.

Chapter 28

Jude held the diamond out on the flat of his palm. It was as if the canteen lights had suddenly grown brighter. A hush fell over the table. Tuesday boggled at the sight of it, and almost spilled his coffee in his lap.

'That's not real,' Jeff said, gaping. 'No bloody way.'

Jude quickly explained how he'd taken it from Pender, and how Pender had later accidentally allowed Khosa to see it when they were all on deck. 'They murdered him for it like stepping on a beetle.'

'He had it coming,' Gerber muttered.

'May I?' Ben took the diamond from Jude and examined it. He'd never seen anything like it before. 'I'd say it's real, all right.'

'Oh, so you're the big expert now,' Jeff said, without taking his eyes off it.

'People are liable to start massacring each other over a lot of things,' Ben said. 'But a lump of cut glass isn't one of them.' He handed it back to Jude.

'What would it be worth?' Jude asked.

Jeff whistled. 'If you have to ask, mate, you can't afford it. Millions? Tens of millions?'

'Hundreds of millions,' Ben said. 'Question is, where did it come from?'

186

'I think Pender stole it,' Jude said. 'Who from, I have no idea. Someone in Oman, I thought. That would explain why he was on the ship, why he bribed his way on board incognito. He needed to get out of the country unnoticed.'

'To Dar es Salaam?' Jeff said. 'Or Mombasa, maybe?'

'Except he had no intention of going that far,' Jude said. 'He could have disembarked at Djibouti just as easily, but he didn't. He wanted to disappear into thin air with the diamond. That's why he set up the attack, to intercept us midway.'

'A staged pirate attack,' Ben said. It made an awful lot of sense. But it also raised more questions, and he could see from Jude's expression that he had already figured that much out for himself.

'Question is, why he'd need to get away in the middle of the Indian Ocean,' Jude went on, frowning. 'Why not just wait until we hit port? It doesn't add up. Unless maybe he was scared that the police were on to him and would be lying in wait to grab him at the docks.'

Ben could see another possibility. 'Or unless there was a third party involved. If we can suppose that Pender was the active partner in the robbery, the one who did the crime and took the biggest risk, it would make sense that maybe someone employed him to snatch it and deliver it to them, either at Mombasa or Dar es Salaam.'

'A sleeping partner,' Jeff said, cottoning on to the idea. 'Mister Big. The head honcho.'

'Who at this point may not even realise that Pender was planning to cut him out and do a runner,' Ben said. 'I don't suppose we'll ever know.'

Gerber took a noisy slurp of coffee. 'Here's another question for you, folks. If this Khosa character and his boys aren't Somali pirates, then who and what in hell's name are they?'

187

'Not Somalis, for a start,' Ben said. 'They speak Swahili among themselves.'

'You speak it?' Gerber said, surprised.

'Some,' Ben said.

'So they're from Kenya?' Jude asked.

'Possibly. Or Tanzania, Uganda, Rwanda, Burundi, Mozambique, the Congo; pretty much anywhere in central or south-east Africa. It's not where they're from that concerns me. It's what they do for a living.'

'Boosting ships?' Gerber said.

Ben shook his head. 'No. Jude's right. These guys are in a whole other line of work. They're PMCs. Private military contractors. Professional guns for hire, most or all with some kind of army or militia training, or what passes for that in Africa.'

'Freakin' mercenaries?' Condor gasped, almost letting go of his stomach contents.

Ben nodded. 'That's who you'd approach if you were planning something like this, or at least, I would. Someone who could bring the necessary firepower to the table and get the job done quickly and effectively. Or at least more quickly and effectively than a band of complete amateurs. All it really takes is a few guys who can yank a trigger, aren't afraid of a little blood and won't run away if anyone starts shooting back. But it seems that Pender slipped up. He obviously didn't reckon on what his mercenaries would do to him if they got an inkling of what this was really about. I've come across men like this Khosa before. Pender made a big mistake with him.'

'And then some,' Condor groaned. 'Jesus Christ. Mercenaries. I heard about these fuckers, man. They'd slit their own sisters wide open from ass to eyeball for something like this.'

'That's right,' Gerber said, scratching his beard. 'The

world's chock full of evil sonsofbitches who'd do anything for even just a few bucks, let alone a rock like that. I wouldn't feel safe with it, that's for sure.'

Jude blanched and stared at the diamond in his hand. 'I can't stand hanging onto this thing any longer. It's too much responsibility for me.' He thrust it towards Ben. 'You take it.'

'What makes you think I want it?' Ben said.

'It'd be safer with you.'

'Safest place for it would be at the bottom of the sea,' Ben said. 'That's the only way you can guarantee it won't do any more harm.'

Jeff interrupted. 'Gents, I hate to break in on this sociological, philosophical or whatever-the-fuck-it-is discussion, but we need to talk about what we're going to do with the prisoners. If we're right and it now looks like we're dealing with a bunch of hardcore warriors led by some nutjob who's pretty highly bloody motivated to slaughter every single one of us on board to get his mitts on a bobby dazzler the size of Manchester, we need to be taking every possible precaution. That storage locker they're in isn't secure enough and I don't feel good about having two inexperienced sailors down there on guard duty. No offence.'

'None taken,' Gerber said. 'I was in the Corps myself, back in the day, final rank of staff sergeant. Most of these boys couldn't guard a Quakers' convention.'

'Jeff's right,' Ben said. 'Ideas?'

Jeff shrugged. 'What about all these containers up on deck? Those things are built like tanks. Empty one out, dump whatever cargo's inside and bung the bastards in there in its place.'

'Sounds good to me,' Ben said.

'In this weather?' Jude objected. 'What if it breaks free

and goes overboard? That can happen. We almost ran into a forty-footer floating adrift just after we left Djibouti. They'd drown inside.'

'Then let them,' Ben said.

'And even if it doesn't, once the storm's over, they'll bake in there.'

'Then let them,' Ben repeated.

'You don't mean that.'

'Don't I?'

'You're not that cruel, surely.'

'There are quicker ways,' Ben said. 'If you're concerned about inflicting cruelty on your fellow man.'

'Meaning what?' Jude said.

Ben just shrugged.

'I can't believe you would even contemplate that,' Jude said. 'What, you want to line them up on the deck, make them kneel, bullet in the back of the head and dump them in the ocean? Execute them in cold blood?'

Ben said nothing.

'No. Absolutely not. That's not who we are,' Jude said.

'Compassion is great, Jude. But if these men had half a chance to get free, do you think they'd show you an ounce of quarter? Have you forgotten what they did to your friends, and almost did to you?'

Jude was silent for a second. 'Fine. I agree that's a risk we can't afford. But I can't accept that we stick them in a container, and we're certainly not going to murder these people. So we find another way.'

'Such as?'

'Such as, we don't keep them on the ship. We let them go.'

'I see. Drop them off at the nearest port, nice and easy, wave bye bye and put it all behind us?'

'Or something,' Jude said.

Ben looked at him. 'Think about who you're dealing with, Jude. Khosa won't give up easily. He's seen what's at stake here. He's had the diamond in his hands once already. And you can be sure he's got the contacts to put together as many men and as much hardware as he's going to need to reclaim it. If you let him go, he'll be back again before you know it, and I don't think he'll be any more interested in negotiating than he was first time around.'

'They're murderers. I know.'

'No, Jude. You don't know.'

'But we're better than that. At least, I thought we were. What happened to you?'

Too much, Ben thought. 'That's just the way it is.'

'Here's what we'll do,' Jude said. 'We'll put them in the lifeboat and cut them loose.'

'Aren't you listening to a word I say?' Ben asked.

'Apart from anything else, it's getting awful heavy out there,' Jeff said.

'No shit,' Condor said miserably.

'That thing's pretty much unsinkable. They'll have a chance,' Jude replied. 'You know, they're still human beings. We owe them a chance, don't we? Or what does it say about us?'

'And you want to make a go of it in Special Forces,' Ben said, looking straight at him.

Jude flinched. 'Who told you?'

Ben pointed at Jeff. 'He did. Apparently that's what you're gunning for, to get into the SBS. Starting with the navy interview in February. Tell me I'm wrong. I'd love to be.'

Jude said nothing. Jeff was frowning.

'Trust me, Jude, you don't want to be a part of that,' Ben said. 'You couldn't be. Because it's shit, and it makes

191

stone-cold killers out of people, and you just proved to me that you're better than that.'

'Hey, thanks,' Jeff said. 'Speak for yourself.'

Ben went on, 'And you also proved to me that you wouldn't survive in that environment. This is not your world, Jude. It's my world and I know what makes it go round and round. So listen to me.'

'We're going to put them in the lifeboat,' Jude insisted. 'It's the only way that we can get rid of them without losing our humanity. We'll make sure they have enough fuel and supplies to make it back to the Somali coast.'

'So they can reorganise themselves and come right back after us with double the forces?' Ben said. 'It's a mistake.'

'It's my decision,' Jude said. 'It's the right thing to do. Everyone agreed?'

'I'm getting too old for this shit,' Gerber said, shaking his head resignedly. 'I've seen enough blood for one day. Let's do what the young fella says and get shot of 'em, and be done with it.'

'Whatever, man,' Condor said. 'I ain't up for no killin'.'

'Not in cold blood, anyway,' Tuesday said. 'Seems like this is the best option.'

'Don't look at me, boys,' Jeff said. 'I'm just a dyed-in-the-wool heartless killing machine.'

Ben held back from saying more. He'd said too much already.

'Then it's agreed,' Jude said. 'The lifeboat it is.'

It had been many, many years since shipwrecked crews had been forced to take their chances at sea in open rowing boats. The *Andromeda* was equipped with a modern MOB, or Man Overboard rescue vessel, a bright orange fibreglass craft some eighteen feet long, with an outboard engine and basic bench

192

seating inside for a whole crew, as well as internal storage space for spare fuel and supplies. Jude had always thought it looked like the submersible Thunderbird 4 from the old TV series. The MOB hung forty feet above the sea from external mountings on A Deck. To release it from its cradle it had to be winched up a few feet, then swung out clear of the ship's side and lowered down on cables using the davit, a small crane used for hoisting materials up and down from the water.

Which was a straightforward enough operation in still and clement conditions. In the middle of a howling tropical storm, it was anything but. The wind was blasting them so ferociously that it was hard to stand up on deck without clinging onto something solid for support. A murky midday had become an even more cloud-laden afternoon, with visibility reduced to almost zero by the time Ben and Jeff had finished loading up the extra water, provisions and fuel that Khosa and his men would need to make it back to the coast.

Next, the prisoners were marched laboriously up from the hold and lined up on the bucking, rolling deck, drenched with rain and spray and closely watched at gunpoint by Tuesday while Ben and Jeff ushered them one at a time into the bright orange craft. One of the men was selected as its pilot and Ben, communicating with him in Swahili, talked him through the basic controls. Jude stood a few feet away, watching.

Khosa was the last to board the lifeboat. He hadn't taken his eyes off Jude the entire time, and they were filled with a crazy fire that made the back of Jude's neck tingle. The African's horribly scarred face twisted into a leer of hatred mixed with triumph. His cheek and brow were swollen and crusted with dried blood. One or two extra scars to add to his collection.

'You will see me again soon, White Meat,' he told Jude as Ben grabbed his arm and shoved him into the boat.

'Not if we see you first, sunshine,' Jeff said.

Ben slammed the hatch and activated the winding gear to crank the MOB off its cradle. The winch took up the slack in the cables. They released the catches holding the craft to its moorings. Then the davit swung the lifeboat outwards from the deck. It dangled, rocking in the gale, before the pulleys began to turn and the swaying craft descended to the water. Once it was floating on the surface, Ben yanked the lever to detach the MOB at the other end, and set the winch into reverse to spool the empty cable back up the ship's side.

In the name of human compassion, the ship was now minus its only lifeboat.

They leaned over the rail and watched as the MOB tossed and bobbed like a rubber duck on the waves. Its outboard motor burbled and churned foam. In minutes, the ship was cleaving away and leaving it behind as it struggled away in the opposite direction, just a tiny orange blob in the midst of the vast, dark, boiling ocean. Ben thought he saw a wild-eyed monstrous face staring up at them from one of the lifeboat's little porthole windows. He might have imagined it, but it was an image that he wasn't able to shake from his mind for a long time afterwards.

'Well, that's that,' Jeff yelled over the wind as they headed indoors to dry off.

And that could have been that. But it wasn't.

Chapter 29

As the afternoon wore on, the storm kept worsening steadily. Waves that before had been as tall as houses now loomed vertically like mountains of water, peaking high above the deck of the *Svalgaard Andromeda* and smashing thousands of tons of water over her bows with a violence that made the ship quiver from stem to stern and every man aboard catch his breath with fearful anticipation. The news from the bridge was grim: the latest weather update from the GMDSS reported that the severe tropical storm that had been lashing the Somali coast was now being upgraded to a full-blown cyclone. And from the readings, it looked as if the *Andromeda* was heading right into it.

Assuming the role of captain, Trent ordered the engine room to crack on under full power while he deviated course to try to outflank the storm. But it was moving so fast and erratically that it was impossible to anticipate where the cyclone might hit.

Sometime after 4 p.m., Jeff Dekker and Tuesday climbed up to the bridge to relieve the exhausted Trent and Lang. Ben had last been seen heading out onto the main deck to check on the fixings holding the fore and aft cargo cranes in place, lest they be torn loose by the incredible wind and start swinging destructively about.

In the galley, plates and cutlery were crashing all over the floor with the wild motion of the ship, and Murphy was squawking and flapping about in a panic. Jude helped Hercules clear up the mess and stow everything safely in place. As he worked, he was feeling unsettled and restless, and not just because of the storm. He couldn't get Pender out of his head. Who was he? Jude wanted to know more. It suddenly occurred to him that, with all that had been happening, nobody had thought to search the cabin where the three mystery passengers had been accommodated.

Jude told Hercules he was going to the head, which was what they called the ship's toilets. Instead, he crept unnoticed up the ladder way to E Deck and made his way to the cabin down the hall from O'Keefe's quarters.

That was where Jude made his discovery.

Pender had apparently been in such a tearing rush to get off the ship with his prize that he'd left a number of items behind. On the bed lay an abandoned holdall containing some clothes and toiletries. There was a yellowed old Wilbur Smith paperback lying propped open on the floor. And a phone.

He found it under a bunk, where it had either been kicked by accident or had slid across the floor with the motion of the ship. Jude fished it out and examined it with a thumping heart. It looked like a normal Motorola cellphone, except for its unusually chunky size and the thick antenna attached to the casing. Jude quickly realised what it was. A satellite phone.

Jude turned it on and the logo IRIDIUM flashed up on its screen. It took him only a few moments to find a menu listing all the recent calls that had been made from it. There had been only two – and both to the same number, with the international prefix code for the USA. Jude redialled the number and pressed the phone to his ear. He wasn't sure if the phone could work in such weather conditions, but he had to try. After a hissing pause, he heard a variety of electronic and static noises as the signal was bounced off the satellite.

His heart jumped as the connection was made. The dial tone was faint, and he had to clamp his hand over his other ear to hear it above the howl of the wind outside and the rain that crackled like fire against the cabin window. After five rings, there was an answer. It was a recorded answerphone message. A man's voice, speaking with an American accent.

'*This is Eugene Svalgaard's phone. I'm not here right now, so do the thing and I'll get back to you.*'

Jude cancelled the call, thinking, Svalgaard, as in Svalgaard Line? Confused, he racked his brain to recall the reading he'd done about the company before heading out to Oman. Its founder, Aksel Svalgaard, a young Danish émigré to New York in the early twentieth century, had ruthlessly built his empire from tiny beginnings in the 1920s. Having grown to become the fifth-largest shipping line in America, it was currently run and owned by his grandson, Eugene Svalgaard. The name had stuck in Jude's mind. He was certain of it.

And Eugene Svalgaard was in communication with Pender? How could that be possible? Jude was thinking he must be getting it wrong. Maybe the lines had got crossed somehow.

He was about to try the number again when the sat phone rang in his hand. After a moment's hesitation, he pressed the reply button and held the phone to his ear without speaking.

'Pender? Is that you?'

The connection was poor, but there was no question that it was the same voice Jude had heard on the answerphone

197

message. Eugene Svalgaard, CEO of the shipping line, owner of the *Andromeda*.

Jude was afraid to speak.

'Talk to me, Pender,' said the voice, sounding irritable and agitated. 'What the hell's going on out there? Hello? Hello? Jesus, it's a godawful connection.'

Jude knew he had to reply if he was to understand what this was all about. He deepened his voice and put on a passable imitation of Pender's accent, hoping that the crackly interference and bursts of white noise would cover up for him. 'Where are you?'

After a delay for the satellite, the voice replied: 'I'm about to leave for Mombasa. Got some business to take care of in Rome on the way. I'll be there to meet you and take delivery as planned. Why are you calling? Is there a problem? Hello? *Hello?*'

Jude cut him off, hardly believing what he'd just heard. He had to go and find Ben and tell him about this. It was incredible.

Clutching the phone, he rushed from the cabin and hurried back down below, zigzagging and slamming into bulkheads as the floor pitched under his feet. The first person he ran into was Condor, who was bent double in a passage and looking as if he was about to expire from seasickness. 'Have you seen my— have you seen Ben?' Jude asked breathlessly.

Condor hadn't.

Neither had Allen, the next person Jude found. Then, a moment later, Lang said he had seen the crazy English guy go out on deck and hadn't seen him come back. That had been just a few minutes ago, Lang reckoned, though he couldn't be sure.

Jude reached the A Deck hatchway and tore it open. The

wind screamed in his ears and he was instantly soaked all over again as he staggered out on deck. He glanced up at the windows of the ship's superstructure behind him, lit up like a tower block behind the curtain of rain, and wanted to be back in the safety of indoors. Out in the open was no place to be. It was as dark as night out there. The gale was frighteningly strong, snatching the air from his lungs and threatening to uproot the hair from his scalp. He ventured a few steps from the hatchway, cupped his hands around his mouth and yelled, 'Ben!'

No reply. Jude battled the wind a few more steps, until he reached the first container stack. The giant cargo crane was a towering black shape against the darkness, like the silhouette of a prehistoric monster disturbed from the deep. He yelled at the top of his voice, 'BEN! WHERE ARE YOU?'

Dread began to grip him. Nobody could survive out here long without getting swept overboard. What if—?

Jude sensed a presence behind him. He turned, clutching the locking bar of the nearest container for support against the gale. 'Ben?' he said, relief flooding through him.

The figure that stepped out of the shadows wasn't Ben.

A sudden flash of lightning snaked and writhed from the sky and glinted off something long and pointed in Scagnetti's hand. His clothes and hair were plastered to him and his muscled arms were gleaming from the rainwater. He came on a step. Another lightning flash; Jude saw the expression on Scagnetti's face, the ragged teeth bared like a snarling dog's.

'Give it to me, Limey boy,' Scagnetti yelled. 'Hand it over. I want it, you hear me?'

Jude's blood turned to ice. Gerber had warned him about Scagnetti. Jude knew what he wanted.

'Don't be stupid, Scagnetti. Put the knife down.'

'Give me that diamond,' Scagnetti shouted over the wind, coming on another step. 'Or I'll spill your guts all over this fuckin' deck.' He raised the switchblade and twirled it between his fingers.

Jude let go of the container and held up both hands to show they were empty. 'I don't have it!' he yelled back.

'I've heard you say that before, you lying fuck!' And before Jude could back away, Scagnetti reached out with the knife faster than a striking cobra. Jude felt the steel bite his hand. A third fork of lightning split the darkness, its strobing white dazzle illuminating the deck. Jude saw the blood streaming from his lacerated palm. He clenched his fist over the cut and staggered back. He was level with the base of the crane now, glancing around him for some place to run, but couldn't see a thing through the sheeting rain.

Scagnetti kept coming. 'I hate people like you,' he shouted. 'Fuckin' rich boys, you're all the same. Want everything for yourself. Well, not this time. Give it to me! It's mine!'

Scagnetti didn't see the shadow that detached itself silently from the darkness, until it was right beside him.

Chapter 30

Ben stepped out from behind the crane and placed himself between Jude and this man who wished him harm. That wasn't going to happen. Not today, not ever, not while Ben lived and breathed.

Ben patted the zipped pocket of his combat vest where the hard lump of the diamond nestled. 'You want it?' he said calmly, just loudly enough to be heard over the roar of the wind. 'It's right here. Come and get it.'

Scagnetti hesitated, and for a moment he seemed to deflate as his confidence wavered. But only for a moment. He was the one with the knife. Ben's hands were empty. In Scagnetti's world, that meant just one thing. It meant *I win*. If this guy facing him wasn't afraid of that, he soon would be.

Scagnetti tossed his head, flicking his straggly wet hair out of his eyes. He lowered his stance like the big knife fighter he was, feet braced, knees bent, arms spread, playing the blade in sweeps and circles. 'You got it, huh? Then do yourself a favour, asshole. Hand it over or I'm gonna carve you up real bad.'

'It's not a fair fight,' Ben said. 'You with a knife.'

Scagnetti laughed. 'Not so fuckin' tough now, are ya?'

'I mean it's unfair on you, Scagnetti.' Ben took a step

closer to him. 'You should have brought a gun if you meant to tangle with me.'

'Yeah? That a fact?'

Ben nodded. 'Yes. It is.'

Scagnetti moved in quickly and lashed out with the blade, low and fast. He was a good mover, even on a badly rolling deck slick with seawater. Footwork was everything in knife fighting, and Ben could see he was practised. He was the kind of scrapper who was tough and mean and wily, with years of experience and many a bloodied bar-room floor to his account. He plied the knife with dexterity, never taking his eyes off Ben, shifting his body weight from side to side, ready to feint and jab, duck and slash. A dangerous man with a blade. Hard to beat.

So Ben took a whole five seconds, instead of three, to break his scrawny neck.

The blade flashed towards Ben's chest. Ben sidestepped the stab and palmed Scagnetti's arm away from him, tried to get control of the knife hand but missed, and had to withdraw fast to avoid the knife as it thrust at his throat. Scagnetti was quick, all right, but he wasn't quick enough to dart out of the way of the low kick that Ben aimed hard and square at an imaginary point about eight inches behind Scagnetti's right knee.

A hard blow is one that connects forcefully with a vital part of the body. A crippling blow is one that goes right through. Which Ben's boot did, with a crunch that folded Scagnetti's right leg in the opposite direction to which nature had intended. Scagnetti would have screamed in pain, but in the same moment he had no air to expel from his lungs because Ben had crushed his larynx with a brutal elbow strike while seizing Scagnetti's knife arm and dashing it against the side of the container stack. The knife whipped away across the deck.

Ben beat Scagnetti's head twice into a container's steel edge. Disarming a man like this wasn't enough, because he would always find a way to come back at you. Brain damage wasn't enough either, because his mind was already deranged. A man like this, you had to end it; and end it decisively and without hesitation. That was exactly what Ben was trained to do. And exactly what he intended to do. No hesitation, no pity.

The secret of a good neck break, one that ensured instant death, wasn't the side-to-side movement you saw in movies. It was a combination twist in two planes, sideways and up at an angle. Ben supported Scagnetti's limp weight in his arms, placed one hand behind his head and gripped his chin with the other, and snapped it clean. Scagnetti never made a sound.

Then Ben flipped him over his shoulder and carried him to the rail and dumped him over the ship's side. Five seconds from the first knife jab, Scagnetti's broken body was engulfed in the leaping, crashing waves and vanished forever.

It was as if the storm gods had been animated into a renewed frenzy by the violence of their fight to the death, drawing in the primal energy and ramping it up to redirect it ten thousandfold stronger. The deafening scream of the wind seemed to have peaked to a new crescendo an octave higher in pitch. The sea was like a wild animal driven berserk, as if all the rage and fury of the world had concentrated itself in the forces of the storm. The deck heaved and juddered under Ben's feet as he turned to Jude.

'I'm sorry,' he wanted to say, but he wasn't sorry. Jude was clinging to the container stack, looking at him with wide eyes in a face that looked ghostly-pale through the murk and the driving rain. Ben started going over to him. Then suddenly, he was pitching forwards as the world seemed to tilt at an impossible angle under him.

For a disorientated fraction of a second he thought that Scagnetti's spirit had arisen from the waves, and come back to attack him, possessed with some inhuman power. In the next, cold water filled his ears and nose and the massive wave that had broken over the deck of the *Andromeda* lifted him off his feet and slammed him headlong against the container stack. His shoulder connected with bone-crushing force into something hard, jolting pain through his body. He gasped, sucked water, couldn't breathe. Couldn't cry out for Jude or see where he was. Then the deck under him was tilting the other way and he was sliding backwards in a torrent of white foam, scrabbling for a hold but powerless against the primal force that was enveloping his body and drawing him back. It was going to suck him under the rail and drag him down into the depths. He kicked and struggled and reached out in desperation for something to hold onto, but his clawing hand found nothing but water. The fear was a pure, burning white light inside him. As the certainty of death closed over him, he thought of nothing but Jude.

He felt a hand close around his own, gripping tightly.

'. . . *en!*'

Jude's voice, a million miles away through the roaring in his ears.

'. . . *ng on! I've . . . you!*'

Ben felt Jude's other hand grip his arm. He kicked against the slippery deck with all the strength he had, and now he suddenly had a foothold against the power of the receding wave. He gasped and blinked the stinging saltwater from his eyes and looked up, and saw Jude's face looking back at him.

'I've got you!' Jude yelled. 'Hang on!' Jude was stretched across the impossibly tilting deck with one foot hooked underneath the bottom edge of the container stack and both arms reaching out with a death grip on Ben's left hand and arm.

Ben opened his mouth to speak, but his voice was lost in the ripping, cracking, groaning, buckling and rending of metal as the crane above them came shearing loose from its mountings and started to topple. Its forty-foot jib swung like a giant arm over the containers as it fell, its momentum carrying it with unstoppable force straight into the windows of the ship's superstructure. The crane buried itself into the *Andromeda*'s bridge as if it had been made of paper mâché, ripping through steel and glass. Wreckage and flailing cables crashed down over the deck. Then the crane ripped itself free as the ship went into another wild tilt, toppled over and smashed down into the container stack, hanging far out over the edge of the deck.

Its unbalanced weight was too much for the ship to bear. The *Andromeda* began to capsize.

As the deck rose into a near-vertical incline, Jude lost his grip and both he and Ben slid helplessly towards the rail. But it was the angle of the slope that saved them from being crushed like insects as the container stack ripped loose of the deck and separated into its individual steel boxes that came bouncing and tumbling down over their heads like loose bricks into the ocean. The wind was screaming all around them now, coming from everywhere at once, more water than air. They were in the eye of the cyclone and there was no force on earth that could stand up to it.

Ben's feet hit the rail as he slid to the edge of the deck. He clung on with his legs and braced himself to avoid slipping through its bars. He wouldn't let go of Jude. No matter what, he'd never let go.

As if in slow motion and with a terrible deep grinding groan, dragged under by the wrecked crane, the *Andromeda* kept rolling over until her superstructure overhung the ocean at a crazy angle, the whole side of her massive hull submerged so deep beneath the waves that the port rail was engulfed in foam.

Ben's head went under the surface. All he could hear for a few seconds was the bubbling roar of the water in his ears. Jude was right there with him, eyes wide and gaping into his under the water. So close, yet so infinitely beyond Ben's power to save him.

Nobody is ever so utterly alone as when death is near – and at that moment it was so near that Ben could taste it. Jude's fingers felt like iron claws locked onto Ben's left hand. Ben could feel every joint in his body stretching as the sea tried to drag him down, but he clung on as he'd never clung to anything in his life. For an instant, his head broke the surface. He spouted water and gasped for air but then the ship gave another lurch as it rolled over further still, and he was plunged back deeper under until his lungs seemed about to burst. Just when he was on the point of drowning he heaved himself free of the boiling foam and managed to snatch more air – but then he realised that his left hand was empty.

Jude wasn't there any more.

'—ude!' Ben's scream tore his throat, but it was soundless in the insane wail of the cyclone.

The giant wave that finally broke the back of the foundering *Andromeda* took its time coming. It seemed to pause above the capsized vessel before it hit, frozen like a mountain face as it gathered its power.

Ben had time to stare up at the sheer wall looming high overhead and say 'Come on, then, you bastard', before a million tons of water crashed down and smashed him under like a fist and everything dissolved into blackness.

Chapter 31

Thirty-seven paces long by twenty-two wide. Those were the exact dimensions of the vast antique Oriental rug that graced the centre of the mosaic floor in Eugene Svalgaard's hotel room. The measurements would remain lodged in his head for a long time to come, after having spent the entire morning pacing up and down and round and round its edge like a mental health patient in the grip of an obsessive-compulsive neurosis. His diary had been wiped clean for the day; all meetings cancelled, the business conference that was his sole reason for being here in Rome in the first damn place now completely unimportant to him.

Eugene halted at the window and glared out at the view beyond his private sun deck, over Via Vittorio Veneto to the splendid panorama of the city and its hallowed and ancient monuments.

What a shit pit. He couldn't wait to get out of the place.

'Damn it all,' Eugene muttered. 'Damn and hell and blast and—' He'd never been much for strong language, but now the occasion seemed to merit nothing less and he could feel the urge rising up from deep inside his restless being like a trapped bubble desperate to escape.

'FUUUUCK!!' He screamed it at the top of his voice, as if he wanted every living soul in Rome to hear it.

There. He felt a little better now, though only a little. His heartbeat still fluttering and his face flushed, he threw his squat frame down into an antique armchair for a few moments before he jumped restlessly up again and resumed pacing the living room.

Needless to say, this wasn't any ordinary hotel room, because nothing Eugene Svalgaard possessed, or merely rented for a single night – whether of the bricks-and-mortar, automotive, airborne or fleshly variety – was ever remotely ordinary. When in Rome, his natural inclination was to take the palatial Villa La Cupola suite that occupied the whole two uppermost floors of the Westin Excelsior. It was the largest hotel suite in Italy and reputed to be the grandest in all of Europe, complete with its own private cinema and wine cellar, magnificently frescoed vaulted ceilings and enough priceless classical artwork to outfit a modestly sized gallery. Eugene had booked the suite complete with the five optional extra bedrooms. He had no intention of using them, but he'd taken them anyway, just because he could, without even blinking at the $20,000-dollar-a-night price tag.

But as much as Eugene Svalgaard appreciated and expected the best of everything, at this moment he could have been cooped up in the city's most pitiful hovel, and barely have noticed the difference. The lavish lunch prepared for him by one of Rome's top chefs in the suite's own private kitchen had gone cold, and he didn't care about that either, oblivious of the hunger pangs that emanated from somewhere deep inside his forty-eight-inch waistline. The fact was, very little in his life mattered to him right now; and that which did matter was in the process of going very horribly wrong.

How, how, *how* could this have happened to him? He'd had it all sewn up. Everything had been going his way. And now, catastrophe.

Eugene contemplated the downturn in his fortunes like a defeated general surveying the devastation of the battle-field. The worst of it all was not even knowing what was happening over there, three and a half thousand miles away where what should have been one of the milestone moments of his life had suddenly turned into a nightmare.

Out of all the vast fleet of cargo ships of the Svalgaard Line, everything hinged on just that one vessel, the *Andromeda*. The disaster had taken shape so bewilderingly fast, within a matter of hours. First the total loss of radio contact with the ship, which was most certainly not part of his carefully hatched plan. Then yesterday's weird call from Pender on the sat phone, with Pender not sounding like himself at all and then hanging up abruptly without saying why he was calling.

Then, just to deepen Eugene's anxiety still further, there had been the email at six that morning from Sondra Winkelman at the Svalgaard Line head offices in New York, reporting the ominous news that not only were the company still unable to make contact with *Andromeda*, far worse, according to their sources the tropical storm tearing up the Somali coast had developed into one of the biggest cyclones seen in those seas for a decade. A decade! Of all the cursed bad luck in the world, this had to land on him now.

Getting straight on the phone to Sondra before breakfast – 2 a.m. there, but the old harridan was getting well enough paid to work around the clock for him – Eugene had learned to his horror that a fresh communiqué from navy destroyer USS *Zumwalt*, which had been patrolling the east coast of Africa and forced to retreat to port by the violence of the storm, reported sightings of large amounts of shipping wreckage floating across a wide area of the Indian Ocean in the wake of the cyclone. So far, there seemed to be no clear evidence that the *Andromeda* was among the victims, but fears in New York were rising. They'd lost vessels at sea before. It was every shipping company's worst nightmare – though Sondra Winkelman could have no idea what the loss of the *Andromeda* would mean for her boss.

'If O'Keefe doesn't resume radio contact in another few hours, we'll have no choice but to mount a search and rescue operation,' Sondra had insisted over the phone.

'Fine, fine. Keep me posted,' Eugene had replied, gut-punched and becoming numb all over. But there had been no more from her since.

Of course, Eugene didn't give a damn about the *Andromeda* herself, or her crew, or her worthless captain. O'Keefe was nothing but a washed-up drunkard whom Eugene would have fired already if he hadn't been useful to his plan. The ship and cargo were fully insured against losses. Let them wind up on the bottom of the ocean, for all Eugene was concerned.

No, the one thing he cared about – the *only* thing he cared about, with an ardour that set his soul afire – was what his hired accomplice Lee Pender was carrying inside that case cuffed to his wrist.

It was the thing Eugene had lusted after all these years. The thing he'd been so close to finally acquiring and holding in his hand.

Eugene Svalgaard had been rich all his life. He'd been born into huge wealth and would die considerably wealthier. Nothing would ever change that. It was just the way things were. As he knew very well, enjoying such vast fortunes was something you actually had to work at, so as not to let the experience go stale. Most of the millionaires and billionaires Eugene golfed with had little trouble fuelling their passions with whatever turned them on by way of ever-fancier jets and superyachts, fast cars, faster women, Bahamian mansions and Scottish castles, all the routine trappings. But that was simply because most of Eugene's super-rich acquaintances were, in his opinion, a bunch of brain-stunted unimaginative Viagra-popping shit-assed numbskulls whose empty pursuits held no appeal for a man of his calibre. From an early age, Eugene had yearned for more. The material objects he lusted after were things of pure beauty: immaculate, eternal, transcendent.

What Eugene loved, more than anything in all the world, more than money, more than power, was diamonds.

Diamond. Even the very word itself seemed to glitter. Cut, uncut, white, pink, red, yellow, he didn't discriminate. He adored them all in equal measure, and over the last thirty or so years had spent gigantic fortunes putting together one of the world's most magnificent collections, one that he revered and guarded jealously from anyone's eyes but his own. The Nizam Diamond, a three-hundred-and-forty-carat colourless topaz that sparkled like all the stars in the sky put together, was one of his favourite pieces. Then there was the Akbar Shah, once part of the jewelled Peacock Throne of northern India's Mughal emperors, now in the hands of an unknown collector: guess who? The Archduke Joseph, a flawless Golconda beauty snapped up anonymously at Christie's in 2012 for an eye-watering twenty-one and a half million bucks – that one was his, too. And there were more, a whole sackload more.

He never displayed them publicly, and God forbid that he should ever resort to gifting any of them to some grasping female in an attempt to gain her transient affections. People just didn't see what he saw in them. While to most folks, diamonds were simply an expression of great wealth, for Eugene their monetary value only mattered insofar as the

211

dollar price required for him to possess them. In no way did he regard them as mere investments, to be cashed in for a profit at some point in the future. Quite the contrary: he intended to hold tightly onto his babies forever, and his will specified that each and every one was to be interred along with him when he eventually shuffled off to a better place. They had come from the earth, and he would accompany them on their journey back.

But as much as Eugene's magnificent collection nourished his soul, the object of his most ardent yearning was one diamond he'd never in all these years managed to possess. For as long as he could remember, it had haunted him. An image of unattainable perfection that brought tears to his eyes and a lump to his throat every time he let his imagination wander. The Holy Grail of precious stones. A legend. Or, as some believed, a myth. But Eugene Svalgaard had long refused to accept the naysayers' claims that it didn't exist. He'd always known it was out there, somewhere, waiting for him.

The lost Great Star of Africa. Possibly the most fantastical diamond in existence. Certainly one of the most elusive, especially to a man who had searched for it for most of his adult life.

The story of the diamond was a long and twisty tale that began in February 1905 at the famous Premier diamond mine in what was then the British-ruled Transvaal Colony of South Africa, with the discovery of an enormous rough stone that would become legendary as the Cullinan Diamond – named after Sir Thomas Cullinan, the mine's owner. When first unearthed, the diamond was so huge that the stunned mine's superintendent didn't at first believe it was real. Weighing in at over three thousand carats, or more than a pound, the sheer size of the monster had a similar effect on the famous Dutch jeweller who would eventually cut it, Joseph Asscher, said to have fainted from the stress of having to cleave such a valuable stone.

The Transvaal Colony government had purchased the Cullinan for the then-huge sum of one hundred and fifty thousand pounds, and presented it as a gift to King Edward VII. Amid rumours of an impending robbery attempt, the British government had a decoy fake replica of the diamond transported under heavy armed guard on a ship to England while, in a flash of insane genius that could have gone very horribly wrong, the real one was sent by ordinary parcel post. King Edward then commissioned the Royal Asscher Diamond Company of Amsterdam to cleave the stone into smaller pieces. Ultimately there were nine of these, the choicest of which found their way into the British Crown Jewels. The largest was set into the head of the sceptre originally crafted for the coronation of Charles II in 1661. The second largest became the centrepiece of the Imperial State Crown. A third was crafted into a brooch often worn by Queen Elizabeth II throughout her long reign. The smallest of the Cullinan fragments adorned a ring designed for Queen Mary in 1911. It was soon after the cutting that the polished pieces of the original diamond became known as the 'Stars of Africa': the Great Star, the Second Star, and the various Lesser Stars. More than a century after its original discovery, all of the pieces of the original 'Star of Africa' were still accounted for.

Except one. One that remained the most exciting and tantalising mystery in the history of the diamond world.

When first discovered in its rough state, it had been noted that one whole side of the diamond was so flat and smooth that it was thought to be only part of a much bigger crystal, separated under the ground by the massive pressures inside the earth. That smooth, flat surface was called a cleavage plane, which theoretically should mate perfectly to that of its enormous half-brother like matching pieces of a puzzle.

Soon the hunt was on, and hopeful prospectors were falling over themselves in the mad rush to unearth the Star of Africa's missing half. For many years, wild yarns had abounded about its possible whereabouts. Nothing was found, until 1934. Eugene possessed a copy of the *Chicago Tribune* dated January 18th of that year, in which an article had appeared headlined: FIND LOST HALF OF CULLINAN DIAMOND.

'*Reports from Pretoria, South Africa, yesterday told of the finding of a massive gem which may be the lost half of the Cullinan diamond,*' the article proclaimed, going on to describe the lucky discoverer as a 'poor digger'. That poor digger had been a black worker named Makani, employed by Johannes Jacobus Jonker, a veteran diamond prospector who had established a claim at a site called Elandsfontein, less than five kilometres from the Premier Mine. On making his amazing discovery on January 17th 1934, Makani had thrown his hat in the air, run to show his boss, and the incredible diamond had been promptly locked in a hut guarded against thieves by men with revolvers until they could decide what to do with it.

This diamond, soon to be named the Jonker, did at first sight appear to be the missing half of the Great Star of Africa; but when carefully examined by experts it was found that its cleavage plane didn't match perfectly enough with casts of the original Cullinan. Moreover, the Jonker diamond had been unearthed such a distance from the Premier Mine that it seemed unlikely they could have ever been related: thus, speculation that they had once been one huge diamond was laid to rest. The Jonker was ultimately divided into thirteen smaller diamonds. Past and present owners of these pieces included the Maharajah of Indore, John D Rockefeller Jr., and one Eugene Svalgaard.

All of which of course meant that, if the missing Star of Africa indeed existed, it was still out there. Did it remain buried deep underground? Had it been found and its discovery kept secret? For years after the Jonker episode, those questions still burned brightly in the minds of many. But as with all things, in time the excitement faded. The advent of World War Two pushed all thought of diamonds aside and the legend soon lost its lustre.

The saga might have ended there, swallowed up into history. But it didn't, not for Eugene Svalgaard who, picking up the trail so many decades later, was undeterred in his quest to find the lost Star of Africa. In 2004 he bolstered the efforts of the small army of investigators he had working on the case by offering a million-dollar reward for information leading to its whereabouts. He was cautious enough to keep his name out of it, of course, setting up a chain of contacts that couldn't lead back to him. Some in the specialist diamond world were scandalised; others scoffed; and everyone soon forgot about it as years went by and nothing happened. Even Eugene began to lose hope as his quest seemed to stagnate.

Then, in 2013, a forty-five-year-old Belgian named Marc Redel stepped into the picture, having only then heard through the grapevine of Eugene's reward. He belonged to a line of jewellers going back to his grandfather, Elias Redel, now deceased, who had been a valuation expert for the Antwerp Diamond Bank from 1936 until his retirement in 1977. It was concerning his late grandfather that Marc Redel had a strange story to tell. He told it, in person to Eugene, on March 4th 2013, in a suite at the Waldorf Towers in New York City, and it went like this:

Old Elias had passed away eight years earlier at the age of ninety-nine, riddled with disease and suffering badly from dementia, though still capable of moments of great lucidity. Marc and his father had been present at the old man's death-bed in 2005 when, close to eternity and ready to make his final confessions, Elias Redel had revealed to them a secret from his distant past that he had kept locked up and never spoken of until now. He related how, late one afternoon in August 1938 as he walked home from work through the streets of Antwerp, he had been approached by a mysterious Afrikaner who introduced himself as Henrik Cornelius Steenkamp and said he had a business proposition for him. At first unwilling, Redel had let himself be persuaded to go for a drink with the man and hear what he had to say.

Steenkamp had come to the point pretty quickly. Over glasses of Witkap Dubbel beer he claimed to be a one-time adventurer, slave trader and now South African diamond mine owner, with a pressing need to have a certain item valued.

'That's what we do at the bank,' Redel had said. 'Why not come to us?' To which Steenkamp had replied that, due to the sensitive nature of the item in question, he wished to conduct the valuation as much under the table and out of reach of government bureaucrats, specifically tax officials, as possible. He was willing to pay a premium for discretion, and had heard through the grapevine that Redel was the best young valuer at the Antwerp Diamond Bank. Would he help?

Elias had sniffed more than a slight tang of illegality here. 'I'm a valuer, not a fence,' he'd said. Steenkamp had laughed at that one. 'I'm not asking you to sell it for me, man. I'm asking you to do your job, privately, just for me, as a special favour. You'll be well rewarded, hey?'

Steenkamp had laid his money on the table. It was an extremely tempting sum for a recently married man of thirty-two saving up to buy a bigger apartment for his growing family. Elias struggled with his conscience. If he declined the bribe and insisted Steenkamp go through the proper channels, he knew the only real loser in the situation would be him. It was just another diamond, after all. What harm could come of it?

Except that it was very far from being just another diamond. When Steenkamp showed it to him, Elias's eyes popped. As he lay dying sixty-seven years later, he could still describe it perfectly.

Even before testing to see whether the smooth, flat cleavage face was a match, there was little doubt as to the identity of the rough stone. It was even bigger than its sibling discovered back in 1905. Bigger than a man's fist, over four thousand carats in weight and absolutely flawless.

An unabashed white supremacist, Steenkamp made no secret of what had happened to the black mine employee who had found the diamond and brought it to him. When Steenkamp had got over his initial shock at the sight of the thing, he'd immediately asked the black digger whether he had told anyone else about this. The answer was 'No, *bwana*.' Whereupon Steenkamp had unholstered his Colt New Service and shot the 'stupid dumb kaffir' in the head to make sure it stayed that way. Steenkamp laughed as he told the tale. 'Don't look so bloody shocked, man. They're animals, nothing more.'

Elias Redel was a Jew who lived in horror of the rising tide of racial persecution in neighbouring Nazi Germany, and Steenkamp's hateful tale had shocked him deeply. But then he went ahead and did the very thing that would most haunt him for the rest of his life. He accepted the Afrikaner's offer and went with the money.

The private valuation took three days to complete. Redel used an exact zircon replica of the original Great Star of Africa to confirm what he already knew: Steenkamp's 4,322-carat stone was the genuine article. That alone pushed its value through the roof. The figure Redel arrived at, after a great deal of soul-searching, was in the region of thirty-five million dollars.

That equated to a present-day value of just shy of six hundred million dollars. Working out the inflation as he sat listening to Redel in the Waldorf Towers suite, Eugene Svalgaard himself had to swallow hard at such an astronomical figure.

That was the end of Marc Redel's story, but it was just the start of the next chapter in Eugene's. Fired with an excitement beyond belief, after paying Redel his million, Eugene had set his investigators back to work. Now that they had a name to chase up and the almost limitless funds to bribe anyone they wanted and find out almost anything, they quickly discovered the trail of the diamond.

Needless to say, it transpired that Henrik Cornelius Steenkamp hadn't kept it for long after August 1938. Suddenly enriched beyond most people's wildest dreams, he had sold up his mine and retired to Switzerland, where he managed to duck the war and lived like a hog in the fathouse until his death, a penniless alcoholic, in 1952. The transaction that had made him fabulously rich had taken place in December '38 after a successful bid at a private, invitation-only specialist diamond auction in Geneva. The buyer, according to the very hard-to-access archive records, had been a sixty-year-old Omani aristocrat named Farouk Al Bu

Said. The sum he had paid was a hair-raising $36,795,000, well above Redel's estimate.

And so the diamond had gone to Oman – and there, as far as anyone could ascertain, it had stayed. Farouk Al Bu Said died in 1964, passing his very considerable worldly goods to his son Feisal. Feisal's own son, Amir, in turn inherited the bulk of the estate on his father's death in 1983 and subsequently passed it twenty-five years later to Hussein Al Bu Said, the elder great-grandson of old Farouk.

Throughout that whole time, the diamond remained hidden, and in 2013 it was impossible for Svalgaard's investigators to tell whether the Al Bu Said dynasty even still owned it, a frustration Eugene found extremely hard to bear. Had those dirty A-rabs auctioned it off on the sly? Eugene disliked and mistrusted all Arabs even more than he hated the Japanese. He only did business with any of them because he had to. By 2015, he had worked himself up into a terrible lather, convinced that the diamond's trail had once again gone cold.

Then, in June of that year, a miracle had occurred when a specialist diamond agent in Zurich by the name of Levin Fiedelholz, part of Eugene's extensive secret spy network, called urgently to say that his firm, Fiedelholz and Goldstein, had been approached by Al Bu Said's 'people' with a view to putting a certain high-value item on the market. Fiedelholz himself had been made privy to confidential photographs that left no doubt about what kind of 'high-value item' they were talking about. For secrecy's sake, for now the piece was being referred to only by a catalogue code number, as 'Stock # 227586'. Reading between the lines, Fiedelholz said, it appeared that Hussein's real estate empire had suffered some bad investments, and he needed to raise cash to bail himself out. The firm had been instructed to begin the process of trawling around for potential buyers.

Eugene was beside himself with excitement, until he was told the reserve price. Seven hundred million was outrageous, beyond even his means. But, Fiedelholz insisted, Al Bu Said would take a lot of persuading to budge. So began a game of chess that had dragged on for several months, until Hussein Al Bu Said's business troubles apparently resolved themselves and he suddenly changed his mind about selling at all.

Fuming like a starving dog cheated out of a bone, Eugene had considered his options. They were few, and they were ugly, but he'd come this far. He would not be denied.

In early September, Eugene had put out cautious feelers to facilitate the plan that was brewing in his mind. Two weeks later, those feelers bore fruit in the shape of a professional criminal and soldier of fortune called Lee Pender. They'd only met once, in October, at which meeting Eugene offered Pender five million dollars to obtain the diamond for him, smuggle it out of Oman on board one of his ships and carry it to Mombasa, where Eugene would be waiting. Pender agreed. If the plan necessitated (as Pender put it) 'pressing the button' on Al Bu Said, then so be it. Eugene had few qualms on that score. Pender certainly had none whatsoever.

It had all seemed so easy, Eugene now reflected miserably as he paced the living room of the Villa La Cupola suite. Pender had carried out the first phase of the plan perfectly, albeit a little messily when he and his hitters had taken it upon themselves to wipe out the whole family. But Eugene hadn't thought twice about Najila Al Bu Said and her kids. He could only think of one thing.

Just like he could only think of one thing now.

Where's my ship? Where's Lee Pender? Where's my goddamned diamond?

But for every problem, there was a solution. And as the initial panic began to subside, and Eugene was able to reflect a little more calmly over the situation, possibilities began to dawn on him that made him realise, with a flash of hope burning brightly in his head like a light bulb, that there might be another way to see this.

He picked up the phone and dialled another number, one that few people knew.

When a voice answered, he said, 'It's me. Is he there?'

The voice replied, 'He's not here.'

'Get him for me. I have a job for him.'

Eugene waited. Nineteen minutes later, the phone burred and Eugene snatched it up.

'Bronski,' said a different voice. Slow, calm, quietly self-assured, infinitely patient. Like the man himself.

'Listen,' Eugene said. Bronski listened. And Eugene told him what he wanted him to do.

Chapter 32

Something was tap-tap-tapping against Ben's head. He opened his eyes, and found himself squinting blearily into the black eye of a seagull. He jerked his head up off the hard, uncomfortable surface it was resting on and shooed the gull away. It flapped off on broad wings, low over the water, then looped up high and circled overhead.

Ben eased his aching body into a sitting position and gazed around him. The sun was rising over a calm, flat ocean and rising slowly into the cloudless sky. It was as if the storm had never happened, except for the absence of the ship and the remnants of the slick of wreckage that floated on the water. The only sound was the soft whisper of the ocean and the creaking of the makeshift raft Ben was sitting on.

His recollection of the cyclone was hazy, like half-forgotten snatches of a nightmare that returned to him in flashes. That last towering wave was still vivid in his mind's eye, and the crush of the water as it crashed down. The pain in his skull was a reminder that he'd whacked his head against something hard as he went under; but after that his memory was blank and there was nothing more until he'd snapped awake, drifting alone on a calm sea under a brightly starlit sky, an arm and a leg still hooked through the piece of deck railing that had somehow become snagged on a half-submerged cargo container and kept him afloat. Just him and the wide open sea and the vast dome of space stretching overhead, its billions of twinkling lights shimmering on the spangled ocean, broken here and there by the bobbing dark rectangles of scores of loose shipping containers that trapped enough air inside their iron shells to keep them afloat, drifting slowly outwards in a spreading circle half a mile or more across. They were a strange, surreal sight. Like floating tombstones, markers for the dead at sea.

At first he'd thought he was the only one to have made it, and his despair almost made him let go and allow the depths to swallow him up, too. Then out of the darkness he'd heard a voice calling his name, pulling him back from the brink.

Jude's voice.

Ben had powered splashing across fifty metres of cold sea and discovered Jude clinging to another container, submerged up to the neck and treading water. Ben had cried as he held him, and Jude had cried too, though that was something neither of them would talk about for as long as they lived.

Then, through the hours of night that followed, the rest of the survivors had gradually come together. Or what was left of them. Two became four when Jude spotted Lou Gerber's white, balding head struggling to stay afloat with the dead weight of the injured, semi-conscious Condor dragging him down. Ben and Jude had swum out together to haul them to safety. Then four became seven when, with a triumphant yell, Jeff Dekker pulled himself to stand on the lopsided top of a container far away in the distance, and waved his arms wildly to show that he had Tuesday and Hercules with him.

Seven was as many as they would ever see again.

It had been the longest time before anybody spoke, too

stunned for words and too occupied with pulling together what pieces of flotsam they could to build some kind, any kind, of raft. The brightness of the stars enabled them to work, without which the wreckage might all have been dispersed on the ocean current before daybreak. The raft consisted of a makeshift, uneven platform that straddled two waterlogged containers like a catamaran designed by a blind man, lashed together out of anything they could harvest from the floating wreckage and their own clothing – bits of electrical wire and cable, bootlaces, belts. It was fragile and would easily break apart at any hint of the sea becoming rough again, but it was all they had, and they were alive, here and now. What little they had managed to save in the way of materials was bundled carefully at its centre, well clear of the water. No medical supplies, signalling equipment or anything edible had survived. Just seven weary men, one diver's knife, one submachine gun, one pistol, a water-damaged short-range radio and the tenuous hope that, somehow, they would get through this.

Then, slowly, as they lay spent with nothing left to do except float under the stars, and wait for dawn to break, and pray, and count and recount their dead, they began to share their stories about what had happened.

Hercules had been bringing a jug of hot coffee up to Jeff and Tuesday on the bridge, the ever-present Murphy perched on his shoulder, when the deck crane had swung loose and crashed through the windows, showering them with glass. Then the floor tilted crazily under them as the weight of the toppled crane dragged the ship over, sending them all sprawling just before the freak wave hit and a wall of water surged through the smashed bridge. Hercules had only just managed to keep Murphy alive by stuffing him inside the empty coffee jug. The three had fought and swum their way out in pitch-darkness, only by luck grabbing three life jackets in the fleeting moments before the ship went under.

Lou Gerber had been making for the outer deck, concerned about Jude's whereabouts after Condor had told him Jude was looking for Ben. Seawater had barrelled through the hatch like a high-pressure hose just as Gerber was opening it to step outside, and almost drowned him. Condor had been less lucky, pummelled head-first against a bulkhead by the force of the water and knocked unconscious. Gerber had grabbed his crewmate by the belt, dragged him bodily up to the next level and the next as the ship tilted over. When the rising torrent of water reached up as far as E Deck and seemed set to swallow up the bridge, Gerber had jumped for it from one of the external walkways, still hanging onto Condor's belt as the two of them dropped clear over the listing rail and into the fury of the sea. How they'd made it, Gerber would never know.

The rest were presumed lost. Trent and Lang had been resting in their cabins when the ship capsized, and might not even have known what was happening until it was too late. Allen and Lorenz were unaccounted for, too. As for Cherry and Peters down in the engine room, once the *Andromeda* began to go down and the holds and passages below filled with water, there was no possible hope of escape as the bowels of the ship became their tomb. The slow, agonising death they must have suffered down there was too terrible to imagine.

Strangely, nobody asked about Scagnetti.

Dawn ground inch by inch into view, the horizon lightening to a pure gold the likes of which Ben had never seen before, as if the sky had been rinsed clean by the fury of the storm. The huge orb of the sun gradually rose over a sea as calm and flat as the day the *Andromeda* had set off from Salalah.

Ben had finally fallen into an exhausted sleep, until the gull awoke him and he was plucked back to the reality of their predicament. Jude lay curled up close by on the raft, with his legs pulled up well clear of the water in case of sharks. None had been spotted during the night, but Ben expected them to make an appearance sooner or later. Each of the three life jackets that Jeff had salvaged from the sinking ship came equipped with a small flashlight and a tube of shark repellent, which were on standby for the first sign of trouble.

It had taken every bit of persuasion Ben could muster to get Jude to put on one of the life jackets. Gerber was wearing another because he was the oldest, something he was unhappy being reminded of. The third jacket had been allocated to Condor, who was still too weak to swim if anything happened to the raft. Ben had examined his head injury and suspected concussion, as his speech was slurred and he kept drifting in and out of consciousness. Gerber was especially worried about him, but there was nothing anyone could do but keep an eye on his condition and hope for the best.

Ben reached over and touched Jude's shoulder. Jude opened his eyes.

'You all right?' Ben asked him.

'I keep thinking about the others,' Jude said softly.

'How's the hand?'

'Hurts a little.'

'Let me see.' Ben inspected the laceration on Jude's palm that Scagnetti's knife had made. It looked worse than it probably was. 'Keep bathing it with saltwater,' he advised Jude. 'Then it won't get infected.'

Tension was high aboard their makeshift little vessel. Ben

could feel it, and it was only a question of time before the stress started getting to them. He wondered who would begin to crack first. Gerber seemed a tough old salt, but he was worn down with fatigue and worry. Hercules was a physically huge and powerful man but, psychologically, Ben sensed a growing strain inside him that threatened to snap if he was pushed much further. Either of them could be the first to lose it.

The only one doing much talking was Murphy, who had recovered from the ordeal of being stuffed into an aluminium coffee jug and now stood perched on the end of the raft, beadily eyeing the gull that was still circling overhead, and breaking out into screeching cries of '*Get the fuck out of here! Get the fuck out of here!*'

'Yeah, right. Wish we could,' Jeff muttered.

'Couldn't you have taught him anything nicer to say?' Tuesday asked Hercules, frowning. He was trying to get the damaged radio working, and had it all taken apart in his lap, sifting through the pieces.

'He didn't get none of it from me,' Hercules protested.

'*Eat my shit, motherfucker!*' squawked the bird.

'Tell you what,' Gerber said bitterly. 'I'd rather be at the bottom of the sea along with the rest of the guys than stuck here having to listen to that feathered sonofabitch.'

Hercules glowered at Gerber and gestured at the waves. 'Be my guest.'

'Can't you shut it up? It's driving me crazy.'

'Bro, you already crazy as a road lizard.'

'Then again, at least we got something to eat, right?' Gerber said, grinning a nasty grin. 'Once you get past the beak, there's gotta be a few scraps of meat on it. You want to pass me that weapon, Jeff?'

'*Kiss my weenie, butt breath!*' Murphy screeched, more loudly than ever.

'Don't even think about it, man,' Hercules said to Gerber. 'I'm serious.'

'One shot. It won't know what hit it.'

'You touch my bird, dude,' Hercules warned him, 'you best hitch yo'self a ride on another boat.'

Gerber laughed. 'You call this a boat? It's the freakin' raft of the Medusa. Like the painting.'

Hercules snorted. 'Painting my ass.'

'Yeah, painting. That's what I said.'

'You got shit for brains, dumbass old geezer. It's *head* of the Medusa. You know, like snakes for hair and shit. Ever'body knows that.'

'Yeah, well, you might have seen that in some knuckle-headed movie, but some of us are educated around here. Even this dumbass old geezer.'

Hercules's face turned to thunder. 'You sayin' I ain't educated?'

'I'm saying, learn your history. The wreck of the French forty-gun frigate *Medusa* on reefs off the coast of Mauritania in 1810. Bunch of the crew managed to get away on a raft before she went down. Picasso painted it.'

Tuesday looked up from the dismantled pieces of the radio handset. 'Uh-uh. Not Picasso. The artist was Géricault.'

Gerber stared at him. 'Jericho? No way. I'm telling you it was fuckin' Picasso.'

Tuesday shook his head. 'Théodore Géricault. Painted the *Raft of the Medusa* in 1818. An icon of French Romanticism, though not strictly accurate in its depiction of the historical events.'

'Listen to m'man there,' Hercules said, nodding.

Gerber blinked. 'How in the world would you know that?'

'I know all kinds of useless crap,' Tuesday said. 'Wish I

knew how to get this radio working again, though. Think the saltwater's got to the circuitry.'

'Did they survive?' Jude asked.

'Who?' Tuesday said.

'The French sailors of the *Medusa*.'

Tuesday shrugged. 'Depends what you mean by survived. There were a hundred and fifty men on board the raft to start with. Fifteen were rescued two weeks later. Storms, suicide, fighting and cannibalism took the rest.'

Which ended the squabble between Hercules and Gerber, but put such a damper on the conversation that everyone shut up for a long time and lapsed into their own thoughts. Jude went back to scanning the water for sharks while Ben kept his eyes on the sky and his ears open for sight or sound of an aircraft, in case the coastguard was out patrolling for shipwrecks in the wake of the storm. The *Andromeda* had been out of radio contact a long time. Someone must surely have raised the alarm by now. But the only thing circling in the air was the solitary gull, following the drifting raft in the vain hope of scavenging any scraps of food.

The presence of the gull told Ben that they were within a hundred miles or so of land. Few seabirds would venture out further than that. They were drifting slowly eastwards, judging by the sun, but in these still conditions they were unlikely to cover more than six or eight miles a day, assuming that the raft held together.

The morning wore on. After a long, cold night of shivering in their wet clothes, the heat of the sun was now baking them. Even Murphy became subdued. Ben used the diver's knife to fashion a makeshift bivouac out of the torn sheet of plastic tarpaulin and a length of wooden pole they'd rescued from the wreckage. Jude and Gerber helped him to move Condor under the shade of the shelter. If the wind

229

came up, as Ben silently prayed it would, the plastic sheet could be hoisted upright to make a sail of sorts that would speed their progress towards landfall.

But if it didn't, and if nobody came to rescue them, the biggest concern was going to be drinking water. Many yachtsmen carried solar stills and desalinisation kits for treating seawater, in case of emergency. But such luxuries were lacking on board the raft, and unless it rained they were going to have a real problem. Depending on the temperature, an adult could just about survive on as little as two ounces of water a day, which would have been hard enough to provide for one man alone. Multiply that by seven and it became an impossible proposition to keep everyone hydrated, especially as bodies began to swelter under the hot sun.

Ration your sweat, not your water, was a piece of wisdom drummed long ago into Ben's mind from his SAS survival training. The secret was to use up as little energy as possible. Day one was less of a worry, as the body carried its own store of water and could get by without extra intake for twenty-four hours. The second day would see the first signs of water deprivation setting in for all of them, especially for Condor, who was already dehydrated from his bout of seasickness during the build-up to the storm.

Using the trimmings from the plastic tarp that he pushed into a hollow in the middle of the raft and secured into place by weighing the edges down, Ben made a rudimentary water-catcher. They had no other receptacles or cups to drink out of, but you could ladle it up with a shoe if you had to. All they needed now was for the heavens to reopen and provide their fill of sweet, beautiful, quenching rainwater. Though judging by the burning white-hot sky and the searing fireball cooking them from the middle of it, that wasn't likely to happen any time soon.

Ben had already donated one bootlace to the raft. Now he removed the other and attached a piece of bent wire to one end to use as a fishing line. Something shiny like a piece of mirror or even a coin could work as 'bait' to attract the attention of a curious fish, and Ben used a spent brass cartridge case. His survival instructors had warned that in an emergency situation, eating without a ready supply of drinking water could increase the threat of dehydration, because the body used up precious reserves of moisture in the digestion process. However, Ben also knew that marine life was more than just a source of food. The aqueous fluids from a dead fish's body could be drained or sucked from its eye as a water substitute. The idea might not go down too well with the sailors, at least initially. But a man would drink almost anything, no matter how revolting, if he got thirsty enough.

Ben crawled to the edge of the raft and lowered his make-shift line into the water. The hook had barely sunk below the surface before Jude called out, 'Fin! Two o'clock, thirty yards.'

'Hello, boys,' Jeff said. 'Wondered when they'd show up.'

'This just keeps getting better and better,' Tuesday muttered.

Ben looked in the direction Jude was pointing, and spotted the ominous steely dark grey triangle of a dorsal fin splitting the water a stone's throw away from the raft. The shark was cruising past them in a lazy curve. It wasn't in a hurry. It had a captive audience, and all the time in the world to check out the floating larder and the juicy life forms aboard it.

'Tiger shark,' Jude said, following the fin under the shade of his good hand. 'See the stripes down his back?' It was the most excited he'd looked all day.

Jude knew his sharks. Before Ben had ever met him, he'd been on an adventure tourism diving expedition to New Zealand, doing the man-in-a-cage *Jaws* thing with the great whites. Coming face to face with a thirty-foot eating machine in its own watery element was some people's idea of a fun leisure activity. Maybe that was because Jude had never seen a man torn kicking and screaming to bloody shreds by one of them, right in front of him. Ben had. It wasn't a sight you could easily forget. Even though the guy in question had had it coming, and the shark in question had been doing Ben a favour, not to mention saving him some effort.

The dorsal fin glided below the surface until its tip vanished under, leaving just a thin streak of bubbles to mark its presence. But the shark wouldn't be far away, that was for sure.

'Looks like I picked a hell of a lousy time to go for my afternoon swim,' Gerber said dryly.

'If it's any consolation, tigers are mostly night hunters,' Jude explained. 'If we leave him alone, he'll probably leave us alone.'

'Thank you. That makes all the difference for me,' Gerber replied. 'And if he changes his mind?'

Jude shrugged. 'Then I suppose he might come up underneath us and tip us all into the water for his dinner.'

'Sorry I asked.'

Ben reluctantly reeled in his improvised line. Fishing with sharks around was just asking for trouble, as was hanging your head and shoulders out over the side of the raft. The first fin was joined soon afterwards by a second, then a third. Impossible to tell how many unwanted visitors there were lurking unseen beneath the calm surface. Like vultures circling, except below them rather than above.

And so they drifted on through the hours, huddled

together, moving little to conserve their energy, trying to shield themselves from exposure to the fierce sun. Condor went on sleeping under the shade of the bivouac, with Gerber watching anxiously over him. Tuesday eventually gave up trying to fix the radio. Jeff occupied himself by stripping their only surviving weapon down to its component parts and carefully cleaning the saltwater residue off each one with a strip of his T-shirt before reassembling it. 'Wish we had some gun oil.'

'Wish we had a bunch of things,' Gerber said.

It was afternoon when they heard the sound of the plane.

Chapter 33

The distant twin-engine drone of an aircraft jerked Ben from his reverie, and he jumped to his feet and shielded his eyes with the flat of his hand to peer up at the sky. There it was, a tiny coloured speck tracking steadily above the horizon.

'Shit, that what I think it is?' Hercules said, and stood up so abruptly that his weight made the raft tilt.

'Easy! You want to tip us over?' Gerber warned him. 'Flinging your lardy ass around like a hippo.'

'You callin' me fat, homes?' Hercules said in a hurt voice.

'Won't be for long, if we don't get rescued any time soon.'

'*Fuck* you, man.'

Jude, Jeff and Tuesday joined Ben in waving their arms and yelling at the tops of their voices to try and attract the attention of the faraway pilot. The speck against the sky didn't grow any larger. The engine drone gradually died away. All they could do was stare in dismay as the plane shrank to a barely visible dot and then disappeared altogether.

'Well, that's that,' Jeff said, scowling up at the empty sky with his face screwed up against the sun's glare.

'They'll be back. We'll see them again soon,' Jude insisted. 'Or someone. It's got to happen.'

'It's a big ocean,' Gerber said.

But Jude was right. They did see someone again soon.

It was less than an hour later when they heard the sound of the second aircraft. It wasn't the flat drone of a plane, but the thump of a helicopter. And it wasn't just a speck bypassing the horizon, but coming their way and growing louder every minute.

They waved their arms and flapped their brightly coloured life jackets in the air and shouted until they were hoarse, but it was unnecessary. The chopper pilot had spotted the raft, and was heading straight for them. As it got nearer, Ben could see it was a large helicopter, like one of the now-obsolete Westland Sea Kings that had been coming to the end of their RAF service life when he was a young soldier. It would have plenty of room on board for all of them.

But something about it bothered him. He wasn't sure what. Not yet.

'Are those coastguard colours?' Jeff asked, standing at his shoulder. Ben was no expert, but he didn't think they were. In America, USCG choppers were generally bright red. In Britain, the Maritime and Coastguard Agency painted their fleet in red and white livery. The same was true of France. The old RAF air sea rescue Sea Kings had been high-visibility buttercup yellow, while in developing countries like Africa, where the fleets tended to be provided by United Nations, the standard colour was UN white. It was hard to tell from this distance with the sun's glare behind it, but the helicopter coming towards them now looked like some kind of military drab olive green to him. He said nothing, kept watching its approach.

'Condor! Condor!' Gerber shook his friend's shoulder, rousing him excitedly. 'We're gonna get out of here. We're saved. You're gonna be okay!' Condor managed a weak smile and a croak.

Hercules and Jude exchanged a jubilant high-five, both grinning irrepressibly and dancing about the raft like kids. 'Boy, is it gonna be good to feel solid ground under my feet again,' Hercules laughed. 'Hear that, Murph? We goin' home, lil' brother.' The parrot looked distressed by the gigantic roaring green monster eagle looming overhead. Hercules held out a finger and Murphy hopped onto it, grasping it tightly with lizard claws and flapping his wings. Hercules gently folded him into the big side pocket of his jacket, where the bird seemed content to ride with just his head peeking out.

The thudding roar of the helicopter filled the air as it drew closer and settled into a hover, the downdraught from its rotors whipping up little white crests of foam off the water and making the raft's plastic sheet bivouac crackle and flap.

That was when Ben realised what he was looking at. It wasn't a United Nations helicopter. And it wasn't any kind of official coastguard rescue chopper, either. It was even older than the scarred Russian dinosaur of a seaplane that had carried him, Jeff and Tuesday from Hobyo. An ancient French Aérospatiale Puma medium transport/utility helicopter that had probably begun its long, hard military service life in the late sixties. It looked exactly like one of those countless thousands of aircraft that were thrashed and abused mercilessly as workhorses for decades on end in their countries of origin before being sold off as obsolete surplus and frequently ending up in the cobbled-together fleets of tin-pot Third World dictatorships and the like. It was painted in nondescript military matt green, but with no markings of any kind on its beaten-up fuselage. A ragged line of old bullet holes ran along its length, where it had been strafed by machine gun fire, once upon a time. Its side hatch was open. Black men with guns were crouched at the mouth of the hatch, looking down at them.

Coastguard rescue helicopters didn't go armed. Not as a rule.

But then, it wasn't here to rescue them. Not as such. Ben realised that now.

The chopper came down lower, sending up a blast of spray off the sea.

'I have a bad feeling about this,' Tuesday yelled over the roar.

From the co-pilot's cabin window, a familiar face grinned down at them. Gleaming white teeth in an ebony face that looked like a vision from the centre of hell.

Jean-Pierre Khosa had said he'd be back. And now he was.

Chapter 34

Hercules stopped jumping around and the smile vanished off his face. He stared up at the chopper. So did Gerber. Jude looked at Ben. Ben looked at Jeff. Jeff looked at the submachine gun and pistol that were stowed next to where he'd been sitting. He looked up at the helicopter, then back at Ben.

Ben shook his head. He knew what Jeff was thinking, because he'd thought it too, as the reality of their situation had hit him. But only for a second. Because the reality of their situation could potentially become a lot worse if either of them made a move for a weapon. There were at least six guns pointing down at them from the open hatch of the Puma, and those were just the ones he could see. Any momentary notions of opening fire on the chopper in the hope of disabling the turbine or piercing some critical engine component or taking out the pilot had to be dismissed in the knowledge that the enemy's finger was already on the trigger and that two or three quick strafes were all it would take to turn the raft into a floating slaughterhouse.

Which, for now at least, left them little option but to stand very still with their hands empty and plainly visible while waiting to see what happened next. Everything depended on Khosa's intentions. If they were of the 'shoot on sight' variety, Ben and the others would find out soon enough. If Khosa's men fired first, then that would change everything. Ben had his first response to that scenario already figured out. Jude was to his right, the guns to his left. The submachine gun was the one to go for. In the instant Ben made a grab for it, he would kick out with his right boot and knock Jude into the water. Then, at least Jude would have a chance of evading the ensuing two-way firestorm. Better to take your chances with the sharks. Jude could survive this, even if Ben, Jeff, Tuesday, Gerber, Hercules and Condor didn't. He could swim like a fish and hold his breath underwater like nobody Ben had ever seen. He could dive deep and come up behind the raft two, three minutes later. In the unlikely event that the gunfight lasted that long, he could use the raft as cover. In the more likely event that everyone else would be dead long before then, Jude could dive back down again and bob up for quick, furtive snatches of air every couple of minutes until Khosa went away.

Because it was easy to figure out that Khosa wouldn't stick around for long, once he had what he came for. Ben knew exactly what that was. It was the same thing everyone else wanted and would die trying to take for themselves. First Pender, then Scagnetti.

Ben could feel the hard lump of the diamond nestling against his thigh. He'd virtually forgotten he was still carrying it. An unimaginable fortune right there in his pocket. Enough money to purchase, equip and crew a large ship to take them all the way home to France, with enough change left over to buy a château or two there. The equivalent of enough stacks of paper money to sink their raft to the ocean bed. More weight than even the Aérospatiale Puma could handle. All things considered, it wasn't so surprising what people would do to make it theirs.

Ben wondered briefly whether the presence of the diamond gave him more options than he'd realised. What would Khosa do if Ben suddenly whipped the little leather pouch out of his pocket? Would he back off, fearful that Ben was about to do the unthinkable and throw it into the sea? At that moment, the diamond would become Ben's hostage. Its value to Khosa would offer some leverage. But like all hostage scenarios, it would be a highly unstable situation. Because once established, the threat either had to be carried out, or not. If it was, then Khosa's next move would be to order his men to kill everyone on board the raft, out of pure rage. Bad idea. If it wasn't, Khosa had only to call the bluff, knowing that Ben couldn't afford to lose the only ace he had up his sleeve.

A no-win situation.

So then Ben wondered what Khosa would do if the diamond was thrown into the helicopter instead, by way of a peace offering. The message would be clear enough: '*Take what you came for and leave us in peace.*' It should work, in principle. Except not with a man like Khosa. Khosa would want his revenge for the humiliation he'd suffered at their hands, for the men he'd lost, and just because he was that kind of guy. He would still execute them all anyway. Another no-win situation.

'What are we going to do?' Jude said, staring at Ben.

'That's what I'm still trying to decide,' Ben said.

'And?'

'And, I don't think there's anything we can do,' Ben said. 'Not yet. We have to see how this plays out.'

'This bastard's beginning to piss me off,' Jeff said, scowling up at the chopper. 'He so much as farts at us, he's the first to cop it.'

'I'm with you on that one, mate,' Tuesday said.

Jude's face was strained with guilt and regret. 'You were right. I should have listened to you back there. I should have let you kill him, while we had the chance. But all I could think about was helping them. I was an idiot.'

'I admired you for your humanity,' Ben replied. 'And I still do. But now we need to think about how we're getting out of this.'

The chopper came closer, and closer, until its scarred olive-green underbelly was almost right overhead, hovering thirty feet above the water. It was turned side-on to them and shifting slightly left and right, up and down. The noise was huge, the screech of the turbine adding a cutting treble to the bass *whap-whap-whap* of the rotors. The downblast was whipping up the sea in a wide circle all around the raft, tearing at their hair and clothes and threatening to rip the plastic bivouac sheet off its tenuous mountings.

Then two things happened.

The first was that two of Khosa's men started lowering a rope ladder from the helicopter's open side. It wobbled and shook, dropping jerkily a foot at a time until it dangled within reach of the raft.

The second was that Khosa himself appeared in the open hatch, grinning down at the survivors. He seemed to have found a replacement for the big revolver that Ben had taken from him aboard the ship, but the weapon was still holstered on his gunbelt. The object he was holding in his hand wasn't a gun. He raised the megaphone to his mouth.

Which made it look to Ben as though Khosa wanted to talk. Which, in turn, meant that his immediate intentions weren't to kill them all. That might come later, but for now it seemed that some kind of parlay was about to begin. Whatever it was Khosa was about to lay on the table, Ben wanted to get there first.

Chapter 35

Before the African could speak, Ben pulled the leather pouch from his pocket and held it up above his head.

'This is what you want,' Ben called up to Khosa. He had to shout hard to be heard over the deafening noise of the helicopter. 'You get no argument from us. It's yours. I let you have it, you spare our lives. Do we have a deal?'

'You're just going to *give* it to him?' Jude yelled at Ben.

'Do we have a deal?' Ben shouted up at the chopper.

Khosa smiled behind the megaphone. 'Oh, yes, we will have a deal. Thank you for keeping it for me, soldier.' His voice was deep and resonant, its sonorous bass tones exaggerated over the loudspeaker. He lowered the megaphone and spoke briefly to the man on his right. Whatever was said, the man stared blankly at Khosa and listened. He didn't show any reaction. He didn't nod, because nodding would imply agreement, and agreement would imply that there was any notion of democracy going on here. If Khosa had told the man to jump into the sea, the man would have done it without hesitation. Or if Khosa had handed him a pistol and instructed him to blow out his own brains, he would have done that too.

Instead, from the man's response, Ben understood that Khosa had ordered him to climb down to the raft. With instant obedience the man slung his rifle over his shoulder

242

on its sling, then lowered himself over the edge of the hatch so that his legs dangled in space. Then he grabbed hold of the sides of the rope ladder and twisted himself out and down and started scrabbling quickly down its length. Ben recognised him as one of the pirates they'd captured on board the *Andromeda*, except that he'd exchanged his loose, ripped T-shirt and frayed shorts for military khakis. He was the one of Khosa's men to whom Ben had shown the controls for the MOB lifeboat before sending them all on their way. Doing the right thing.

The man kept descending the ladder. He was only a skinny little guy, but the laws of physics were immutable. The further down he reached, the more his weight, combined with the side-to-side motion of the hovering chopper, made him sway like a pendulum. As he got to the bottom, he twisted his neck to look down, waiting for the right moment to let go. If he misjudged it, he'd be in the sea. Ben wanted to see that happen, especially if one of the sharks circling hidden beneath the surface happened to get lucky.

But the man judged it correctly, and he let go of the ladder just as it was swinging towards the bottom and middle of its arc, and landed like a gymnast on his feet on the edge of the raft. The impact made the whole makeshift construction shake. The man quickly unslung his rifle and pointed it at Ben and the others. Technically unnecessary, with several more guns already aimed their way from above, but it was a dramatic gesture and Ben guessed the man wanted to look properly ferocious and aggressive in front of his commander. Or maybe he was just stupid.

If he was, Khosa certainly wasn't. Even from a position of complete strategic superiority, he was being careful. He raised the megaphone back to his mouth and called down, 'Throw your weapons in the water.'

Ben shrugged. It wasn't as if he could do much anyway, under the circumstances. The guns were one step to his left. He replaced the leather pouch in his pocket, then held his arms out from his sides, palms splayed, and slowly crouched down. He could feel the hard lump of the diamond pressing against his thigh. No sudden moves. With great delicacy he reached for the weapons and picked one up in each hand, holding them by their barrels, butt-down, making a show of how harmless and well-intentioned he was. Not without some regret, he tossed the submachine gun over the edge of the raft and into the sea. Followed by the pistol. The smaller, lighter weapon made a smaller splash than the first. Ben gazed at the ripples and wistfully visualised the guns spiralling down to the ocean bed. Then he splayed out his arms again and stepped back, and glanced up at Khosa aboard the chopper as if to say, 'Okay, what next?'

'Now hand over my diamond,' Khosa ordered from above.

My diamond. As if it had been his all along. As if all he was doing here was rightfully reclaiming his lost property. Ben wondered if Khosa somehow actually believed that. Was he really that crazy?

Ben thought so.

But he had no idea at that moment how crazy Khosa truly was. That was all set to change.

Ben took the leather pouch back out of his pocket. Again, no sudden moves, no surprises, no whipping out of a concealed weapon with which he might miraculously redress the situation and save the day. Ben held out the pouch at arm's length and took one step towards the man on the raft, who was watching Ben's every twitch with his finger on the trigger. His face was covered in sweat and his eyes were wide with fear, as if he thought Ben could break his neck at any moment. Ben would gladly have proven him right. But even

244

the most fragile deal was still a deal. For now, at any rate.

The man wedged the butt of his rifle under his right armpit to support its weight, holding it one-handed while he edged forward and reached out with his left hand to snatch the leather pouch from Ben's fingers. He did it furtively, anxiously, like a nervous but hungry dog over-coming its suspicion to accept a titbit from a potentially menacing stranger.

In that moment, the diamond was back in Khosa's posses-sion. Ben's pocket suddenly felt strangely empty. The man with the rifle stuffed the pouch into his pocket, slung his weapon back over his bony shoulder and turned to clamber up the rope ladder. Three seconds later, he was back aboard the helicopter and handing the pouch to his commander, who snatched it from him with imperious disdain and opened it to peer inside.

A great glowing smile spread over Khosa's scarred face. *My diamond.* Reunited at last.

'Outstanding. There goes our only tactical advantage,' Jeff muttered from behind Ben's shoulder.

Ben glanced back at him. 'What would you have me do?'

But Jeff was right, too. Now they were left with nothing. No weapons, no bargaining chips. Just their trust in the forbearance of their fellow man. It wasn't a great feeling.

Ben turned back to look up at the helicopter. Any moment now, he thought, they would find out whether or not Khosa was going to honour his side of the deal.

And a moment later, they had their answer.

Chapter 36

Even at this distance, Khosa's victorious smile was brighter than the burning hot sun that was bearing down on them out of the cloudless sky. He gave the leather pouch a loving squeeze in his fist, as if savouring the knowledge of what was inside. Then he tucked the pouch into the pocket of his combat jacket and raised the megaphone to his mouth once more.

'Thank you, soldier,' the big voice boomed out over the blast of the chopper. 'Now you will all come with me.'

'Oh, shit,' Tuesday said. Gerber and Hercules exchanged terse glances. Jude turned suddenly pale. Jeff ground his jaw tighter.

'That wasn't the deal,' Ben shouted up. 'You have the diamond. Now leave us.'

Khosa's amplified laughter roared down at them like thunder. 'I said we would have a deal, soldier. My deal. Take it, or die. It is your choice.'

Ben looked at Jeff. Jeff wasn't saying anything.

'Good,' chuckled the booming voice from above. 'Now you will all climb aboard. Starting with the boy.'

Ben looked uncertainly at Jude. Jude returned his glance. *What do I do?* his expression read.

'The boy first,' Khosa repeated over the megaphone. 'Or

he dies first.' Without looking back over his shoulder, he snapped his fingers theatrically and two of his men instantly appeared to the left and right of him, rifles shouldered and trained on Jude. With the up-down, side-to-side drift of the chopper their aim couldn't be that steady or precise. But with their weapons set to fully-automatic fire, it didn't need to be.

'Remember I said I had a bad feeling about this?' Tuesday said. 'It just got worse.'

'What does that maniac want with us?' Gerber asked.

Ben said, 'I don't know.'

'I do,' Hercules said. 'He's gonna put a bullet in our asses one by one.'

Jeff shook his head. 'Nothing stopping him from doing that right now. He doesn't need us in the chopper for it.'

Hercules gave a snort. 'Then he's plannin' to chop off our fuckin' arms and drop us in the sea for sport with the fuckin' sharks.'

Ben looked at them. 'Whatever we find up there, whatever his intentions are, we'll deal with it. One step at a time. Jeff's right. If he wanted us dead, we'd be dead. Something tells me he has something else in mind.'

'We're wasting time here,' Jude said. 'Let's get this over with.' He stepped to the edge of the raft and reached out for the swaying ladder. Using his uninjured hand to grab hold of the bottom aluminium rung, he pulled it towards him. He put a foot on the rung and tested it with his weight, like testing a stirrup before mounting a horse. The thick nylon cord stretched and wobbled, but it could have held many times Jude's weight.

Jude began to climb, a little gingerly because of his cut palm. Ben's heart was in his throat and his fists were clenched at his sides, and there was nothing he could do but watch helplessly as Jude ascended rung by rung towards the open hatch and the pointing rifles above him. As Jude reached the top, sinewy hands reached down and grabbed him by the arms and hauled him aboard the helicopter. Jude and Khosa disappeared from view. For a terrible moment or two, Ben was frightened that the aircraft was going to fly away. But then Khosa reappeared at the mouth of the hatch and pointed down at Jeff. 'Now that one,' he boomed down through the megaphone.

'Whatever happens,' Jeff said to Ben.

Ben nodded. 'Whatever happens.'

Jeff climbed, with the practised ease of a guy who had shinnied up a thousand ropes and ladders into a thousand helicopters in his time. He reached the top quicker than Jude had. With two rifles at his head he was yanked inside the hatch and disappeared as well.

Next, it was Tuesday's turn. Then Condor's. Ben and Gerber helped him to his feet and steadied him as he stumbled towards the waiting ladder.

'I can't do it,' Condor gasped.

'You gotta try, buddy,' Gerber told him, clutching his shoulder. 'I'll be right there behind you.'

Condor inched his way up the ladder like a half-crushed spider crawling up its web in search of a place to die. Khosa was frowning impatiently down at him. Twice, Condor lost his footing and almost fell into the sea. When he eventually made it to the top rung, the Africans dragged him roughly aboard and virtually threw him inside. Gerber went next. Then Hercules, his bulky weight making the ladder swing wildly, the bewildered parrot still peeking its head out of his pocket.

Ben was the last man off the raft. He wasn't sorry to leave it behind, but he wasn't happy about where he was going, either. At the top of the ladder he batted aside the guns that pointed in his face, and clambered to his feet inside the cargo area. He looked around him.

The interior of the Puma was exactly how he remembered them from his military days. The exact opposite of Auguste Kaprisky's Gulfstream. Even more spartan than the Soviet seaplane. The inward-curving interior walls and riveted seams of the fuselage had been painted the same dull olive green as the outside, but many years ago, and were mostly worn and scuffed down to the bare metal. The floor was sheet aluminium, grimed with layers of filth and oil. Rudimentary folding seats were bolted along the length of the cargo bay, either side of a narrow aisle that passed through a narrower hatch into the cockpit. The inside of the chopper was completely uninsulated from the noise of the turbine. Totally utilitarian in every respect. Nothing much in the way of creature comforts, especially with a bunch of aggressive Africans pointing loaded and cocked automatic weapons at you.

There were five of them, including the skinny one who had come down to the raft. The ubiquitous AK-47s all round, except for the fat one who was armed with a black Remington combat shotgun. All were attired in the same thrown-together military uniforms. Ben couldn't remember all their faces, whether they'd been with Khosa aboard the *Andromeda* or whether they were fresh troops he'd picked up ashore. If fresh was the right word to describe them. They looked as worn out with fear as they looked desperate as they looked ragged.

Their weapons jabbed and prodded Ben to an empty fold-down seat between Hercules and Gerber, opposite where Jeff was already sitting with Jude to his right and Condor to his left. Jude was staring blankly into space, apparently lost in his own thoughts.

Condor wasn't looking good. He could barely sit up and kept listing sideways to his left to lean on Tuesday, who was leaning forwards with his elbows on his knees, rigid with tension and all keyed up, glancing constantly at Ben and Jeff for some kind of guidance. *What do we do?*

Khosa had made his way forward to the cockpit and returned to the co-pilot's seat. All Ben could see of him was one wide shoulder and the back of his head from a rear-three-quarter angle as he turned to give some unheard instruction to the pilot. What was going on inside that head, Ben still had no idea. But whatever Khosa had planned for them, at least they were still alive.

Right now, that seemed about as much as anyone could wish for.

Chapter 37

One of Khosa's men hauled the rope ladder aboard and flung it carelessly into a corner. The fat one with the shotgun slammed the hatch shut, and then they all stalked forward to fill the four remaining seats at the front of the facing rows while the fifth made do with the floor.

The pilot had had his orders. He worked the controls and the turbine screech grew even more deafening inside the bare metal fuselage as the helicopter broke out of its hover and wheeled and banked away, nose down and tail up under acceleration, carving upwards into the sky and pressing rapidly on towards its unknown destination. Unless Khosa had an aircraft carrier cruising somewhere off the east African coast, Ben presumed they were heading for land. There was none of that for fifteen hundred miles to the south, when they would hit Madagascar. None of it for over three thousand miles due east until Sumatra, and north would take them straight back towards Oman. In any case, the Puma's fuel capacity wouldn't allow for a fraction of that distance, especially taking into account the large quantity that Khosa must have already burned up in searching for them over thousands of square miles of ocean. The chopper must be pretty much running on fumes by now, which strongly supported the logic that they must be heading west, back to the Somali coast.

Except that neither Khosa nor his men were Somali. That implied that their ultimate destination lay further inland. Ben had the map of Africa pretty well imprinted on his memory from all the times he'd been deployed there, back in the day. Neighbouring Kenya was the nearest of the Swahili-speaking countries. The furthest away was probably Zambia, though the southern tip of Mozambique lay as far to the south as Johannesburg. An enormous distance away, half the length of an enormous continent. There was no way to know the answer, except to wait and see.

But to passively await whatever fate Khosa had in store for them all was something Ben had no intention of doing. Glancing across the narrow aisle at Jeff and Tuesday and seeing the looks on their faces, Ben knew that both of them were thinking exactly the same thoughts as he was.

Whatever we find up there, we'll deal with it.

Nobody spoke. The noise levels inside the helicopter would have made conversation impossible anyway. Ben looked at Jude and tried to catch his eye so that he could say, or mouth, something reassuring like 'Everything's going to be okay.' But Jude seemed lost in another world, slumped in his seat with the same thousand-yard stare directed at the green metal wall opposite him.

Ben was worried about Condor. He wasn't at all well, and had lapsed back into unconsciousness. As the pilot shifted course a few degrees and the aircraft banked a little to the right, Condor suddenly pitched forwards. Before anyone could stop him, he slumped right out of his seat and flopped to the bare metal floor like a sack of washing. The nearest of the guards rose half to his feet, pointing his weapon as if ready for the sick man to spring up at him with a knife.

'Our friend is injured,' Ben told the guard in Swahili, yelling to be heard. 'He needs a doctor.'

The guy just stared at Ben, then shrugged as if it were nothing, and sat back down. Hercules and Gerber helped Condor back to his seat, watched closely by all five guards. 'You're gonna be fine, bud,' Gerber shouted in Condor's ear. 'Hang in there, you hear me?' Whether Condor heard or not, it was hard to tell.

The chopper thudded on. Sea miles passing beneath them. The old Puma had a never-exceed speed of 147 knots, or 169 miles per hour. Its cruising speed was 134 knots, equating to 154 miles per hour. Still pretty damn fast, even if the pilot took it easy for the sake of fuel economy. By Ben's very rough calculations, the Somali coast couldn't be more than an hour away. If his guess was right, Khosa was planning on landing as soon as possible, to refuel or else to transfer his prisoners to some other form of transportation.

Either way, when they landed they were sure to be met by more of Khosa's troops. Ben couldn't believe that the African had come looking for them with just five soldiers and one helicopter. The RV could be with ten more men, or it could be with thirty, or more. And as much of a slackly trained raggle-taggle militia as they might be, the kind of force that real soldiers would laugh off, it would be a lot harder for Ben, Jeff and Tuesday to deal with upwards of thirty or forty men than with just five, plus Khosa and the pilot.

That knowledge was in Jeff's expression, too. They both knew that if they were going to make a move, it had to be sooner rather than later.

With that in mind, Ben and Jeff struck up an urgent back-and-forth dialogue, the way that only two people who knew each other so well and were tuned to the very same wavelength could. The conversation was all contained in tiny shifts of head carriage and body language and eye movements that would have been all but undetectable to anyone watching them, but it was as clear and precise as if they'd been two top brass officers discussing military strategy across a table in a war room, with maps and charts spread out between them and little models placed here and there to denote the movement of enemy troops.

Jeff's eyes said, *The clock is ticking, mate. Now or never.*

Ben's said, *I know.*

Jeff's said, *We can do it. So are you up for it?*

What about Tuesday?

We make our move, he'll follow us. Trust him.

All right. But it's got to be quick.

It'll be quicker than quick.

Ben cast a quick glance down the aisle at the soldiers. All five of them were relaxed and off their guard. The four who were seated were twiddling their thumbs like bored commuters on their regular subway train ride to the office. The one sitting on the floor had his AK butt-down on the floor between his feet, with the barrel resting loosely against his shoulder. He had a finger up his nose and seemed entirely focused on retrieving and eating whatever he could ream out of his nostril. Not the most finely tuned fighting unit Ben had ever seen. Which potentially made things very much easier, if this was to have any chance of a favourable conclusion.

Ben's eyes darted back to meet Jeff's. *All right. You take the nearest one on the left and use his gun to shoot the fat one at the end of your row. I take the nearest one on the right and use his gun to shoot the skinny one at the end of my row.*

Jeff's chin rose and fell by about half a millimetre. *That'll work.*

Ben's eyes said, *That just leaves the nose picker on the end. Whoever's finished with the others first gets to him before he gets to his rifle. Agreed?*

Jeff threw a discreet look in the nose picker's direction, and the nasty twinkle in his eyes said, *He won't be a problem.*

Ben took another glance, this time up the narrow aisle and through the hatch into the cockpit. Khosa and the pilot were still talking. Eyes front, completely distracted by whatever they were looking at through the windscreen. Ben looked back at Jeff and gave a tiny, almost imperceptible nod that was as expressive as if he'd jumped to his feet and screamed, 'Fuck it, let's do it.'

Jeff nodded back. It was agreed. For a few seconds the two of them prepared themselves, mentally and physically, to explode into action. Each had his own way of handling it. Jeff was winding up like a steel spring, as intense as a racehorse waiting for the gate to open on Derby day. Ben's own heartbeat was dropping. His muscles relaxing. A familiar calm descending on him, in the certain knowledge that he would move fast, and hit hard, and strike with accuracy. Getting the weapons from the guards was theoretically going to be the hardest part, and the biggest danger was from the fat one's shotgun. One blast from that thing could kill all of them. But surprise was on their side. Once the five were permanently out of action, it would just be a question of getting to Khosa before Khosa could draw that big revolver of his and get his bulk twisted round in the co-pilot's seat to be able to get off a shot. A lot depended on Khosa's speed of reflexes and combat readiness. Risky, but not impossible. Not by a long stretch. Ben didn't foresee too many problems there. As for the pilot, he'd have a gun to his head before he'd fully registered what was even happening.

255

Hijack complete. Five seconds from start to finish. Six, on the outside.

Ben felt ready. He moved his right hand to his right knee and splayed three fingers. *On my count of three.*

Jeff nodded.

Ben mouthed, 'One'.

Jeff waited.

Ben mouthed, 'Two'.

Tuesday was watching them with huge eyes, understanding that something was about to happen, and holding his breath. He knew. He could feel it. He'd been there before. It was the pulse-pounding moment before the eruption into all-out balls-to-the-wall combat, when the lips were dry and the whole body was tingling and the senses were ready to burst with anticipation of the green light and the command *GO GO GO*, from which there was no turning back. Adrenalin running so thick and fast through your blood that you could taste it, just one of a whole hormone cascade pushing alertness and reflex speeds through the roof, pumping blood to the skeletal muscle, preparing the body to ignore pain and injury, dilating the pupils to draw in maximum light. Excitement and terror intermingled into a heady cocktail like no other sensation on earth.

Ben pursed his lips to mouth, 'Three'.

Then something happened that nobody had expected.

Chapter 38

Khosa suddenly did something very strange. He broke off as sharply from his conversation with the pilot as if a rifle shot had cracked out behind him. He turned in his seat, leaning so that he could peer back out of the cockpit and down the aisle. His eyes went straight to Ben and fixed him with a look of complete knowing. Seeming to bore right through Ben's head and penetrate his mind. A brief, peculiar smile twisted his grotesque features.

Ben stared back at the African, feeling as if he'd been caught out. The conspirators nabbed red-handed around their table as the secret police kicked in the door and burst in on the clandestine meeting.

Khosa's smile dropped. He got to his feet quickly, ducked out of the cockpit and moved up the aisle, steadying himself against the pitch and sway of the helicopter. His revolver was out of its holster and clenched in his fist. It was a monster handgun, a .44 Magnum Colt Anaconda, an exact duplicate of the one Ben had flung off the deck of the *Andromeda*. His men all snapped to attention like soldiers on inspection, and snatched up their weaponry. Khosa barely glanced at them, instead glaring at Ben, then at Jeff, then up and down the facing rows of seats at the rest of the prisoners. His gaze seemed to linger on Jude for a moment.

Sensing that something was up, though oblivious of what it could be, Jude was startled out of his reverie and looked up in confusion. Gerber and Hercules did the same. Condor was too out of it to be doing much of anything.

Khosa barked a command to his men that Ben couldn't make out over the noise of the turbine. But his men heard it fine, and obeyed instantly. The nose picker and the skinny one stalked over to where Jude was sitting, grabbed his arms, one either side, and yanked him out of his seat and dragged him to his feet and started marching him up the aisle towards the nose of the aircraft. The other three had their guns up and pointed straight at Ben. Ben froze. Not breathing. Heart stopped.

Khosa's little smile was back. He pointed at Jude, then barked another command, and the two men shoved Jude roughly against the curve of the fuselage just behind the cockpit bulkhead and pressed him down to the floor. Jude thought they were going to shoot him. He raised his hands to protect his face and head, in that instinctive way people do under threat, as if their hands could stop a rifle bullet.

Jude wasn't the only one convinced that he was about to be shot. Ben was certain of it. His heart restarted, pulse racing, and he felt himself redden as he half-rose out of his seat with his guts twisting and fists clenched. Whatever happened, he wouldn't, couldn't allow that to happen to Jude.

Khosa pointed his .44 Magnum at Ben, with the same half-smile curling his lips. Now it was Khosa's turn to shake his head and say *Don't even think about it.*

Ben froze. There were just too many guns. And there was nothing he could do, except die a futile death trying in vain to save his son. He lowered himself into his seat. In that moment, he wanted this man Khosa gone more than he'd ever wanted anything in his life. Sooner or later, one way or another, it was going to happen. Khosa had just sealed his own fate.

The rifles pressed against Jude's head. Jeff's face was drawn so tightly that the bunched muscles in his jaws looked as if they were about to snap. Tuesday's eyes were wide and his face was as pallid as it was possible for an Afro-Jamaican's face to be.

But Khosa's men didn't shoot Jude. That wasn't Khosa's intention. Not yet.

The two who had grabbed Jude stepped back and steadied their backs against the fuselage with their rifles still pointing at his head, holding him in his uncomfortable curled-up position on the floor, jammed up against the curve of the opposite wall and the bulkhead next to him. The other three resumed their positions at the ends of the facing rows of seats, guns aimed at the rest of the prisoners, and especially at Ben.

Khosa nodded to himself in satisfaction, holstered his revolver and returned to the cockpit. His orders were clear. *If they try any of their tricks, the boy dies.* As if he really had been able to read their thoughts and predict their intentions down to the last detail.

It was uncanny. Ben was shaken by it.

Jeff looked at Ben with a 'what now?' expression.

Ben shook his head. *Stand down. Mission aborted.* Their one chance had come, and now it was gone again. There was no longer anything they could do, except sit very still, and wait to find out what Khosa planned for them, and hope that another chance might come their way. That didn't look very likely right now.

The helicopter thudded on.

An hour passed. Ben kept his eye on the cockpit and

noticed the way the pilot's head kept dipping, as if he was anxiously checking his gauges. Ben could guess which gauge in particular. The chopper must be literally running on fumes by now. And they must have passed over the Somali coastline by now, too, although there was no way to tell from where he sat. All he could see through the cockpit windows up ahead was clear blue sky.

Ben was still counting the minutes a little while later when he saw Khosa, up front, turn to the pilot and say something. He was pointing through the glass. The pilot nodded and they seemed to exchange a few words.

The chopper began to descend. The view through the windscreen changed from open clear sky to an arid and endless semi-desertified rock-strewn landscape dotted here and there with sparse, sun-withered vegetation. They had passed over the coast, that was for sure. They were some indeterminate distance inland, apparently far from any kind of civilisation, which in Somalia accounted for the vast majority of the country's land mass.

Minutes later, the helicopter finally touched down. There was a bump as the skids settled on solid ground. Back on land again for the first time since driving Geedi's Land Cruiser off the beach and into the sea at Hobyo. For Jude and his fellow *Andromeda* crew survivors, it was their first landfall since Djibouti. But there wasn't one of them who wouldn't rather still be drifting at sea aboard their raft with only sharks for company.

The chopper pilot began shutting everything down. The screech of the turbine slackened to a roar, then to a rumble. Khosa's men burst into action, over-enthusiastically pointing their weapons here and there as they jabbered in Swahili. The fat one with the shotgun yanked open the side hatch. Searing-bright sunlight flooded into the Puma. 'Up! Up!' he yelled in English, jerking his big black autoloader at the prisoners. The nose picker and the skinny one standing guard over Jude seized him by the arms and hauled him to his feet.

The rotors were winding gradually to a standstill as the seven prisoners were made to disembark at gunpoint. Condor was just too sick to jump down unaided from the edge of the hatch. Ben and Jeff took charge of helping him down to the ground. Within moments, the glaring white heat of the late afternoon sun was already sticking their T-shirts to their backs. The air was still and oppressive and almost too thick to breathe. After the shade and cool of the draughty aircraft it was like stepping into a kiln.

'Hurry! You hurry!' the fat soldier yabbered impatiently at them, looking as if he wanted to loose off a whole magazine of twelve-gauge buckshot.

'Tell that bastard if he doesn't get out of my face, I'm going to skin him and wear him as a fucking wetsuit,' Jeff said between clenched teeth as they carried Condor down from the edge of the hatch and set him carefully on his feet.

'Ten sizes too big for you,' Tuesday said.

Ben said nothing, but gave the fat soldier a look that made him back off a step.

The Puma had landed inside a large compound that at first glance appeared to Ben to be a deserted government installation or military base. The ground was pounded earth that had been levelled flat and cleared of rocks, everything lightly covered with a layer of sandy dust blown in from the deserts of the north. Roughly in its centre, arranged into two strung-out blocks either side of a long, broad avenue like a street, there stood a dozen or so cinder-block buildings of different sizes and in different states of repair ranging from more or less undamaged to crumbling ruin. The wider compound was a stretched-out rectangle, maybe a hundred metres across at its narrowest, and maybe three times as long. Its outer perimeter was ringed with sagging wire mesh hung from concrete posts and topped with curls of razor wire. Outside the fence, the rocky ground stretched out flat to infinity, dotted here and there with sparse clumps of bush and the odd stunted-looking tree standing sad and alone.

At some time in its history the place could have been a base for government troops, or for one of the many rebel factions that had been vying for power in Somalia during the country's civil war years. But, much like the hopes of most of those same factions that they could create from the ashes of war a better, happier Somalia for themselves and their children, it had been abandoned years ago and was on the fast track to becoming completely derelict. The largest of the buildings had a long, windowless side wall that was as heavily pocked and bombarded with so many bullet craters that it resembled the lunar surface. Africa was full of walls like that, where you could only guess at how many poor souls, the young with the old, had been lined up and then executed by firing squad.

Khosa's Puma wasn't the only aircraft on the ground within the compound's perimeter. A second and a third helicopter rested on their skids a short distance away, parked in ragged single file close to the buildings on one side of the broad beaten-earth avenue. They had got there long enough ahead of the Puma for their rotors to have stopped turning, the heat shimmer from their engines to have faded away and their heavily armed occupants to disembark and hang around waiting for their commander to arrive.

Ben's guess had been right when he'd thought Khosa wouldn't have undertaken a search of a vast spread of ocean with a single aircraft. He'd evidently marshalled his whole private air force. Which, even by African standards, was nothing to write home about.

The choppers were a matched pair of antique Bell Iroquois that looked as if they'd been in service through the whole of the Vietnam war and gone on to see heavy action in every African conflict of the last forty or so years. They were in even worse shape than the Puma, and seemingly just as low on gas after what must have been a long, intensive search launched from the moment that Khosa had reached shore in the MOB lifeboat. The fourth vehicle in sight was a battered commercial truck with a ripped canvas soft-top and oversize wheels. It too was parked alongside the buildings, tucked in to the side of the avenue with its rear backed up close to the leading Iroquois. Hitched up behind the truck was a long trailer with a pair of large, rust-streaked metal tanks bolted to its flatbed, which Ben realised was a trans-portable fuel bowser for the choppers. A rubber hose was connected between the nozzle on the fuel bowser and the first Iroquois. A motorised pump was roaring and grinding away. The rubber hose was twitching and pulsing on the hard-packed dirt like some bloated snake as fuel flowed through to the helicopter's tanks. Some of the men were attending to the refuelling. Others lounged nearby, talking and joking among themselves and smoking cigarettes with reckless disdain for the flammable fumes Ben could smell all the way from where he was watching.

In his time Ben had seen a lot of military units that could have been described as 'irregular'. Spit-and-polish parade-ground perfection and exact adherence to regulations meant little to him in the real world, because some of those irregular units had contained the best fighting men anyone could wish to have on their side, or fear to have as their enemy. He'd seen Delta Force guys on operations in Sudan and

Afghanistan who looked like bearded hobos. SAS operatives in deep-cover missions in the Middle East whom you couldn't tell apart from the insurgents they were hunting. He'd been one of those men himself, in another life.

But there was a line. Irregular on one side, tin-pot on the other. On the right side of the line it didn't matter how the soldiers looked, because underneath they were all about iron discipline and unflinching professionalism. Men you could stake your life upon in even the direst of circumstances. On the wrong side of the line, they were just a disorganised rabble that would crumble into chaos at the first shot fired.

And Khosa's unit was exactly that: an undisciplined, untrained, unsoldierly bunch of clowns with guns. Ben had seen it during the storming of the container ship. He was seeing it now. Most of the men were draped in bandoliers of gleaming pointed rifle cartridges looped diagonally around their torsos or draped around their necks like a kind of twenty-first-century lion-tooth necklace. Wraparound Ray-Bans and mirrored aviator shades were pretty much standard issue in this squadron, along with the gold chains and gold teeth on display when they laughed, which they were doing a lot of. Several had clusters of grenades fixed to their vests like bunches of strange fruit. Others had machetes thrust into their belts, like pirate cutlasses of old, or dangling sheathed from leather baldrics slung over their shoulders. In a nod to proper military dress a few were wearing red berets, and several had the four-colour DPM combat jackets of the pattern Ben had seen on Kenyan UN-affiliated peacekeeping troops in Sierra Leone, back in the day.

But even a tin-pot bunch of clowns with guns were dangerous, if there were enough of them. Worse than dangerous.

Ben did a quick head-count. He could see eleven of the enemy around the Bells, plus four more around the truck. Plus the five soldiers from the Puma, plus the pilot, plus Khosa himself, made twenty-two. Not counting any who might be inside the buildings. Not one man he could see wasn't armed with some variety of automatic weapon. Mostly Kalashnikovs, naturally, which in their tens of millions were the most abundant piece of hardware in Africa; a few American M16s, a few ancient FNs, a couple of Uzi submachine guns, plus a couple of heavy machine guns. It all added up to an awful lot of bullets that would be coming their way, if any of the prisoners made any rash moves.

Not good. Not the most sensible thing at this point.

Then as Ben watched, Khosa jumped down from the co-pilot side of the Puma's cockpit and went to meet his troops.

Chapter 39

The crews from the two Bell Iroquois and the men by the fuel truck all turned as Khosa made his appearance. He strode across the avenue between the rows of buildings, kicking up clouds of dust with his boots. As he neared the gathered crowd of his men, he reached into his pocket and brought out the diamond in its leather pouch for all to see. He held it high in the air like a trophy and yelled 'I have it! You see? I have it!'

His men greeted him like a conquering hero returning from a victorious military campaign. Laughter and yells and whoops of triumph echoed around the compound, and a few did the tin-pot army thing of stabbing their rifles straight up like spears and loosing off a string of shots in celebration. The crackle of the gunfire sounded hollow and flat in the oven-dry air.

'Are you all right?' Ben asked Jude, squeezing his shoulder.

Jude gave a nod and managed a smile. 'I'm fine,' he replied. 'I never really thought they were going to shoot me. Just playing around, acting tough. I wasn't worried.'

'Nor was I,' Ben lied. 'It'll all be fine. Just you wait and see.'

'Move! Move!' barked a voice behind them. It was the fat soldier again, joined now by the skinny one and the nose picker, jabbing gun muzzles at them and motioning urgently towards the buildings.

Jeff pointed a warning finger at the fat one. 'Hey. You. Back off. I'm telling you. Before I ram that shotgun down your throat so hard it'll come out of your arse, butt end first.'

'I wouldn't provoke them, Jeff,' Tuesday advised him with a frown. 'Especially chubby cheeks there. He's just itching to blow us away, first chance he gets.'

Gerber and Hercules each had one of Condor's arms, without which the sick man couldn't have remained upright for long. 'What the hell is this place anyway?' Gerber said. 'Why'd they bring us here?'

Hercules nodded grimly towards the largest of the buildings, the one with the heavily bullet-cratered wall. 'You blind, homes? Don't you see that wall right there? It's a mother-fuckin' execution yard, is what it is. They ain't takin' us inside. They's gonna line our asses up along that there wall and put us down like a buncha dogs.'

'We're not dead yet,' Jeff said.

'Move! Move! You walk!' the fat soldier barked, urging them on. Then, scowling at Condor, 'What wrong with him?'

'He needs a doctor,' Ben told him in Swahili. 'Either leave him alone or go and fetch one, right now.'

'No doctor! No doctor!'

'Then get us some water,' Ben told him. 'For God's sake, these men are thirsty.'

'No water! No water!'

'Yeah, right.' Hercules shook his head. 'No doctor, no water, 'cause why waste it on a dead man? This is it, my friends. End of the line, I'm tellin' you. But not for all of us.'

Releasing Condor's arm for a moment, Hercules opened

up the flap of his baggy jacket pocket and let Murphy clamber out onto his hand. Hercules raised his arm up high.

'Go, Murph. Get out of here. Go!'

The parrot blinked at Hercules, then flapped its wings and took off. Hercules watched it go, nodding wistfully to himself.

Then the boom of the fat soldier's shotgun cut through the desiccated air like a grenade blast. The flying bird exploded in a cloud of feathers. Murphy's mangled carcass dropped to the earth floor of the compound. Laughing, the fat soldier walked over to it and crushed what was left of it into the dirt with the heel of his boot.

That was the last thing the fat soldier would be doing for a while. Because when he turned back round to grin at the prisoners, he was met by Hercules's ham-sized fist coming at him like a wrecking ball with two hundred and fifty pounds of muscle behind it. The punch spread his nose into a bloody pulp across his face and slammed him hard to the earth. With a roar of pure rage, Hercules was about to finish the guy off with a stamp to the head when Jeff and Tuesday rushed forwards and grabbed Hercules by the arms to restrain him.

'You want to die, big man?' Jeff said in his ear. 'Keep it up.'

'Gonna die anyway. Fuck'm! Fuck'm all!'

The fat soldier was stone unconscious. His comrades were all yelling and screaming and jabbering and waving their guns. Khosa turned to see what was happening. More of his men came running. In two seconds, Hercules was surrounded by rifle muzzles. Ben, Jude, Jeff and Tuesday stood shoulder to shoulder with him. Ben eyed the nearest yelling African and got ready to make a grab for his rifle. If this was how it was going to end, then so be it. You could have death, or you could have glory, but sometimes you had to settle for both at once.

Then Khosa shouted, 'Stop! Hold your fire!'

The circle of guns backed off and opened up to lead the way.

The seven prisoners were marched towards the large building. Hercules shooting glares of grief-stricken hatred at every man who dared come within punching distance. Jude helping Gerber to steady Condor on his feet. Ben and Jeff glancing at each other and both wondering the same thing. Why had Khosa stayed his men?

Ben was worried. Because he had a feeling he knew the answer.

Hercules had been wrong. The soldiers didn't line them up along the wall to be shot, but instead prodded and shoved them inside the building. It was a bare one-room shell inside, long and low, cool and dark and dank. The compacted earth floor was littered with broken glass and garbage, but most of all it was littered with empty cartridge casings. Piles of them, two or three deep in places, trodden into the dirt. Ben felt them underfoot as he stepped inside and instantly knew what they were, even without looking. Just as he knew that the fired shells would be mostly concentrated at one end of the room. Just as he knew why, without needing to peer into the shadows to examine the far wall and make out the craters that scarred the inside of the blockwork as well as the outside.

Bad things had happened here. Maybe even worse things than could be done out in the open of the compound. The earth floor had soaked up the stench of it. The indelible scent of death from the terrible, inhuman atrocities that he could imagine taking place on this spot. And perhaps some that he didn't want to imagine.

Ben wasn't surprised. It was all pretty much what he expected, and the reason could be summed up in the same three neat little letters he'd been running through his mind while observing Khosa's soldiers. *T.I.A.*

The acronym was a wry old saying often repeated all over this continent, by people who knew the score. To remind others that things here didn't work the way they did elsewhere. To encourage them never to forget that when you set foot in this land you were suddenly in a very different place, where you had to forget everything you thought you knew about the world and the people in it.

T.I.A. This Is Africa.

All that really needed to be said. If you knew, you'd get it. If you didn't, you soon would.

The tall, broad figure of the commander filled the doorway, silhouetted against the dust-hazed light from outside. His booted feet braced a little apart, hands clasped against the small of his back, chest thrust proudly outwards. He nodded to his men, and they drew back from the prisoners. He walked into the building. More of his soldiers crowded through the doorway in his wake and spread out behind him with drawn weapons and scowling faces. Khosa himself was wearing a contented smile. As well a man should be, with an incalculable fortune in precious stones bulging his pocket and his enemies subdued and powerless before him.

'I am General Jean-Pierre Khosa,' he said to them. 'Welcome to my army.'

Chapter 40

It was what Ben had been afraid Khosa was going to say. Why else hadn't he ordered them to be killed after he'd got the diamond, or left them to die of thirst on their raft, or let his men shoot them to pieces after what Hercules had just done to one of their comrades?

Ben took a deep breath. So now his suspicions were confirmed. He had to tell himself it wasn't the end of the world. There were worse things than this, torture and execution being two of them. But there weren't many.

Gerber was the only one of the seven who spoke in the stunned silence. 'You gotta be kidding.'

Khosa turned to look at him. His smile had gone. He didn't look at all as if he was kidding, and he didn't look like someone used to being challenged or questioned, either. His men flashed glances at one another. A couple of them repressed grins. They knew their commander's ways. They were looking forward to what would happen next.

Ben was thinking the same thing they were. *Keep your mouth shut, you bloody fool.*

Khosa walked slowly over to Gerber, stepping close until their faces were just inches apart. Except Khosa was a good four inches taller, so he was looking down and Gerber was looking up. Khosa's eyes seemed to bore deep into him. Gerber swallowed. He couldn't maintain the eye contact. He looked down at his feet and cleared his throat nervously.

'This one is very old,' Khosa pronounced after a long silence. 'His legs are bandy, his belly is round and his beard is white. I have no use for a weak old man.' He turned to his men. 'And he looks like a goat. Do you not think he looks like a goat?'

The men nodded and murmured their concurrence with the General's wise opinion that the old man did indeed look just like a goat. Khosa seemed pleased. He gave a low chuckle. 'Goats are for eating,' he declared loudly. 'They are animals to be slaughtered. For what do I need a goat man in my army?'

Gerber kept looking down at his feet. He was gulping and sweating profusely.

Ben had to speak out. 'He's a veteran of the American armed forces. A former non-commissioned officer of the United States Marine Corps. Marines don't get weaker with age. They get tougher. He's a more worthy warrior than half your men put together, General. Do yourself a favour.'

Gerber looked at Ben in horror. Ben raised an eyebrow back at him. *I just saved your life, old fellow.*

Khosa pursed his lips thoughtfully. 'That is interesting. United States Marines. Interesting.' He considered Gerber a few moments more, then nodded. 'We will see about you, Goat Man. Yes, we will see.'

Khosa moved up the line, hands still clasped behind his back. The senior officer inspecting his troops. Next he stopped at Hercules. Now it was Khosa who had to look up. Hercules was shaking, but not for the same reason as Gerber. He looked ready to tear Khosa's head off.

'This one is very dangerous,' Khosa said. 'Perhaps we

should not take a chance with him. Or perhaps he may still be of use to us. I have not decided.'

The guards thought this was funny, but nobody laughed too loudly.

Khosa moved along the line. Now he reached Jude, and smiled down at him with a look that could have been mistaken for benevolence if everyone in the room hadn't known better. 'He is a fine boy,' Khosa said. He grinned at the soldiers. 'Do you not agree he is a fine boy?'

The soldiers all readily agreed that he was.

'Yes, yes,' Khosa chuckled. 'Did I not tell you we would meet again soon, White Meat?'

'Go to hell,' Jude said, staring Khosa straight back in the eye. 'I'm not a boy. And I'm not anybody's meat.'

Khosa boomed with laughter. 'I like you, White Meat. You have *changarawe*. In my country, this means "guts". I need men with guts.'

Khosa moved on. He stopped at Tuesday, scrutinised him long and hard and then passed on without comment.

Next Jeff. Jeff stared back at him with calm fury in his eyes. 'This one is interesting too,' Khosa said. 'Look how he defies me. Many men would be very frightened of such a man. What is your name?' he asked Jeff.

'Dekker,' Jeff said. 'Remember it.'

Khosa narrowed his eyes and the terrible scars on his face crinkled like rubber. 'Do you think I am frightened of you, Dekker?'

Jeff said nothing.

'Are you frightened of me, Dekker?'

Jeff said nothing.

'You will be,' Khosa said. 'Soon, you will be.'

Condor had been standing unaided too long. His knees gave way under him and he collapsed to the earth floor. He gave a heave and then lay still, his arms folded under him and one leg splayed outward.

'What is the matter with this one?' Khosa demanded, pointing down at the unconscious man.

Ben spoke out again. 'He has a severe concussion. He was injured when our ship went down. He needs a doctor, and rest. He'll be fine in a few days. He's a good man.'

'He does not look fine to me,' Khosa said, peering down. 'Concussion. I know all about this. He does not need a doctor. I will test him myself.'

What happened next was a surreal parody of a medical examination. Khosa crouched down next to Condor, leaned close to his ear and asked, 'What is your name?'

Condor made no reply. Not a sound. His eyes were closed and he barely even appeared to be breathing.

Khosa looked up. 'He does not know his name,' he said with a look of consternation that Ben couldn't tell was real or put on. 'Who is the president of your country?' Khosa asked Condor.

No response.

Khosa looked up. 'He does not know who the president is?'

'He's unconscious,' Ben said. 'Give the man a chance.'

Khosa grunted. Then asked Condor, 'Now tell me. Look at me. Who am I?'

Once more, Condor gave no response. His eyelids opened a glimmer, then closed again.

'How can he not know who I am?' Khosa said, straightening up and shaking his head with what Ben now believed was genuine incredulity. 'It is very serious. The man has brain damage. You do not need to be a doctor to know this.'

'With respect, General,' Ben said, choosing his words cautiously. 'It's just a grade three concussion.'

Khosa shook his head once more, gravely. 'He is a cripple. No. How do you say? He is a vegetable. I have no use for a vegetable in my army. This,' he declared, pointing down at Condor, 'is not acceptable.'

Then Khosa signalled to his men. 'Kill him.'

'You can't do that,' Ben said. He took one step towards Khosa and half a dozen Kalashnikov rifles instantly snapped in his direction, and he froze before he could take a second step.

'Are you telling me what I can and cannot do, soldier?' Khosa asked in a voice silk-lined with menace.

'Please,' Gerber said. 'You want to kill someone, then kill me. I'm old. Just like you said. I'm no use to anyone.'

Khosa laughed. 'Maybe you are right, Goat Man. Perhaps afterwards we kill you too. What do you think?'

And then they dragged Condor into the middle of the floor and got started on him.

Ben had seen plenty of men meet a bad end before now. He'd witnessed ugly, brutal death up close and personal, more times than he cared to remember. But he'd never seen anything like this. And he never wanted to see anything like it again.

Chapter 41

Condor didn't regain consciousness right away. Not when the four men grabbed him by the wrists and ankles and hauled him like a sack of rice across the floor. Not when they rolled him over on his back, and not when all four of them drew their machetes from their belts and stood around him in a circle, grinning down at him with glints of dental gold catching what little light was inside the building.

But when the first chopping blade cut into his flesh, the pain and shock jolted Condor out of his semi-coma and he started to scream.

The screaming went on for several minutes. It could have been much quicker, but Khosa's men were experts in prolonging things.

Lou Gerber sank to his knees and vomited. Jude had his eyes screwed shut and his fingers in his ears to block out the chopping sounds and the awful tortured wailing. Hercules had his head bowed with his chin on his chest and his big fists clenched and trembling at his sides. Even Jeff had to look away. Tuesday watched it all from beginning to end, unable to tear his gaze away, as if frozen into a trance of horror.

Ben's eyes stayed on General Jean-Pierre Khosa the whole time.

The blades kept rising and falling and hacking and chopping in the hands of the silent killers. Condor's screams reached a sickening pitch that didn't even sound human any more. Then, mercifully but much, much too long afterwards, they died to a gurgling whimper. Then finally to nothing.

By the time Khosa's four men stepped away, panting with exertion and mahogany-shined with sweat and sheathing their bloody blades, Condor wasn't Condor any more. He was an unrecognisable heap of diced meat and exposed innards and separated body parts and tattered shreds of clothing at the centre of a huge dark stain that soaked deep into the earth.

Gerber was curled up on his knees with his arms wrapped around himself, racked with sobbing. 'Tell the goat man to stand,' Khosa ordered, pointing at him. Slowly, very slowly, Ben and Jeff took Gerber's arms and gently pulled him upright. Gerber stood bent and bowed, suddenly a very old man.

'I want you to look,' Khosa said, swivelling his pointing finger away from Gerber and towards the remains of Condor. 'Look, and remember. This is what happens to men who do not make the grade in my army.'

None of them did look, but they would always remember.

It's nothing next to what will happen to you, Ben was thinking. The stench of death and vomit in the building was sharp and acrid and he had to control his own desire to throw up. He put a hand on Jude's shoulder. Jude's muscles were as tight as rope and his skin felt cold through the damp material of his T-shirt.

'And now,' Khosa said brightly, spreading his arms wide like a TV conjuror who'd just wowed his audience with a spectacular trick, 'the show is over. I am sure that my new recruits are hungry and thirsty. We have a long journey ahead of us and I want all my soldiers to have their strength.'

Seven prisoners had gone into the building. Six came out. Now it was Gerber who needed to be held by the arm to steady him as he walked, like a survivor pulled unscathed but badly shaken from the rubble of an earthquake. His eyes were glazed and he was still trembling violently. Ben was trembling too, not with shock but with rage. He couldn't look at Jeff. He knew that if he did, that if they exchanged even the slightest glance, the two of them would do something reckless. Nobody spoke. Nobody could find words to say what they were feeling.

Khosa strode out ahead of them and went off in the direction of the fuel truck to attend to whatever business he needed there. A V-formation of his soldiers trailed closely in his wake, including the four who had just finished hacking a sick, defenceless man to death. Now they were back to their regular duty, until the next time. The General's personal guard, rifles held in the low-ready position as if expecting a horde of assassins to attack the perimeter at any moment.

A larger group of soldiers led by the nose picker escorted the prisoners across a stretch of open ground to another long, low, windowless building on the same side of the avenue. The prone body of the fat soldier that Hercules had laid flat was no longer there. He'd either managed to crawl away, or he'd been dragged away. The only remaining sign of him was a patch of blood on the dusty ground. Ben gave it a brief glance and then looked away. He'd seen enough blood-soaked earth today.

But however sickened he might have felt by what they'd all just witnessed, the smell of cooking wafting out of the open doorway as they approached the building made Ben feel dizzy. He couldn't remember the last time he'd eaten anything.

This building wasn't in much better condition than the first, but at least there were no dismembered bodies inside. Ben was beginning to realise that Khosa's unit had adopted the derelict compound as a forward operating base away from home, wherever home was. Ben's army unit had set up camp in a hundred similar locations in a dozen countries. The avenue between the buildings most likely served as a rough kind of drill or assembly ground. One of the buildings either side of it was probably being used as a barracks hut for the men. The best of them was presumably the CO's personal quarters, while the worst of them would be the camp latrines.

This one was being used as a makeshift cookhouse and mess, Africa-style. The building's dank, dark interior was dimly lit by oil lamps hanging from nails in the walls. Some wooden tables and benches had been knocked up out of whatever bits of timber had been lying around. A large battered cauldron of some kind of homogenous brown stew was bubbling and simmering on a portable stove. The smell of the food was mingled with the petroleum fumes of what-ever fuel the stove was burning up, and the unmistakable oily stink of paraffin lamps being run on diesel. A fog of smoke drifted and swirled overhead.

They were made to sit at a table. Guns surrounded them. Not the most comfortable mess facilities Ben had ever seen, but marginally better than the slaughterhouse they'd just come from. The nose picker marched over to their table carrying an aluminium water canteen, which he slammed down on the tabletop in front of them. 'You drink.'

Ben picked it up, unscrewed the nozzle and tasted the water first, to ensure it was fit for consumption. It was, just about. 'Go easy,' he told Jude as he passed the canteen to him. 'Take it in small sips or you'll be sick.' Standard SAS survival advice to any trooper who had been deprived of water for too long.

Jude refused the water, even though his lips were parched and cracked from dehydration. He took the canteen from Ben and passed it across to Gerber. Gerber ignored the offer and kept doing what he was doing, which was staring emptily at the tabletop like a man who'd just been told he had inoperable cancer.

'Drink it, Lou, for God's sake,' Jude said strongly. 'You want to end up like Condor?'

Gerber flinched at the words. He shot Jude a hesitant glance. Then slowly reached out with a hand that was still shaking from traumatic shock, took the canteen and raised it to his mouth for a few choking sips. He wiped the nozzle with his hand and then passed it to Hercules.

'I won't take water from these motherfuckers,' Hercules said, crossing his huge arms and leaning back on the bench. 'Not one solitary drop. I'll die first.'

'Then the rest of us know who we can rely on,' Ben said. 'Or not. If you want to live, you're one of us. If you don't, you're on your own. That's how things are going to work between us from now on. Because we need to be able to depend on each other one hundred and ten percent if any one of us has a chance of getting out of this alive. We need to be strong for each other. We need to be a team. And team members all drink from the canteen, or they get left behind. I want you on my team, Hercules. What do you say, Jeff?'

'Damn right,' Jeff growled. 'Every inch of the way.'

'And me,' Tuesday said.

'Your choice,' Ben said. 'Live or die. Starting now.'

Hercules stared at him. He nodded. Took the canteen and drank from it, spluttered and sighed and smacked his lips and passed it on. The canteen went all around the table. Jude was the last to drink.

When the canteen was empty, the nose picker came back over to the table carrying a mess tray. He banged it down in the middle. On it were six bowls of the steaming concoction from the cauldron. A tin spoon had been stabbed into the centre of each bowl and stood upright in the thick stew.

'I hope this guy's not expecting a tip for service like this,' Jeff said. 'He could get a job at the greasy spoon caff I used to go to in Islington.'

'You eat,' the nose picker said, jabbing a finger at the bowls.

Ben peered at the food. It was a thick, glutinous, lumpy morass of boiled-down beans and some kind of shredded dark meat.

'It is goat,' the nose picker said. He smiled and pointed at Gerber. 'Like him.'

The rest of the soldiers thought this was hysterically funny. Laughter filled the mess hut.

'I'm not hungry,' Jude said.

'Nor me,' Hercules growled. 'And if I was, I wouldn't touch this shit nohow.'

Normally, Gerber would have waded right in there with a crack about Hercules's cooking. He said nothing.

Ben grabbed a bowl off the tray and slid it across the table towards himself. Snatched up the spoon and took a mouthful. The trick was not to think too much about how it tasted, or what it might contain apart from goat and beans. He chewed and swallowed and shovelled up another steaming spoonful. Jeff grabbed a bowl and dived in, eating hungrily. Tuesday hesitated, then followed their example.

Jude watched the three of them in horror. 'How can you eat? After we just saw Con— after what just happened?'

'I'd advise you to get it down you,' Ben said between spoonfuls. 'Number one rule is, eat when you can, drink when you can, sleep when you can. Your future trainers in Special Forces will tell you the same thing.'

Jude made no reply.

'I went to Sweden once,' Jeff said through a mouthful of stew. 'If you can swallow their *surströmming*, you can swallow this stuff. It's really not all that bad.'

'Everyone eat,' Ben urged them. 'Khosa's right when he says we're going to need our strength. Like he said, this isn't the end of the line. We have a trip ahead of us.'

'Where is he taking us?' Jude asked.

'Beats me,' Jeff said.

'We'll find out soon enough,' Tuesday said.

Jude reluctantly took a small spoonful of stew and ate it, pulling a face. 'I'm not waiting. I want to know.' He stabbed the spoon back into the bowl and turned to face the nose picker, who was standing over them like a kennel-hand at feeding time. 'Hey, you. What's this journey we're being taken on?' Jude asked him.

'The General is bringing you home,' the nose picker replied with a grin that was more like a sneer. 'Long, long way. Very far from here.'

'Well, there's your answer,' Jeff said.

But it wasn't good enough to satisfy Jude. 'Home? What's home?' he said to the nose picker. 'Hey. Oi. Didn't you hear me? I asked you where your so-called general is taking us.'

'Watch it, Jude,' Ben said softly. There was a ripple of annoyance passing through the crowd of soldiers, and too many Kalashnikovs pointing at Jude for him to start getting arsy.

'Ask him yourself, White Meat,' the nose picker said.

The soldiers filtered aside as their commander appeared

in the doorway and walked into the mess hut. Khosa strode up to the table. 'I am pleased to see you eating. The food is to your liking?' He laughed, then waved a hand at Ben as if to order him to stand. Ben ignored him, scraped up the last spoonful of stew from his bowl and took his time eating it. Only when he'd swallowed it did he lay down his spoon and slowly rise to his feet.

'Come with me, soldier,' Khosa said. 'I wish to speak to you. Alone.'

Chapter 42

Jude, Jeff, Tuesday, Gerber and Hercules all watched in silence as Ben followed Khosa towards the doorway. The General paused to snap a command at the soldiers in Swahili. 'Guard them closely. Especially the boy.'

Outside, the sun was sinking and cooling a little as evening set in. Ben's T-shirt didn't immediately stick to his skin, and he didn't have to shade his eyes with his hand. The four men acting as Khosa's personal guard formed a tight semi-circle behind him, their weapons pointing at his back. Khosa led the way from the mess hut, across the beaten-earth avenue and past the parked choppers and the fuel truck to the smallest of the buildings on the far side. It was the one in the best state of repair, the one Ben had guessed a unit using this place as a forward operating base would designate as the CO's temporary quarters.

He'd been right about that, though the place was less than palatial. Like the others, the building consisted of a single, unpartitioned room. It smelled of mildew, stale cigar smoke and another tangy odour that was familiar to Ben but which he couldn't put his finger on. The floor was concrete, the walls bare. It was minimally furnished, even by military standards. There was no bunk. Maybe Khosa didn't sleep here, Ben thought. Maybe he never slept at all. A folding metal table was set up in one corner, with a folding metal chair next to it. On the table lay a walkie-talkie handset, a GPS navigation device, a half-smoked Cohiba Gran Corona resting in a carved ebony ashtray, and the assorted rods and brushes and solvents of a cleaning kit for a handgun. Now Ben recognised the odd smell.

'Hoppe's Number Nine,' Khosa said grandly, picking up a small labelled bottle and brandishing it as though it were the elixir of life. 'The finest bore-cleaner in the world, manu-factured since 1903, specially imported from America. I never travel without it. It removes all trace of powder fouling, lead and copper and brings everything up so nicely. Do you not say so, soldier?' To make his point he drew the magnum revolver from his holster, twirled it cowboy-style around his finger and gazed lovingly at the bright, burnished stainless steel of his cherished weapon.

'I'll have to make a note to get myself some for Christmas,' Ben said.

Khosa chuckled. 'For Christmas. That is a good one. You know, soldier, you have upset me very much. This was a matched pair of Colts. Custom engraved and specially accur-ised, with handles of genuine mammoth ivory. Now I only have one, thanks to you. But I am prepared to find it in my heart to forgive you.'

'That's awfully decent of you, General,' Ben said.

Khosa twirled the Colt back into his holster and stepped towards Ben, until he was less than a foot away. He was an inch taller than Ben, maybe two. Ben's shoulders were broad from the regular routine of two hundred press-ups a day that he'd stuck to for years, but Khosa's were broader by at least four inches. He was a powerful man and an imposing presence, even more so up close. The horribly scarred face topped it all, like a nightmarish mask from which his wide-set eyes bored penetratingly into Ben's. The temptation was to look away, but Ben had never looked away from a challenge in his life.

Instead, Ben was thinking of how easily he could kill this man. If Khosa was a tiger, Ben was a panther. Ben could have killed him before he even knew he was dead. An elbow to the throat, crushing his trachea. Faster than fast. Then the revolver would be out of the holster and in Ben's hand, and one of those big forty-four-calibre slugs would be on its way to Khosa's brainpan at about fifteen hundred feet per second. One shot was all it would take to end this and go home.

But then Ben thought about the four, or six, or eight high-powered rifles that were pointing at Jude's head at this moment.

Not good. Not wise.

It would have to wait, just a little longer. The time would come.

'You would like to kill me,' Khosa said with a knowing look.

'Whatever gives you that idea?'

Khosa smiled. 'I perceive many things, soldier. It is my gift to understand what goes on inside a man's head. I can see much in you. You are a warrior of great skill, and you do not fear any man. I respect this very much. That is why I wished to talk to you alone. Because you and I have business together.'

'I doubt that,' Ben said.

'Never doubt me,' Khosa said. 'I am a man of my word. What is your name, soldier?'

'Hope. Ben Hope. Not that it's any of your damn business.'

Khosa nodded. 'You are named after a mountain in Scotland. Perhaps this is what makes you strong. Are you from Scotland, soldier?'

'My mother was from Ireland. Not that that's any of your damn business, either.'

'A fine country. I know it very well. This surprises you, I see. You think I am just a stupid, uneducated African peasant, do you not, soldier? You will learn that I am nothing of that kind.'

'Nice place you have here,' Ben said, looking around him. 'Very swish. Like your air force. State of the art. The envy of the world and enough to make any superpower tremble in its boots. I take it you see yourself as some kind of great military leader. But all I see is a murdering sack of lowlife shit in a mongrel uniform. And someone I wouldn't do business with in a thousand years. So whatever it is you have to say, you can save your breath and stick it up your arse instead.'

Khosa's smile dropped. The wide-set eyes seemed to burn with a dark light Ben could almost feel on his face. 'Very few men would speak to me this way. Those who have dared to defy me now lie rotting in the dirt, their bones scattered and chewed by animals.'

'Except this one,' Ben said. 'And that's the way it's going to stay. I'll still be here a long, long time after the world's had the pleasure of forgetting your ugly mug ever existed.'

Khosa boggled at him in utter astonishment. Then he threw his head back and roared with mirth. His laughter boomed and echoed through the building. His whole body shook and doubled up with it. He laughed so hard that he choked and spluttered and had to rest his hands on his knees as tears rolled through the furrows of scar tissue on his cheeks.

'Oh, oh,' Khosa gasped, and wiped the tears away. 'You are a very unusual fellow. Such boldness and insubordination, I have never seen. I should have my men take you out there and put you against a wall and shoot you as a punishment. But there is a time and place for everything. Do you not think?'

'I couldn't agree more,' Ben said.

'And this is not your time. I like you, soldier. Yes, I like you very much. I wish for you to live for many more years. Just as you say.'

'I'm so delighted to hear it,' Ben said. 'But you're wrong about me, General. I'm just a man. I'm not a soldier. Not any more.'

Khosa wiped away the last of his tears and studied Ben intently. 'A man cannot hide what he is. Nobody has ever defeated me the way you did on that ship. You appeared from nowhere. You exploded my boat and killed many of my men. Zolani Tembe was my best fighter, yet you squashed him like a worm.' Khosa clapped his hands together to illustrate the point. 'Three men did this. Three! It takes a special kind of adversary to get the better of me. Tell me, Ben Hope. Your accent is not American. You served in the British army?'

'For a while,' Ben said.

'I knew this must be so. For how many years did you serve?'

'A few.'

'What was your unit? What was your rank?'

'Catering corps,' Ben said. 'I was a pot scrubber. Sometimes they let me make the tea for the troops.'

Khosa eyed him warily, and wagged a finger at him. 'No, no. I think you are lying. Come, tell me the truth.'

Ben eyed him back. 'All right, then. I will tell you the truth. I served with a regiment called 22 Special Air Service. You might have heard of it. Final rank of major.'

'Ah. Much better. This is very acceptable. And you have fought many battles, yes?'

'More than you can count,' Ben said. 'Against much better men than you.'

'And killed many enemies?'

'These days I only kill the ones who deserve it the most,' Ben said.

Khosa chuckled and clapped Ben on the shoulder. 'I will have to watch out, hmm? Now, tell me about Dekker. He is a warrior like you, yes?'

'The best,' Ben said. 'Worth a hundred of your soldiers at least.'

'A hundred. That is many. And this young black man you have in your group. He is African?'

'His name's Tuesday and he's from Jamaica. He also fought with the British army. He was the best sniper they've ever had. He can kill a man from two miles away with a rifle.'

Khosa raised his eyebrows. 'Two miles! This is a man of extraordinary skill.'

Ben had no idea whether his wild claim was anywhere near the truth. He only knew that the more he played up the martial prowess of his companions, the less likely this lunatic might be to have them summarily chopped up into mincemeat.

'And what about the goat man?' Khosa asked. 'Is he really a veteran of the United States Marine Corps, or were you only trying to protect him?'

'He was a staff sergeant,' Ben said. 'In Africa, he'd have been made a colonel.'

'And the big one? You can vouch for him also, or should I have my men kill him? I did not like the way he looked at me.'

'They call him Hercules,' Ben said. 'And he's as strong as his name implies. He could tear this building down with his bare hands. A man like that is worth keeping alive, well fed and well cared for.'

'Hercules,' Khosa repeated thoughtfully. 'From Greek mythology. Interesting. Very interesting.' He looked at Ben. 'It surprises you that I am so educated, yes?'

Ben chose not to reply to the question.

Khosa's eyes twinkled. 'Ah, soldier. I am happy. It is good that we can talk like this, you and me.' He waved a hand towards the doorway. 'We are not ordinary men like the others out there. They are loyal to me, but they have no understanding. They are just mindless vassals who do what I command them.'

'Like hack a defenceless man to death,' Ben said.

Khosa shrugged, as if to brush off such trivial accusations. 'You are speaking about the cripple? I have done him a favour by ending his misery in this way. But I do not think he is your main concern, is he, soldier? You are thinking about the boy. There is a special reason for this. He is your son.'

Chapter 43

'He is your son,' Khosa repeated slowly, as if enjoying the sound of the words. 'Tell me it is not so.'

Ben felt the muscles in his face tighten as if steel hooks, cables and pulleys were reeling them in.

Khosa smiled. 'I know I am right. He has your eyes, soldier. But I see deeper than this. It is what we can see behind the eyes that counts, for that is where we find the essence of a man. He is young, but he has much spirit. Like his father. Come, no more lies. Do not deny it. I can already tell the answer from your expression.'

Ben said nothing.

'It is as I thought,' Khosa said, pleased with himself. 'I told you, nothing can escape me. He is a fine young man. Of course you wish for him to stay alive. There is nothing you would not do to save him.'

'You want to talk,' Ben said, 'then let's talk. You have the diamond. I don't know where it came from, or who that guy Pender took it from, or what kind of crimes he committed to obtain it from them. Whatever the case, none of it was legitimate. Which makes that diamond stolen goods, and means you'll be lucky if you get one percent of its value from whatever fence you try to sell it to. But even one percent of what that thing is worth is enough to make you a very rich man. What can you possibly stand to gain from me that you don't already have or that you can't buy? Why are you doing this?'

Khosa didn't answer immediately. He turned away from Ben and began pacing around the room, hands clasped behind his back, head bowed in deep thought, like a philosopher in search of inspiration while contemplating some abstruse concept of metaphysics. But the greatest inspiration for Khosa at that moment happened to be nestling in his jacket pocket. He paused mid-stride to take out the leather pouch. He drew open the string fastener and rolled the diamond out onto his palm. The light was slowly fading outside, and the interior of the windowless building was growing darker. But the diamond seemed to shine like a lantern on Khosa's hand.

'You ask why I am doing this,' he said, turning back towards Ben. 'The answer is clear. Because when fate smiles on Jean-Pierre Khosa, he takes everything she has to offer. You say I am wealthy, and you are right. Before I had this, I was already a rich man. Now that it is mine, I will be the *richest*. It is true, I cannot sell it on the open market. But that is not your concern, soldier. I am a businessman with many connections. I will be meeting an associate and arranging the sale at a very good price, once we have returned home to my kingdom.'

Ben looked at him. 'Your kingdom.'

Khosa swept his arm towards the south and west. 'You heard me correctly, soldier. My kingdom. It lies a long way away from this worthless desert. There is nothing here but rocks and sand, scorpions and goats. My kingdom is filled with beauty and rivers and forests and mountains. Its soil is fertile, its mines are the richest in the world and its territory is bigger than England, France and Germany all put

292

together. It is a paradise. One that you will see soon, I can assure you. We will cross the Somali border westwards into Kenya. Then across Kenya into Uganda. Then across Uganda into Rwanda. My kingdom lies to the west of there. The beating heart of Africa.'

Ben scanned the map of the continent in his mind. Twenty percent of the planet's total land area, some thirty million square kilometres, home to nearly a billion people and some of the last great wildernesses on earth, divided into countries of a size that many of them made major European states look like tiny principalities. He pictured the journey that Khosa was describing, like a thin red line tracking roughly south-westwards across the map from Somalia across four borders. Skirting the southern edge of Ethiopia before passing through the Great Lakes regions, leaving behind the arid, dusty yellow-scorched plains for the equatorial humidity of dense grasslands and jungle. It was an enormous distance to travel, half the width of Africa, the equivalent of crossing almost the whole of Europe. Closer to two thousand miles than one. Like driving from Le Val to Budapest.

And the journey's end was a place that Ben had been to before. Back when he had made his first unofficial military excursions into Africa the country had gone by its former name Zaire, until the civil war and mass genocide that had spilled over from neighbouring Rwanda finally tore that nation apart in 1997. It was one of the most notoriously unstable, corrupt and violently blood-soaked regions of Africa, with vast tracts that were still generally seen as no-go areas and carefully avoided by anyone not motivated by a deathwish.

The DRC. Democratic Republic of Congo. It was when a country took special pains to include the word 'democratic' in its name that you knew it was anything but.

A paradise, for sure.

'The Congo,' Ben said. 'That's where you're taking us? That's what you call your kingdom?'

'Because it belongs to me,' Khosa said grandly. 'All of it. Or I should say, soldier,' he added, clasping the diamond tightly in his fist, 'it *will* belong to me. And you are going to help me to gain the power that is rightfully mine.' Khosa paused, thought, shifted gears and then added with a sly smile, 'You see, I knew you would come to me. I saw you in a vision. I have been waiting for you, Ben Hope.'

Ben stared at him, but could see nothing but plain earnestness in his eyes. The man was being completely serious.

Khosa's disfigured face was lit up with triumphant joy as he went on, 'And now you have been brought to me, as this diamond has been brought to me. All these things that have happened – that fool Pender and his lies. You and your men, appearing like a vision from the sea. My defeat, and your mercy towards me. The storm that sank your ship and made it possible for me to find you again. You do not see it, because you do not have my gift. But I, Jean-Pierre Khosa, *I* now understand that these things were meant to happen.'

Ben went on staring, not saying anything.

Khosa held the diamond out in front of him like a trophy, and shook it in his fist with a fierce grin. 'And now, with this power that has been given to me, you and I together are going to reclaim what is mine. You and Dekker and Tuesday from Jamaica are going to train my army into such a force that it cannot be defeated by any enemy. Then nothing can stop me from achieving my destiny.'

Chapter 44

Ben said, 'Were you born this crazy, Khosa, or did your mother drop you on your head as a child? Either way, there's a straitjacket and a padded cell out there somewhere with your name stencilled on them.'

Khosa glared at him. 'You speak to me frankly. You have *changarawe*, like your son. But you should also be careful not to strain my tolerance too far. Do you understand?'

'I understand,' Ben said.

'Good,' Khosa said, his expression softening.

'I understand that you're a man of rare vision and exceptional ambition.'

'Yes. That is what I am, soldier.'

'I understand that you enjoy having innocent people put to death in front of you, and strutting about in that uniform pretending to be a general. And that in your twisted fantasies you'd love nothing more than to lead your country to freedom, so that when you've butchered and bribed your way into the presidential palace in Kinshasa and you've covered yourself in phony medals and gold braid, you can add a few more million notches to your belt by slaughtering your own citizens in the streets before you run off like a filthy coward into exile somewhere like every cheap little thug of a dictator before you. The ones that don't end up

295

in front of a UN war crimes court or dangling upside down from a tree with their balls stuffed in their mouths and their throats slashed open by their own henchmen, that is. And you want me to help you on your way to that? Forget it. Not in a thousand years. Next question.'

'You are the one who is forgetting, Ben Hope. I have only to lift this finger, and your son will die.'

'He dies, you die,' Ben said. 'That's what's called an impasse.'

'I do not believe you can kill me so easily as you think.'

'Then I die trying. Which puts the kibosh on your plans, whichever way it goes down. Whatever happens, it's in your interest to keep him alive. I advise you to let us go, Khosa. If you don't, you're inviting more trouble on yourself than you can even begin to imagine. You've been warned. I won't say it again.'

Khosa was speechless for a moment. Then he slapped his thigh and started laughing harder than ever, roaring and booming uncontrollably until the tears were dripping from his chin.

'Such defiance is incredible!' he declared when he could talk again. 'You stand here in my camp, with armed soldiers all around you, and the life or death of your own son in my power, and *you* warn *me*. You are truly the bravest man I have ever known. You are not afraid of death at all.'

'Why be afraid of something I can't change?' Ben said. 'If it happens, it happens. But to die killing you, that would be a pleasure.'

Khosa was impressed. 'This is the creed of the warrior. You should know, I have studied history for many years. Tales of great heroes, like King Leonidas of Sparta who stood with only three hundred men against the might of the whole Greek army at Thermopylae. The Bushido tradition of the

Samurai. The great clans of Scotland. The dog soldiers of the American Cheyenne. Geronimo and Sitting Bull of the Sioux. The Code d'Honneur of the French Foreign Legion. And now there is Ben Hope.'

'That's quite a list,' Ben said. 'Should I be flattered?'

'Do not be modest. If you are still alive now, it is because you have shown me that you have the same virtues that the true warrior has shown through history. The virtue of courage. The virtue of mercy. And the virtue of loyalty. This last virtue, you will now prove to me by becoming my military advisor. You will teach my men these same qualities and make them strong. The training will begin as soon as we reach our home base.'

'All the way to the Congo, in a ratty truck and three antique helicopters that look like they'll fall apart before they've covered half the distance,' Ben said. 'If that's the best you can do to mobilise this army of yours, you're even more deluded than I thought.'

'Do not underestimate me, soldier. This would be a very grievous mistake.'

Khosa carefully replaced the diamond into its leather pouch, and tucked it away safely into his pocket. He looked at the gold Rolex on his wrist. 'I have spoken enough. Come. It is time.'

Ben said, 'Time for what?'

The African smiled, but there was no humour in it. 'Time for me to show you the next part of my plan, soldier. Then you will begin to understand who you are dealing with in Jean-Pierre Khosa.'

Khosa stepped out of the building and into the fading sunlight. Ben followed, with no idea what Khosa was talking about. But whatever it was, Ben didn't like it.

The General's personal guard had assembled outside the

doorway and gave Ben hostile looks as they all walked out across the compound. Ben glanced over at the mess hut and could see no sign of Jude and the others. It worried him to lose sight of them, but he reasoned with himself that they were still in there, eating. Or Jeff and Tuesday eating, and the other three still being stubborn about it, with Jude being the most stubborn of all.

He is young, but he has much spirit. Like his father.

Ben looked away from the mess hut and watched Khosa. He was gazing up at the sky, into the west where the sun was dropping fast towards the horizon, like a giant orange slowly turning to vermillion red as purple and gold streaks of cloud drifted across its swollen disc.

Khosa said, 'Listen.' He cupped a hand behind an ear and cocked his head. He looked around, turning wide eyes on his men, who were all rapt with attention. 'Can you hear it?'

Ben listened, but all he could hear was the chirping of a billion insects from all around, reaching a shrill crescendo in the last hour of daylight. The men all nodded, as if they could hear it too.

Ben had extremely sharp hearing, which he'd depended on more than a few times to save his life. However much he strained his ears, he still couldn't make out anything except the incessant surround-sound chirp-chirp-chirping. He was sure the men were just humouring their leader, out of fear of what he might do to any vassal who appeared to contradict him.

If Khosa really could hear something, Ben thought, he must have the ears of a German shepherd. The aural senses of a bat. Or else, he only imagined he could hear something. Ben wondered about that. Could a crazy person have auditory hallucinations, as well as strange prophetic visions? Ben

298

was no psychiatrist, but he'd crossed paths with a few nutcases in his time. If a disturbed individual could persuade themselves that they could hear voices from inside their heads telling them what to do, or whispers calling their name from the darkness, then Ben reckoned just about anything was possible.

Thirty seconds went by. Khosa stood rooted as a statue, listening and nodding to himself. A full minute. Ben began to wonder how long he was going to keep the show up. Maybe he was getting ready to proclaim, '*Yes, God. I hear Thee. I will endeavour do Thy bidding, oh Lord.*' Then turn around with eyes glowing like an evangelist preacher's and relate to his blinking, staring men what the Almighty had said to His chosen one. Maybe next would come the laying on of hands, or Khosa would suddenly produce snakes from his pockets, for the taking up of serpents in Mark, Chapter Sixteen.

Or maybe Khosa didn't talk to God. Maybe it was the other guy he had conversations with.

But then, Ben was startled. To his amazement, now he *could* hear something, though it was so faint and faraway that it seemed impossible that human ears could have detected it more than a whole minute ago.

The sound was coming out of the west, in the exact same direction towards which Khosa was gazing and nodding. A soft, ever so distant rumbling drone that seemed to emanate from some invisible point in the red-streaked sky. Ben listened hard. He closed his eyes to focus on the sound as it grew clearer and louder. With his eyes shut, he suddenly felt as if he was back on that raft drifting in the middle of the Indian Ocean, desperately straining his ears for the minutest whisper of a sign that rescue was coming.

And then he knew what it was, and opened his eyes.

Chapter 45

'There,' Khosa said, and swung up an arm to point towards the sunset.

It was a moment before Ben spotted the distant speck in the sky, but by then there was already no doubt in his mind what he was going to see up there. The aircraft was still a few miles away, gently dropping altitude as it droned closer. The speck grew larger as they watched, then larger still. Coming right towards them. Even at this distance Ben could tell it was a sizeable plane, a big flying tank of a thing, broad in its wingspan and much larger than Kaprisky's sleek private jet. An aircraft of that size coming in to land in the middle of nowhere, in a desert of rubble and scattered brush miles from any kind of airport, should have been an unreal, improbable sight.

But Ben was realising what he'd missed before.

Now he understood what the disused compound really was. It was much more than just an old abandoned military base for embattled government or rebel forces to hole up in during a civil war nobody talked about any more. It was the lack of any kind of smooth, level, metalled runway that had fooled him into never twigging until now that the place was an airfield. The broad avenue between the facing rows of buildings wasn't any kind of drill or parade ground. It had

300

been hammered out and levelled into a rough landing strip. Nothing like the one that he, Jeff and Tuesday had landed on at Obbia, which looked like Heathrow by comparison. Nothing you could remotely call an airport, not even in African terminology.

And Ben hadn't reckoned either on the kind of plane you could land on a rough, rutted strip of compacted earth in the middle of the arid, rock-strewn arsehole of nowhere.

He hadn't reckoned on a Dakota. Two mistakes in one. He was angry with himself for not thinking of it before.

It was the sound that gave it away, even before he recognised it by sight. Nothing like the ear-ripping high-decibel screech and whistle of an incoming jet. The thrumming, clattering rumble of the approaching plane sounded like a thousand pneumatic drills all pounding away at once. It sounded exactly like what it was, the roar of twin nine-cylinder air-cooled radial piston engines driving a pair of massive three-bladed propellers towards them out of the falling dusk. It sounded like something out of World War Two.

Because it *was* something out of World War Two, literally.

The Douglas DC-3 Dakota, or 'Old Methuselah' as it was often called by the pilots who both loved and hated it, was like no other plane ever built. The first one had rolled off the production line at the Douglas factory in Santa Monica in 1935 and the last one just ten years later at the close of the war. But in that short production period it had become legendary as the most versatile and durable airliner ever made, and quickly found useful service all over the planet. It was the only airliner still flying that could take off and land on runways of dirt and grass, making it the hot ticket for developing countries everywhere. The landing distance it required was much shorter than modern airliners, and could take off in little more than half that. It was also one of the toughest warbirds ever made. It could go anywhere, in any weather. It could fly on one engine if needed. Ben had heard of one US Air Force Dakota during WWII that had been riddled with over three thousand shells from Japanese fighters and not only reached base safely but been put back in service just hours later, patched up with canvas and glue. Despite its supposed maximum passenger load of just thirty-five, a hundred Vietnamese orphans had been crammed on board one Dakota that had scraped out of Saigon under heavy fire during the city's evacuation in 1975.

Ben had only ever seen two of them in his life, one in the air over Sierra Leone many years ago, and another smashed into a mountainside high up in the Hindu Kush, not far from the Khyber Pass near the Afghanistan–Pakistan border, pillaged and looted for anything the local militias could strip out of it and reduced to little more than a skeleton. But he knew that hundreds of these living dinosaurs were still in daily use in Third World countries everywhere even after seventy-odd years of hard service, and that you could still pick up a battered but sturdy example for a couple of hundred thousand US dollars.

Jean-Pierre Khosa had apparently done just that.

Do not underestimate me, soldier. Ben was suddenly beginning to wonder if that was another mistake to add to his account. And he was wondering what other surprises the man had in store. It was a deeply uncomfortable thought.

The Dakota came down low and slow, a huge lumbering monster with the falling sun casting red glints along its fuselage, scarred and battered and dull olive green like the three helicopters in the compound, but dwarfing them completely in size. Over sixty feet long and almost a hundred feet from wingtip to wingtip. Its undercarriage was lowered, those two wheels so huge that they couldn't be fully retracted below its wings, attached to massive hydraulic struts that canted forwards like the legs of an eagle swooping down on its prey.

The Dakota's clattering roar filled Ben's ears, and the hurricane from its propellers and slipstream filled the air with a storm of dust and loose particles of dirt whipped up from the sun-baked ground as it cleared the perimeter fence by a matter of feet and came down to earth in the broad open space between the buildings.

The huge wheels hit the dirt with a jarring crash and an explosion of dust. The aircraft juddered and bounced, the wings slewed at a crazy diagonal angle, and for a second Ben thought the pilot had come in too hard and fast, and that the starboard wingtip was going to plough a massive furrow into the ground and flip the whole plane over and round in a circle and tumble it over end to end, wreaking a giant trail of exploding carnage right through the middle of the compound.

But whoever was at the controls was a cool and experienced hand who must have done this a thousand times before. The Dakota dropped back from its erratic bounce into an even landing, its tail settling, its rear wheel touching down with hardly a bump. The aeroplane roared down the beaten-earth runway with its wings just a few yards clear of the buildings either side, making Ben and Khosa's soldiers step back out of the great slap of wind and cover their eyes and noses against the choking dust. Khosa himself didn't flinch as the giant wing passed right over his head. The Dakota roared on, past the parked helicopters and the fuel truck that Khosa's men had, Ben now realised, tucked in close to the buildings to make way for its landing. The pilot backed off the throttle and the deafening roar of its engines rapidly subsided as the Dakota slowed.

Khosa watched with a beaming smile and his hands on his hips while the plane rolled by for another fifty yards, reached the open ground beyond the buildings and then began to taxi back round on itself in a wide circle, steering by its pivoting rear wheel, barely visible for the clouds of dust swirling around it like smoke. The Dakota rolled to a halt, stones crunching and popping under its gigantic front tyres. The engines shut down with a splutter, first one and then the other. The three-bladed props with their yellow-painted tips and silver nose-cones clattered to a standstill. The drifting dust began to settle back down to earth.

Khosa turned to face Ben, his demon's face split by that beaming white smile of triumph. He pointed at the Dakota.

'You want to know how we will return to my kingdom, soldier?' Khosa said, laughing. 'That is how.'

Ben looked at him. 'I warned you. I hope you listened to me.'

'Say goodbye to the world you have known, soldier. You are mine now. We leave at first light.'

Chapter 46

Serena Beach
Mombasa

From where Eugene Svalgaard was lying fully clothed on the king-size bed, cellphone in hand, he was able to raise his head and peer through the glass doors and out over the balcony and the low-rise cluster of mock-thirteenth-century something-or-other luxury hotel complex to take in the whole mawkish picture-postcard thing that scads of dumb schmucks from all over the world paid good money to come see. Waving coconut palms against the balmy sunset. The surf rolling in over the ribbon of white sand that was the last land eastwards between here and . . . wherever. The hotel manager had told him a lot of couples came here to be married. Ha. Good luck to 'em. The stupid suckers would still be paying for it after they were divorced.

What Eugene was in fact raising his head off the bed to stare at through the glass windows and over the balcony was the infinite stretch of the Indian Ocean beyond. Somewhere out there was his diamond. The only possible reason why he'd have dragged his weary ass all the way to godforsaken fuckin' *Kenya*, for Chrissakes.

The long-distance call over, Eugene tossed the phone away

and closed his eyes to digest the news that Sondra Winkelman in New York had just broken to him. Not good news, but hardly unexpected. It was the confirmation of what he'd already more or less accepted to be the case.

'Well, there it is,' he muttered to himself. 'Shit happens.'

The rotten old harridan had just informed him that the wreckage picked by the navy destroyer USS *Zumwalt* off the Somali coast in the aftermath of the typhoon was now officially confirmed as belonging to the cargo of the MV *Svalgaard Andromeda*. Eighty miles east of where the *Andromeda*'s course should have taken it, the patrolling warship had winched aboard a floating forty-foot shipping container that was half-full of seawater, half-full of soggy electrical equipment bound for Mombasa.

The computers had done the rest. Every container transported anywhere in the world was logged with its own unique BIC code. BIC stood for 'Bureau International des Containers', a horrible bit of Franglais that would have language purists tearing their hair out in outrage, but which was nonetheless the name of the head office located in Paris where all such information was processed. The BIC code of the recovered container had been checked against the Svalgaard Line's own data records, and there was absolutely no doubt any longer that the *Andromeda* was one of several vessels (though none of them anywhere near as large or valuable) that had fallen victim to the monster storm that had wreaked havoc up and down five hundred miles of the Somali coast.

As Sondra had gone on to notify him, the Svalgaard shipping line had already begun the long and painful proceedings to recoup their loss. Insurance company lines were buzzing. Salvage crews were already en route to locate the wreck. Less importantly, but even more of a chore for the Svalgaard executives, also underway was the process of contacting the relatives of the ship's captain and crew to inform them of the tragic news that the vessel had been lost at sea, apparently with all hands. There would be the usual coolly corporate expressions of sympathy and commiseration. *Our thoughts are with you at this terrible time, you'll get over it, they knew the risks, life goes on.* Not necessarily in those exact words, but that was the gist of it. Shit happens.

None of which was allocated much room in Eugene's turbulent thoughts at this moment. He was far too consumed with his own private interests. Over the last few days his mind had been working through a sequence of logical twists and turns that would have bamboozled even him, if he hadn't been so obsessively driven to find his way through the maze. It all went something like this:

If the *Andromeda* had indeed sunk to the bottom of the Indian Ocean with all hands, then the most obvious and immediate conclusion to draw was that Lee Pender had gone down with it. It wasn't the idea of Pender being at the bottom of the ocean that had been giving Eugene heartburn. The guy was a Grade A shitsack and it was very unlikely that a living soul existed who would mourn his passing. What had been knotting Eugene up inside was the idea of the diamond being down there with him. Gone. Lost. Chances of recovery, virtually nil. Barring a miracle.

It got worse.

Because even *if* a professional marine salvage crew did manage to locate the sunken ship somewhere on the ocean bed at some indeterminate point in the future, and *if* one of their divers just happened to find the lost diamond down there among a million tons of wreckage, the possibility of preventing that lucky individual from a) reporting it to the authorities or b) more likely, simply pocketing it for himself, was even more outside Eugene's control than the typhoon that had taken the ship down in the first place.

The way Eugene saw it, in such a case it would be infinitely preferable for the marine salvage diver to just quietly take the damn thing for his own retirement fund. Because *if* the authorities did by chance learn that the world's currently most valuable and therefore hottest piece of stolen property, linked to a notorious quadruple murder, had been discovered on board a Svalgaard ship, and *if* some clever dick managed to put that information together with the little-known but not entirely undiscoverable fact that the ship's owner happened to be one of the world's most avid diamond collectors, then it didn't take much imagination to see how the trail could lead straight back to Eugene's door and wind up with him being locked away for the rest of his life. He'd rather the diamond was never found at all.

But those were only the most obvious conclusions. They weren't the only conclusions. If they had been, Eugene would have been throwing himself out of the window around now. As it happened, he wasn't.

In fact, he was smiling.

Because the glimmer of optimism that had first dawned on him back in Rome had steadily grown stronger since then. That single-minded ray of hope was what had been keeping him going, against all the odds, for one simple reason. Namely, the whole unthinkable worst-case scenario that would have had Eugene flinging himself to his death, or beating his own brains out against the wall, or spending the rest of his days in jail, all depended on Pender having gone down with the ship. But there was a flaw in that assumption. It failed to take into account one very crucial factor, which was the fact of Eugene's prior suspicions back in Rome that his man might be playing a tricksy little game with him.

The weird call on the sat phone. Pender hanging up on him like that. Something not quite right about the way the guy was acting.

If Pender hadn't been a dirty thieving crook, Eugene wouldn't have given him the job in the first place. Then again, the possibility of his being additionally a dirty thieving *double-crossing* crook, one who might try and take the diamond for himself, had been a major source of concern. Though only a temporary one. Soon after that initial panic, it had dawned on Eugene that Pender's double-crossing ways could actually be the best thing to come out of this situation.

Eugene being something of a crook himself, it wasn't hard for him to put himself in Pender's place. If Eugene had been Pender, and if he'd wanted to run out on his employer and grab the rock for himself, then he'd have no intention of being still aboard the ship when it sailed into Mombasa port with his employer there on the dock waiting to meet him. No, he'd want to get off the ship before then, slink off somewhere at sea and disappear, laughing his pants off at how he'd suckered his boss. And for a guy who'd just been paid millions of dollars to pull off a heist and home invasion involving multiple murders, there had to be a thousand ways to get off a ship mid-ocean. You could hire a helicopter to whisk you into the blue. You could arrange a rendezvous with another vessel. You could even escape in the damn lifeboat if you couldn't find another way.

Which potentially changed everything. Because a sneaky conniving double-crossing sonofabitch who'd high-tailed it to a life of wealth and luxury was not at all the same thing as a sneaky conniving double-crossing sonofabitch lying rotting on the ocean bed with Eugene's diamond in his pocket. If Pender had got off the ship before the storm hit, then there was every chance the bastard was still out there somewhere, alive and well.

And if Pender was still out there somewhere, then Eugene could find him. Because Eugene could find anything and anybody. He'd found the diamond, after all. Nothing was impossible, when you had money. More specifically, Eugene himself wouldn't find Pender; rather, he'd get someone else to do the legwork. Someone efficient, dependable and hard as galvanised nails who, for the right price, would scour the earth for as long as it took to sniff the little scumbag out. And who, when he found him, would pin him like an insect to a board and return the diamond to its rightful new owner, with no questions asked. Nobody was more suited to that job than Victor Bronski, and that was precisely why Eugene had called him from Rome to set him on the trail.

And was precisely also the main reason Eugene was smiling, instead of jumping out of the window. Because Sondra Winkelman hadn't been the first person with whom he had spoken on the phone that day.

An hour before she called, Eugene's cell had buzzed and a different voice had spoken to him. Slow, calm, quietly self-assured, infinitely patient. Like the man himself. Ex-NYPD. Ex-FBI. Ex a lot of things that Eugene didn't know about and didn't need to know about. The most diligent, most careful and most ruthlessly efficient private investigator money could buy. Lots of money, in fact, but price was no object here.

'Are you alone?' Bronski had said.

'We can talk. Where are you calling from?'

'Nairobi. You in Mombasa yet?'

'Since last night. Well, have you got anything for me?'

'News.'

'Good or bad?'

310

'I found him.'

'What! Where?'

'Keep your hat on, boss. Pender's dead.'

'Down with the ship?'

'Maybe. Maybe not. No way to tell. But he's history, all right. As sure as you live and breathe.'

'Bronski, what are you talking about? You just said you found him.'

'I found his trail, which adds up to the same thing.'

'Only if it leads to the right place.'

'Like I said, keep your hat on. How I know your guy's dead, is that he left tracks that a blind man could follow. A few weeks before your ship sailed he had a meeting with someone that nobody ever has a meeting with without ending up that way, sooner or later.'

'That sounds like an assumption. I don't pay you to make assumptions, Bronski. An assumption is just one small step up from a guess.'

'You want to hear this or not?'

'Of course I want to hear it. What meeting?'

'Right there where you are, in Kenya. The Fairmont The Norfolk Hotel in Nairobi, top-floor suite. Very nice. You might want to check the place out yourself some time. Best wine selection in Africa, or so I'm told.'

'Cut to the damn chase, Bronski. You're killing me here.'

'This'll kill you, all right. You ever hear of one Jean-Pierre Khosa?'

'Should I have?'

'Okay, well, you ever hear of Joshua Milton Blahyi, otherwise known as General Butt Naked?'

'I think so. He's some kind of African warlord, right? Ivory Coast? Ghana?'

'Close enough. Liberia. He called himself Butt Naked

because that was how he went into battle. Thought he had magic powers, all that kind of shit. People said he was a satanist and a cannibal. Killed about twenty thousand people during the first Liberian civil war. Or maybe it was the second. You lose count.'

'Okay. So?'

'So, this guy Khosa makes Joshua Milton Blahyi look like Mahatma fuckin' Gandhi. My advice, don't try to read his résumé on a full stomach. I'm guessing that your man Pender must've read it too, because that's who he called the meeting with in Nairobi. This nutjob calls himself *General* Khosa. Born June third, 1972, in some little village near a place called Lingomo, south of the Congo River. Killed his first man at the age of eight and never looked back. He and his brother were said to have hooked up for a while with Joseph Kony and the Lord's Resistance Army, while they were still in their teens. Uganda, Zaire, Sudan. Lots of very, very nasty shit going on. Then a few years later they split from Kony. Apparently he was too humanitarian and touchy-feely for their tastes and ambitions, and they wanted to go their own way. You want the details?'

'I just want to know what the hell this has to do with me and my diamond.'

'No problem, boss. Khosa turned up at the Fairmont The Norfolk in a black limo full of badass African dudes in black suits. Very hardcore. Packing lots of heat, but hey, we're talking Kenya, right? Two of them were guarding the door while Pender and Khosa talked inside for nearly three hours. Had the hotel staff in a hell of a twist, wondering what kind of big-shot player this white guy must be to call a meeting with these fellas. One of them got curious enough to listen in through the wall of the room next door. Air vent, or something.'

'How do you know all this?'

'What do you pay me for, boss? I told you, Pender left a trail like a goddamn slug. I know because I was there. Poked around, asked a few questions, spent a few bucks. I got the hotel employee on tape. He didn't catch all of their conversation, but he caught enough, even if he didn't understand what it was about. Stuff about a ship, one that Pender was going to be on, and how he wanted to be taken off it before it reached port. He kept on about some bullshit regarding a bunch of sensitive legal papers that some client didn't want to fall into the wrong hands. An obvious crock of crapola. I'd be surprised if Khosa was dumb enough to swallow a word of it. Anyway, then we get to the interesting part. Right there, Pender offers Khosa one and a half million bucks to intercept the ship and get him off it, "legal papers" and all. Khosa must surely already be seeing through the bull if he's got any sense, because when he bumps the price up another half a mill, Pender apparently doesn't blink. Who pays two million dollars for a bunch of papers? And where'd a lowlife like Pender get that kind of money from?'

'From me.'

'My thoughts exactly. You were set up, boss. He used your own cash to sell you out, thinking he could score a whole lot more of it. Just like you thought. Which makes you almost as cynical and hard-boiled as I am.'

'I love it.'

'I thought you might. Because I'm pretty sure you're also thinking what I'm thinking. Forget Pender, right? That's more than an assumption. And it sure as hell ain't a guess. The moron was dead the moment he set foot in Khosa's garden. He just didn't know it yet. Dollars to doughnuts, Khosa snapped up his two mill, then grabbed the diamond too, first chance he got. No prizes for guessing what

313

happened to our friend after that. Which takes him out of the frame entirely, but keeps the diamond still very much in it. Just with a whole new set of characters involved.'

'Find Khosa, find the diamond.'

'Sounds simple enough. There's just one small hair in the soup. Namely, Khosa's not your regular kind of guy. You can't just walk up to him and ask him for it back. I guess if you offered him enough, he might sell it. But I'm not sure I'd want to do business with this fucker.'

'We'll cross that bridge when we come to it,' Eugene said. 'You've done a magnificent job, Victor. I'm more than impressed.'

'It's what I do.'

'Why the hell didn't I hire you instead of Pender?'

'You know why, boss. Because you're a cheapskate at heart, and because I'm not some lousy burned-out mercenary asshole who kills kids.'

'I told you, I didn't know he was going to go that far.'

'Sure, boss. Whatever. That's between you and your own conscience. Nothing to do with me.'

'Anyway, I'm hiring you now.'

'Thought you already did that.'

'I mean, I'm giving you a new job. I don't need to tell you what it is. Just go do it.'

'I'm an investigator. Go find someone else.'

'You're the only guy I can trust.'

'That's what you thought about Pender. Anyway, if I wanted to kill myself, I already got enough pills and whiskey to do it with twice over. I don't need to get myself shot up in the freakin' Congo or wherever. Not for this daily rate.'

'Then increase it.'

'Have to do better than that, boss. I'd have to multiply it too. Times the number of extra guys I'd have to take on.'

'You know the right people?'

'Do bears shit in the woods?'

'Call me when you get some results. And Bronski?'

'I'm listening.'

'You find me that diamond, you hear?'

Chapter 47

As Ben stood watching and the dust settled around the now-stationary DC-3 Dakota, the main hatch on the left side of its green fuselage, halfway between the rear edge of the wing and its tailplane, swung open and a ladder was lowered out. Moments later, he watched as more of General Jean-Pierre Khosa's soldiers spilled out of the hatch and came stampeding down the ladder to meet their commander.

By the time the last man had climbed out, his Kalashnikov slung over his shoulder, Ben had counted thirteen of them. An unlucky number, especially as it now brought the strength of Khosa's ground force up to over thirty, and brought Ben's chances of making the slightest move against them to less than zero. The odds just kept getting steeper. The disused airfield was now beginning to look like a real military base again, full of bodies and activity and a lot more guns. It wasn't a welcome development.

The nose picker and a few other soldiers emerged from the mess hut, grinning and waving at the new arrivals. The nose picker ducked back inside, then reappeared at the head of a larger group of his comrades herding the remaining five prisoners outside at gunpoint. Jude, Jeff, Tuesday, Hercules and Gerber all gaped at the plane, slackening their step only to be prodded on from behind with jabbing rifle barrels.

Ben felt a similar jab in the back and a voice behind him said, 'Move! Move!' He let himself be marched across the compound to rejoin the others.

'What the hell's going on?' Gerber said.

'Our transport just arrived,' Ben said. 'At least now we know where we're going.'

'Where?' Gerber said.

'What did he want with you?' Jude asked.

'I'll tell you inside,' Ben replied. The soldiers were ushering them back towards the hut where Condor had been killed.

'I ain't goin' in there,' Hercules said. But he wasn't going to argue with three rifles at his back. The six of them were walked across the dusty ground and through the doorway into the bullet-cratered building. The stink of death hit them as they stepped inside. It was bad enough to make them gag and cover their faces with their hands, but not as bad as it would be by tomorrow, when the morning sun began to blaze afresh and the flies arrived in their millions to feast.

'You clean up,' the nose picker ordered them.

'No chance,' Hercules told him resolutely. 'We ain't touchin' it.'

'I'll do it,' Ben said. 'I get the feeling we're going to be spending the night here.'

'Not like we haven't done it before,' Jeff said.

'Bring a shovel,' Ben told the nose picker.

'No shovel. Use hands.'

'Then bring me a sack,' Ben said.

They brought a wooden crate. An old but sturdy oblong box nailed together out of pine slats and fitted with rope handles at either end, painted olive green and stencilled with faded white Cyrillic lettering. All the way from the Lugansk Cartridge Works in the Ukraine. If it could fulfil its original

317

purpose of holding two thousand rounds of Soviet 7.62x39mm assault rifle ammunition, it could hold the weight of a hundred-and-sixty-pound corpse, albeit in pieces.

Gerber couldn't face it. Nor could Hercules. It was left to the other four to place the empty box in the middle of the floor and kneel in the drying blood and scoop up what remained of poor Condor. The guns were pointing at them the whole time. The gruesome work took ten long minutes, by which time the pine slats were slippery with blood and Ben, Jeff, Jude and Tuesday were stained up to the elbows with it. 'You got water?' Ben asked the nose picker.

'You already drink.'

'Not to drink. To wash with.' Ben held up his bloody hands. 'See?'

The nose picker pulled a face and turned to grunt an order at another soldier. Khosa's army must have had some notion of rank hierarchy, because the other soldier ran off and returned a moment later with a begrudging half-cup of water and a filthy rag for the four of them to clean up with. Once they'd done the best they could, Ben pointed at the box and said to the nose picker, 'We can't leave him here.'

'Okay, okay, bring out, bring out,' the nose picker said, waving impatiently towards the doorway.

'This isn't exactly the kind of funeral I'd have in mind for myself,' Jeff said, trying to joke. Gallows humour was how he'd always coped with the worst situations, but for once it failed him and he couldn't raise a smile as he went to grab one of the rope handles.

'Let me do it,' Jude said. 'I knew him.' Ben grabbed the other handle, and he and Jude carried the sloshing, dripping box outside into the falling evening. The sun was dropping fast. The temperature would quickly follow.

Ben said to the nose picker, 'Now tell your man to fetch us that shovel.'

The nose picker frowned as if he'd been asked a long division question. 'Why do you need it?'

'To bury him, idiot.'

'No shovel!'

'Why, did you think I was going to use it to smack the side of your thick skull in?'

'Now, where did he go getting an idea like that?' Jeff growled from the doorway.

'Quiet!' The nose picker pointed across to a far corner of the compound near the perimeter fence. 'Leave it there.'

'We're not just going to dump him,' Jude said, outraged.

'Rats also must eat,' the nose picker said with a guffaw that was picked up by a few of the other soldiers.

And so, veteran merchant mariner Steve Maisky, a.k.a. Condor, found his final resting place. Unburied, unmarked, left to rot in a crate behind a clump of weeds next to a chain-link fence in a forgotten no-man's land many thousands of miles from any home he'd ever known.

Ben turned his back on the rifles and muttered a quick prayer, and then all that could be done for the dead man had been done, and nothing remained but to walk away and prepare for whatever lay in store next.

It wasn't long coming.

As Ben and Jude were being escorted back towards the bullet-cratered building that was to be their dormitory for the night, a pair of soldiers moved in on Jude and grabbed his arms, one on each side. They started hauling him away in the other direction, towards another of the buildings opposite.

'Hey, hey, what do you think you're doing?' Ben said. He

took an angry stride towards them and was instantly halted by three rifles in his face.

'General's orders,' the nose picker said with a sneer. 'He will not stay with you tonight. We will look after him.' He laughed.

'It's okay,' Jude said. 'I'll be fine.'

Ben's hands balled into fists. 'No, it's not okay.' He glared so hard at the three men holding the rifles in his face that they backed off a step. But the rifles kept pointing right at him as the soldiers led Jude away.

'Move, move!'

Night fell. The building cooled. Its dark, empty shell felt like a grave. Just a milky shaft of moonlight shone in through the doorway, broken by the shadows of the two sentries standing on watch outside. Down to five, Ben and the others huddled in a circle on the cold, hard compacted earth. In a low voice, Ben related to the others what Khosa had said to him earlier.

'The Congo,' Tuesday muttered, shaking his head. 'That's bone.'

'Bone?' Gerber said.

'Technical term,' Tuesday explained. 'British army expression meaning "totally fucked up".'

'I'm with you there, brother,' Gerber said sullenly. 'It's bone, all right. Christ. I could use a drink around now.'

'I could use a whole damn bottle,' Hercules added. His big form was a slumped shadow in the darkness, exuding defeat.

A long hush fell over them as each man sank into his own thoughts. It was Gerber's voice that finally broke the silence.

'Jesus, guys. What are we going to do?'

'Two sentries on the door,' Jeff said in a lowered voice. 'Am I the only one thinking "easy meat"?'

Ben shook his head. 'One gunshot. That's all it'll take to raise the alarm. Then it's over before it even started.'

Jeff shot a furtive glance at the doorway. One of the guards had just lit a cigarette. They could see the glow of its tip burning in the night, like the red dot of a laser sight marking its target. 'Who's talking about shooting them? We can take them down in a second, quiet as a mouse. Won't be like we haven't done it before. Then we grab their guns and go and find Jude, and get the fuck out of this place.'

'I'm not taking that chance,' Ben said softly. 'Not when there's thirty more of those bastards out there in the darkness, and a gun to Jude's head with someone's finger on the trigger. That's just the way it is.'

'Then what are we gonna do?' Gerber repeated.

'Stay alive,' Ben said. 'All of us. This is about survival now. We play it cool, we don't do anything stupid, and we wait.'

'Wait for what?' Gerber said in a strained whisper. 'Wait for this lunatic to decide to let us go?'

'For the right moment,' Ben replied.

Hercules gave a bitter chuckle. 'Sure. They got us sewn up tighter than a fish's ass, man. You just said it yourself. What right moment?'

'It'll come,' Ben said. 'We'll know it when it does.'

'And when it does,' Hercules said. 'What then?'

Ben said nothing.

It was a long, cold night. Ben moved to a corner of the building and curled up on the floor. More than he wished he had his cigarettes, and a tot of his favourite scotch to console him, he wished he had a blanket to wrap himself up in. What sounded like a pair of hunting jackals were roving somewhere outside the perimeter, deep in the darkness. He lay huddled up, trying to relax his tense, aching muscles, and listened to the haunting cries of the nocturnal predators. Doing what they were evolved to do, flitting through the night in search of their quarry. The same thing Ben was evolved to do. The night was his element, always had been.

But now he was no longer the predator.

He had never felt so powerless in all his life.

Chapter 48

Ben was woken by the sounds of activity outside. He opened his eyes and sat up, stiff and aching. The first light of dawn was creeping in through the doorway.

Another day. Ben already knew it wasn't going to be a good one.

The night sentries were gone, replaced by a fresh guard of Khosa's men standing inside the building and another three outside, all cradling rifles in their arms except for the fat soldier with the shotgun, who seemed to be in charge. The middle of his face was plastered with a dressing, and to Ben's pleasure the bruising had spread outwards from his busted nose and his eyes had swollen to the size of pears. He could barely open them wide enough to shoot vengeful looks at Hercules, who was still sleeping on the floor a few yards from Tuesday and Gerber. Jeff was already awake, sitting against a wall. He gave a dark smile. 'Morning, chief. How was your night?'

Ben gathered himself up to his feet and approached the doorway, watched every step by the guards. Outside in the red dawn, the soldiers who weren't on sentry duty were busily refuelling the Dakota from the second tank on the truck trailer. The whole base was swarming with preparation for the onward journey.

'How about getting us some coffee?' Ben said to the fat soldier, but all he got in reply was a surly look. Then the nose picker came bustling into the building, shouting, 'Awake! Awake! Up! Up!' His English vocabulary might have been limited, but he could use it to good effect.

Within moments, the five prisoners were hustled outside. Hercules yawned and stretched his big arms, then very deliberately passed within a step of the fat soldier, paused to give him a contemptuous stare and then suddenly tensed as if he was about to hit him again. The fat soldier flinched away like a beaten dog. Five rifles were instantly pointing at Hercules and the air was filled with nervy shouting and yelling.

'Easy, brother,' Gerber said softly, putting a hand on Hercules's broad back. Hercules gave the fat soldier a nasty smile and then walked on through the doorway.

The burning heat of the new day hadn't started bearing down yet, but it soon would. Stepping into the dawn light, Ben saw that Jude was already outside, flanked by the two exhausted-looking guards who had evidently been sitting awake all night watching him like hawks, kept awake by their terror of what their commander would do to them if the prisoner escaped. By comparison to them, Jude looked as fresh as a daisy.

Eat when you can, drink when you can, sleep when you can.
Jude was learning.

Moments later, Khosa himself emerged from the relative luxury of his own quarters, smoking another of his long cigars as his personal guard gathered round him. The General looked in high spirits, issuing commands here and there, rubbing his hands in expectation of an eventful and productive day ahead and surveying with satisfaction the bustling activities of his troops.

Even the most basic forward operating base runs on a minimum of kit. The men were busy collecting it all together into a stockpile next to the plane. Weapons, crates of ammunition, jerrycans, the portable cooking stove, pots and pans and mess tins and oil lamps, the medical first aid kit from which the fat soldier's dressing must have come, the folding table and chair from Khosa's quarters, plastic water jugs, more crates containing food and sundry other supplies. Soldiers were swarming like ants up and down the ladder to and from the open hatch of the Dakota, loading all the gear on board.

Ben walked across the compound towards Khosa, who saw him coming and turned. He smiled, smoke jetting from his nostrils.

'Did you sleep well, soldier?'

'Like a baby,' Ben said. 'I've been thinking, General. If we're going to be soldiers in your army, then you have to equip us.'

'I cannot allow you to be armed, soldier. I am not yet so sure I can trust you.'

'I was thinking more along the lines of bootlaces,' Ben said, pointing at his feet. 'As well as uniforms. Jackets, at the very least. We need five of them. For me, for Jeff, for Jude, for Tuesday and for Gerber. Hercules already has one, and I don't think you'd have anything in XXXL size anyway.'

Khosa considered Ben's request with a grave nod, and then gave a sharp command to one of his personal guard. The soldier scurried over to the stockpile by the Dakota, rummaged through a crate and came scurrying back a few moments later with a set of laces and an armful of green and brown clothing. The uniforms were a mix of plain khaki and disruptive-pattern camouflage combat jackets that might have been raided from any cheap and nasty army surplus store in the world. Khosa inspected them before passing them on to Ben. 'This is good thinking, soldier. Now you are becoming one of us. I am pleased.'

'Get them on,' Ben said as he handed the clothing out to Jude and the others. 'It's going to be a long and chilly flight.' The one he picked out for himself was a DPM pattern jacket. It was old and tatty and greasy to the touch, but it had all the right button-down pockets in all the right places. You never knew what you might have to conceal in there, when the opportunity came.

Ten minutes later, Ben's boots felt reassuringly tight again, the fuel pump had stopped pumping and it looked as if the old Dakota was ready for its long flight inland. Khosa issued his final orders to his air crews. Six men clambered into the Puma and the two Bell Iroquois, a pilot and co-pilot apiece. Khosa climbed the ladder to the aeroplane's hatch and disappeared inside, followed by the Dakota pilot. Ben glimpsed the General through the co-pilot window of the cockpit, his eyes hidden behind mirrored shades and the cigar clenched in his teeth, talking animatedly to the pilot as the guy busied himself flipping switches and powering up the aeroplane.

Things moved quickly from there. The three helicopter turbines started up with a triple out-of-phase whine that grew into a lazy *whap-whap-whap* and then into a howling chorus as the rotors slowly picked up speed. Then one after another, the Dakota's engines gave a wheezing cough from their starters and a puff of smoke, and then the big three-bladed propellers began to crank into motion. The clattering drone of the plane mingled with the rising howl of the choppers, until the whole base was filled with noise and wind and dust and the rich smell of exhaust fumes and, to Ben, the familiar tension and anticipation of an airborne squadron preparing for action.

The prisoners, now six again, now all clad in military jackets, were forced at gunpoint up the ladder and through the Dakota's hatch. The aeroplane's interior closely resembled that of the Puma that had brought them here, but on a much larger scale. Just like before, they found themselves being herded into a bare metal fuselage of bolted-together sections with exposed seams and fitted with facing rows of fold-down seats. Just like before, they were made to sit with the fat soldier, the nose picker and the skinny guy close by, guns at the ready, eyes never leaving them. Only this time, they were six and not seven. And this time, they were surrounded by a far greater enemy presence. Minus the half dozen men on board the choppers, minus Khosa and the pilot up front, that still left nearly thirty heavily armed soldiers to contend with. Ben and Jeff exchanged the same glances they had exchanged on board the Puma. But this time around, there was going to be no chance of taking over the aircraft in mid-air. No chance whatsoever.

The rumble and vibration of the engines resonated through the whole aircraft as the Dakota began to roll. The engines revved up to takeoff speed and Ben felt the acceleration press him sideways in his seat. It was a bumpy ride, and the faster the Dakota lurched and hammered over the uneven ground the bumpier it got, until they were being jolted out of their seats and everyone was clinging on tight to whatever support they could find.

Then, just as it seemed as though the lumbering dinosaur would never get off the ground, the crazy bumping ride suddenly smoothed off and Ben felt the stomach-sinking sensation as the Dakota gathered the wind beneath its wings and its wheels left the ground. And they were airborne.

Chapter 49

The droning, clattering flight went on and on. Even if it had been physically possible, there wouldn't have been a lot of scope for conversation. An hour passed. With no window to see out of, and with the overwhelming noise of the Dakota's engines and the whistling blast of cold wind rushing through the draughty, unpressurised interior, Ben could only wonder whether the choppers were managing to keep pace with them, or whether the Dakota had already left them far behind.

For the same reason, Ben could only imagine the landscape passing by below, gradually changing as they progressed westwards for another interminable hour, and then another again. They must have covered at least six hundred miles by now. Almost certainly avoiding major centres of civilisation, which wasn't a hard thing to do in Africa. From the dust bowl of Somalia to the great plains of Kenya, overflying shanty towns and thatch-hut villages and rivers and the tail end of the great migrations of teeming herds of wildebeest and zebra as they drifted towards the Serengeti in Tanzania before the worst of the rainy season began. Then further westwards and southwards, over sweeping savannas and into thickening forest so dense that a man could wander lost for days, weeks, and barely ever see daylight squinting through the canopy of trees far overhead. Then further still, scraping the high western plateaus that soared over three thousand metres before they sloped down to the vastness of Lake Victoria, like an inland sea the size of Ireland, the source of the White Nile River, where giant herons and eagles glided over the water, and shore villagers fished the way they had been fishing for a thousand years, and hippos bobbed and basked in the water, and Nile crocodiles as huge and ancient as dragons lurked in the reeds and hunted through the depths. Then onwards, and onwards, heading inexorably towards the verdant heart of what the early colonial explorers had dubbed 'the Dark Continent'. Much of it still as dark and dangerous, in some parts infinitely more dangerous, than in the time of Livingstone and Stanley.

A whole different world.

Khosa's world.

As Ben watched the hours tick by on the face of his watch, he was working out the logistics of the journey in his mind. Fully fuelled and not exceeding its cruise speed too recklessly, the DC-3 Dakota was good for a range of maybe fifteen hundred miles, perhaps longer if it had been fitted with the extra-large tanks that many of the old workhorses had. Those could extend their range by as much as another five hundred miles or more, enough to take them all the way to their final destination. If indeed the three choppers had followed them from Somalia, there was no way they could make even a third of the ultimate distance without taking on more fuel. They would have already had to land long before now. Which implied that Khosa would already have everything set up waiting for them in advance, planning for the choppers to make the journey in several well-orchestrated hops. The more Ben learned about the man, the more disconcertingly aware he became of how much smarter and more organised he was than Ben had first reckoned on. That wasn't a reassuring thought to hold in your mind when where was nothing else to think about and nothing you could do to make a difference.

Another hour dragged by, then another. Going by the Dakota's typical cruise speed, that meant anything up to two hundred more miles travelled for each full rotation of the minute hand on Ben's watch. They must have covered something like a thousand miles by now. Ben closed his eyes and revisited his mental map of Africa. If his idea of Khosa's flight plan was anything close to accurate, that distance would have taken them over Lake Victoria. Beyond Kenya into Uganda, as Khosa had intended, taking a line approximately midway between the Ugandan capital of Kampala, to the north, and the Rwandan capital of Kigali, to the south. The journey must be nearly three-quarters over by now. Ben wasn't looking forward to its end.

He opened his eyes and gazed across the aisle between the rows of seats. Jude, sitting facing him, was fast asleep. Good for him. Gerber and Hercules, the same. Jeff was sitting staring into space, apparently lost in whatever thoughts were knitting his brows into deep corrugated ridges of anxiety. Tuesday's eyes were closed, but judging by his posture he was awake, conserving his energy, staying calm.

To the left and right of them, many of Khosa's soldiers were managing to remain much more alert even after all these hours in the air, and Ben knew why. They all had dilated pupils and were as jumpy as a hardcore caffeine addict after four pints of Turkish coffee. They were chewing khat, an amphetamine-like stimulant derived from a flowering plant widely found across the Horn of Africa and even more widely used to stay mentally zoned in at times of great stress or boredom. Ben had tried it once in Sudan, didn't get on with it, and resorted back to his time-honoured tobacco. Along with tremors and constipation, its side effects could include manic or even psychotic behaviour.

Shut in a flying coffin with thirty potential psychopaths armed with loaded assault rifles. Things just kept getting better.

But only a few short minutes after that, even those not chewing khat suddenly had a much better reason to become wide-eyed and alert.

The steady monotonous drone resonating through the Dakota had abruptly changed in pitch. First there was a wheeze, followed by a strange kind of death rattle, both clearly audible over the roar of the wind. Then came a peculiar sensation as if someone had turned the balance knob on a sound system all the way to one side, directing all the signal through only one speaker. Like going suddenly deaf in one ear. At the same moment, the aircraft started juddering and shuddering as though it had hit air turbulence.

Ben knew from experience that air turbulence was unlikely to be a problem below the high troposphere, between about 23,000 and about 39,000 feet up. Which in the former case was right on the Dakota's maximum service ceiling, and in the latter case far exceeded it.

And that, along with the strange and sudden change in sound pitch that had coincided precisely with the jerky motion that was making the aircraft lurch like a drunkard through the air, was enough to tell Ben they hadn't hit turbulence at all.

He wasn't the only one thinking it. Tuesday had opened his eyes, and he and Jeff were staring right at him. They knew it, too.

The old Dakota had just lost one of its engines.

It wasn't cause for total panic. Not yet. A Dakota could

331

still fly on a single engine, like the one that had made the eleven hundred miles from Pearl Harbor to San Diego back in 1945 with one propeller out of action. Even on one wing, like the one that had collided mid-air with a Lockheed bomber and still made it safely home. The loss of an engine didn't seem to worry the soldiers unduly. Maybe the old machine had played this trick on them before. Maybe this happened all the time.

But when a second wheezing rattle was followed moments later by eerie silence except for the roaring, howling rush of wind streaming past the fuselage, it was clear that the situation had just changed dramatically for the worse.

Because there wasn't a Dakota yet built that could fly on no engines at all.

Chapter 50

It is said that the experience of war is defined by long periods of mind-numbing inactivity, interspersed at random intervals by brief, sharp periods of intense terror. Ben could pretty much testify to the wisdom of that old saying. It was about to be proven true yet again.

When the second engine cut out, three things happened. First, total shocked silence as every one of Khosa's men on board sat there frozen and speechless, rooted to their seats as the seconds ticked by and all ears strained for the sound of the engines cutting back in again. Then, mayhem and panic. Soldiers springing from their seats and yelling and screaming and waving their arms in terror, while others curled up and tucked their heads between their knees.

Thirdly, the awful sensation of weightlessness as the aircraft began to fall from the sky.

Amid the chaos, Jeff flashed Ben a crazy grin. Maybe they wouldn't have to wait for the right moment after all.

Ben launched himself out of his seat and grabbed hold of Jude, who was suddenly very awake and looking around him with wild eyes. 'Hang on tight!' Ben yelled in his ear. But there was very little to hang onto as the plane went into a gliding nose-dive. Nothing to do but count down the seconds until impact.

Ben fought his way through the frenzied crush of Khosa's men and ran down the centre aisle towards the cockpit. He saw the pilot desperately yanking on the controls as he struggled to bring the Dakota's nose up. Through the twin panes of the split windscreen he saw a blanket of green rushing towards them. The plane was plummeting at a steep angle towards what looked like an unbroken canopy of tree-tops stretching as far as the eye could see, maybe four hundred feet below and closing fast.

Three hundred feet and dropping.

Two hundred feet and dropping.

The pilot had both feet braced on the control panel and both hands on the stick as he hauled with all his might to get the flaps down and create as much lift under the wings as he could, while bringing down their airspeed by whatever margin he could for the inevitable crash landing. The plane's electricals were still working fine. A light was glowing in the instrument panel to indicate that the undercarriage was lowered. Clusters of dials and gauges were going crazy. Sweat was pouring down the pilot's face and his teeth were clenched.

Jean-Pierre Khosa just sat calmly in the co-pilot's chair and puffed on his cigar as if nothing were happening.

One hundred feet and dropping. Ben could almost make out the individual leaves on the branches of the trees hurtling towards them. Then, down there below the green canopy, half-screened by the treetops, he glimpsed a tiny meandering ribbon of ochre brown. At first he thought it was a muddy river. A full second later, he realised it was a dirt road.

The pilot had spotted it too. He was desperately trying to steer the stalled aircraft towards it.

Seventy feet and dropping. But not dropping as fast now. The pilot was winning his battle to keep the Dakota's nose up, though only by a few critical degrees. Airspeed was falling. The flaps were cranked down as far as the pilot could muscle the lever. The dirt road grew larger in the window, appearing like a narrow ravine flanked on both sides by tropical forest, just barely wide enough to squeeze the plane into without ripping off both wings and smashing the aircraft into a thousand fiery pieces.

Fifty feet.

Forty.

Thirty.

Jude. Ben turned away from the cockpit and rushed back along the aisle, fighting his way through a wall of bodies.

He was halfway there when the impact knocked him off his feet and he went sprawling backwards.

CRUNCH.

The plane hit the dirt road with a violent slamming jolt that shook it from nose to tail, bounced and then came back to earth harder still in a wild bumping slithering skidding ride that seemed to go on forever. The tunnel of the fuselage twisted one way, then twisted the other. It felt as if the whole landing gear had been ripped off, wheels, struts and all. As if the whole aircraft was coming apart at the seams. A deafening cannonade of hurtling rocks and stones and dirt pelted its underside.

Then, at last, the plane's momentum was spent and its brakes brought it to a bumping, lurching halt. Then a stunned silence, before the wild cheers and the whooping broke out.

Ben called Jude's name and heard Jude's voice reply, then Jeff's. He shoved and elbowed his way through the melee to get to them. Tuesday had a bleeding cut above one eyebrow and Gerber and Hercules were badly shaken up. Jude and Jeff were both without a scratch. It seemed a miracle that none of them had been hurt.

335

Neither, apparently, had any of Khosa's people. That seemed less of a miracle to Ben. A broken arm here, a sprained wrist or cracked collarbone there, anything to compromise the enemy's strength however minutely, would have made his work that little bit easier down the line.

Khosa emerged from the cockpit, unruffled, still calmly smoking his cigar and clutching the GPS navigation device Ben had seen on his table back at the base in Somalia. Khosa quickly marshalled his men, issuing commands left and right. The hatch was opened and the ladder lowered to the ground for everyone to disembark. The six prisoners were made to lead the way, then shoved and prodded to one side and held at gunpoint while the rest of the soldiers came rattling down the ladder and crowded beside the Dakota. The air was heavy with the scents of the forest around them, mingled with the tang of hot oil and hot exhaust.

Up close, what had looked from the air like a dirt road was nothing more than a rutted track. Even before the emergency landing had carved long, deep trenches in the loose soil, it would have taken a four-wheel-drive vehicle and a fairly committed driver to negotiate.

Ben looked up at the sky, shielding his eyes from the searing midday sun. As he'd fully expected, there was no sign of the helicopters. No sign of anything, except the track winding away through the trees, one very grounded DC-3 and thirty or more soldiers milling around and checking their weapons for damage, lighting cigarettes, bantering and joking among themselves like tough guys and trying to act as if they hadn't just moments ago been screaming in panic for their lives.

'Where the hell are we, anyway?' Jude asked.

'Somewhere hot and damp, is all I can tell you,' Tuesday said.

'I think we're in Rwanda,' Ben said. 'Which puts Khosa still an awful long way from home.'

'One thing's for sure,' Jeff said, pointing at the Dakota. 'If he's going to get there any time soon, it won't be in that.'

But Khosa seemed to have different ideas. Once the last of his troops had clambered down to the ground, he ordered for the boarding ladder to be moved from the hatch and leaned up against the port wing. At his command, one of the soldiers climbed up the ladder and walked along the wing to peer into the circular mouth of the engine cowl, as if he could figure out what the problem was just by gawking at it.

The engine yielding no immediate diagnostic clues, the soldier hurried back to clatter a few rungs down the ladder, until his head was just below the level of the wing and he was able to crane his neck and examine the huge aluminium fuel tank attached to its underside. He hung off the ladder with one hand, reached up and prodded around, then drew his machete from his belt and used the flat of the blade to give the nearest end of the tank a judicious tap. It produced a telling, hollow-sounding *clang*.

Empty.

Problem solved. Or diagnosed, at any rate.

It looked as if the Dakota hadn't been fitted with those longer-range fuel tanks after all, Ben thought.

'Just as I reckoned,' Jeff said. 'Silly buggers kept on flying until they ran clean out of gas. Anyway, that's the least of their worries now. Look at that wheel.'

Ben had already noticed it, because it wasn't easy to miss the fact that the whole aircraft was listing to one side on its undercarriage. The starboard wheel had hit a rock on landing, hard enough to explode the monster balloon tyre, which was now hanging in black shreds from a naked steel rim buckled badly out of true by the impact. But it wasn't just the wheel. The whole hydraulic strut was bent out of shape, causing the out-of-balance tilt. Until the old Dakota received some serious attention in a well-equipped workshop, it wasn't going anywhere again. Not even if they'd had five hundred yards of glass-smooth concrete runway to take off from.

'Looks like it's Shanks's pony for us,' Jeff said. 'Whoever the fuck Shanks was.'

Ben had to smile at that thought, knowing Jeff was right. They'd have no choice but to progress on foot. It wasn't the idea of a long march in the hot sun that made him smile, but the knowledge that maybe Khosa wasn't that organised, after all. And a long march on foot might just present the six of them with unexpected opportunities. Escape, for one.

The soldier climbed sheepishly back down the ladder to where Khosa was waiting for him at its foot, arms crossed and no longer looking as placid. The guy was shaking his head and spreading his arms and shrugging his shoulders and offering all kinds of excuses as his commander stood glaring at him.

'Who's he anyway, the unit mechanic?' muttered Jeff, who didn't understand Swahili. 'Not much cop, if he is.'

'Sounds like he was in charge of refuelling the plane,' Ben said.

'Wasn't exactly his fault, though, was it?' Jeff said. 'Pilot should've been watching his gauges. Assuming they work.'

'Still, I wouldn't like to be in his shoes,' said Gerber.

Hercules gave a snort. 'Like we give a shit what happens to the guy.'

But nothing could quite prepare them for what did happen to the guy, three seconds later.

Khosa waited in silence for the man's excuses to dry up.

The soldier just stood there, cringing, shoulders slumped, head hanging in mortification. Then, still without a word, Khosa drew the .44 Magnum from his holster and in a rapid sweeping motion he raised it up at arm's length and shot the man once, point-blank range, right in the middle of the face.

Chapter 51

Once was enough. The soldier jerked back like a shirt on a washing line caught by a sharp gust of wind. He hit the dirt on his back and slid two feet, spreadeagled on the ground with a shattered mess of teeth and exposed brains and sinus cavities where his face used to be. The crashing boom of the pistol shot rolled away across the countryside. A thin wisp of smoke curled out of the barrel of the revolver in Khosa's hand.

'Shit!' Jeff burst out.

'Oh, Jesus,' Tuesday said. 'He executed him.'

Jude turned away. Gerber and Hercules just stared in horror.

Ben said nothing. It was one enemy down. How or why it happened, fair or not, humane or cruel, was all the same to him. They all had it coming, each and every one of them.

Still clutching the gun, Khosa pointed at another of his terrified men. 'You! Come here!'

The soldier stepped forward with his eyes shut, face contorted into the grimace of a man facing imminent sudden violent death. *At least it will be quick*, he must have been thinking. By the General's standards, a supersonic large-calibre handgun slug to the head was a pretty sanitised and painless way to meet your maker.

'Get on the radio,' Khosa ordered him. 'Raise my helicopter pilots and give them our position. Tell them we are two hundred and forty miles north-east of the Rwanda–Congo border. These are our coordinates.' He tossed the soldier his handheld GPS device. The soldier hurried off to obey, grinning with relief at the stay of execution. But his grin didn't remain in place long, when he came creeping a few moments later to report that the helicopter pilots must be out of radio range.

Either the guy must have been a hell of a radio operator the rest of the time, or Khosa had simply lost interest in blowing people's brains out for the moment, until the next time. Instead of putting a bullet in his head, Khosa turned to the rest of the men and commanded them to start unloading all essential items from the aircraft. The soldiers were instantly galvanised into the same frenetic bustle of activity they had shown first thing that morning, at the air base in Somalia. Except now it was in reverse, scurrying up and down the repositioned ladder to and from the open hatch with armfuls of everything that would be needed for the long trek ahead, and stacking it on the ground. The stack was much smaller than the one that had been loaded into the Dakota at the start of the journey. Essentials only: water, light food rations, first aid kit and all the ammunition they could carry.

And so the march began. The dirt road was running roughly east to west, and it was towards the west, towards his kingdom, that Khosa led them. He set off at a fast stride, swinging his arms like a man going for a Sunday stroll, without a backward glance at his abandoned aircraft or the body of the man he'd just murdered. Behind him walked his personal guard, fanned out across the width of the road, eyes alert and scanning the trees and bushes for any enemy that might spring out to threaten their leader.

The remaining troops filed behind in a tail, two or three abreast, lugging the supplies. The group of prisoners were made to walk in between, strung out single file a short distance behind the spearhead of Khosa's guards and a short distance ahead of the rest of the column, with thirty guns behind them as a constant reminder that anyone who made a break for it would be shot in the back before they'd made it halfway to the tree line.

The Dakota was soon out of sight and forgotten as the track twisted through the forest. The first couple of miles were covered in silence, apart from the steady tramp of boots on loose dirt. October through November was the short rainy season in this part of the world, when sheeting downpours of spectacular intensity could alternate with roiling heat that quickly baked the moisture back out of the earth and reduced it to a fine red dust that found its way like sand into every crevice. After just a few hundred yards Ben was sweating under his jacket, and the dust was stinging his eyes and crunching between his teeth. But like all soldiers he was used to walking. This wasn't the first long, hot, gruelling march he'd been on in his life, although it was the first military column he'd been a part of with neither a heavy bergen strapped to his back nor a weapon hanging from his neck. The sixty-pound kit bag, he was happy to be free of. The weapon was a different matter.

He was lost in his brooding thoughts when he felt a presence at his side. Jude's face was shiny with perspiration and his hair was powdered with dust. Ben was glad of his company, but said nothing. They walked side by side without speaking for another mile or so. Then Jude got too hot and peeled off his jacket, slinging it over his shoulder.

'I was meaning to ask you about that bracelet,' Ben said, pointing at the little string of name beads around Jude's right wrist.

'Oh, that,' Jude said, barely glancing at it.

'Helen. You never mentioned her.'

'No point,' Jude said. 'If you'd asked me six months ago, that was a different story. All in the past now.'

'Forget I asked.'

'These things happen.'

'Yes,' Ben said. 'They certainly do.'

Jude said nothing, feeling uncomfortable because of the way the thread of conversation was inevitably heading towards the subject of Ben and Brooke. He fell silent for a while as they trudged on.

Then Jude suddenly said, 'I think about them all the time. The others, I mean. Mitch, and Diesel, and Park, and Lang and Allen and all the rest of them. And now Condor, too. So few of us left.' He forced a smile. 'Like an endangered species.'

'Then it's a species we're going to preserve,' Ben told him. 'With everything we've got. Because it's all we have.'

'I suppose that's how it must be, in the military. Remembering all the ones who didn't make it.'

Ben paused before replying. A lot of faces, names and memories were flashing up in his mind. He said, 'No, you never forget them. But at the same time, that's what keeps you moving forwards. To honour what they gave up.'

'And so you don't end up like them.'

'That, too,' Ben admitted.

'I'm frightened.' The tightness in Jude's voice wasn't just from the choking dust that the column of men were kicking up from the road.

'Everyone gets frightened,' Ben said.

'You too?'

'More than you know.'

'I'm sorry,' Jude said. 'I wanted to tell you on the ship, but we were never alone long enough to talk.'

'Sorry for what?'

'A lot of things,' Jude said. 'Such as, it's my fault you got into this whole mess. I should never have dragged you into it. I just didn't know what else to do.'

'You did the right thing and I wouldn't have it any other way,' Ben replied. 'Now I'm here, we're going to get out of it. You, me, all of us.'

'And I'm sorry that I hid things from you. I should have told you what I was doing.'

'At Le Val?'

Jude nodded.

'If it's what you truly want to do with your life, Jude. It's yours to live however you choose. I just have to accept that. Who the hell am I to stand in your way?'

'I'm not sure what I want. Not any more. I think that's why I told people my father was dead.'

Ben looked at him, not understanding. 'Simeon was your dad in a lot more ways than I ever was, or could have been. Not everyone gets to have a father they can be proud of, but he was a very special person. If you want to hold onto that, I would never blame you for it.'

Jude shook his head. 'That's not what I meant. What I'm trying to say is, it's like I needed him to be my real father, so that my father could be dead, so that I could go on pretending to myself. You know what I mean?'

'I can't say that I do.'

'So that I wouldn't have to fight against what's inside here,' Jude said, touching a hand to his chest. 'It's like something in me trying to get out all the time. Like a wild animal that wants to break free of its cage, but part of me is afraid to let it.'

Ben felt a twinge of sadness, but most of all guilt. Because he understood exactly what Jude was feeling. And because the wild animal Jude was talking about had been put there by him, by the Hope genes that were all Ben had ever been able to pass on to his son.

'Sometimes I think I want to,' Jude went on. 'That's where this screwy idea of joining the navy came from, out of the blue. Other times I just don't know *what* I want. Sometimes I just don't know who I am, even.' He glanced at Ben. 'I'm not like you that way. You knew who you were, right from the start. You set out on that path, and you never looked back or had doubts.'

'Is that how you see me? Then you don't know me as well as you think, Jude. I've spent my whole life trying to figure out what I wanted. I still haven't got the answers I was looking for.'

Jude mulled that over for a while. 'Then that's something else to be sorry for,' he said at last. 'That we never communicated much. About the important things. We had to find ourselves in this situation before we could talk. I mean, *really* talk.'

'There'll be time,' Ben said. 'All the time in the world.'

Jude looked back at the soldiers and the guns.

'You think?'

'How could I think otherwise?'

It was another eight or nine miles before Khosa slowed his pace and then held up a hand to halt the column. By now the thick of the forest was far behind them and the road was twisting between banks of tall, yellow grass and thorny scrub with just the occasional flat-topped acacia tree standing alone. They had seen no sign of a living creature along the way. The afternoon sky had grown overcast, with heavy clouds rolling in from the higher ground to the south of them. Rain might threaten for hours, and then come all at once. When it finally did come lashing down, it would pound the parched earth into mud and cleanse the dust from their bodies and hair in a welcome cooling deluge.

But Khosa hadn't halted them to shelter from the incoming weather. Just visible over the crest of a high grassy ridge some eighty or so yards ahead was the top of a rickety wooden fence marking the perimeter of the first habitation the marching column had seen all day. Beyond the fence, Ben could see the domed thatch roofs of some dwellings. He could hear the bleating of goats.

'He wants you,' Jude said, nudging Ben's elbow and nodding in Khosa's direction. The General was waving and beckoning for Ben to come over. To give him an accolade, perhaps. Or maybe just to shoot him in the face. There was only one way to find out. No other choice.

'Soldier, I have chosen you to enter this village ahead of the regiment,' Khosa told Ben. 'If they have transport, we will requisition it.'

So the rag-tag rabble was a regiment now. 'I thought I was a military advisor,' Ben said.

'Now you are a scout as well,' Khosa told him.

'Then give me a rifle,' Ben said.

'Why?'

'Because that's what army scouts carry, as a rule,' Ben said. 'Some of these villages are armed and might be inclined to shoot first and ask questions later. Especially when they see approaching units of soldiers who could be rebels come to give them a hard time. Or steal their vehicles, even.'

Khosa eyed him carefully. 'You wish to have a rifle, so that you can shoot me?'

'With all these soldiers around?' Ben said, gesturing at the guards. 'You think I'm that stupid?'

Khosa shook his head. 'You will go without a rifle. I have

been thinking, soldier. We spoke earlier of trust. If you wish to gain my favour, you must first prove yourself to me.'

'I see. And this is how I prove myself, by walking unarmed into a potentially hostile village. I take it that if I come out in one piece, you'll start trusting me?'

'This is a small test,' Khosa said, and swatted at a buzzing fly. 'After you have passed this one, I will think of another that is more worthy of a warrior of your skill.'

'I'm honoured.'

'Now go. And remember, soldier. I have your boy here with me.' With a sinister smile, Khosa drew the heft of the Colt Anaconda from its holster and aimed the heavy barrel towards Jude. 'If you do not return, he dies first. If you try any tricks with me, he also dies first.'

Ben stared at Khosa. In his mind he saw himself twist the weapon out of the African's hand, using the leverage of that long barrel to snap his finger like a twig in the trigger guard. Then Khosa would be eating one of his own bullets before he or his men had the slightest inkling of what was happening.

It would have been so easy.

And then the last thing Ben would see before he died was Jude being shot to pieces in front of him by thirty assault rifles.

Not happening.

He obeyed.

No other choice.

Chapter 52

The column stayed back as Ben walked on alone in the sultry, overcast heat. The dirt road split off into a narrower path that led through a divide in the grassy rise and past the rickety wooden fence into the village. He knelt to inspect the ground for signs of tyre tracks, but either there were none to find or they'd been washed away in the last deluge of rain.

Back in the day, Ben had found himself in African villages not so very different, in Sudan and Sierra Leone. It looked like a well-tended settlement, extending over maybe a couple of acres on the edge of a thicket of trees and long grass and thorn bushes. To the other side, a further couple of acres were fenced off and cultivated, though he had no idea what kind of basic crop could be produced here. Last time he'd ventured into such a place had been many years ago, an in-and-out sortie as second-in-command of an SAS unit hunting a marauding guerrilla force called the Cross Bones Boys who had been kidnapping and butchering UN aid workers. People had died that day. He hadn't had a lot of time to study rural African agriculture.

Ben kept walking, and the track took him deeper into the village, past little areas of garden and some wire-and-post enclosures where chickens scratched at the dirt and goats bleated nervously at his approach. The homes were traditional mud-walled roundhouses with carefully crafted domed roofs woven from sticks and thatch, each supported at its centre by a stout wooden pole where a primitive dwelling in a less tropical climate would have had a stone or clay chimney.

So far, nobody had taken a pot-shot at him from one of the huts. Everything seemed peaceful. Strangely peaceful, because apart from the few goats and chickens the place appeared deserted. As he walked on, he was beginning to wonder if a lookout had spotted the soldiers coming and the entire population of the village had fled. Which would most certainly have been the sensible thing to do.

It wasn't until he followed the track around a bend and reached the very centre of the village that Ben saw a living soul. Then he understood why the place had seemed so deserted.

The heart of the settlement was a village square, except it was circular, about thirty yards in diameter, with the largest of the thatched dwellings at its northern edge, which Ben took to be the home of the chief or headman. Or head-woman, for that matter. It seemed as if the entire village, men, women and children, had gathered in the middle of the square in a big crowd of some fifty or sixty people, but not for any kind of happy or ceremonial occasion. Ben saw right away from the distressed looks on the villagers' faces that some sort of commotion was going on, hidden from view at the centre of the crowd.

He felt like an intruder as he approached. A strange white man in a dirty army jacket appearing out of nowhere couldn't be good news. Faces turned and fingers pointed and one or two people shied away. Ben held up his hands to show he was unarmed, smiled and tried to look as unmenacing as he could.

Rwanda had three official languages: French, English and Kinyarwanda. Of the two he knew, he reckoned that English was the most universally understood and his best bet.

'What's happening here? Can I help?'

An unarmed and unthreatening white man in the middle of rural Africa could be many things, but was probably most likely to be a doctor or an aid worker. The crowd parted to let him through. Many looks were darted at him, a few suspicious, some anxious, most of them trusting. Ben heard the sound of a child crying and howling in pain. 'Can I help?' he repeated. '*Je peux vous aider?*'

He soon saw what the commotion was. The crowd had gathered around an injured child, a small boy of maybe nine or ten. Women were weeping and men were frowning as they kneeled on the ground next to him, trying to stem the bleeding from his left arm and leg, which were badly lacerated and ripped open. The wounds were as fresh as they were ugly. They were nothing like the injuries made by a bullet or a knife. Ben had seen ones like these before, once, long ago, on a dead man. If these had been caused by the same thing, then this young boy was incredibly lucky to be alive.

Claw marks. Made by something very large and very powerful.

Ben bent over the child and asked, 'What did this to him?'

From a chorus of explanations, he was quickly able to piece the answer together. The boy had been attacked by a lion that had started appearing in the thicket of woods near the village. It had been hanging around for weeks, stalking among the huts at night. First it took just a couple of goats. Then it started focusing its attentions on people. It killed a woman who was washing clothes down by the river. Now it had attacked this boy while he was out gathering firewood.

A tearful woman who seemed to be the child's mother pointed at the thicket beyond the edge of the village and said the animal was still in there, hidden and lying in wait for its next victim.

Ben knew that a rogue male, separated from its pride and taken to hunting alone, could do this. Especially if something was wrong with it – if it was old, or sick, or weakened in some way that had affected its ability to go after normal prey. Thin-skinned, weak, defenceless and slow-moving humans were an easy catch by comparison.

Crouched next to the bleeding child and holding his hand with a tortured expression of concern was an African man of about thirty, whom Ben took to be the boy's father. He wore khaki shorts and a tattered sleeveless sweatshirt from which his powerful shoulders protruded broadly, as lean and muscled as a human anatomy chart. From his left lobe hung a single earring fashioned out of beads and braided cord, with a pendant disc of copper wire that shone like gold even under the overcast sky. He looked up at Ben with pain in his eyes and asked, 'Are you a doctor?'

'British army medic,' Ben said, which was partly true as all SAS soldiers received basic medic training. He asked to take a look and kneeled on the ground by the boy. 'What's his name?'

'Gatete,' the father said.

Ben spoke gently. 'Gatete, I need you to keep still while I take a look, okay?' This was one brave kid. He held in his tears while Ben inspected the wounds. They were deep, but no major blood vessels had been severed. The main concern was infection, because a lion's claws were covered in bacteria from the bits of rotting meat that collected behind them.

'I can stitch these,' Ben said. 'But he's going to need antibiotics.'

Gatete's father got to his feet. 'You have medicine?'

'I think so,' Ben said. He was thinking of the first aid kit back there with the column. But it wasn't that simple. He said, 'My name's Ben. What's yours?'

'I am Sizwe.' The boy's father pointed at another large, muscular African standing behind him. 'This is my brother, Uwase.'

'Sizwe, I need your help too. Does this village have any kind of motor vehicle?'

Sizwe thought for a moment, then nodded and told Ben that Gahigi, the richest man in the village because he had the most goats, used a truck to take them to market in the nearest town. Also his friend Ntwali – pointing at another of the men in the crowd – had a four-wheel-drive. Why was Ben asking this?

'Because I'm going to have to take them from you,' Ben said. 'I'm sorry to do it. But the man who brought me here is a dangerous man and I need to persuade him to move on from here as fast as possible, in everyone's best interests. That's why I need the trucks. You understand?'

'Who is this man?'

Ben said, 'His name is Khosa.'

The mention of the name caused a ripple effect of fear among the villagers. Suddenly, everyone was looking at Ben with hostility.

'I'm not one of his people,' Ben reassured them. 'I promise that, and I mean you no harm. You have to let me help you. Look—' To make the trade more even and show his good-will, he took off his watch and handed it to Sizwe. 'It's an Omega Seamaster. Swiss made. A new one would cost you over a thousand dollars. And it's automatic, so it will keep going forever and never need a battery. Take it. It's yours.'

After a brief conference with the others, Sizwe nodded

and said Ben could have the trucks if he could bring the medicine for his boy. The deal was struck.

Now all Ben had to do was get Khosa to honour it.

He left the village at a run and sprinted back down the dirt track to where the General was waiting impatiently.

'Well, soldier?'

'Trade,' Ben said. 'Two trucks, for some penicillin and a surgical needle and thread. I'll need that first aid kit.'

Khosa narrowed his eyes. 'For what you need this?'

Which forced Ben to have to explain the situation with the injured child. Khosa showed little interest, until he heard about the lion. His eyes lit up with fascination. He turned to his gathered soldiers and issued the command that Ben hadn't wanted to hear.

'Move on. We are going into this village.'

'I did a deal with these people, General,' Ben protested. 'I just need a few minutes to treat the child. Then we take the trucks, and we go. Fair's fair. There's nothing else to gain from your going in there.'

'You are not in authority here, soldier. And Jean-Pierre Khosa does not trade with cockroaches. We go.'

Chapter 53

The column advanced up the track and marched into the village. Ben and the others could only watch as Khosa led his troops along the path between the huts to where the villagers were gathered. There were cries of fear as they saw the soldiers coming. The crowd scattered, but were quickly herded back together at gunpoint.

Khosa planted himself in the middle of the village square and lit a fresh cigar. Wreathed in a swirl of smoke he shouted, 'I am General Jean-Pierre Khosa! If there are strong men and boys in this village, they will now have the honour of serving in my army!'

Next, Khosa ordered for all the men and women to be rounded up separately. It was a task his soldiers completed in under a minute, jabbing their rifles and yelling wildly at the terrorised villagers.

'Only the fittest can fight for me!' Khosa declared loudly. 'There is no room in my army for the old and the weak. Kill them.'

'He can't do this,' Tuesday said, and looked imploringly at Ben and Jeff.

But he could do it, and he did. Because nobody had the power to stop him. Moments later, the village echoed to the crackle of small-arms fire and screaming as every man deemed too old, too infirm or in any way unfit for service was gunned down. A one-legged man on crutches, shot three times in the head and chest. A white-haired elder of about seventy, blasted in the back as he tried to escape. And on, and on. When the firing stopped, there were eighteen dead bodies on the ground.

And every one of them, Ben felt as if he'd murdered himself. He was shaking with a rage he could hardly contain. Women wailing, children crying and screaming, Khosa's soldiers surrounding them with guns and roaring at them to shut up. Sizwe, Uwase and the other men of the village all staring at Ben as though he'd betrayed them.

It was unbearable.

But it wasn't over. It was just beginning.

Next, Khosa had all the remaining men and older boys lined up for his inspection. He strutted down the line, puffing smoke, the sunlight glinting off the revolver at his side and the mirrored lenses of his shades, and took a long, slow look at each one in turn.

'This one is big and strong,' he said, pointing at Uwase. 'He is acceptable. And this one is even bigger. You! What is your name, cockroach?'

'Sizwe.'

Khosa nodded with satisfaction. 'This Sizwe is the strongest of them all. I will take him too.'

Like a flesh trader of old picking out the choice goods at the Zanzibar slave market, Khosa selected four more of the tallest and fiercest-looking males of the village, asking each his name in turn. Ntwali, who owned the four-wheel-drive. Gasimba, his friend. His number five and six choices were named Mugabo and Rusanganwa.

'These are very good,' Khosa declared. Then he turned to his soldiers and said, 'Take the rest and kill them. But do not waste more bullets.'

355

The soldiers used their machetes.

Ben had heard of carnage like it, and often. In Africa, and especially here in Rwanda, there was a long and depressing record of man's senseless brutality against his fellow man. He'd seen the aftermath of such slaughter, on one occasion that he had tried very hard for many years to close out of his memory. But to be forced to witness it taking place in front of his eyes felt like being dragged to the brink of losing his mind. Almost the very worst thing was the way the villagers took it, many of them barely resisting as though they accepted their fate with a calm, dignified, almost detached resignation. It was more awful to watch than if they'd fought and struggled.

Ben watched through a stinging, clouding veil of tears until he couldn't stand it any longer and closed his eyes. But he couldn't close his ears to the keening screams of the womenfolk and the terrible repetitive chopping of sharpened steel on flesh and bone as Khosa's soldiers carried out their bloody work.

When the massacre was over and the ground was littered with the severed body parts of the dead, Khosa strolled calmly up to where Ben stood with his head bowed, and revealed his plan.

'I have thought of a better test for you, soldier.'

Khosa took off his sunglasses. His eyes bored into Ben's, as though he could read every thought that was in there. 'Do you see these scars on my face?'

As if it were possible to miss them.

'These were made when I was just a young boy, to show my courage. Do you know how I earned these marks? By proving myself in combat against two strong warriors from another tribe, who were sent to hunt me in a forest. These men were prisoners. If they killed me and cut off my head, they would be let go. But I killed them both, with nothing but a spear in my hand, and I carried their heads back to my village to show to the elders. This was how a boy became a man. And now, soldier, you will prove yourself to me in the same way.'

Ben said nothing.

'You and you,' Khosa said, motioning at Jeff and Tuesday in turn. 'You are his comrades in arms who will join him in this test. Three against six is the same as one against two. This is why I have chosen the six strongest men from this village. They will be given weapons to fight with. If they wish their women and children to be spared from the blades of my soldiers, they must kill you in combat.'

Khosa smiled his demon smile at Ben.

'But if you kill them, soldier, you will save the life of your boy. Lose, and his head will be the next to be cut off.'

Ben said nothing. He could feel the tension coming like waves of heat from Jeff and Tuesday.

'Clear this space,' Khosa commanded with an imperious sweep of his arm. 'The contest will take place here, before me. Let the fighters be given their weapons.'

Then Khosa paused, and rubbed his chin, and his eyes narrowed, and he nodded and chuckled to himself. 'No, I have a better idea. Yes, yes. Much better. This will make the contest more interesting, I think.'

He pointed at the thicket of scrub and thorn bushes just beyond the edge of the village.

'There is where you will hunt and kill each other,' he announced. 'Where the lion awaits its prey. To be a true warrior, one must confront many different dangers.'

Ben found the words to speak.

'The biggest danger is you, Khosa. I can't decide whether you're a lunatic or just evil. But I promise you one thing.

357

Whatever happens to me, my friends or my family, the worst end will be the one that comes to you. Sooner or later, you'll be looking it right in the face. And no man would deserve it more than you.'

'It is not a matter of who deserves,' Khosa said. 'It is only a matter of who wins, and who loses.'

'I won't fight,' Ben said. 'Not like this.'

'Think carefully, soldier. You should not forget that you have much to lose.' Khosa pointed at Jude. 'His life is in your hands. He is your son. Look into his eyes and tell him that his life is not worth the lives of six poor villagers? Six strangers who are nothing to you?'

Ben didn't reply.

'If you will not fight, soldier, it means that you are a coward. And I have no use for a coward in my army. Refuse my command, and it is the same thing as if you fail the test. I will have the boy's head cut off. Is this what you wish for? I do not think so, soldier.'

Ben still didn't reply. He looked over at Jude. Jude was looking at him. Two of the soldiers were holding him by the arms. A third was pointing a gun to his head. A fourth was standing behind him with a machete, poised and ready for the swing. Its blade caught the sunlight.

Jude shook his head. 'Don't do this for me,' he called out. 'I can't have six innocent men die on my account. Let the bastard do to me what he has to do. Let go.'

But Ben would not let Jude go.

Sizwe, his brother and their friends stood shoulder to shoulder, arms crossed, eyes averted from the slaughterhouse that was all that remained of the rest of the village menfolk.

'We will not kill,' Sizwe said. 'We are not animals.'

At a signal from Khosa, the nose picker and another of the soldiers stepped up to the huddled, whimpering crowd of women and children. They homed in on Sizwe's wife, who was clutching their injured son tightly against her, his blood soaking into her plain cotton dress. The boy howled both in terror and in pain as they tore him out of his mother's arms. The nose picker drew a blade and held it to the child's throat while the other held his squirming body down. A third soldier restrained Sizwe's wife as she flew at them, screaming in anguish. He used his rifle butt to slap her hard across the face, then kicked her to the ground and pointed the weapon at her.

'This little cockroach is bleeding all over my uniform,' the nose picker said with a grin, just itching for the command to make him bleed some more.

'I will count to three,' Khosa said. 'Then we will add his head to the pile. One.'

Sizwe said nothing.

Khosa said, 'Two.'

Sizwe remained silent. He glanced at his wife, then at his son, then at Khosa, then at Ben. Uwase, Ntwali, Gasimba, Mugabo and Rusanganwa were all looking to him, their eyes wide and white and bulging.

Khosa said, 'Thr—'

But Sizwe spoke before he could finish.

'We will kill.'

Chapter 54

Before the test, came the preparations. Sizwe, Uwase, Ntwali, Gasimba, Mugabo and Rusanganwa were each given a loaded semiautomatic pistol, as well as a set of pressed tin dog tags on thin chains to hang around their necks. Many of Khosa's men wore them like jewellery to show how big they were, and were happy to lend them for the occasion.

Another three sets of tags were allocated to Ben, Jeff and Tuesday, along with three machetes wrapped up in a sack-cloth bag from one of the soldiers' packs.

'You three men are the superior warriors,' Khosa told them in a booming, grandstanding voice for all to hear. 'So it is right that you must have the lesser weapons. To pass the test, you will bring me all six sets of tags and the head of Sizwe inside this bag. Do you understand?'

'Six sets of tags and the head,' Ben said. 'If that's what you want, that's what you'll get. And when it's over, you let these people go back to what you've left them of their lives. And you let Jude and my friends go. You can keep me, if you want. I don't care.'

'Are you trying to negotiate with me, soldier?' Khosa asked with a smile. 'I do not remember offering these terms. Now, there has been enough talking. You, you, you, you and you,' he said, waving his arm at a group of his soldiers and

360

jabbing a finger at the big hut overlooking the village square, 'will make sure that all of these female cockroaches and the little cockroaches are closed inside this hut. Guard them closely. Any man who allows a cockroach to escape will pay the price of one hand.' Then he waved his arm towards another group of soldiers, which included the nose picker. 'You, you, you, you, you and also you, will escort the fighters to the trees where the contest is to take place. Release the three warriors first. They will have one minute to take their positions and prepare, before you release the six hunters. You will stand guard and kill any man who tries to run away. Do you understand this duty that I have placed on you?'

The nose picker and his comrades enthusiastically chorused that they understood this duty very clearly. They'd just been given a ringside seat and couldn't wait for the games to begin.

'And I will stay here, and rest my feet for a while, and finish this very good cigar all the way from Havana, Cuba,' Khosa said, rolling the Cohiba Gran Corona lovingly between his fingers. 'While I keep both my eyes on this boy and make sure he does not try any more of his tricks. Come, White Meat. You will stay beside me as your father fights for your life, and tell me some of your white man jokes.' He roared with laughter. The soldiers thought it was deliriously funny, too.

And so it began.

The combatants were escorted out of the village in two groups, Ben, Jeff and Tuesday in front and the six village men some way behind. The nose picker and the skinny soldier were in charge of the lead group. Two against three. Theoretically pretty good odds, and under normal circumstances there was no question that Ben would have gone for it. Even unarmed, against a pair of trigger-happy killers who were weighed down with as much armament as they could carry. The nose picker had been helping himself to the munitions supplies since Somalia. In addition to his AK-47, a nine-millimetre Browning pistol and the machete he'd held to little Gatete's throat, he was decked out in extra bandoliers and had a cluster of hand grenades rattling like a bunch of coconuts on his belt.

'You must be a real hard guy,' Jeff said to him. 'The African Clint Eastwood. The way you handled yourself against that little kid back there. I mean, you've got me shaking in my boots, matey.'

'I am Captain Terminator,' the nose picker said. 'So fuck you, asshole. And keep walking or I will shoot you in the back.'

'That sounds about right,' Jeff spat at him.

The soldiers stopped them at the edge of the thicket. The nose picker grunted to the skinny guy, who was carrying the bag and at his comrade's command tossed it deep into the bushes. It landed out of sight with a rustle and a clatter. Then, leering, the nose picker pulled out his nine-millimetre and fired a single shot in the air, like a starting pistol being fired to announce the beginning of a race. Pointing the pistol at the three men, he said, 'Go.'

Now the clock was ticking. Just sixty seconds before Sizwe and the others were released into the thicket after them, armed with much more than an armful of machetes.

Ben, Jeff and Tuesday went ploughing into the dense vegetation. The grass was eye-high to an elephant in places, making it hard to see beyond a few yards in any direction. Ben spotted the bag and snatched it up, drew out one of the three machetes inside for himself and tossed one each to Jeff and Tuesday.

Fifty seconds.

362

'This is fucked,' Jeff said.

'That's one way of putting it,' Ben replied.

'He's insane. He's got every intention of killing us all anyway, no matter what, sooner or later. You know that, don't you? This is all just a fucking game to him. Like a blood sport.'

'I know,' Ben said.

'He's lost his mind. He's completely off his rocker.'

'I know that too.'

'What are we going to do, mate?'

Ben looked at his friend. They'd been through a lot together. Faced all kinds of dangers, all kinds of death, and they'd come through it. But he'd never seen such an expression of doubt and worry and fear in Jeff's face before.

'Whatever works,' he replied. 'That's all we can do.'

Forty seconds.

Tuesday was scanning the bushes, eyes darting in all directions. 'I hate to put a downer on this happy moment, guys, but did someone say something about a man-eating lion on the loose in here?'

'Least of our worries, under the circumstances,' Ben said. 'A rogue male isn't like a normal lion. He doesn't have his pack to hunt with any longer, and he won't go after herds. He's become a solitary predator who goes for solitary prey. One-on-one kills, easy meat. He sees a crowd of us, he'll leave us alone. As long as we stay together, we should be okay.'

'That's so reassuring,' Tuesday said with a shudder.

'Enjoy it. In about half a minute, we really will have something to worry about.'

'How do you want to handle this?' Jeff asked.

'You heard the man,' Ben said. 'Six sets of tags and a head in a bag. That's what he asked for, and I aim to deliver it.'

'It's not right. They're just trying to protect their families.'

'So am I,' Ben said.

The seconds pounded by. Tuesday wiped sweat from his eyes. Jeff moistened his lips with his tongue. Ben stood completely immobile, listening, watching, merging with the stillness of their surroundings. He felt his heart slow. Forty-five beats a minute. Forty. He held the handle of the machete loosely in his right fist and thought about the six men who were being sent to kill them. He thought about the soldiers fanning out to encircle the thicket, surrounding them with watchful eyes and sharp ears and fingers on triggers. He thought about heads in bags, and wondered whose it would be.

Ben bent down and picked up a stone that was lying at his feet. He clenched it in his left hand.

'They'll be on us any moment,' Tuesday whispered.

'They're already here,' Ben replied.

Chapter 55

They came stalking through the thicket with a soft footfall that would have been perceptible only to the senses of the keenest predator. Or the keenest prey. These were men who had grown up in the wilds, most likely never seen a city or walked on a pavement or ridden on a train. They belonged to this place, and they could move through it without sound or trace.

Many years ago, Ben had been taught how to hunt such men. He'd spent many more years honing the skills his teachers had conferred on him. In his mind's eye, the screen of thorn bushes and tall yellowed grasses and gnarled trees and branches that made visibility impossible didn't exist. He could sense the approaching men as clearly as if he were in an empty, featureless desert landscape observing the enemy through high-powered binoculars from two miles away. He could smell them, reach out and touch their fear and desperation.

'Get down,' he whispered. He dropped into a press-up position, knuckles and toes in the dirt, legs out straight behind him, his chest pressed deep into the long grass, neck craned upward in the direction of the incoming enemy. Jeff and Tuesday did the same, both instantly disappearing from sight in the grass to his left.

A second and a half later, a ragged volley of gunshots rang out. Half a dozen nine-millimetre pistols all blazing away at once, four or five sharp reports from each of them in rapid succession, pumping fire into the bushes as fast as their shooters could squeeze the triggers. The swarm of bullets burned a scything sweep through the thicket that was chest-high to a man standing, clipping leaves from twigs and chopping stalks of grass, singing off tree trunks iron-hardened by heat and sun. Sizwe and his friends were firing blind into the thicket in the hope of hitting something or flushing out their opponents.

Tactically, it was the behaviour of frightened, inexperienced men. The Africans were afraid. But they were even more afraid of what would happen to their women and children if they failed.

The gunfire fell silent. Ben sensed the Africans spreading out. They would be listening hard for signs that one of their bullets had found its mark. A cry of pain, the crackle of twigs as a man fell dead or rolled in agony on the ground. The more they spread out, the less they would chance another blind volley, for fear of hitting one of their own group.

Ben waited, perfectly still. To his left, unseen in the grass, he could feel the presence of Jeff Dekker and Tuesday Fletcher doing the same. He gripped the handle of his machete a little more tightly. It was a crude affair of probable Far Eastern manufacture, two roughly shaped slabs of cheap wood riveted together either side of the untempered tang of the blade. The blade was thick and heavy to compensate for the weakness of the steel. An unsophisticated instrument. More axe than sword, its single sharpened edge fashioned by some underpaid Chinese factory worker with an angle-grinder and its back edge a spine of rusty metal an eighth of an inch wide. Ben rotated the handle between his fingers and went on waiting.

He did not have to wait long for what he anticipated would happen next.

The Africans were growing more nervous by the second. Nervous of the hungry big cat they fully expected to come charging at them out of the thicket at any moment with the taste of human blood still slathered on its lips. Even more nervous of the unseen, unheard enemy that had shown no response to their opening gambit.

And Ben knew very well from long experience that nervous men unaccustomed to being in life and death situations often found it hard to remain still in a moment of serious do-or-die crisis, with legs like jelly and pounding hearts flushing adrenalin through their bodies and every muscle taut and twitching with fight-or-flight reflex. The mad itch to go bolting and yelling either towards or away from anything that moved was virtually irrepressible. That was how Ben knew that the flitting shape of a man he'd just glimpsed stalking through the thicket, no more than a ripple in the long grass ten yards dead ahead of where he lay crouched and ready, was about to break cover at the first sign of movement.

Ben pressed his left knee to the ground so that he could take some weight off his left hand. The hand clutching the stone. In a quick, small flick of the wrist he tossed the stone a few feet to his right, where it fluttered the bushes.

And got exactly the response he expected.

The African who came bursting out of the cover of the long grass was Uwase, Sizwe's brother. With a wild roar of pent-up fear and aggression and a crackle of undergrowth he came bounding and leaping with his pistol thrust out in front of him in both fists, blasting a salvo of shots at the spot where the stone had landed. His rushing, panic-stricken charge took him within three feet of where Ben lay hidden.

All Ben had to do was sweep his feet out from under him with the thick blunt edge of the machete, and let the African's momentum do the rest.

The blade caught Uwase's ankle just below the shin, in the crook of his ankle. It wasn't a hard enough blow to break bones, but Ben delivered it with more than enough force to send him sprawling on his face with a yell of pain and surprise. Uwase didn't have time to react before Ben was on him, pinning him hard in the grass, an elbow in his face to stun him and the sharp edge of the machete against his throat.

All too fast for Sizwe to even aim his pistol as he burst out of the bushes in pursuit of his brother.

Ben said, 'Stop.' And Sizwe stopped.

'Drop the gun,' Ben said. And Sizwe dropped the gun.

'Call the others, so I can see them,' Ben said. But Sizwe didn't have to. Gasimba, Mugabo, Ntwali and Rusanganwa all stepped out, pistols hesitantly half-raised as they looked to Sizwe for guidance.

'Tell them to drop their guns too,' Ben said. Sizwe gestured to his friends. The pistols fell into the dirt with dull thumps.

To Ben's left, Jeff and Tuesday were back on their feet, tense and silent. Uwase struggled and tried to throw Ben off him, but Ben had him tight. The crude blade hard against his throat. Ground to an edge by some Chinaman in a factory thousands of miles away. Not shaving sharp, by any means. But plenty sharp enough. That much had already been demonstrated too many times that day.

'Do not hurt my brother,' Sizwe said. There was no pleading in his voice, only stoic pride.

'Kill or be killed,' Ben said. 'No mercy, no quarter. That's what Khosa said. But it doesn't have to be like that, Sizwe.'

'You and me fight!' Sizwe roared.

'Like champions,' Ben said. 'Single combat. May the best man win. Is that your idea?'

'This is the only way.'

Ben stood up, hauling Uwase up with him. He shoved Uwase away, scooped up Uwase's fallen pistol and tossed it to Jeff. Jeff transferred his machete from right hand to left and aimed the pistol in a swinging back-and-forth arc, covering all six men with a look on his face that said, 'Don't make me.'

'You want to fight me?' Ben said to Sizwe. 'Then you'll need a weapon. Take mine. I don't want it.' He flipped the machete, caught it by the tip of the blade and threw it. It twirled through the air with a hiss and speared point-first into a tree trunk four inches from Sizwe's left ear and stuck there, juddering.

Those four inches had been a deliberate aim-off, and Sizwe knew it very well. 'You could have killed me,' he said slowly.

'Nearest I'm going to get,' Ben replied. 'Now it's your turn. Give it your best shot.'

'Don't be fucking stupid, Ben,' Jeff said from behind the gun.

'Stay out of it,' Ben said. 'I owe him that much.'

Sizwe looked at Ben, then looked at the machete buried in the trunk. He hesitated. Then grasped the handle and twisted and wrenched the blade free. He took a step towards Ben with the machete raised.

'I'll shoot him,' Jeff said.

'You'll do no such thing,' Ben warned him.

Sizwe came on another step, then another. His face was contorted with confused rage. Ben didn't move.

Sizwe faltered. The blade sank as if it had suddenly become much too heavy for him to hold. He let it droop weakly to

369

his side and then slip from his fingers and clang dully to the ground as he stood there, chest heaving, not from physical effort but from the emotional turmoil that was tearing him apart inside. 'I cannot kill a man who does not fight back,' he said, looking at Ben with the crazed, bloodshot eyes of a torture victim.

'Then don't do it,' Ben said. 'There has to be a better way than for innocent men to gut each other.'

Uwase said, 'What way is there for us? We cannot all win this fight.'

'Better that than we all lose,' Ben said. 'You trust Khosa to keep his side of the deal?'

Sizwe shook his head, mournfully. 'No. Everyone has heard of this man. There are many stories of the things he does. He will never stop until there is no more blood to spill.'

'Unless we can make him stop,' Ben said. 'Nobody else has to die. Only those who deserve it. If we work together, we can beat him.'

'What are you thinking, mate?' Jeff asked, lowering the pistol.

'I'm keen to hear it myself,' Tuesday said.

Rusanganwa said, 'Why should we trust you? You said we would make a deal. Now many are dead.'

Ben felt the knife go deep with those words. 'We won't get a second chance at this. We do it once, and we do it right.'

Sizwe said, 'Tell us your plan.'

Chapter 56

Captain Terminator was becoming agitated. After the initial burst of gunfire that rocked the thicket had quickly dwindled into silence with nothing since, his expectations of a good, bloody human cockfight had shrivelled up into disappointment, boredom, and now into restless indecision as he paced up and down beyond the thicket's edge, trying to peer here and there through the impenetrable screen of leaves and thorns. He was wondering whether he should venture in there himself to make sure everything was okay, or whether it would be better to skirt around the edge of the thicket to find the others, for strength in numbers, in which case they'd be leaving most of the thicket's perimeter unguarded and an easy escape route for the prisoners, which could be a mistake; or again whether he should run back to his general and fetch more men.

The latter idea wouldn't be a wise decision either. He had already been informed of the consequences of failure to perform his allotted task. While by contrast, courage and leadership initiative would surely be rewarded.

So on balance, Captain Terminator felt that his best option was to venture in there alone, like the brave warrior he indisputably was, see for himself what was what and kick the necessary ass to get it all sorted out. The General would be proud of him; might even offer him a cigar. What a feather in his cap that would be, to stand shoulder to shoulder with his commander and light up a Havana in front of all his jealous comrades! Better still, the General might let him have first cut at that squirming little cockroach of a kid, later, when they finished the job they'd started.

With a smile at the promise of these future rewards, Captain Terminator racked the bolt of his AK, drew his machete and went striding into the crackling undergrowth, hacking and chopping his way through.

He was twenty yards into the thicket when a soft rustle among the bushes up ahead froze him mid-step and turned his blood suddenly cold.

The lion. He'd forgotten all about the damn lion. It was in there. Stalking him. Getting ready to charge him. He could almost feel its hungry eyes on him, measuring him up from head to toe.

He levelled his rifle and swallowed hard. Backed away a step, then another, then turned in panic and started rushing and crashing back the way he'd come.

But he hadn't taken three steps before a force as solid and hard as a brick wall hit him with a savage violence that exploded like white lightning inside his head and slammed him to the ground, driving the air from his lungs. He tried to scream, convinced as he was that the lion's teeth were about to close in on him and rip his throat out.

But it wasn't the lion. The lion would have been better.

Ben stood over the nose picker and kicked him once more in the left temple, not hard enough to kill him, just enough to render him all the way unconscious.

'So much for Captain Percolator,' Jeff said with a fierce grin. 'Not so cocky now, are we?'

'What are we going to do with the bastard?' Tuesday asked, gathering around the prone soldier with the six Africans and looking down.

'Sizwe, please give me your earring,' Ben said, holding out his hand for it. Sizwe hesitated, then unhooked the ornamental pendant from his left earlobe and passed it over without question. Ben took it from him and laid it out flat on his palm to examine. The business end of the earring was an S-shaped wire fishhook with a blunt point, much like any of the earrings Ben had had cause to see up close in his time, during those few periods in his life when he'd been sufficiently domesticated to cohabit with someone more inclined to wear the things than he was.

An equally quick examination of the left earlobe of the unconscious nose picker, a.k.a. Captain Terminator, unsurprisingly revealed no kind of pre-pierced hole through which to insert the wire hook. But Ben was good with that. Crouching in the dirt beside the prone body, Ben stretched the guy's earlobe as far as it would go, like a flange of dark rubber, and stabbed the hook through the flesh. There was a little blood, but that wouldn't be a problem, under the circumstances.

Jeff was staring at him. 'Ben, what the fuck?'

It was a detail of the plan that had only just come to Ben. He was making it up as he went along. 'Trust me,' he said.

'Okay, then what next?'

'The Hi-Power,' Ben said, and held out his hand.

Hi-Power was the name given in the trade to the Browning nine-millimetre GP35 pistol, or *Grande Puissance* model of 1935, made by Fabrique Nationale in Herstal, Belgium, that had long been a staple weapon of armies worldwide. Jeff handed the nine over to Ben.

'Now, everyone, please stand back a little,' Ben said. 'This could get a little messy.'

And he pointed the pistol muzzle right up close to Captain Terminator's face, averted his own to avoid the worst of the spatter, and pulled the trigger. Just as Khosa had done to his own soldier earlier that day, except with slightly less spectacular results. Only slightly. The remains of the man's face wouldn't have been instantly recognisable to his own mother.

'Christ, Ben,' Tuesday breathed when the ringing in their ears had subsided.

'Whatever works,' Ben said grimly.

'This is the man who wanted to kill Gatete,' Sizwe said through bared teeth. 'You should have let me shoot him.'

Ben applied the pistol's safety catch and stuffed it into the baggy side pocket of his combat jacket. 'I'm not leaving you out, Sizwe. If you're up to it, that is.'

'I do not understand.'

'Six sets of tags and a head in a bag,' Ben said. 'That's what the man asked for. That's what we'll give him. Do you want to do the honours, or shall I?'

Sizwe was only too happy to perform the service, clutching his machete with a look of animal ferocity while Ben stepped away to give him room. Sizwe was a very strong man. It took only two strokes of the blade to sever Captain Terminator's head from his shoulders.

After what they'd all witnessed that day, the horror of the moment barely even seemed to register.

Ben held the bag out, and Sizwe dropped the head into it.

'Tags,' Ben said. The six Africans unlooped the strings of military dog tags from around their necks and dropped them into the bag, now heavy and dripping in Ben's hands. Ben knelt back down beside the headless body, set the bag down for a moment and unclipped the bunch of grenades from the dead man's belt. Five of them would do fine for what he had in mind. He stuffed them in his jacket pockets with the pistol.

'Now what?' Tuesday said, staring aghast at the bag.

'So far, so good,' Ben said. 'Now we move to the next phase.'

As it turned out, none of the remaining sentries scattered around the edge of the thicket had shown the same initiative as their comrade Captain Terminator. Not that it did them any good.

Ben and the others found each of the five in turn either lounging smoking or half-asleep against a tree trunk with his rifle between his knees, or standing in a daze with his back to the thicket and a mouthful of khat cud. The sounds of gunshots evidently hadn't bothered them. All part of the game.

But now they were sitting ducks. One after the other.

Ben and Jeff killed two each. Sizwe killed the last. It was quick, it was quiet, and it was bloody. No mercy deserved and none given. They dragged the bodies into the heart of the thicket, laid them out in a row and collected their weapons into a pile.

'We've been out here long enough,' Ben said. 'Khosa will be wondering what's going on. It's time for us three to return to the village, before he sends more soldiers out here.'

This was the part of the plan that Sizwe and his friends still weren't convinced about. 'If you tell him you have won, he will kill our families.'

'No more innocent blood,' Ben said. 'Not today.' He dug the grenades out of his pocket and handed one each to the village men. 'You remember what I said about how these things work? Pull the pin and throw, and keep your head

375

down. And for the love of God, don't fumble and drop them at your feet.'

'We remember.'

'What about those?' Ben asked, pointing at the Kalashnikovs on the ground.

Sizwe nodded. 'Even a child can shoot a gun.' It went beyond a figure of speech. Sizwe was more than old enough to have seen at least some of the mass genocide that had rocked Rwanda only a few years earlier, in the wanton bloodbath of the so-called civil war. He had probably seen plenty of child soldiers just as proficient with automatic weapons as adults.

Ben pointed at his Omega, now on Sizwe's wrist. 'Give us four minutes. Count them exactly on the second hand. During that time, the six of you split up into pairs, with the rifles and the grenades. Work your way around the edges of the village. When the four minutes are up, Sizwe throws the first grenade. That's the signal. When you others hear the explosion, you let loose as fast as you can, one after another.'

'We will destroy our huts,' Uwase protested. 'The village will burn.'

'A few outer huts you can rebuild,' Ben said. 'And it's the rainy season. The thatch is still damp. It won't burn easily. Now, once that last grenade has gone off, I want you to start firing your guns. Point them up in the air, and keep firing until they're empty.'

'I do not see what good is firing in the air,' Rusanganwa said with a doubtful frown.

'I'm not asking you to get into a fight with these people,' Ben reminded him. 'And we can't afford for a stray bullet to go anywhere near the hut where your families are, or near any of our people. I just want you to make as much noise as you can. Make it sound as if the village is under attack by many fighters. Do you understand?'

Sizwe nodded. 'We can do all of this.'

'Then, when your guns are empty, I want you to stay hidden. All hell will break loose in there. Most of Khosa's troops will panic and run. Only a few will stay near their general. We'll take care of those.'

'And Khosa?'

'You leave him to me,' Ben said.

'You are going to kill him?'

Ben nodded. 'Most definitely. And then I'll get started on him.'

Chapter 57

In war, as in life, nothing is guaranteed. Few combat strategies, however carefully planned, ever survive first contact with the enemy. Military tacticians had been saying it for centuries, and Ben was acutely aware of it at this moment as he, Jeff and Tuesday made their way back towards the village.

His scheme wasn't perfect, by any means. It was a desperate, last-resort, seat-of-the-pants kind of deal that he didn't want to over-analyse for fear that all the potential holes in it might put him off. But it was all they had. Another chance like this might never come. There was only one thing he knew for sure: if he did nothing, if he didn't grasp this one tiny fragile opportunity and give it all he had, sooner or later Jude and all the rest of them would be dead men.

Ben, Jeff and Tuesday walked into the village square to find Khosa sitting on an upturned bucket as though it were a golden throne, still luxuriating in the cigar he'd promised himself, and surrounded by twenty of his men. Jude was kneeling on the ground at the General's side, looking ashen and sick to the stomach. A few yards away, Gerber and Hercules had been made to kneel with guns to their heads. All around them lay the pitiful body parts and hacked corpses of the villagers, red slowly turning to russet brown.

'You have returned victorious, soldier,' Khosa said with a smile. 'I knew it would be so. Though it took you longer than I thought. I was beginning to wonder what tricks you were playing, hmm?'

Ben dropped the soggy, heavy sackcloth bag on the ground between Khosa's feet. 'There's what you asked for. We passed your stinking test. Now let us go.'

Khosa flicked ash from his Cohiba, then reached casually inside the bag. He rummaged around as though it were a lucky dip, then came up with a bloody fistful of the dog tags. Counted one, two, three, four, five, six. He nodded. Tossed them away.

Next he reached back inside the bag and pulled the head out by a handful of its owner's short, wiry, Afro-textured hair. He raised it up in front of him at arm's length, like holding a lantern to light the way. Blood dripped from the ragged stump of the severed neck, not yet congealed and pattering into a small pool between his feet. He peered closely into the ruined features of the disembodied face, then rotated the head a few degrees clockwise to examine the earring hooked through the left earlobe, with its beads and coiled wire pendant. He nodded once more. Then, much to his soldiers' amusement, he plucked the half-smoked cigar from his mouth and stuck it between what was left of the head's open lips.

'This cockroach Sizwe looks much better now,' he proclaimed to the laughing soldiers, raising the head higher to display it to them. 'Do you not think?'

Khosa plucked out the cigar and replaced it in his own mouth, puffing clouds of smoke. He dropped the head back into the bag and kicked it away like a football. It rolled a few yards and came to a rest in the dirt.

'You have indeed passed the test, soldier,' Khosa said to Ben. 'But I cannot let you go. That was not the agreement.'

Ben was counting down the seconds in his mind. He'd told Sizwe to hang back for four minutes. That left one minute and forty-five seconds to go before Sizwe and his companions kicked off the diversion. Ben could feel the weight of the Browning Hi-Power in his pocket. He was mentally running through the motions, visualising every detail. Khosa would be the first to die. To shoot him now would be suicide for Ben himself, and certain death for the others. But to shoot him when all hell started breaking loose: at least then there was a good chance that all six of them would survive it.

Khosa frowned, gazing left and right. He blinked as if he'd suddenly remembered something, and raised a hand. 'Wait. Someone is missing. Where are the guards I sent with you?'

'The lion got one of them,' Ben said. 'Isn't that right, Jeff?'

'Happened right in front of me,' Jeff said. 'Most horrible thing I've ever seen in my life.'

Khosa blinked again. 'The lion took one of my men?'

Ben shrugged, as if such things were a daily occurrence for British army soldiers. 'What did you think would happen, sending men in there with a man-eater? You want to send a team to find the remains, that's up to you. Personally, I'd let it go. That's not a happy cat in there.'

'One man,' Khosa said. 'Where are the others?'

One minute, twenty-eight seconds to go.

Ben shook his head. 'Sorry to be the one to tell you, General, but your men have deserted you. I heard them talking. It's a coup. They're probably still out there right at this moment, conspiring how to kill you.'

It might have been a flimsy psychological thread to hang a whole strategy on, but it was every bit as effective as Ben could have wished. Khosa leapt to his feet, propelled into an all-consuming hurricane of outrage, a raptus of seething, foaming psychotic fury. He jumped up and down. He ripped the cigar from his lips and dashed it to sparking pieces in the dirt with the heel of his boot as though it had personally offended him. He tore his Colt Anaconda out of his holster, cocked its hammer and waved it like a man possessed at his terrified soldiers.

He screamed so loudly that his voice was distorted. 'YOU, YOU, YOU, YOU, AND YOU FOUR. GO AND FIND ME THESE DESERTERS AND BRING THEM BACK TO ME ALIVE! *GO! RUN! GO!*'

Eight of the soldiers jumped to it, clutching their rifles, probably glad to have been ordered off the scene of what could be an imminent massacre.

Ben kept counting. Sixty seconds to go.

'WHO ELSE WANTS TO BETRAY ME?' Khosa bellowed, waving his revolver at the rest of the soldiers. 'YOU?'

Not me, General.

'YOU?'

Never, General. We swear.

Forty seconds. Ben watched and listened to the raging fury that was the General storming up and down and pointing accusing fingers at his men. His enraged bellowing diminished in volume as his rage passed its apoplectic peak and began to hit the downslope. He was now merely screaming very, very loudly. 'Am I not a fair and generous leader? Do you not enjoy many privileges thanks to my kindness?'

Of course, General.

Twenty seconds.

'You! Do you want to lead this army in my place? What about you?'

We follow only you, General.

Amid all the noise, Ben counted down the last remaining seconds. So far, the plan seemed to be going all right. But Sizwe was taking his precious time. The four minutes were up.

Then they were more than up.

Nothing was happening, except that Khosa was beginning to calm down. Which was more frightening than the peak of his rage. There was no telling what he would do next. And there was a limit to how long Ben could keep this lunatic distracted with mind games.

Come on, Sizwe, Ben thought. *Where the hell are you?*

Nothing happened.

Not until twenty seconds later, when Ben knew that his plan had started to go badly wrong. From one instant to the next, it was suddenly unravelling worse than he could have possibly anticipated.

Half a dozen of the soldiers Khosa had sent out to hunt for the deserters were marching back into the heart of the village. They weren't alone.

Walking in front of them, heads bowed in defeat and arms raised in submission, were Uwase, Ntwali, Gasimba, Mugabo and Rusanganwa.

Chapter 58

'We caught these five cockroaches just as they were going to attack us, General,' the lead soldier reported. 'And we found these.'

The captured rifles and grenades clattered to the ground.

An electric shock prod stabbed at Ben's heart. Outwardly he let nothing show, but it was the collapse of everything. All hope was gone. Sizwe was on his own now, alone and running scared, having seen his companions caught and marched away at gunpoint, and probably convinced that more soldiers would be combing the brush for him at any moment. There was no way he was going to launch a diversionary attack on the village single-handed.

Run, Sizwe, Ben was thinking. *Run like hell and don't look back, no matter what.*

If the soldiers caught him too, Khosa would soon find out for sure that Ben had tricked him. Things were bad enough already.

Uwase, Ntwali, Gasimba, Mugabo and Rusanganwa were thrown down on their knees and made to grovel in a line as Khosa strode up to them, gnashing his teeth in rekindled fury.

'Where did you get these?' he demanded in a roar, and pointed at the weapons and grenades. When he got no reply, he spun around to face Ben with bulging eyes.

383

'What kind of deception is this, soldier? I ordered you to kill these men. Do you take me for an idiot? Is this how you repay my mercy?'

Ben's right hand was just inches from the pistol in his pocket. The urge to make a grab for it and start shooting was hard to suppress. If he put a bullet in Khosa's head, right here, right now, before the soldiers cut him down, what would happen next? Without their general to give the order, would they fall into disarray like the rabble they were, or would they simply open fire on the prisoners and not stop shooting until every single one of them was dead? If Ben pulled the trigger, was he saving Jude or was he killing him?

It was just too great a chance to take. Ben knew he couldn't risk it. In the blink of an eye, the gun in his pocket had now gone from being his best chance to being his greatest liability. Khosa had only to order the men to search Ben, and the jig would be up.

'Your orders were to bring back one head and six sets of tags,' Ben said, gazing coolly into Khosa's blazing eyes. He was having to use every last bit of his training and discipline to remain outwardly calm. 'That's what we did. I killed one and let the other five run. As your military advisor, I would respectfully suggest that a commanding officer's orders should be as clear and specific as possible, to the letter. If you meant differently, you should have said so.'

Khosa stared at him, clamping his jaws so hard that Ben half expected to see blood foaming out of his mouth.

'Where did they get the grenades?' Khosa demanded.

'From the dead body of the soldier the lion killed,' Ben said. 'That's my best guess. Maybe they chased it off.'

Khosa stared at him for ten long, drawn-out seconds. Ben could almost feel the rage from those bulging eyes boring into his head like beams of energy, scouring his mind, ransacking his thoughts for any trace of a lie. To look away now, to show the slightest sign of doubt or weakness, would be fatal.

Khosa said, 'Hm.'

Then turned back to point at the five kneeling Africans on the ground. 'I want these cockroaches DEAD!' he screamed at his soldiers. 'But first, kill the women and children. Every last one of them! Bring them out here and chop off their arms, legs and heads! I want this village razed to the ground! Let it be removed from the earth as if it had never existed! Spill their blood! SPILL THEIR BLOOD!'

The soldiers cheered and waved their guns in the air. They took up their general's chant, over and over, like a chorus from hell.

SPILL THEIR BLOOD!
SPILL THEIR BLOOD!

Jeff and Tuesday were standing rooted to the spot. Jude was staring wildly at Ben. Gerber and Hercules both had their eyes closed, as if trying to shut out the nightmare unfolding around them, just wanting it to be over.

SPILL THEIR BLOOD!
SPILL THEIR BLOOD!

Ben felt the weight of the pistol like a brick inside his pocket. In that moment, he very nearly thought 'Fuck it' and went for the weapon.

But before Ben was able to do anything that crazy, the explosive rattle of gunfire from beyond the outskirts of the village startled him back to his senses. The terrible chanting faltered and stopped. Khosa and his soldiers all turned towards the gunfire, momentarily distracted.

Ben's immediate thought was, *Sizwe*. He hadn't made his escape after all. He was back. The man was mounting a heroic solitary assault to claim back his village. The diversion was happening, after all. It could change everything.

And that could be all the chance Ben needed. He slipped his hand inside his pocket. His fingers closed around the butt of the Browning.

Now or never, he thought. *Do it.*

But he hadn't got the weapon half out of his pocket before everything changed again. And got worse. Much, much worse.

The gunfire had stopped as suddenly as it had begun. Two more of Khosa's soldiers were running back into the village, bursting with news to report to their commander.

Ben thought, *Shit, they've caught Sizwe.*

He was wrong. They hadn't caught Sizwe. Sizwe was still out there somewhere. But they had caught something.

The soldiers had caught the lion.

Chapter 59

The lion had been in the thicket all along. Watching, hiding, waiting. When the soldiers had gone in to search for the deserters as Khosa had ordered them, two men split from the main hunting party had accidentally flushed the animal from its hiding place. It had tried to attack one of them but been driven back by a volley of gunfire and gone crashing off through the thicket. In its blind panic, it had fallen into a ditch with steep banks from which it could not escape.

The soldiers breathlessly reported to Khosa that it was still there, trapped.

The General's eyes widened in enthralment at the news. 'I must see it!' he exclaimed. 'Show me the way!' His fury had abated instantly, like a child's tantrum appeased by some placatory gift. From one second to the next, he seemed to completely forget about the villagers he'd been just about to have chopped into pieces, and about the attempts at treachery and deception that had so enraged him just moments earlier. Gripped by fascination to see the lion, he ordered for some of his soldiers to stay behind and guard the five village men while everyone else accompanied him to the spot where the animal had become trapped.

The two who had found it led the way, Khosa striding after them with a rapt smile on his face. Ben, Jeff, Tuesday,

Jude, Gerber and Hercules were marched along at gunpoint in the General's wake. Few of the soldiers seemed particularly excited to see the lion. There were looks of disappointment that their fun had been interrupted, if no actual grumbles of dissent. Nobody would have dared push it that far. In any case, the fun would resume soon enough. The villagers weren't going anywhere.

As the procession of men headed deeper into the thicket, Ben exchanged anxious glances with Jeff and Tuesday. But their worry that Khosa was about to be led right past the spot where the headless Captain Terminator and the bodies of the other soldiers lay stretched out in the long grass soon left them when the procession instead veered off in a dogleg to the right, into an area thick with thorn bushes where the ground was loose and crumbly and the terrain rose and fell steeply in a series of natural ridges and troughs. Ben first made sure that none of the guards was watching him, then slipped the pistol from his pocket to discreetly lose it in the bushes.

A tough decision to make. It felt as if the last flimsy thread connecting him to the world had just been snipped.

They heard the animal's frantic roars before they got within sight of it. The soldiers bent back a tangle of thorny growth for their general to duck through, followed by the rest of the contingent, and then there it was. A big male, with a shaggy mane and a tawny coat streaked with dust and dirt. Just as the two soldiers had reported, it had got itself trapped between the steep earth banks of a deep trough that was closed off at both ends by thorn bushes so dense that not even a rhino could have ploughed through them.

Peering through the crowd that assembled at the edge of the ditch, Ben watched the frightened animal trying to get free. To his eye it looked thin and emaciated, its ribs too visible through its fur. Every time it hurled itself in an attempt to scramble up the bank, it could only rake desperately for a purchase using its front paws and kept slithering back down to the bottom time after time in a small landslide of dirt and stones and ripped plant roots. Ben saw right away why the poor beast was unable to climb or leap its way out. The same reason it had turned to preying on people. It had a withered and dragging hind leg that was too weak to help give it the push it needed to escape. An old injury, maybe, or the result of disease. The kind of debility that no wild animal, prey or predator, could hope to survive in the long term. That accounted for the emaciation, too. The lion was a desperate animal that was slowly starving and living on borrowed time.

Nature is cruel. But even a lame, starving lion was still a lion. Five hundred pounds of muscle and teeth and claws and killer instinct. If this thing had made an appearance earlier, things might have gone quite differently for Ben and the others.

Khosa stood on the edge of the ditch and shook his head in awed admiration. 'I would like to have this magnificent creature as a pet,' he announced to his men. Motioning at two of them, he added, 'You and you. Go in there and bring it to me.'

The men hesitated, not quite certain at that moment which frightened them more, Khosa or the lion.

'Wait,' Khosa said, holding up a finger. He thought for a moment; then a smile spread over his face. 'No. I have had a better idea.'

He turned to Ben.

'I have thought of another test, soldier.'

'I thought we had passed the test.'

'This test is not for you,' Khosa replied, and pointed back through the crowd of soldiers at Hercules. 'It is for him.'

Ben said nothing. His stomach had turned into a ball of molten lead.

Holding up his hands and smiling widely, Khosa seemed to address the sky and proclaimed the words '*Of all creatures that breathe and move upon the earth, nothing is bred that is weaker than man.*'

Down below where they stood, the lion charged at the bank and crashed its claws into the earth and fell back, roaring in rage and frustration.

'Homer, *The Odyssey*,' Khosa said to Ben. 'I told you, soldier, I am a very learned man. I have read all of Greek mythology. One of my favourites is the legend of the warrior Hercules. Do you know it?'

Ben knew it. That was why he said nothing. Because he was beginning to realise where this was going and it made him feel even sicker than before.

'If you do not know it, I will tell you. According to the legend, the great warrior Hercules was commanded by his king to carry out twelve labours, tasks so difficult and dangerous that no ordinary man could perform them. His first task was to slay a lion so mighty that its teeth could penetrate any armour, and it could not be killed by normal weapons. To prove himself, Hercules had to make the king an offering of its skin.'

Khosa beamed, liking his idea more and more. He pointed again at Hercules, the real Hercules, surrounded by Khosa's men with guns. 'You say he is strong, soldier. Now let us see how strong he is. You! Big man! Go down there and kill this lion and bring me its skin.'

Ben began, 'General—'

'Quiet! I have given an order. I am this man's king. He is my vassal. He must now do as I tell him. There is to be no discussion!'

'If you want to be a king,' Ben said quietly, 'then act like one. I can't let you do this.'

Khosa gave Ben another of his lingering, mind-scouring stares. 'This is the last time you will dare to tell me what I can and cannot do. Let me show you, soldier, what I can do.'

He motioned to his men. 'Kill the boy.'

Chapter 60

The soldiers instantly raised their rifles. Over the roars of the trapped lion below them came the metallic rattle of actions being cocked, safeties being released. Jude stood very still, very stiff, very pale. He raised his chin and looked resolutely into Ben's eyes, as if to say 'It's all right.'

'No,' Ben said.

Khosa slowly turned back to gaze at Ben. 'No?'

'Don't kill him.'

'Are you commanding your king?'

'I'm asking,' Ben said, fighting to keep his voice steady. His eyes were locked on Jude's.

'Does one now ask a king, as an equal?'

'All right,' Ben said. 'I'm begging.'

Jude gave a single shake of his head. *It's okay. Really.*

Khosa smiled and said, 'Better. Now tell me why I should not kill him.'

'Because if you do, it ends our arrangement,' Ben said.

'Then you have accepted my offer, soldier? Because I was not sure that you had, in your heart. I am not sure that you did not try to trick me before. A clever man like you is full of tricks, hmm?'

Ben said, 'Yes. I accept and agree.'

'With all your heart?'

'With all my heart.'

'Am I a wise and just king?'

'Yes,' Ben said. 'Very wise and very just.'

'You will serve me with loyalty?'

'To the last,' Ben said.

'And obey my orders?'

'Without question,' Ben said.

Khosa looked pleased. He glanced at the soldiers still pointing their rifles at Jude's head, then looked back at Ben. 'As you are my military advisor, let me ask your advice. Should I order my men to kill the boy, or should I send Hercules into combat with this lion?'

The huge tawny cat was still struggling to escape from the ditch. It was clawing and raking at the earth banks in a desperate attempt to clamber up and away to safety, but without the power in its hindquarters it still couldn't gain the momentum to scramble up the sheer slope. The bank was becoming eroded away by its efforts and becoming only more vertical as the lion dug itself in deeper.

Ben said nothing. He could feel Jeff's presence behind him, and Tuesday's, and Gerber's. He could sense the grim strain coming off all three of them like electric charge from a high-voltage cable. Nobody spoke. Ben looked down at the lion. Looked across at Jude. Then at Hercules.

'I am waiting for my advisor's counsel,' Khosa said with a raised eyebrow.

'Shoot me,' Jude called out. 'It's my choice. Go ahead and shoot me and let Hercules live.'

Khosa kept his eyes on Ben as he said, 'It is not your decision to make, White Meat. It is for my advisor to choose. But I hear nothing from him. Perhaps he is not a good advisor after all. Perhaps I have misplaced my faith in his judgement, and should replace him.'

Ben looked again at Hercules.

There's nothing I can do, he said with his eyes.

Hercules looked back at him. *I know.*

I'm so sorry.

I know.

Forgive me.

'I don't want my son to die,' Ben said to Khosa.

Khosa asked keenly, 'That is your choice?'

Ben swallowed hard. 'Yes. That's my choice.'

Khosa nodded. 'So it will be. For the moment.' He turned to the soldiers by Jude and waved down the rifles. Then he turned to the soldiers by Hercules.

'Put him in the hole.'

The soldiers closed in around Hercules. Hands grabbed his thick arms. He didn't try to resist. His shoulders sagged and his eyes were full of nothing but sadness.

Ben bowed his head as they shoved Hercules to the edge of the ditch and toppled him down the slope. The big man went slithering and sliding downwards, throwing up a plume of loose dirt and grunting as he hit the bottom.

The lion saw him and turned. Sensing a new threat, it lost interest in trying to escape. The law of nature. Flight was impossible. Now it had something to fight, instead. It lowered its maned head close to the ground and its shoulder muscles coiled and rippled under the matted fur. Its black lips gaped open in a snarl, showing fangs like devil's horns.

Hercules backed away. He threw a helpless, wide-eyed glance up at the crowd above him.

'In the legend,' Khosa declared, 'Hercules used a club to kill the lion. Even a mighty warrior should have a weapon. Throw him a club.'

One of the soldiers jerked the magazine out of his AK-47, jacked the round from the chamber and then tossed the rifle into the ditch. Hercules hesitated and then picked up the empty weapon, holding it by the barrel with the triangular wooden buttstock raised shoulder-high like a bat.

Ben's knees sagged under him. He wanted to curl up on the ground and sleep, but he knew he couldn't sleep again for a long time. Maybe for the rest of his life.

Hercules faced the lion. 'Come on then, motherfucker!'

The lion's snout wrinkled into another snarl. It made explosive huffing sounds from its chest and blew from its nostrils and pawed at the ground. Its great amber eyes gazed impassively at its trapped prey.

Then it attacked with all the massive force and shocking aggression of the most dangerous land predator in Africa. A lame, sick, starving lion. But still a lion. Five hundred pounds or more of muscle and teeth and lashing claws. Twice Hercules's weight. Ten times the strength of even the strongest human. It was only in the story world of old legends that a man armed with nothing but a club could defeat such an animal.

Hercules never had a chance. His first and only swing of the empty rifle struck the lion with what to a human would have been a skull-crushing blow across the side of the head, but the cat barely flinched and kept on coming. It swatted Hercules to the ground with one swipe of a forepaw the size of a dinner plate. Then it crushed him with its weight and closed its jaws around his thick neck and shook him from side to side like a terrier shaking a rat.

The screaming didn't last very long. Hercules was soon almost dead, although he was still moving, the fingers of an outflung and bloody arm flexing and twitching in the dirt. The lion backed away, sniffing at him, one paw cocked to prod and roll him to test if he was still alive. Then it closed back in and bit him again, ripping into his flesh. Hercules's arms and legs flailed and jerked spasmodically as the lion tore into the muscles of his shoulder and back, but ninety percent of it was just nerve response. He couldn't feel much any longer.

At least, Ben hoped he couldn't.

Khosa watched with a smile as the lion pulled Hercules apart. It ripped off one arm, tossed it aside, then ripped off the other. Then it buried its face into what was left of his throat. Chewing, tugging, tearing, swallowing.

By now Lou Gerber was on the ground, weeping openly.

'Make the goat man watch,' Khosa commanded. The soldiers seized Gerber's arms and yanked him back to his feet.

It was another long, agonising minute before Khosa got bored with the bloody spectacle. 'He has failed the test,' he declared. 'It is as I thought. This man was never a true warrior. Now let us return to the village. I have more business to attend to there.'

Chapter 61

Ben was barely conscious of the presence of the soldiers around him as he walked back to the village. He could only dimly sense that Jude, Jeff and the others were looking at him. He couldn't return their looks. He felt as though he had lead weights attached to his legs. His head was filled with a kind of buzzing and everything seemed somehow distant and unreal.

Back at the village, the rearguard of soldiers left behind stood over Sizwe's five companions, still kneeling on the ground with their heads bowed so low that their hair brushed the dirt. Sizwe himself would be long gone now. If he had any sense. Running through the bush, stricken with grief, streaming tears in the knowledge that his friends and family could no longer be saved, and there was nothing he could do but try to stay alive himself.

Trust me, Ben had said. And Sizwe had trusted him. And now it had come to this.

Khosa ordered for the village's vehicles to be brought, and soldiers hurried off to fetch them. Moments later, the grunt and snort of diesel engines filled the air. This was Africa, where fuel stations were so few and far that even the poorest man kept his truck fully gassed, if he could afford one at all, and loaded it with all the spare jerrycans he could fill. The vehicles lumbered through the village: a scarred and rusted-out old Mercedes-Benz L-series nineteen-ton heavy truck, and an even more ragged long-wheelbase Land Rover with a spare wheel mounted on the bonnet and a canvas top so ripped by thorns and branches that it was hanging in tatters. Both were blowing clouds of smoke, and their engines clattered and rattled.

Ben didn't have many prayers left in him, but he was praying that the arrival of the vehicles would spur Khosa to get out of here before he wrought worse carnage on the blighted village.

Once more, Ben's prayers went unanswered.

After Khosa had surveyed the vehicles and seemed satisfied with them, he turned his attention back to Uwase, Ntwali, Gasimba, Mugabo and Rusanganwa, the five them all kneeling silently in the dirt. 'I have tried to show fairness to these men,' he proclaimed, in a tone that conveyed both his greatness as a leader and his hurt at their betrayal. 'I have offered them the chance of freedom, for themselves and their families. What do they offer in return? Treachery. They have proved to me that they are nothing more than cockroaches. Unworthy of mercy. Unworthy of life.'

Khosa paused. He shook his head, solemnly, like a judge weighing up the gravity of the moment before passing sentence.

'You will bring the women and children,' he told the soldiers. 'You will make them kneel here before me. Then you will kill the children in front of their mothers. Cut off their heads. Then cut off the heads of the mothers. Then you will kill the last of the men. Kill them all.'

And they did.

Chapter 62

Afterwards, the dark clouds that had been gathering like battlefield smog in the air finally burst, as if a giant knife had reached up to the heavens and slashed their guts open. The rainstorm came down in solid sheets, lashing and pounding the ground. It washed the blood into the earth, and washed the earth into rivers of purple mud. But nothing would ever wash the stench of death from this place.

A dismal hush fell over the remaining prisoners as they let themselves be herded into the Mercedes box truck. They moved slowly through the rain. Their clothes and hair were soaked, but they didn't care. The soldiers barked and shoved and jabbed. They didn't care about them, either.

Soon afterwards, the heavily laden trucks were bumping and lurching away in tandem from the silent village, down the muddied track towards the dirt road. Heading west, big tyres crashing through flooded potholes, headlights poking beams through the deluge, wipers slapping back and forth as fast as they could bat the rain aside. Khosa had made Ben ride with him in the lead vehicle. The General lounged in the front of the Land Rover with one elbow crooked on the door sill, laughing at his own jokes and smoking and talking away happily.

Khosa, the victor. Khosa, the king. The unquestioned lord

of all he surveyed, wherever he went. With the diamond in his pocket, a gigantic fortune at his fingertips. And nothing to stop him.

Ben sat still, silent and numb. He felt as though his heart had broken, for Jude, for the villagers, for Hercules, for all of them. It was as if all his strength had left him and would never return. A feeling he'd never experienced with such overwhelming intensity before. He played back in his mind things that had happened in the course of his life. The grief of losing loved ones. The bitter wrench of failure. The worst times he'd come through.

He'd thought he'd known what it felt like to be swallowed up in absolute black despair.

He'd been wrong.

He'd had no idea what it felt like. Not until this moment.

The trucks rumbled on through the rain, and then through the night, and on through the first glimmers of morning when the sunrise turned the light the colour of blood. Deeper and deeper into a different world. One in which human life was cheaper than dirt. Where a man with absolute power and the ruthlessness to wield it could do anything he liked, unchecked.

This was not Ben's world any more.

Ben was in Khosa's world now.

Later that day, they crossed from Rwanda into the Congo, over a flimsy river bridge at a point on the border where there were no checks, no stops, no authorities within fifty miles. Soon after that, as they rumbled along an arrow-straight dirt highway that shot ahead to infinity through a vista of rolling green plains and faraway hazy mountains, they were met by a contingent of Khosa's forces that had been contacted by radio to rendezvous with them.

They appeared at first like a shape-shifting spectrum of colour through a heat shimmer where the road met the sky, moving fast at the heart of a great swirling dust cloud that resembled an approaching sandstorm. Moving fast, detail falling into focus as they sped closer and closer. The dull glint of sunlight on matt-painted bodywork and bull bars and dusty windscreens. Big brutal tyres crunching the road surface. The line stretched out far behind the lead vehicle. There must have been thirty or forty of them. It was a whole fleet of what irregular armies called 'technicals', which were civilian pickup trucks modified for warfare. Most of them crudely spray-painted in splodges of green and brown camouflage. Several were equipped with half-inch-calibre American Browning heavy machine guns or Russian-made anti-aircraft cannons fixed on swivel mounts behind the cab. The kind of firepower that could level a forest or decimate a whole town. They were the only vehicles in sight, as if they owned the road. Perhaps they did own it. Nobody, not even regular government troops, would have stood in their way in any case.

The approaching convoy blasted a symphony of honking horns as they recognised their leader. Khosa had the Land Rover pull off the road, followed by the Mercedes box truck, and moments later they were surrounded by a roaring, bouncing mass of vehicles that skidded to a halt on the rough ground and spewed scores of Khosa's militia fighters all running to greet and welcome him like a returning hero. The force of thirty that had travelled from Somalia had now swelled to over two hundred heavily armed soldiers. Ben hadn't seen this many guns all together in one place in a long time.

Then the final vehicle at the tail end of the convoy came into view, still far off, a speeding black dot trailing a dust cloud and gradually growing larger. As he stepped down from the Land Rover and tried to spot Jude, Jeff and the others among the crowd disembarking from the box truck, Ben detected a palpable sense of excitement among the soldiers and heard exclamations of 'Here he comes!' and 'Masango is coming!'

The car wasn't an armoured pickup, nor a four-wheel-drive of any description, but a long Mercedes limousine, shiny black coachwork stained with the dirt of a long drive on unmade roads. It slowed as it reached the mass gathering of vehicles and pulled gently off the road, wallowing and rocking on its soft suspension. Its windows were a smoky tint just short of black, and Ben could make out no more than dark shapes in the front seats and nothing at all in the rear.

The limousine rolled to a halt. The driver stayed where he was and kept the engine purring while the front-seat passenger got out. He looked like a bodyguard. A tough, burly African, incongruously well dressed in the midst of all the military khaki. Italian silk draped over planes of sculpted muscle. Dark glasses. Stubby Uzi submachine pistol. He stalked around to the rear door and opened it, and out stepped a tall, thin and elegant black man with silvering hair and an expensive light grey suit.

This would be Masango, Ben thought. But who was he?

Khosa had been doing an exultant victory lap of his two-hundred-strong fighting force when he saw the limo pull up and broke away from his men to come striding to meet it. He and the tall man in the grey suit shook hands and patted each other's shoulders like old friends.

As much as Ben wanted to go and find Jude and his friends, he wanted to know who this man Masango was. He walked around the front of the parked Land Rover and leaned on its square wing, watching and listening.

'You had us worried, Jean-Pierre,' the tall man was saying. 'When I heard about the plane—'

'It was nothing,' Khosa laughed, brushing it off. 'I decided to take the scenic route.'

The scenic route, Ben thought, and went on watching the two men in disgust as they laughed and backslapped and bantered some more. Khosa seemed to sense Ben's eyes on them. He turned and guided the tall man by the elbow to meet him, as if doing polite introductions on the country club lawn at a society party.

'Soldier, I want you to meet César Masango,' Khosa said, curling an arm around Masango's shoulders. 'He is my political attaché. He is the man who is going to help put me into power one day very soon.'

Masango offered his hand to Ben. 'Pleased to make your acquaintance, Mister—?'

Ben ignored the hand and didn't move or speak.

'The soldier is my military advisor, but sometimes does not say very much,' Khosa said, flashing a look at Ben.

Masango shrugged, as if saying, if he doesn't want to talk, fine, fuck him. They clearly had more important matters to discuss. 'So, Jean-Pierre. Is it true? You have it?'

'I have it,' Khosa said with a slow smile that he couldn't suppress, and took out the enormous diamond to show his colleague. Under the bright sunlight, the unreal fist-sized rock seemed to be filled with dancing fire.

Masango shook his head in awe. 'May I hold it?'

'Careful, or my men will shoot,' Khosa said, and they both laughed.

Masango clenched the diamond in his hands, gaping. 'With this,' he said, 'anything is possible.'

'And everything is within our grasp,' Khosa said with a fire dancing in his own eyes.

Masango asked, 'Can I take it to show my wife? She will be amazed.'

'Of course. Take it, take it. Just make sure that you bring it back in the morning.' Khosa burst out laughing and punched Masango's arm playfully. Just two guys messing around. What a double act.

'And now,' Khosa said, turning his attentions back towards Ben, 'the time has come to say goodbye.'

Ben stared at him, not understanding.

Khosa snapped his fingers. Two soldiers immediately hurried off towards the box truck. They came hurrying back seconds later, now three. They had Jude by the arms. His wrists were cuffed in front of him.

Jolts of alarm shot through Ben. What was happening here? 'Jude?'

'Ben? I don't know where they're taking me.'

'What's this about, Khosa?' Ben demanded.

'Where we are going, you will too busy to look after your son,' Khosa said. 'So my friend César will be looking after him now.'

Ben's heart was skipping beats and his hands were beginning to tremble. The sun was burning hot, but a chill like a freezing fog was descending over him. 'Where are you taking him?'

'Somewhere safe,' Khosa said. Then he chuckled and added, 'Safe from his father. Do not worry, soldier, we will not let him come to too much harm. He is there to protect our investment.'

'Investment in what?' Ben snapped.

Masango said, 'In you, Mister Hope.' The political attaché made a big show of checking his watch. 'Now, we have a long drive back, so . . .'

'Do not let me keep you, César,' Khosa said warmly. 'Safe journey. We will talk soon, hmm?'

The soldiers transferred Jude into the hands of the body-guard with the Uzi. He held Jude's arm in a pincer grip and began steering him towards the limo, but Ben blocked his way and ignored the nine-millimetre snout of the machine pistol pointing at his midriff.

'Let it go, Ben,' Jude said. 'You'll only make it worse.'

'This isn't over,' Ben told him. 'You hear me? This is not over. I'll find you.'

'Put him in the car,' Khosa said.

'I'll come for you, Jude,' Ben said. He couldn't disguise the catch in his voice.

'Dad—'

Dad.

And then Jude was being dragged towards the open back door of the limo. The man with the Uzi climbed in beside him, reached for the door handle and shut it with a soft clunk. Ben stared at the black-tinted rear window but could no longer see Jude inside.

César Masango gave Khosa a last wave and climbed into the other side of the limo's rear. The car purred slowly off, bouncing and lurching over the rough ground until it reached the road, then accelerated smartly away.

Ben watched it go.

'You will see him again, soldier. One day. Perhaps alive, too.' Khosa walked away laughing.

Ben watched the limo shrink into the distance. He watched until all that could be seen was a tiny rooster-tail of dust on the horizon where the road melted hazily into the sky.

Then it was gone.

Jude was gone.

Ben closed his eyes and the ice wave of despair broke over him.

Then he opened them again. Said out loud, 'No.' Looked

405

at his clenched fists and felt the power of his rage surging through him, as if it could boil his blood in his veins.

Khosa hadn't won this thing yet. He just thought he had.

Ben pictured Khosa's face in front of him, and made his promise to the man.

I will finish you. Sooner or later. No matter what. You're a dead man walking. You might as well start digging your own grave.

And Ben didn't know if he was imagining it or not, but from somewhere inside his mind he thought he could hear the echo of maniacal laughter.

END OF PART ONE

To be continued . . .

THE DEVIL'S KINGDOM

Sequel to STAR OF AFRICA and the
concluding part of

Ben Hope's epic African adventure

Available November 2016

Read on for an
exclusive extract . . .

Chapter One

South Kivu Province,
Democratic Republic of Congo

It was a rough road that the lone Toyota four-wheel-drive was trying to negotiate, and the going was agonisingly slow. One moment the worn tyres would be slithering and fighting for grip in yet another axle-deep rut of loose reddish earth, the next the creaking, grinding suspension would bump so hard over the rubble and rocks strewn everywhere that the vehicle's three occupants were bounced out of their seats with a crash that set their teeth on edge.

At this rate, it was going to be some more hours before they reached the remote strip where the light plane was due to pick up the two Americans and fly them and their precious cargo to Kavumu Airport, near Bukavu. Once safely arrived at the airport, the pair intended to waste no time before jumping on the first jet heading back home and getting the hell out of here. But safety and escape still seemed a long way beyond their reach right now. They were still very much in the danger zone, a fact that didn't escape them for a moment.

The battered, much-repaired old Toyota was one of the few possessions of a local man named Joseph Maheshe who now and then hired himself out as a driver and guide to tourists. Not that many tourists came here any more, not even the thrill-seeking adventurous ones. It was a precarious place and an even more precarious trade for Joseph, but the only one he knew. He'd been a taxi driver in Kigali, back over the border in neighbouring Rwanda, when the troubles there twenty years earlier had forced him and his wife, both of them of Tutsi ethnicity, to flee their home never to return. Joseph had seen a lot in his time, and knew the dangers of this area as well as anyone. He wasn't overjoyed that the two Americans had talked him into coming out here. He was liking the grinding sounds coming from his truck's suspension even less.

While Joseph worried about what the terrible road surface was doing to his vehicle, his two backseat passengers had their own concerns to occupy their minds. They were a man and a woman, both dishevelled and travel-stained, both shining with perspiration from the baking heat inside the car, and both in a state of great excitement.

The man's name was Craig Munro, and he was a middlingly-successful freelance investigative reporter based seven thousand miles from here in Chicago. In his late forties, he was nearly twice the age of his female companion. They weren't any kind of an item; their relationship was, always had been and would remain professional, even though the lack of privacy when camping out rough for days and nights on end in this wilderness sometimes forced a degree more intimacy on them than either was comfortable with.

The woman's name was Rae Lee, and she had worked for Munro as an assistant and photographer for the last eighteen months. Rae was twenty-five, second-generation Taiwanese American, and she'd been top of her law class at Chicago University for two years before switching tracks and studying photography at the city's prestigious Art Institute. She had taken the job with Munro more for the experience, and for ideological reasons, than for the money – money being something that wasn't always in good supply around her employer's shabby offices in downtown Chicago. The camera equipment inside the metal cases that jostled about in the back of the Toyota was all hers. But as expensive as it was, its true value at this moment lay in the large number of digital images Rae's long lens had captured last night and early this morning from their concealed stakeout.

It was an investigative journalist's dream. Everything they could have wished to find. More than they'd dared even hope for, which was the reason for their excitement. While at the same time, it was also the reason for their deep anxiety to get away and home as fast as possible. The kind of information and evidence they'd travelled to the Democratic Republic of Congo to acquire was precisely the kind that could get you killed. And the Congo was a very easy place in which to disappear without a trace, never to be seen again.

The hammering and lurching of the 4x4's suspension made it impossible to have any kind of conversation, but neither Munro nor Rae Lee needed to speak their thoughts out loud. They were both thinking the same thing: that when they got back to the States, that was when their work would begin in earnest. The physical danger would be behind them, but the real grind would await, and Munro's endless desk-bound hours of writing the sensational article would be just part of it. There would be scores of calls to make, dozens more contacts to chase, many facts to verify before they could go live with this thing. It was serious business. While what they'd found would cause a substantial stir in certain quarters, not everyone would be pleased. Including some very wealthy and powerful people who would use every ounce of their influence to block the publication of this information in every way possible. But what they had was pure gold, and they knew it. They were going to be able to blow the lid off this whole dirty affair and open a lot of eyes to what was really happening out here.

'How much further?' Munro yelled, leaning forwards in the back and shouting close to Joseph's ear to be heard.

'It is a very bad road,' the driver replied, as if this were news to them. He was a French speaker like many Rwandans past a certain age, and spoke English with a heavy accent. 'Three hours, maybe four.' Which put them still a long way from anywhere.

'This is hopeless,' Munro complained, flopping back in his seat.

Rae's long hair, normally jet black, looked red from all the dust. She flicked it away from her face and twisted round to throw an anxious glance over her shoulder at the camera cases behind her. The gear was getting a hell of a jolting back there, though it was well protected inside thick foam. 'We'll be okay,' she said to Munro, as much to reassure herself as him. 'Everything's fine.'

But as the Toyota bumped its way around the next corner a few moments later, they knew that everything wasn't fine at all.

Rae muttered, 'Oh, shit.'

Munro clamped his jaw tight and said nothing.

The two pickup trucks that blocked the road up ahead were the kind that were called 'technicals'. Rae had no idea where that name had come from, but she recognised them instantly, because they weren't hard to recognise. The flatbed of each truck was equipped with a heavy machine gun on a swivel mount, with ammunition belts drooping from them and coiled up on the floor like snakes. The machine guns

412

were pointed up the road straight at the oncoming Toyota. A soldier stood behind each weapon, ready to fire. Several more soldiers stood in the road, all sporting the curved-magazine Kalashnikov assault rifles that Rae had quickly learned were a ubiquitous sight just about everywhere in the eastern Congo and probably all across the entire country, over a land mass bigger than all of Europe.

'Could be government troops, maybe,' Munro said nervously as the Toyota lurched towards the waiting roadblock. In a badly decayed and impoverished state where even regular army could closely resemble the most thrown-together rebel force, sometimes it was hard to tell.

'Maybe,' Joseph Maheshe said. He looked uncertain.

There was no driving around them, and certainly no way to double back. Joseph stopped the Toyota as the soldiers marched up and surrounded them, aiming their rifles at the windows. The unit commander was a skinny kid of no more than nineteen. He was draped in cartridge belts like a rapper wears gold chains and had a semiauto pistol dangling against his ribs in a shoulder holster. A marijuana roll-up the size of a small banana drooped from his mouth. His eyes were rolling and his finger was on the trigger of his AK47.

'Let me handle this,' Munro said, throwing open his door.

'Be very careful, mister,' Joseph Maheshe cautioned him. Anxiety was in his eyes.

As Munro stepped from the car two soldiers grabbed his arms and roughly hauled him away from the vehicle. Rae swallowed and emerged from the other passenger door, her heart thudding so hard she could hardly walk. She'd heard the stories. There were a lot of them, and they generally ended the same way.

The soldiers in the trucks and on the ground all spent a second or two eyeing the Oriental woman's skimpy top, the honey flesh of her bare shoulders and as much of her legs as were made visible by the khaki shorts she was wearing. Her attractiveness was an unexpected bonus for them. A few exchanged grins and nods of appreciation, before the teen commander ordered them to search the vehicle. They started swarming around it, wrenching open the doors and tailgate and poking around inside. Munro and Rae were held at bay with rifles pointed at them. Joseph Maheshe didn't try to resist as they hauled him out from behind the wheel.

The soldiers instantly took an interest in the flight cases in the back of the Toyota. The unit commander ordered they be opened up.

'Whoa, whoa, hold on a minute,' Munro said, putting on a big smile and brushing past the guns to speak to the commander. 'You guys speak English, right? Listen, you really don't need to open those. It's just a bunch of cameras. What do you say, guys? We can come to an agreement. Nothing simpler, right?' As he spoke, he reached gently into the pocket of his shorts, careful to let them see he wasn't hiding a weapon in there, and slipped out a wallet from which he started drawing out banknotes marked BANQUE CENTRALE DU CONGO, the blue hundred-franc ones with the elephant on them.

The commander grabbed the wallet from him, tore out all the Congolese money that was inside as well as the wad of US dollars Munro was carrying, his credit cards and American driver's licence, and stuffed it in his combat vest. He tossed away the empty wallet.

'Hey. I didn't mean for you to take all of it,' Munro protested.

'Shut up, motherfucka!' the commander barked.

'Give me back my dollars and my cards, okay? Come on, guys. Play fair.'

Rifles were pointed at Munro's head and chest. Beads of

414

sweat were breaking out on his brow and running into his eyes. He held up his palms.

'What is your business here, American bastard?' the commander asked.

'Tourists,' Munro said, his face reddening. 'Me and my niece here. So can I have my dollars back, or what?'

Rae was thinking, *Please be quiet. Please don't make this worse.* How could she be his niece? For such a gifted investigator, he was a hopeless liar.

The commander shouted orders at his men. Two of them stepped up, grabbed Munro by the arms and flung him on the ground. Rifle muzzles jabbed and stabbed at him, like poking hay. Rae screamed out, 'Don't shoot him! Please!'

More of the weapons turned to point at her. She closed her eyes, but they didn't shoot. Instead, all three of them were held at gunpoint while the soldiers went on ransacking the Toyota. They opened up the camera cases, spilled out Rae's gear and quickly found the Canon EOS with the long lens. The commander turned it on and flicked through the stored images, calmly puffing on his joint, until he'd seen enough to satisfy him. He shook his head gravely.

'You are not tourists. You are motherfucka spies. We will report this to General Khosa.'

At the mention of the name Khosa, Rae went very cold. That was when she knew that nothing Munro could say or do would make this situation worse. It was already as bad as it could be.

'Spies? What in hell are you talking about? I tell you we're tourists!' But it wasn't so easy for Munro to rant and protest convincingly while he was being held on the ground with a boot sole planted against his chest and a Kalashnikov to his head.

'Kill this *mkundu*,' the commander said to his soldiers. 'When you are finished with the whore, cut her throat.'

Rae felt her stomach twist. She was going to be gang-raped and left butchered at the roadside like a piece of carrion for wild animals to dismember and gnaw on her bones. She wanted to throw up.

She had to save herself somehow.

And so she said the first thing that came to her.

'Wait! My family are rich!' she yelled.

The commander turned and looked at her languidly. He took another puff from his joint. 'Rich? How rich?'

'Richer than you can even imagine.'

He showed her jagged teeth. 'Rich like Donald Trump?'

'Richer,' Rae said. That was an exaggeration, admittedly. It might have been true back in about 1971, twenty years before she was born. 'If you don't harm us, there will be a big, big reward for you.' She spread her arms out wide, as if to show him just how much would be in it for him.

The commander digested this for a moment, then glanced down at Munro and kicked him in the ribs. 'This mother-fucka says he is your uncle.'

Munro grimaced in pain and clutched his side where he'd been kicked.

'He's my friend,' Rae answered, fighting to keep her voice steady.

The commander seemed to find this hard to believe, but his main concern was money. 'Is his family rich too?'

'We're Americans,' she said. 'All Americans are rich.'

The commander laughed. 'What about him?' He pointed at Joseph Maheshe.

'He is just a stupid farmer,' another of the soldiers volunteered. 'How can he pay?'

416

'This man is our driver,' Rae protested. 'He has nothing to do with this. Leave him out of it.'

The commander stepped closer to Joseph and examined him. Joseph had the classic Tutsi ethnicity, with fine features and a rather narrower nose, slightly hooked, that generally, though not always, distinguished them from Bantu peoples like the Hutu. During the Rwandan genocide it had been the worst curse of the Tutsi people that they could often be recognised at a glance.

'This one looks like a cockroach,' the commander said. It wasn't the first time Joseph had heard his people described that way. Cockroach was what the Hutu death squads had called his brother and their parents, before hacking them all to death.

'Get on your knees, cockroach.'

Without protest, Joseph Maheshe sank down to his knees in the roadside grass and dirt and bowed his head. He knew what was coming, and accepted it peacefully. He knew the Americans might not be as lucky as this. He was sorry for them, but then they should not have come here.

The commander drew his pistol, pressed it to the side of Joseph's head and fired. The sound of the shot drowned out Rae's cry of horror. Joseph went down sideways and crumpled in the long grass with his knees still bent.

'We will take these American spies to General Khosa,' the commander said to his men. 'He will know what to do with them.'

The soldiers tossed the camera equipment into the back of one of the armed pickup trucks. The two prisoners were shoved roughly into the other, where they were forced to crouch low with guns pointed at them.

'You saved my life,' Munro whispered to Rae.

Eventually, that would come to be something he would

417

no longer thank her for. But for now, they were in one piece. Rae looked back at the abandoned Toyota as the pickup trucks took off down the rough road. Joseph's body was no more than a dark, inert smudge in the grass. Just another corpse on just another roadside in Africa. The vultures would probably find him first, followed not long afterwards by the hyenas.

As for Munro's fate and her own, Rae didn't even want to think about it.

Chapter Two

At various and frequent points throughout the ups and downs of what was turning out to be an unusually eventful existence, Ben Hope was in the habit of pausing to take stock of his life. To evaluate his current situation, to consider the sequences of events – planned or not – that had got him there, to ponder what lay ahead in the immediate and longer-term future, and to reflect on how he was doing generally.

All things considered, he had always thought of himself as being a pretty normal type of guy, and so he figured that this stocktaking exercise must be something most normal folks did, even though most normal folks probably didn't tend to find themselves in the kinds of situations that invariably seemed to keep cropping up in his path. Just like most normal folks didn't have to do the kinds of things he had to do in order to get out of those situations in one piece.

In his distant past, Ben's stocktaking had involved thoughts like *'Okay, so passing selection for 22 SAS might be the toughest challenge you've ever taken on, but you will not fail. You can do this. You will be fine.'*

Many years later it had been more along the lines of *'All right, so you've walked away from the military career you struggled so hard to build and the future looks uncertain. But it's a big world out there. You have skills. You will make it.'*

Or, some years further down the line again, *'So she's left you for good this time, and you feel like shit. But you won't always feel this way. You'll survive, like you always do.'*

If there was one thing Ben had learned, it was this: that wherever the tide might carry him, whatever fate might throw at him, however desperate his situation, however impossible the task facing him, however dark his future prospects or slim his chances of survival, he would live to fight another day. He would not be defeated or deterred, not by anything, not by anyone. That spirit was what had driven him, bolstered him, enabled him to be the man he was. Or the man he'd thought he was.

But not now. Not any more.

Everything had changed.

Because at this moment, as he sat there helpless and surrounded by aggressive men with guns, slumped uncomfortably on the dirty open flatbed of an old army truck with his knees drawn up in front of him and his head resting on his hands and every jolt of the big wheels and stiff suspension on this rough road somewhere in the middle of the Congo jarring through his spine, he was fighting a rising black tide of emptiness.

If there was a way out of this one, the plan had yet to come to him. And if there was a tomorrow, it wasn't one that he was sure he wanted to face.

Sitting next to Ben in the back of the truck, staring silently into space with a pensive frown, was his trusted old friend, Jeff Dekker, with whom he'd survived so many narrow scrapes in the past and come through in one piece. Beside Jeff was the tough young Jamaican ex-British army trooper named Tuesday Fletcher, on whom Ben had quickly learned he could absolutely depend. But Ben was barely even aware of their presence. All he could think about – all that really mattered to him at this moment – was that his son Jude, just at the point in their troubled relationship where it looked as if they were finally bonding, was lost to him and there wasn't a single thing Ben could do about it. And that riding happily at the front of the irregular militia convoy speeding along this dusty road, wearing a self-satisfied grin and probably smoking another of his huge cigars in victory, was the man who had taken Jude from him.

That man's name was Jean-Pierre Khosa. Known as 'the General' to the army of heavily-armed Congolese fighters who both feared and loyally served him. Khosa had every reason to be smiling. Most men would be, when they were carrying inside their pocket a stolen diamond worth hundreds of millions of dollars and there was nobody to stop them from gaining every bit of power that wealth like that could afford.

Ben knew little about Khosa, but he knew enough, and had seen enough, for the seeds of doubt inside his own heart to grow into a chilling conviction that here, now, at last, was an enemy he couldn't defeat. That Khosa could beat him.

And that maybe Khosa had already won.

Has Ben Hope met his match at last?

Read *The Devil's Kingdom* and find out...